THE ADVENTURES OF
LADY HARPUR

The Adventures of Lady Harpur

Wordsworth Classic Erotica

This edition published 1996 by
Wordsworth Editions Limited
Cumberland House, Crib Street
Ware, Hertfordshire SG12 9ET

ISBN 1 85326 636 1

Typeset by Antony Gray
Printed and bound in Great Britain by
Mackays of Chatham plc, Chatham, Kent

EDITORIAL PREFACE

The large and increasing demand for this unpretentious little work proves that the plan adopted by our fair author, of making free use of all the common terms and expressions indicative of sexual enjoyment, is in accord with the almost universal feeling of our nature.

This work possesses also the peculiar and unusual advantage of being an account of such matters from the female point of view. Anyone familiar with the working of the feminine mind will not fail to recognise the delicacy of touch and ingenuity of contrivance, combined with boldness of statement, which eminently characterise the actions of the gentler sex.

Women are supposed to take a narrower view of most subjects than men, but if they do, they grasp them more firmly, maintain their ground with more tenacity, and utter their judgement with more fearlessness in this narrative in a very marked degree.

But we do not write to enlist the sympathy of our readers. It would be unnecessary. This little work stands on its own merits; and unless we are much mistaken, its interesting details and graphic descriptions will not fail so keenly to excite their emotions as to cause all that is manly in them to stand also.

It is important to note that, in spite of its title, Queenie is still plain Mrs Harpur in the present volume.

CONTENTS

PART ONE

My Parentage and Early Life

PART TWO

Safe Haven with the Governor

PART THREE

My Life of Free Enjoyment and Ecstatic Love

Part One

**MY PARENTAGE AND
EARLY LIFE**

CHAPTER ONE

First Experiences

My father possessed a large and flourishing estate on one of the West Indian islands before the emancipation of the slaves.

My baptismal name is Charlotte, but from the fancied likeness to a picture of the English queen of the name, my father called me Queenie, which pet name has clung to me ever since.

The first event of any importance in connection with my subject which I can remember occurred when I was about ten years old. I had then a black nurse called Dora, in whose charge I was especially placed. It was from her I learned that my mother, who died soon after my birth, had been a favourite and very handsome slave, nearly as white as a European, and that I greatly resembled her.

My father was kind to me, though I did not see much of him, for he was often away on business; when he was at home, he used to send for me to come to him after dinner, when he would set me on his knee and make me sip sweet rum toddy. He liked tickling my thighs and pinching my bottom, he said, as it made me laugh and look merry; but one evening after his second glass he placed me astride his lap with my back towards him and my dress pulled up, that he might feel the warmth of my bottom there. I laughed and thought it funny and let him settle me as he wished. Then in a short time I felt a hot stiff thing poking up between my thighs and rubbing against my slit in such a way as even then to cause such a strange tingling there that I told my nurse of it when she was putting me to bed. She laughed and said massa wanted to do to me what he had done to my mother before me.

'Oh, nurse, do tell me what papa did to mamma.'

'Never mind now, missy, you'll know time enough.'

'Tell me now, nurse, you know I am past ten and the other day, when you were wiping me after the bath and were looking in between my legs, you said that I was grown quite a little woman; look at me again, nurse,' I said, lifting up my nightdress and spreading my legs, 'had mamma a little slit in here, like I have, and did she let papa rub it for her?'

'What a funny child you are, Miss Queenie! You're indeed a large and well-made girl for your years and your mamma did enjoy a rubbing there more than anyone I ever saw and, unless I am very much mistaken, you will be just the same,' then, stooping down, she put here hands under my bottom and raised me up and plunging her face between my thighs began to kiss the lips and lick around the inside of my little slit.

I was greatly surprised at first, but soon the motion of her warm pliant tongue in that most sensitive spot, made me press up against her mouth and cry, 'Don't stop, dear nurse, that is so nice!'

A thrill of pleasure passed through me, then feeling tired and heavy I closed my eyes and soon fell asleep.

Nurse was a noted herb doctor and she used to boast that she could cure any sick person, or make them sleep, or even kill them if she liked. There was one herb which she often gathered when out walking with me, which, she said, was good for tea and made people sleep afterwards. She sometimes used it for our own tea. It was nice and pleasant to drink but always made me sleep heavily after taking it. She had steeped some that evening and filled my cup, but as it tasted more pungent then usual, my stomach turned against it and when she was not looking I poured it into the slop basin; but when she helped me again it was not so strong and I drank a little.

I suppose it was the effect of it which made me go to sleep so quickly, but it did not last as long as usual, for I awoke after a few hours; the moon was shining brightly through the curtains drawn across the open window and I could see by the clock that it was only a little after twelve. I felt hot and restless and the excitement in my slitstill continuing, I involuntarily put my hand to it and felt its smooth lips and the little slippery lump between. Then I rubbed with my finger the little hot chink below, which throbbed under my touch and which I felt to be connected in some mysterious way with the very mainstring of my being. I knew not then of that wondrous key which could enter in, wind up the spring and put all the hidden machinery into motion; but my eyes were partially opened, my curiosity aroused and many things I had previously heard and witnessed recurred to my memory with a startling significance unknown before. I settled in my mind therefore to lose no opportunity of enlarging my knowledge of these interesting matters.

I was lying quietly in my bed while these thoughts were fermenting in my mind, when a low whistle to the window arrested my attention.

Nurse sat up and softly asked, 'Is that you, Dandy?'

The whistle was gently repeated.

'You may come in,' she replied, 'the child is fast asleep and the coast is clear.' A dusky form then passed through the window and I recognised one of the assistant overseers, a good-looking mulatto, who was much chaffed as nurse's follower and admirer.

She took him in her arms and gave him a mighty hug; on being released he turned towards me and asked, 'Is she fast asleep? Might I look at her little cunny?'

'You might, for I gave it to her strong last evening.'

He came softly to the side of my bed and, lifting the clothes, pushed his hand between my thighs. I pretended to be asleep though at first I found if very hard to remain still for his fingers tickled me, but he quickly aroused the sensation of pleasure I had felt before, and that made me firm as a rock. He then pulled down the clothes and opening my legs said, 'What a fair little cunt she has, Dora. I wonder who will be the first to ravish its sweets?'

'I would not be surprised if her own father had the first of her himself,' and she related what I had told her.

'I would not put it past him for he is the greatest man for women I ever met. Does he often come to you, Dora?'

'Yes, he does; he takes a turn when he wants a black cunt for a change.'

'And you give him enough of it too, Dora?'

'Why not,' said the nurse as she kissed the top of his red-headed tool which she had drawn out while they were talking. She seemed to be supporting its bag with one hand while she moved the other up and down the dark-skinned shaft.

Meanwhile Dandy had frigged my cunt into such a state of excitement that he was able to push the tip of his finger through the passage and though the pain was so considerable that I had to bite my lips to prevent myself crying out, yet the sensation was so overpowering that I willingly bore it while he forced his whole finger up; then I felt something snap inside and to my great relief he moved it in and out without hurting me.

'I declare she is fit to be fucked,' he said 'although there is not the slightest sign of hair on her mount yet. See the whole of my finger goes in without waking her.'

'So I see, but don't meddle further with her now; come here and I'll finish you off, then go to bed like a good fellow.'

Still holding him by the pego, she drew him towards her bed and sat down on the edge with him standing between her legs. He put his hands under her thighs and tilted her back. She at once spread herself like an open book, giving me a clear view of her enormous gap.

The outsides of the great fat lips were dark and covered with black, woolly hair, but the inside was a flaming red and seemed to be brimming over with unctuous juice.

'Let me put it in, Dandy!' she said as she directed with her hand the glowing head of his now rampant tool into what seemed to me the huge mouth of some all-devouring creature.

'Push, you villain,' she cried, as she clutched the two polished cheeks of his bottom with her hands, driving her nails into his quivering flesh, 'send home your prick and fuck me like a man.'

Dandy, bending to his work, was not slow in obeying her command and fucked with such fury that the whole room shook with the vigour of his strokes. Then his job being done and having lain on her a few minutes, he got up and went away.

The events of that night completely changed the current of my life. I was no longer an innocent child. A new sense had arisen in my nature; I felt a want of something, I scarcely knew what. At that same time I had become as knowing and suspicious as one of long experience in the ways of men.

I had learned to read and write from a schoolmaster who attended me for an hour each morning. I was fond of reading but had few books at my command and they were chiefly novels of light description and such books of poetry such as *Don Juan*, Tommy Little and Burns; all these I now read with renewed interest and enlightened comprehension of the meaning of the numerous hints and allusions.

But my attention was especially directed to the living characters with whom I mingled in daily life and the strange events which were continually occurring around me and which were so highly calculated both to stimulate and gratify my eager and prurient curiosity.

I began life in the midst of an atmosphere pervaded by sensuality and self-indulgence and how I remained in comparative innocence so long is to marvel at now.

My father was a man of robust health and unbridled passion; he had absolute control over a large number and variety of women; and as he was generous in conduct and had a most winning manner and address, they were only too ready to gratify him in every way that he desired. Nor was he selfish in his pleasures, for he allowed his overseers – and he had several, mostly European – to enjoy the same licence he claimed for himself; so that, in a word, unbounded and promiscuous intercourse seemed the order of the day.

A son of the head overseer was allowed to play with me when he was home from school. His name was Dick and he was sixteen years of age. He had often tried to make free with me, but hitherto I had always repelled his advances, but now I felt quite prepared to meet him half-way. The next time he came to play with me, he started his old tricks of running his hand up under my petticoats.

'Where are you putting your hand? I have no pocket there for guavas or nuts.'

'No, but you have a sweet little flower which I could very much like to see and unfold.'

'What nonsense you talk. How do you know that I have a flower or anything else there?'

'Oh, I know very well. I was watching my sister who is about your age taking her bath the other morning and she has the prettiest little mouth between her legs that I ever saw.'

'And what have you got there yourself, Master Dick?'

'Oh, I will show it to you; look here, Queenie, there it is, won't you take it in your hand?'

'No, I'd be sorry to touch the ugly little thing – all the time, however, looking at it with fixed attention.

'Why do you call it ugly – you just mean the contrary. Look how stiff it is getting,' and he drew down the covering skin, 'see its red top peeping out. Do you know what it is for, Queenie?'

'No, what would I know about it?'

'Perhaps you may know more than you would like to say; but anyway, I will tell you: it is just made to go into the mouth between your legs – ah, do; there's a good girl.'

After much laughing, dragging and pushing he succeeded in getting his hand on my chink of delight.

I enjoyed watching how his face beamed with satisfaction as he felt with eager fingers the swelling mound and soft, rounded lips which formed the outer portion of my little unfledged cunny. He praised and kissed me and pressed hard against me, but all the while the knowing young dog was forcing me back and quietly pushing in between my legs. He pinched my clitoris and his fingers rubbed the slit, as he softly pulled up my frock and opened my drawers until at last I allowed him to get what he desired – a full view of my rosy chink. How his eyes then sparkled. How he kissed its lips and thrust in his tongue. He was leaning over me on one side and somehow my hand strayed up his thigh. His trousers were open and I took hold of his prick, it stiffened up as my fingers closed up around it. He seemed greatly pleased and lifting himself up, he pushed it forward for a closer inspection. He showed me how to frig it, as he called the moving of its loose skin up and down, and with a gratified air watched the operation.

He gradually moved his prick towards my mouth and then asked me to kiss it. I put its head to my lips and rubbed it to my nose. It had a slight and peculiar smell, which to me was pleasant and exciting. I let it enter my mouth and twined my tongue around its neck. He put my hand on the little bag that held its stones and told me to feel them and then pushed on my hand until my fingers reached the little round hole in his bottom.

Dick was in fact, quite a little European and, young as he was, he had seen and even participated in many of the various modes of sexual enjoyment.

'Queenie, you are a brick, you know how to please a fellow and you have a lovely cunt; now let us have perfect confidence in one another; we shall have great fun and I shall tell you all sorts of queer things; do you agree?'

'Yes, Dick, you are a good, clever boy and I am very fond of you,' and we sealed our bargain with a kiss.

'Queenie, you shall be my true love and I will marry you when you are grown up and I have an estate of my own. But now tell me, do you know the name of what you are now holding in your hand and petting so nicely?'

'It is called a prick and this, you know, is called a cunt and putting the prick into the cunt is the nicest feeling in the world and is called fucking. Now lean back, raise your knees and open your thighs as widely as ever you can and let us fuck together; if I can get my prick into your cunt you will know what a delightful thing fucking is.'

I lay back, spread my thighs and putting down my hand, tried to open my cunt as much as I could, while he knelt between my legs and pressed the head of his tool against the opening. He pushed and worked away and I heaved up and helped by every means in my power, but all in vain, he could not get in; at last some white juice spurted out of his prick and he had to give up, almost crying at his want of success.

I fully sympathised with him and said, 'But Dick, how do you know that it is meant to go in there at all?'

'Why, I have seen it go in many a time; shall I tell you what I saw only last week?'

'Do, Dick, I would like above all things to hear it.'

'You know, old Snigger keeps the plantation cat, and flogs the slaves when they are sent to him with a note from my father. Last week our Sally was lazy and impudent and he resolved to give her a lesson by sending her to Snigger. So he wrote: "Give this girl a round dozen to teach her better manners," and sent the note with her. I knew what was in the note and why she was sent. So I followed quietly after her and going to the rear of the punishment house, I was able to look in and see all that passed. The old fellow led her in and fastened the door. When the poor girl knew why she was sent there, she seemed quite dumb-founded and burst out crying. He tried to comfort her by saying, "I know you, Sally, and if you are good and quiet, I won't hurt you much."

'He then tied her hands and placed her leaning over a beam so that her bottom was well cocked up. Then he raised her petticoat and flung it over her head and shoulders, and putting his hands between her legs, forced them wide apart – at which she squealed out and threatened all sorts of things.

' "Very well," he said, "if you won't keep quiet you must only suffer for it,' and bringing down the cat he gave her a smart cut across her naked posteriors.

'She jumped and gave a yell.

' "All right," he said, giving her another, "now perhaps you will be quiet and behave yourself."

' "Oh, yes, Mr Snigger, I will be as quiet as I can, but don't hit so hard, you hurt me terribly."

' "I don't want to hurt you at all, Sally," he said, rubbing his hands between her fat thighs, spreading them further apart and gazing up at her cunt. He then loosened his pants and brought out his tool. You would have wondered at the big prick the old fellow has. He made it wag its great purple top as he shook it in his hand. Then holding her by her hips, he drove it at her cunt.

But when she felt it between her lips she cried, "Stop, you mustn't do that."

' "You want another taste of the cat, my lady?" he said, drawing back and giving her a lash.

' "Oh, Mr Snigger, don't whip me any more and I'll let you do anything you please."

' "Now, you speak like a sensible girl," he said, coming up close again. He opened the glowing lips of her cunt, inserted the head of his prick and pushed it slowly up. As it disappeared, he leaned on her back, put his hands down under her belly, spread them over her cunt and made his prick pass in and out through his fingers. You would have been surprised, Queenie, to have seen with what ease the great prick passed up into her belly; and as soon as he began to fuck with regular back and forward thrusts, she pointed her bottom out to meet every push. When he finished he made her promise never to tell anyone what he had done to her. "If you do and I have you here again, maybe you won't catch it, that's all." She knew that was no idle threat, so she let him kiss her and then went quietly away.

'Would you have liked to see that, Queenie?'

'Oh, dear yes, almost every day.'

'I will tell you the next time and we can go together. Won't it be fun?'

I promised to go with him and after some more handling, looking and kissing, he departed.

CHAPTER TWO

My Strange Dream

The next time my father sent for me after dinner, I made an excuse for not going, as my newly awakened feelings caused me to shrink from him now. But that same night, nurse made some of her peculiar tea. I tried to avoid drinking it, but she pressed it so strongly upon me that I could not help taking some. Soon afterwards, I fell into a heavy sleep and out of that for some cause or other, I passed into a curious state of half-consciousness and either saw or dreamed that papa was in our room lying on nurse's naked body. Then I seemed to be carried over and laid on my back by her side, in such a way that he could see and kiss my cunny as he worked his bottom up and down over her. All this time I was quite powerless and totally unable to move or speak, though I had a dreamy perception of all that was going on.

Nurse then got over him with her bottom towards his face, her breast, resting on his belly and her hand between his raised thighs. After a while she said, 'Hah, I have got him into life again; what shall we do with him now?'

'Could we get him into Queenie?'

'Isn't she too young as yet, it would hurt her I fear.'

'She is going on eleven and I have often fucked girls as young as she is, for in this country, as you know, girls mature very early. We will grease her little crack and this poor fellow not being over-strong, will not hurt her too much.'

She then brought cold cream and anointed my cunt, while he worked his finger in and out and at last forced up two together; then he got nurse to go all fours on the bed and placing me on her back, held up my legs and knelt between. After working his tool a few turns in her receptacle, he put its well moistened head in my little chink and holding me firm by the shoulders, gradually forced it in. I felt a dull sensation of pain as it entered and passed up, yet I could neither stir nor cry out; but when it was all inside, it seemed to fill me with warmth and satisfaction. I heard nurse asking if he had got it in. 'Oh, yes, easily,' he replied, as he lifted me in his arms, staked on the engine of bliss and began to carry me round the room. The motion was so delightful that it partially aroused me, for the action of the prick fairly convulsed my cunt with delicious throbs as I clung round him with my arms and legs.

He soon laid me in my bed and I was conscious of nothing until the morning, when a feeling of soreness in my cunt brought back the dream to my recollection.

Nurse examined my nightdress and noticing some ensanguined spots, took it away and said I must have been scratching myself in the night. I kept my own counsel and said nothing.

My father always had young good-looking slave girls to do the housework and wait on him; but they also had other functions to discharge, which I now began to find out about and understand. I soon learned, moreover, that all the planters round whether married or single were similarly supplied and that they were not thought any the worse of for it as it was the universal custom.

My father, being the wealthiest among them, only carried on matters on a grander scale. When he invited his friends to dinner – and he never had any but gentleman's parties – after they had imbibed a sufficient quantity of drink, he used to call in a number of these girls and make them strip and dance naked; then would follow a regular orgy, which would end only when they all rolled off to bed together.

I heard all this from a pretty slave girl named Zilla, whom papa had lately appointed as my special waiting-maid. She attended me in the bathroom and nothing seemed to please her more than when I let her kiss and suck my cunt. She told me that my father had a splendid prick and fucked so delightfully that the girls were always contending who should go to him at night; and that he loved to have his prick petted and sucked. While telling me these things, she kept on playing with my cunt, probing and frigging it and inserting the tip of her finger in the little round hole behind, which I found excited me greatly.

I asked her if she went to him often.

'As often as I get the chance,' she replied.

'But are you not too young – would it not hurt you to have such a big thing pushed up into your belly?'

'Not in the least, missy, I was not nearly so tall as you when I was first fucked. Put your finger in and feel how open I am now.'

To my surprise her cunt admitted three or even four fingers with the greatest ease.

'You are much more open than I am. Now tell me, do you find fucking so very pleasant as they say.'

'Oh, yes, it is grand. There is nothing like it in the world. How you would enjoy it, missy. Ah, if you only saw two people fucking, you would never rest until you were fucked yourself.'

'At all events, I would like very much to see how it is done; could you not contrive, Zilla, to let yourself be fucked while I was looking on – of course, concealed.'

'Well, missy, if it would gratify you, I think I could manage it safely and pleasantly. But first I want to show you something; massa is not at home today. Come, let us explore his rooms.

She led me to a room which I had always found locked, but of which she had the key. It contained only some broad couches, some very lascivious pictures on the walls and a tall roomy press. Several large mirrors were fixed on either side and a splendid chandelier hung from the ceiling.

'This is the place where massa and his friends hold their orgies,' Zilla said, 'but he will be alone this evening, I am told.' She opened the press which was full of loose gauze robes hanging up and continued, 'We sometimes hide in here to see what is going on, but he does not mind and never looks in himself; what would you think of hiding in it tonight – you would see all sorts of funny things and no one would know that you were here.'

'But what should I do if I was found out?'

'There would be but little chance of that; anyway I could disguise you, so that you would not be recognised even in the full glare of all these lights. You would only have to let down your hair, put on the same light dress we wear and stain your face and arms with a dye which can be easily washed off next morning. Do missy – try it – you will have more fun than I can describe and really no risk. I will be there and you will see me fucked and probably several others. You can tell nurse that you are going to pass the evening with your papa. Come here before he leaves the dining-room and I will settle you in the press and stay near it and take out any dresses that might be wanted.'

At last I consented and in due course found myself standing almost naked among the gauze dresses in the press, while Zilla peeped in now and then to tell me that everything was all right.

After some time papa came in looking very flushed. He had only a dressing gown on and was followed by three girls, one of whom was Zilla, with nothing whatever on them but their stockings and boots. He threw himself on his back on the couch opposite the press, and saying he was tired, asked the girls to dance and play before him.

Two of them embraced and commenced waltzing about the room. They pushed their legs in between each other's thighs and displayed their cunts and bottoms as much as they possibly could. As they went on they grew more excited, smacking each other's rumps and pulling the hair of each other's cunts. They then lay over one another and pretended to fuck. Anon they kissed each other's cunts.

All this time, Zilla knelt at my father's side, petting his prick and smiling towards the press as she made it stand up stiffly. She even winked when she drew down the soft skin and uncovered its large swelling head, red and shining like a ripe plum. But papa soon directed her to get over his face and called the others to come and manipulate his prick and bottom. Zilla then knelt with her knees on each side of his shoulders to enable her to place her cunt full on his mouth. While one of the other girls lay between his legs and lifting them up, pressed back his hams and thus got free access to his upturned bottom into which she thrust her tongue as far as she could. The other held his prick in her mouth, but without frigging it, which, I observed, she carefully avoided as she sucked the head and gently stirred the balls.

After a few moments he cried, 'Enough, my pets, now ring the bell.'

Zilla jumped up and pulled the bell-rope and immediately the door opened and three lusty black fellows sprang in, perfectly naked, and began chasing the girls about the room. Sometimes they would catch them and flinging them down would feel and kiss their cunts and try to fuck them but they always managed to break away from them before they could finish.

Suddenly the girls disappeared, leaving the three men looking very foolish with their black pricks sticking up like ship's bowsprits before them. Then they too rushed out to hunt after the women; and soon one of them returned dragging one of the girls with him. He laid her on a couch, turned her up and was into her in a moment. He had only fucked her a few strokes when another pair rushed in and dragged him off; then the newcomer took his place, thrust his prick into the open cunt and fucked away. The man who was dragged off seemed in no way put out, for he seized the girl that came in last, laid her on her back and charged into her cunt. Then in came the third pair; the second man was now pulled off in turn, only to be replaced by the third. So they went on, each girl being only partially fucked by each of the men one after the other; which Zilla afterwards informed me, is a most agreeable way of fucking.

In the midst of the confusion the lights were suddenly put out and we were left in total darkness.

I held the press door firmly from the inside, but Zilla came whispering, 'Open, missy, and let me slip in.'

I opened the door and she slipped in and clasping me in her arms pressed her naked body against mine. Immediately I felt a hand moving about my bottom and cunt and asked, 'Is that you, Zilla, squeezing my bottom?'

'Yes, dear, open your legs more – more still, now lean against me and poke out your behind, I want to play with it.'

'Oh, Zilla, that's not your hand – what are you pushing into me? Stop, its hurting me. Oh, my, Zilla, what do you mean? You are holding me for somebody to – what are you doing? You horrid man – Oh, Zilla, he is splitting me up.'

'Be quiet, missy, don't make so much noise or you will have the whole of them in on us.'

Meanwhile I felt what I knew was a large prick forced into my cunt from behind; while a pair of strong arms held me firmly round the waist and a hairy chin pressed on my shoulder. Zilla put her hand between my legs, chuckled and whispered, 'Now missy, you have it in and no mistake, right up into your maiden cunny; how does it feel – crammed with a fine prick. Oh, yes, wag your little bum, that's the way to enjoy a fuck.'

Just then the press door was forcibly pulled open and one of the black fellows caught hold of Zilla, crying out: 'Here she is, I have her again.' Her back was towards the door and in a trice his prick was darted into her cunt and by the impulse of her body against mine I knew that she was being fucked with tremendous vigour. Whoever was behind me now fell to again and each time Zilla was banged against me in front, my bottom got a shove behind as the prick darted into my cunt.

Zilla, panting with excitement, kissed me and said: 'Darling missy, put down your hand and feel Sambo's prick fucking me.'

I lowered my hand to the bottom of her belly and felt the fat hairy lips of her cunt clinging round a sturdy prick. Both prick and cunt were reeking with moisture which made my fingers smell for hours after. Sambo speedily discharged and retired; so did my friend behind, who then passed out quickly in the dark and we were left alone.

'Zilla, take me to my room,' I said, 'I am tired and frightened to death; you are a bad girl and I won't trust you again.'

'Forgive me, darling missy, I only meant to give you a treat; you surely have not been hurt, nor really vexed. A good fuck never does any harm.'

I was soon in bed and fast asleep, for I was tired and exhausted. Next morning, however, after being refreshed by my bath, I was more inclined to laugh with Zilla over the matter; but I could not prevail on her to tell me who it was that came behind me in the press, though I had my suspicions.

I had now been twice fucked, but somehow not in the regular way, and I longed for Dick to come and give me a more satisfactory lesson. I was soon gratified, for that afternoon Dick came with a radiant face and told me that a lazy, impudent girl and two others were to be sent to Snigger at four o'clock, by my father's directions; that he had got the key for the door which opened into the loft over the punishment room; it was half filled with dry flax, he said, but by shifting some a famous view of all that passed below could be had through the loose boarding in the floor. 'So clap on your things and come along; we have just got time to get comfortably settled before the play begins.'

We hurried to the left and when we had entered Dick carefully closed the door, locked it and took out the key. We then made a comfortable nest for ourselves amid the flax, over a large aperture in the floor through which Dick said we could have a clear view of Snigger's operations on the bottoms and cunts of the poor girls.

He then raised my dress and I opened his trousers and we lay head and tail together, so that he could see and explore all the secret crannies between my legs while I was able with equal facility to investigate the fascination of his prick and balls.

While thus engaged, I gave him a full account of what had happened the night before, with the exception of the fact that I had been fucked myself. In return he told me how he had seen his father fucking slave girls scores of times; that on one occasion he stole out of his bed at night when he heard sounds of great revelry in the house and, on creeping to the parlour door which was slightly open, he saw his father chasing with a birch rod four naked women round the room, hitting at their bottoms as hard as he could; that when he caught one, he make her lean forward on the table with her bum cocked up and her legs widely apart; that the others then ran up, opened the lips of her cunt, pushed in his father's prick and tickled his bottom while he fucked; that as he was intently watching this performance, the door suddenly opened, which startled them and one of the girls, running to it, caught him and drew him into the room.

His father told them to take off his shirt and give him a good whipping for peeping when he should have been in bed. This direction they at once began to carry out, but one of the girls whose cunt he had often tickled seized him by the prick as she was taking off his shirt and proposed that one of them should lie down with Dick on top of her and that she should hold him tight while the others played with his bottom. To this they all agreed and told her to lay herself down, as it was she who proposed it; she complied and Dick was placed over her, most willingly indeed, for he was longing for a fuck, but they tantalised him at first by holding his prick in their hands and rubbing its head about the lips of her cunt. He heaved up and down, hoping to drive it in, but they always pulled it aside as his father and all the rest of them laughed at his frantic efforts to get it in.

'Do let me in,' he implored, 'I cannot hold off any longer.'

'Yes, do,' cried the girl, 'I want it too.'

At last they placed it aright; and with one plunge of his prick, Dick rushed it up the hot recess. Oh, what delicious heat. How she bounded under him at every stroke. Lifting her legs, she crossed them over his back, while they touched up his bottom with the rod.

'You may lather away now,' he said, 'as hard as you like.'

All the feeling in his body seemed concentrated in his prick and that felt as if it were bathed in bliss. He finished with a roar of delight; and they all said he fucked like a man and was worthy of admission to the ranks of love.

'Oh, Queenie, you give me such pleasure. I think a good suck when you play with the balls and so delightfully finger the bottom is equal to any fuck. Did you swallow my seed?'

'Yes, Dick, every drop.'

'That's right. Now I must give you a new pleasure in return. Let me fix this bundle of flax under your bottom to raise it up; now put your hands down on each side and hold open its cheeks while I tickle it with my tongue.'

Then lying along the floor, he sucked my bottom-hole, pushing his tongue, so that I felt its tip moving round and round inside and stirring up most delicious sensations throughout the whole regions of love.

I did not know until then what an amount of feeling there is in our bottoms and how closely connected they must be with our cunts. After a few moments he asked, 'Do you like having your bottom sucked, darling?'

'Yes, very much, I think it is the nicest feeling I ever had.'

'Does it increase the feeling in your cunt?'

'Yes, my cunt and bottom feel all in a glow, a very little more sucking or frigging would make me come.'

'Well, now, darling, I want you to put your hands down again and this time to hold open the lips of your cunt and show me where you have the most feeling and how best to excite it.'

I put my hands down and spreading open the lips I pressed the clitoris and rubbed the tip of my finger up and down over it and between the inner lips of my cunt.

'That's where I have the most feeling.'

'Very well, I'll suck the entrance while you rub the clitoris, but meantime go on telling me how you are feeling and especially when you are just about to spend.'

'Yes, Dick, my cunt is growing hotter and hotter while you suck, and I frig the clitoris. Oh, it is getting very nice – I can't keep quiet – I must twist my bottom about – Oh, and heave up my cunt; now, now, Dick; suck my cunt, push your tongue into it; squeeze my bottom, move your finger inside; there! Oh!'

I rolled in ecstasy, while Dick supped up the soft effusion that distilled with so much pleasure from my fountain of delight.

Just then – but what happened must have a chapter to itself.

CHAPTER THREE

Lizzy

In the midst of our sweet delirium, we heard steps on the stairs leading up to the loft and Disk had only time to draw the flax stalks over us, when the door was opened and to my horror my father's voice sounded in my ears.

He had a lady with him whom I did not then know, but whom he called Lizzy. He carefully arranged a snug corner for her within a few yards of our hiding place and said, 'Now Lizzy, my pet, we are perfectly safe from observation here and we can enjoy ourselves without fear of intrusion while we watch Snigger and the girls. The old fellow, I am told, gloats over their naked bums and always fucks the fattest before or after whipping them. Would you mind taking off some of your dress, the loft is so hot; and this corset of yours is always in the way.'

'Are you sure, Robert, that no one can see us here?'

'How could they, when we found the door locked and I re-locked it after we entered.'

He then spread his coat for her to lie on while she divested herself of everything but her chemise and let down her hair. I could see through the flax that she was young, of fair complexion and exceedingly pretty.

Dick told me afterwards that she was the wife of a neighbouring Planter named Hobbs, who was a worn-out debauchee; that he was said to be very jealous of her, but in other respects did not seem to care for her, as he was much more attentive to his numerous black mistresses.

'It was very good of you, Lizzy, to come today when you heard I was anxious to see you, but how did you get away from the Ogre?' meaning her husband.

'I told him I wanted to make some purchases in town and, to satisfy him, said I would enquire about cigars he was expecting – having done which I rode on here.'

Papa took her in his arms, kissed her and said, 'Take him out yourself, my pet. He loves the touch of your soft fingers; it always puts life into him.'

She pretended to look shy as she unfastened his trousers, opened them down the front, put her hand inside, felt around and drew out his fine handsome prick. Although it was my own father's prick, from which my natural instinct inclined me to turn away my face, in my then excited state I could not help regarding it with the greatest interest. I especially admired the milky whiteness of its shaft and the look of pride with which it upreared its purple head as she drew down the covering skin. As she kissed its glowing top and sucked it in her mouth, he said: 'Tell me its name, Lizzy.'

She looked up and answered: 'Prick.'

'And this soft mouth with its silky moustache, what is it called?' he asked as he separated her yielding legs.

She replied, dwelling most lasciviously on the two last letters, 'My cu–n–t.'

'That's a pet, now what shall we do with this prick and cunt?'

'Let them fuck, to be sure, what are they made for but fucking.'

'Does the Ogre often fuck you?'

'No, but he sometimes wants to put his nasty prick into my bottom and then he hurts me terribly.'

'He is a brute; and yet fucking the bottom is not so bad when it is done gently and nicely.'

'Oh, I would let you fuck me anywhere, Robert.'

'Thanks, my pet, we will try that way soon. Does he ever fuck any of his girls before you?'

'Oh, dear yes, he has often tied me down and fucked them so close to me that I could not avoid seeing all that was done, then he would take his prick fresh out of their cunts and make me kiss it and when I refused one day, he brought in a slave and having stripped me naked he held open my legs while the fellow rammed his prick into my cunt and fucked me before them all.

'Oh, he is a horrid beast and I hate him.'

'How I wish I could take you from him altogether, but it is better for you to bear with him and come to me as often as you can. But here comes the first girl, a saucy impudent hussy. I wrote to give her two dozen and I hope he will cut into her well; get on your knees, pet, and while you are watching them through the slit in the floor, I will try this other slit between your legs.'

Snigger took the note from the girl, read it with a grin and commenced tying her hands.

'Oh, Mr Snigger, this is the first time I was ever sent here, won't you be good and not uncover me?'

'Well, I must place you here at all events.'

He secured her as usual, leaning over the beam, but when he attempted to raise her petticoat, she screamed and kicked with all her might.

'Ah, my lady, I will soon stop that,' and taking a long flat piece of wood, he fastened her feet to each end, thus fixing them at their widest stretch. Then, not heeding her cries, he thew up her clothes and passed his lecherous hands deliberately over her belly and bottom and the inside of her thighs, then opening the lips of her cunt, he looked in and poked his finger up. She threatened him at the highest pitch of her voice, but her abuse only seemed to add zest to his pleasure, for he laughed as he took out his prick and placed its rebicund head between the thickly covered lips of her cunt and slowly drove it up.

'What is he doing?' I heard papa asking Mrs Hobbs.

'He is admiring her great black buttocks and hairy quim; now he is putting in his prick – there – he has driven it all inside and his belly is pressed against her rump; now he is holding her by the hips and pushing away as hard as he can.'

'And we too will have a turn, Lizzy – there – does your cunt relish the taste of my prick in its soft mouth?'

'Yes, Robert, it likes it dearly; your prick fills my cunt with rapture and bliss. Oh, yes, it is very pleasant being fucked by the man we love. Does my cunt hold your prick as you like?'

'Yes my darling, the pressure of your sweet cunt is most delicious, I can feel it nipping the head of my prick far up inside; put back your hand and let it slip in and out through your fingers.'

Meanwhile, Snigger, having discharged, had taken out his tool and after wiping it said, 'Now, my lady, I will pay you off for all your hard names and abuse: how do you like that, and that?' each time giving her a cut across the bottom with the cat.

'Oh, Mr Snigger,' another cut, 'Oh, have mercy,' another slash.

'You vile strumpet to call me a dirty black nigger,' and down came the cat harder than ever.

'Oh, Mr Snigger, I will never call you names again.'

'Won't you? What else will you promise?' Cut – slash – cut.

'I will let you fuck me whenever you wish.'

'And how am I to fuck you again,' he said, lashing away.

'Any way you like.'

'Oh, yes, fuck your arse?' Slash, slash, slash.

'Yes, my arse or anywhere, only stop whipping.'

She had now received about a dozen and a half and he drew back to observe the effect of his work.

Her bottom was all marked across with red streaks while a few drops of blood appeared on her thighs.

'Oh, Mr Snigger, pity my poor bottom, unfasten and let me go.'

'I am not done with you yet, you want me to fuck you again, don't you?' he asked raising up the cat.

'Yes, my bottom is all in a glow and my cunt is just burning; you may fuck me as much as you like, I would really enjoy it now.'

He went up to her and having moistened two fingers in her cunt, he pushed them into her bottom; when she started he cried, 'What, do you want more of the cat?'

'No, I want your nice prick, dear Mr Snigger, in my cunt.'

'What?'

'Well, in my arse or anywhere, only let me down.'

'That's right, now push out your arse, I will fuck your cunt first.'

She poked out her behind as much as she could; he took off his pantaloons and shirt, and after rubbing up his tool with his hand, he drove it up her cunt.

'Is that good?' he asked with a grunt.

'Yes, dear Mr Snigger, it is delightful.'

After a few long deliberate strokes, he drew it out and holding open the cheeks of her bottom, he thrust its head against the little round hole. 'Open,' he cried, 'open your arse, I say.'

She groaned and let in the head. He then pushed the whole prick up into her bottom and clasped her round the waist; then drawing it all out except the head, he plunged it in again and so went on till the paroxysm came and he spent.

'Well, Lizzy,' papa asked, 'what is he doing now?'

'I declare he is fucking her bottom and she likes it.'

'Why not? May I fuck yours now, Lizzy?'

'You may, dearest, I could refuse you nothing; but will you do it gently, Robert?'

'You may be assured of that; now try and open it as much as ever you can – there now, it is in, does it hurt?'

'No, my love, your dear prick would not hurt me anywhere.'

Papa leaned on her back with his hands over her cunt and they both panted as his prick passed slowly in and out.

This scene excited Dick greatly. He wetted his fingers and began to frig my bottom. I knew what he wanted and whispered, 'You may'; for the sight of father's fine prick slipping in and out between the beautiful white globes of Lizzy's bottom had stirred up all the lust of my nature, and even made my bottom itch for a prick.

'I will moisten it first in your cunt,' he whispered in reply. 'Now put back your hands and open your bottom as if you were going to do something.'

I did so and he squeezed in the head of his prick.

'How do you like it?'

'Pretty well – frig my cunt – that is nice; fucking in the bottom is not so bad after all.'

'Oh, it is grand,' replied Dick.

The sensation of pleasure was so great that we could no longer restrain ourselves and we groaned aloud together.

'Hallo,' cried papa, 'here's Queenie and young Dick fucking away like mad. Dick, you rascal, you should have asked my leave before fucking my daughter; however, I'm sure you did your work well and I must forgive you.'

In fact, I have not the least doubt that he was pleased rather than otherwise, for should any mischance occur to me, it would be very convenient to have Dick to lay the blame on.

So when I hid myself in the flax, he pulled me out, and kissing me, told me not to be alarmed, as he was not at all angry; then putting his hand under my bottom, he raised it up so that Mrs Hobbs could see my cunt.

'Has she not a pretty cunt, Lizzy, so fat and smooth and beautiful red inside?'

Mrs Hobbs looked at it and kissed it; in doing so she elevated her own plump posteriors. Papa winked at Dick, and pointing to them said, 'My friend Dick is admiring your splendid array behind, and is no doubt wishing to be allowed a closer inspection, but I fancy Queenie has pumped him dry for this time.'

Dick only laughed, and putting his hand on the well-rounded cheeks of her bottom said, 'May I feel you, dear Mrs Hobbs?'

'Well, Dick, as you have seen all that has passed, it can't make much difference, and if you promise to be discreet, and never tell, I have no objection to your sharing in our amusements.'

Dick was delighted to have access to a new cunt; and he patted her bottom and kissed its cheeks, while he poked his fingers into the recesses of her cunt and drew open the fat moist lips, ornamented with light curly hair.

Meantime, papa played with my chink of love and said that he always admired a cunt more before the hair grew than afterwards. 'These plump smooth lips, so round and white, look so innocent and inviting.'

'Yes,' Mrs Hobbs replied, 'I quite agree with you; I think my own cunt would be much nicer without hair.'

'No,' cried Dick from behind. 'It could not be nicer than it is – this silky hair is lovely'; and he prolonged his delight by rubbing his prick over and about the soft lips of her cunt.

Mrs Hobbs laughed and pleased with his attention she spread her thighs and protruded her bottom and said, 'Well, anyway, it looks like a good fuck, Dick, so put in your prick and fall to work.'

Papa smiled at her ardour, and taking my hand placed it on his own affair saying: 'I warrant that young rascal has taught you how to frig a prick too.'

I now held in my hand that engine which some twelve years ago had deposited into my mother's womb the germ of my being; and I shall confess it, the idea rather added to my pleasure. I smiled as I watched it recover its strength, swell up and stiffen while I frigged its smooth shaft and drew back the skin from its head.

Lizzy laughed and said, 'Look how she cuddles her father's prick. You seem well acquainted with it, dear. Did you ever give her a taste of it in her cunt, Robert?'

'Now, Lizzy, you know the old saying: Ask no questions, and you will hear no lies.'

'Well, try it now, at all events; I have got possession of her sweetheart, and it would be only fair exchange that she should have mine.'

'Shall I, Queenie,' papa asked, leaning over me.

'You may, papa, if you like,' I said turning on my back and spreading open my thighs.

'Hold on, Dick,' cried Mrs Hobbs, who was on her hands and knees with Dick fucking away at her rear. 'Wait until they begin, and put something under her bottom, Robert, that we may better see your prick working in her cunt.'

Then supporting herself on her left hand against the strong pressure of Dick's action behind, she caught papa's prick in her right and placing its head between the lips of my cunny watched it disappear amidst its rosy folds.

Papa's large prick now slipped in with the greatest ease and satisfaction to us both. As he drove it home, I involuntarily gave that peculiar spread of the thighs, and sympathetic heave of the loins which women cannot help doing when they are truly enjoying a fuck.

My father noticed it and whispered in my ear, 'My darling Queenie, do you like my fucking?'

'Yes, dear papa, I do very much,' I said, compressing his prick in my cunt and squeezing him in my arms. 'Why should you not fuck me if you like; you have given me all I have, and I love you very much.' Then, pressing him closer, I asked: 'Does the thought of fucking your own daughter increase the feeling of pleasure, papa?'

'Yes, my darling, it does. I don't believe I ever enjoyed a fuck so much before in all my life.'

Here let me pause to remark I simply relate certain incidents in the early life of an untrained and uneducated girl, of warm temperament and loving disposition, but wholly in a state of nature and surrounded by a variety of evil influences.

I do not insert this, however, as an excuse, for my object is not to moralise or teach, but only to gratify and excite. I therefore record the facts of what occurred, and leave my readers to think and feel just as they like.

But to return. A great commotion was heard in the room beneath, which arrested the attention of all of us. Peeping down, we saw that two new girls had come in and they being sturdy women had proved more than a match for old Snigger.

One had caught him in her arms, while the other tied his hands together. They then dragged him to a rope which hung from a pulley in the rafters, and having fastened his hands to one end, they hoisted him up until he was standing on tiptoe. Meanwhile they laughed and hooted at his threats and cries, declaring that it was their turn now and that they would pay him off in kind, by letting him feel the scratches of his own cat, and also, as one of them merrily proposed, by drawing out of his wicked old tool, every drop of spunk he possessed, so that he would not be able to fuck for a month at least.

So after letting down his trousers, and tucking up his shirt, one of them commenced behind by vigorously operating on his rump with the cat while the other, in front, frigged his prick with her hand. The heat behind and the friction before, soon made him spend, which he did not object to; but when they went on to a second bout, and after that to a third he complained terribly, while his prick seemed to have shrunk to nothing.

So the one who was frigging exclaimed, 'It is no use going on, his old tool has gone completely dead.'

'Show him your cunt,' cried the other from behind, still pounding away.

She held up her frock, and spreading open the fat lips of her cunt, showed him its red inside glistening with heat and moisture, but he, perhaps for the first time in his life, turned his face away from the luscious sight, and languidly closed his eyes.

'Make him smell it,' cried she with the cat. 'There is nothing like the scent, Sambo tells me.'

The one in front then drew up a table that was near and getting on it stood so as to bring her cunt close up to his face, and rubbed it against his nose.

The other pushing her hands between his legs from behind, made the unfortunate man spend the fourth time by frigging.

He seemed now utterly exhausted and ready to faint, so they let him down, and as he lay on the floor, they warned him most emphatically: 'Remember, if you dare to say one word about us, we will tell everybody all that has happened, and then you will be the laughing stock of the whole plantation.' After which they departed with great glee at their success. We too laughed at the scene, for we all agreed with Mrs Hobbs that the old fellow only got what he deserved.

CHAPTER FOUR

My Departure from Home

In a warm climate, frequent bathing becomes not only a luxury, but a necessity of life. My father fully understood this, and being a man remarkable for his attention to personal cleanliness, he impressed his habits on his household; and, to afford them greater facility, he had several bathrooms fitted up in his commodious habitation.

I took my bath regularly every day – as regularly as I took my meals –

and sometimes a second or even a third when the day was hot.

I liked to have Zilla with me in the bath, as she was sprightly and full of fun; and afterwards, before resuming our clothing, we usually reclined together on a couch to rest and to luxuriate in the freedom of our limbs from the constraints of dress, with all its botheration of hooks, buttons and ties.

The sight and feel of our naked bodies would then naturally suggest subjects of conversation of an amatory and confidential character; and Zilla seemed always to make it a point to introduce such subjects and both by words and acts draw me on to lascivious talk; she even induced me to describe my sensations at the different times when I had been fucked, and how I liked to feel and handle the pricks. Then she would kiss and pet my cunt, and place me in different positions, and turn me up and, in short, play all sorts of pranks both with herself and me.

The reason of all this, as I found out afterwards, was to please and gratify my father, who, by means of a spy-hole which had been specially constructed, was able to watch our proceedings, and hear all we said.

On one of these occasions I asked her which gave her the most pleasure, a black or white fuck? She replied that though the colour did not much matter, provided they were equally strong and active, she preferred being fucked by a white man; but some of the blacks, and especially Sambo, had the most enormous tools. 'Oh, missy, at first sight, you would almost think that he would split you up, but somehow, after the head gets in, you by no means object to its large size.'

I said, 'I would like very much to feel what fucking by a black man's prick would be like.'

'Then, missy, take my place tonight, and you will be fully gratified; for I have promised Sambo to let him in for an hour, and he won't recognise you in the dark.'

So we arranged to exchange beds for the night.

Then I asked her to give me some idea beforehand of his usual mode of proceeding.

She replied, 'He will expect, of course, to find the dooropens easily, and he has promised to enter very quietly without making any noise, not even to speak. As soon as he finds the side of the bed, he will be sure to push his hands under the clothes and feel your bottom and cunt. He will then very likely draw you to the edge of the bed, lift up your legs on his shoulders and kiss or suck your cunt. If you wish to gratify him, then put down your hand, and you will find his big tool sticking up; rub it with your fingers, and when he stands up, put it to your mouth, it will find its way in, after that, you must let things take their course.'

She prepared me in the evening by rubbing some strong-scented herb into my cunt. 'For Sambo likes a good smell,' she said, 'and plenty of it too.'

Zilla had a nice clean bed in a comfortable room that opened on the veranda not far from mine; so as soon as it was dark, I took her place, and I had not occupied her bed many minutes before the door was gently opened and I heard someone enter and cross the room as if familiar with the way.

On his reaching the bed, the clothes were raised and I felt a large warm hand pulling up my shift and nestling in my cunt. The other hand then passed under my bottom, lifted me up, and drew me gently to the edge of the bed, with my bottom turned out; then all the coverings were pushed aside, and I felt a curly head between my thighs, and a nose sniffing about my cunt, then a pliant tongue licking round within the lips.

When Sambo perceived by my twisting and turning and panting that the pleasure tide was rising in my cunt, he sucked more eagerly, and grasping the cheeks of my bottom with his hands, he squeezed them so strongly that he hurt me, and I could hardly help crying out, but I quickly found that the smart of my bottom had a great effect in increasing the excitement in my cunt.

Putting my hand on his head, I pressed it in between my widely extended thighs, and opening my cunt, I moved it up to meet the probing of his tongue as I poured forth my effusion in a hot oozy stream.

He licked it up with evident relish while I lay back in a half-panting state; the suction of his lips, however, and the pressure of his fingers soon recalled me to life and feeling. I then put down my head and encountered the fiery head of his charger. It was full, hot, and erect but not so large as I expected, for my fingers were able to close around it as I frigged it up and down.

He raised himself up to bring it nearer to my face, just as Zilla had described, and pushed it on until its head touched my lips. It felt soft as velvet and had a good deal of that subtle perfume which I had before observed to exhale from the pricks of both Dick and my father and which I found by experience had a powerful effect in stimulating my amorous desires.

I parted my lips and it immediately passed in and filled my mouth. I twined my tongue around its indented neck, and sucked as hard as I could. I held his balls with one hand while with the other I played with the cheeks of his bottom, and as I became more excited, I felt for the little round hole in the furrow and pushed in the tip of my finger.

I felt a thrill pass through Sambo's frame, his prick bounded in my mouth while his hot spunk poured down my throat in quick gushes of rapture and delight.

The intensity of the feeling forced him to exclaim, to my confusion and amazement, 'Darling Queenie, it is I; what extraordinary pleasure you have given me. How deliciously you have sucked my prick.'

'Oh, papa, I thought you were Sambo. I am glad to have given you so much pleasure, but how did you know I was here?'

'Well, to tell you the truth, I was close to you this morning when you were taking your bath with Zilla, and I heard your arrangement with her to enable you to get a taste of Sambo's prick; and I am not surprised at your curiosity, for he certainly has an enormous tool, as big as that of any jackass, and all the women on the estate are mad for it. I knew that he would be here shortly, and my intention was to steal a march upon him, and to have you first myself, so as to smooth the way for his huge affair and prevent your being hurt by its unusual dimensions; but the suction of your mouth was so delightful, that I could not withdraw my prick in time. However, I don't expect that you will suffer much inconvenience, as your cunt is unusually large for so young a girl.'

But while he was talking another pair of hands commenced playing about me, and I found that Zilla had been present with us all the time.

'Dear missy, I have brought you some nice ointment, let me put a little of it inside your cunny; it will prevent Sambo tearing it with his powerful machine.'

She pushed a quantity of the softening unguent up my cavity of delight and then, suddenly pausing, said, 'Hush, he comes.'

They slipped noiselessly round to the other side of the room, as Sambo opened the door and entered the room.

I was almost terrified by all these warnings and preparations, and began to repent of my undertaking, but it was now too late to change my mind for in less than a moment I felt his great paws groping round my cunt. But he stopped all at once, as if much surprised, and with a low chuckle, said, 'Golly, Miss Zilla, what hab you done with your cunt? It had lose all of its hair. It smooth as de palm of my hand.'

It now occurred to me for the first time, that although I was nearly the same height and stoutness of Zilla, yet, of course, he would find a great difference in our cunts, for mine had only the suspicion of the growth which now so luxuriantly covers it.

'But all de same,' he went on, 'dis leetle smooth cunt is very nice – no matter to Sambo, whether you be Miss Zilla, or missa some oder body; and it hab good smell too,' he said, kissing my cunt and thrusting in his tongue with considerable force. 'Now, missa, where you lettle hand? Put him here on Sambo's tool.'

He took my hand, and placed in on his huge affair. Oh, that was a prick. I am certain I don't exaggerate when I say it must have been more than a foot in length, and thick in proportion; but the head was tremendous, it was as big as my two fists together. I felt it with amazement and began to fear for my cunt in good earnest.

'Hah missa, what you think? Will him get in? You not need afraid – though very big, he slippery as snake, and creep in like possum through the cane patch. S'pose we try, but first gib him one smack of de lips, that make him bery lubbing and tender.'

He pushed his huge prick towards my mouth. I held it in both hands: it felt very muscular, and seemed instinct with life.

I rubbed the large soft head to my lips. I did not suppose that my mouth was large enough to take it in, however, the moment my lips opened, he pushed it in. It filled the whole aperture inside, and kept my jaws at their widest stretch. I certainly never had so large or so strange a mouthful before.

'Golly, how nice,' he grunted, moving it slowly back and forward through my lips.

I had tasted Dick's seed several times, and I had just swallowed a quantity of my father's; now the desire got possession of me to taste what Sambo's was like.

So I sucked the head, while I frigged the stiff column of his prick and felt about his enormous cods, more like a stallion's than a man's.

The whole prick grew larger, stiffer and hotter, until, all of a sudden, a mighty flood of steaming spunk burst into my mouth faster than I could swallow, and bubbled out at the corners; it seemed very hot and thick and had a strong aromatic flavour.

Sambo's grunts were now almost alarming, 'Oh–ah. Wah–oh. Ee–augh!'

Then with a great sigh he sank on one side.

All this time there was a rustling and shaking going on at the opposite side of the bed, and I heard Zilla's suppressed titter, so I knew they were at prick-and-cunt work too, and were enjoying all that was going on.

I was afraid to say a word lest I should betray myself, so I quietly wiped my mouth, and awaited the further progress of events.

Sambo speedily recovered, and putting his hands under my bottom, and his head between my thighs, he again kissed and sucked my cunt; then rising, he flung himself over me on the bed between my uplifted legs.

Now came the ordeal which I at once dreaded and longed for; I felt the huge prick poking its head strongly against my cunt; the tender opening seemed already over-stretched by its attempted entrance, but I was resolved to endure any amount of pain provided the passage was finally effected. So I put down my hand, and opening my lips widely with my fingers, placed the slanting top at the critical spot. He then made a downward shove, forcing the monstrous head just inside the inner lips; I spread my thighs to their widest stretch, and heaved against him, but still it stuck fast in the entrance. A sudden thought seemed to strike him, for he drew his prick back and daubed its head and my cunt plentifully with spittle, then he replaced it in the mouth of my cunt and renewed his efforts; this time with better success, for the huge well-moistened head gradually forced its way in, and at last I enjoyed the supreme pleasure of feeling that grand specimen of a manly organ passing into and filling up the whole of my femine recess. For the life of me, I could not help groaning out with a sigh of relief, 'Oh, it is in. At last I have it. I feel it all inside.'

Zilla laughed outright, and cried, 'Hold it, missy, hold it fast. Now Sambo, fuck.'

'Who dat – dat you Zilla? Hah, you just one big rogue, you humbug Sambo! Sambo humbug you noder time.'

'Fuck, you fool,' cried Zilla, coming behind him, and pushing her hand between us, she felt the lips of my cunt stretched round the mighty shaft of Sambo's prick; 'you should go on your knees and bless me for getting you the nicest cunt on the whole island.'

'Oh, Missa Queenie, you very kind to poor Sambo; you hab lubly leetle cunt,' and he commenced a series of slow but all the more delicious up and down heaves, making the huge tool pass most luxuriously in and out through the clinging lips of my throbbing aperture.

Zilla's fingers greatly increased the sensation, as she felt the lips and pinched my clitoris; and I thought I felt my father's hand besides playing about my bottom. Hearing a stir on my right, I reached out my hand; it met my father's and he placed it on his prick.

It sometimes happens in the experience of us all, that after long waiting, our desires are accomplished, and then fortune, as if to make up for the past delay, heaps her favours on the happy recipient, and, to use the old saw, it not only rains, but it pours; so in this instance, I was now at last gratified to the uttermost: I had in my cunt the largest prick I ever saw, in my hand I held my father's fine tool and Zilla's fingers roved about my cunt and bottom; still, I wanted more, so I turned my head to one side, and drew on papa's prick until I got its head into my mouth, that I might at the same time enjoy its fragrance and velvet softness as I twined my tongue round its palpitating end. Thus while

Sambo fucked my cunt, I sucked my father's prick, and Zilla frigged us all, and as she frigged, she cried – like one intoxicated with delight – 'Go to it, pricks; suck cunts; heave bottoms; smack bellies; fire away, gods; over prick, cunt and bottom; and we all rolled together in one mass of intermingled life and pleasure.

After a while we recommenced feeling around and the effect of the neighbouring hands meeting together as they felt the different pricks and cunts was curious and exciting.

Sambo had taken father's prick in his mouth and was trying to suck out something more, while father played in my bottom with his tongue and licked my cunt.

Meantime Zilla had managed to get over me with her cunt on my face and enjoyed the titillation of my lips, for she quickly favoured me with a soft effusion.

We all felt now tolerably used up, so after a few moments rest we separated for the night, and in our beds sought the repose we so much needed to recruit our exhausted powers.

From this time forward my father's manner became more tender and affectionate. He obtained the services of the best teachers on the island to impart to me instructions and accomplishments. By day he was most guarded, but at night I often slept in his arms, and we indulged freely in every kind of sensual enjoyment. After some time, he decided to send me to a ladies academy in the Southern States of America, and told me that a friend of his, a Captain St John who commanded a trading vessel, would take charge of me as far as New Orleans and that we were to sail in a fortnight. I thanked him, commended his plan, and promised to lose no time in getting ready.

I was, of course, sorry to leave him, especially now that I knew him better, but I felt that he was doing well in sending me away, and the thought that I could improve my learning and enlarge my knowledge of the world reconciled me to the change.

Dick too, had to leave, as his father had arranged to send him to one of the island colleges as a medical student. We engaged to correspond regularly, and he assured me that he would remain faithful to me forever; but he laughed when, in reply, I asked him to promise to give me a true and exact account of all the girls he fell in love with, and also a full description of any *amours* he might engage in and of any love scenes he might witness, for I will knew he could not live without some amusement of the kind. 'And remember,' I added, 'I don't care how many girls you go with provided you retain your confidence in me, and report everything that happens.'

I may add that Dick was faithful in his promise, and he did send me from time to time very amusing accounts of his love adventures. I have his letters still, and as some of them are exceedingly graphic in their detail, I may in their place transcribe portions of them for the gratification of my readers.

The events related above, though massed together, really occupied a period of three years. I have selected only the most remarkable as types of the rest and because they made a deeper impression on my memory and produced a corresponding effect in the formation of my character.

We are all very much what early teaching and examples have made us; and those who have met with experiences similar to mine in their youth know how impossible it is in afterlife to resist the bias and change the tone they received, when impressions thus produced are as lasting as life itself.

I refer to this fact because it throws light on the development of my character as delineated in following pages.

CHAPTER FIVE

The Voyage

All preparations being completed, I was taken by my father aboard the good ship *Cammarilla* and given in charge to Captain St John. My maid Zilla accompanied me; she was in great spirits, not only on account of the new life before her, but because my father had promised her her freedom if she served me faithfully until I was twenty-one.

I was glad to find on board the vessel when I arrived a pleasing and very good-looking young lady who was introduced to me by the captain as his niece Laura.

The ship was to sail next morning so our first thought was to make ourselves as comfortable as we could. A small cabin was allotted me next to Laura's. On the opposite side of the saloon were two similar cabins, occupied respectively by the captain and Mr Yeats, the mate, a gentlemanly young man who made himself agreeable to us ladies.

Zilla had a snug cabin assigned to her in the fore part of the ship near the petty officers, which pleased her well, for she was in inveterate flirt.

The captain seemed a plain honest seaman, a little hot-tempered, yet exceedingly kind and genial in his nature. He was a widower about fifty years of age, but still in the prime of his life. He always professed himself an all-round admirer of the fair sex, which I soon verified so far as sex was concerned.

Laura was very friendly and communicative, and as the captain and mate were busy getting the ship in order for an early start, we were left the first evening almost alone. She showed me how to stow away my belongings in what she called 'ship-shape', fashion that is, making the most of the very limited space at our disposal. She told me this was her first trip with her uncle, who was her guardian; that, as she had no settled home, she preferred to be at sea with him to living on shore by herself; but that he had many funny ways and was fond of making free with any girl who would let him, but that I need not be afraid for he really meant no harm. 'And Queenie, after all, how very dull life would be if we were always to be straightlaced and never enjoy a little fun – when we can do it safely you know.'

I said that I quite agreed with her, and that though very young, I had seen enough of the world to prove the truth of the poet's words, "Every woman is at heart a raker", not that I quite understand what that means,' I added.

She laughed and promised to instruct me more fully if I wished and said she thought I had come to a very good school for acquiring any learning that I needed in that respect.

When it grew dark the captain and mate came down, mixed some grog, and prevailed on us to take a little; after which the captain said it would be well for us to turn in, as we should most likely be wakened early when the ship got well under way. He wished me good-night, called me 'his dear child' and told me he liked me not only for my father's sake, who was one of his best and only friends, but still more for my own, as he found me innocent, pretty and good. (I fear that like most men he was taken with a pretty face, and thought that all the rest must follow suit.) Then drawing me towards him, he kissed me on the cheek, and directed Laura to see me comfortably settled in my bed.

Next morning I was awakened at the first dawn of day, by a great tramping of feet and rasping of cables on the deck overhead. Soon afterwards the vessel began to heave and plunge as she felt the wind acting on her wide-spread canvas.

At first I thought the motion agreeable, but I quickly found that it produced most unpleasant effects in my internal economy, and I felt for the first time that dire distress called seasickness. As the motion went on the seasickness increased, and I lay tossing and moaning in my bed.

At length the cabin-boy peeped in and enquired when I wished to have breakfast.

I told him I wanted nothing, but to send for my maid, Zilla, as I was very sick.

He replied that she was quite as bad as myself, and so was Miss Laura too, but that he would tell the captain.

The captain soon knocked on my door and asked might he enter. I said, 'Come in.' He came up to the side of my bed, looked kindly at me and told me to cheer up, and take some breakfast, and that I would be all right by and by.

'Oh, I feel too sick to take anything. I feel as if I were just going to die.'

'Not at all,' he said, raising me up. 'You have plenty of life in you yet.'

He held me up with his arm around me, and sick as I, I remarked how his eyes glistened as he caught a glimpse of my bosom through the opening of my dress.

'Lay me back,' I muttered. 'Oh, I am so sick.'

He laid me down, and as he smoothed my dress, passed his hands lightly over my breasts. 'You are very hot; shall I remove some of this thick covering?'

I grunted approval and he moved his hands over my thighs and rested them on my stomach and asked, 'Is it here that you feel uneasy?'

'Oh, yes, captain. Oh, I am so sick.'

'You are very bad, my poor child, but I know what will do you good; a glass of hot stiff grog – and I will go and mix it for you.'

'Oh, no, I would not be able to drink it.'

However, he went off and soon returned with a steaming hot tumbler in his hand. After much coaxing and entreaty on his part, I gulped down a good portion of its contents. It speedily threw me into a kind of stupor, the excessive sickness moderated, and I lay back helpless and exhausted and with a spinning in my brain that made me almost unconscious.

The captain then proceeded to arrange the clothes about me and finding I made no resistance, passed his hand up under my shift between my thighs until he reached my mount, on which the hair was just beginning to appear. He felt about the lips and rubbed his fingers in the chink between them. Then pulling up my shift, he separated my thighs and kissed my cunt. I muttered, 'What are you doing?'

'Taking care of my little pet,' he said, as he drew the covering over me, kissed my forehead, and went away.

I lay in a stupor the whole of that day; I felt so weak after the sickness and was so stupefied by the brandy that I was unable to move and did not care what happened to me.

I was just conscious that the captain came in several times to see and enquire how I was getting on, and I think he took every possible liberty with my helpless person, so far as feeling, kissing and examining all my secret nooks and crannies.

In the evening Laura paid me a visit and brought some tea which I found refreshing. She said that she had been very sick herself as it was unusually rough and the ship had had to beat to windward. She asked if the captain had been to see me, and whether he had taken good care of me.

I said he had come in several times to enquire how I was, and had brought me brandy and water, which made me quite stupefied, and that then he took care of me after a fashion.

'Oh, I understand,' said Laura laughing, 'that is an old dodge of his, and I may as well tell you myself what you would soon find out, that my uncle regards me as something nearer than a niece; and that is the way he commenced. I expect he showed his care for you by taking a liberty or two when perhaps you were scarcely able to oppose him; but you don't mind it, do you my pet?' she said, lowering her hand and passing it up between my thighs. 'What a charming little love-trap you have got, Queenie. I don't wonder at the captain coming to you again and again, after he had found a way of getting at it; but how roomy it is. Queenie, you are not so innocent as you appear; you must tell me all about yourself, and we will have such sweet confidences together. Now put your hand on me here, and feel me while we seal our bargain with a kiss.

Lifting up her dress as she stood at the side of my bed, she took my hand and placed it between her firm, smooth thighs up to an immense bush of hair that clustered at their junction. In the midst of it, I felt the projecting ridges of two fat lips, and to please her I pressed my finger into the moist slit between.

'I guess you are a little roomy yourself, Laura,' I said, as I pushed two or three fingers up the passage.

'Why not?' and Laura laughed, and with a knowing wink said, 'It's well to suit all comers you know.'

'No, I don't know; what do you mean by suiting all comers?' I asked, looking very simple.

'Now, Queenie, don't put on the innocent with me; you know, I am sure, just as well as I do, what kind of comers we like to visit us here, and I would venture a good sum that you know the names too. Now suppose I give you the first letter – P; tell me the second.'

Turning away my face, I answered, 'R'.

'That's right, then I – now go on.

'C.'

'And I will finish with K, and pronounce PRICK; and then its friend and companion, which you and I are more familiar with: C.'

'U,' I supplied.

'N and T. Now say the word.'

'CUNT.'

'Good,' said Laura, 'so far for the agents, now for the act: F-U-C-K, Fuck.'

'You'll do, you are quite up to the mark; just as I thought, you don't want teaching, you want practice, and the captain will give you enough of that, or I am mistaken. But now my dear, you ought to get some sleep, that you will be strong and fresh tomorrow.'

She then got me a cup of excellent coffee with beaten up egg in it, which quite set me up; and as the motion of the ship was more easy, I soon fell asleep.

When I awoke next morning, to my surprise, I felt myself in the arms of a naked man, who stopped my cry with a kiss.

'Be quiet, darling Queenie,' he said, getting over me, and half smothering me with his weight, 'it is only your friend, the captain. I heard all your conversation with Laura last night, and I could not resist the temptation of visiting you this morning, that you may find out what my comer is like; where is your hand?'

He caught my wrist and forced my hand on his prick, while he pushed his knee between my thighs.

'Captain St John, I can't permit that – you had no right to come in here without my leave – let go my hand – no, I won't hold it – I don't want to know how big it is – I won't let you put it in – you are hurting me – Oh.'

'Well, take your hand out of the way – now open your legs more – Oh, my love – let it in – there,' he said as he pushed his prick into my cunt and drove it forcibly up.

When I felt the dear thing enter the region of love, and penetrate to my centre of delight, every other thought passed away, and with the utmost abandon I threw my arms around him and pressed him to my heart.

'That's the way to do it, my darling, heave your sweet little bun. Oh, isn't that good?' he asked, working his prick rapidly in and out of my throbbing cunt.

'Have I permission to fuck you now, Queenie?' he asked as he paused for a moment with the whole length of his prick deeply embedded in my cunt.

'You may fuck away; how could I refuse you, captain, while your prick is filling all my cunt.'

My ready use of the words prick, cunt and fuck surprised him into fresh delight, and with successive grunts of satisfaction, he darted his seed into my glowing recess.

After lying on me for awhile, he moved to one side, and having wiped his tool, he placed my hand on it again.

The touch of a new prick was certainly pleasant and exciting; so I said nothing, but quietly played with its head, and frigged the soft skin up and down.

'Queenie, you are a darling, and I am delighted to have you on board. Laura and I will do our best to make your voyage pleasant and agreeable; and maybe we'll have fun together; get over me now, my pet, and I will fuck you from beneath.'

He drew me on top of him, with my thighs straddled across his hips, then, with his hands round my bottom, he opened the lips of my cunt with knowing fingers and directed the head of his prick into the hot chink.

'Now, Queenie, ride the cock-horse, while we heave up and down together. How do you like this style of fucking?'

'It is delicious,' I replied, moving up and down.

'You do it splendidly,' he grunted, driving up his tool; then raising his voice, he cried: 'Laura, Laura, come here, and see how Queenie is fucking me.'

Laura must have been listening close by, for in half a minute she was alongside the bed, and without ceremony she drew off the clothes and laid my bottom bare.

'For shame, Laura, get away you horrid girl; let me up captain,' but he held me round the waist with one of his hands, while he shoved the other up Laura's petticoats.

She stooped over us and said, as she played with her fingers about my bottom and cunt, 'Take it easy, Queenie, you will get used to it in time; why need you mind my seeing your little fanny enjoys a visit from a newcomer? If you have not learned it before, you must know now how much additional pleasure is derived from a change of pricks; go on again, there's a dear, my looking on will only add to your pleasure.'

'Pull up your shift, Laura, and show Queenie that you are not ashamed to let her see how well prepared and ready you are for the sports and enjoyments of love.'

She at once pulled up her clothes and showed her fine bushy cunt with the captains's fingers buried between its pouting lips, and as she withdrew his hand, she pushed it close to our faces, and with a merry laugh, said: 'Look at it, Queenie,' and drawing aside the hair she separated the lips and continued, 'see how red it is inside. If it could speak it would say – Get me a prick – fuck, fuck, fuck – What is the use of having a cunt if one does not use it as it was intended to be used; so commence again,' and poking her fingers into my cunt alongside the captain's prick, she nearly set me wild with excitement.

'Never mind, Miss Laura,' I panted out, as I recommenced heaving up and down, 'I'll have my revenge on you yet.'

She stooped down behind me and said, 'You shall, darling,' at the same time giving me a cruel bite on my bottom just as the captain with a yell of delight shot his spunk up my enraptured cunt, and my own spending poured over his belly and thighs –

I felt quite ashamed to look the captain in the face when I next met him but he drew me into his cabin. At once he passed his hand up under my clothes, and reaching my cunt said: 'My sweet little pet, you have a delicious quim, and can give a man more satisfaction than any girl I ever fucked. You shall be queen of the ship, while you remain on board. You have only to command, it will be my pleasure to obey. Is there anything I can do to gratify you and prove my devotion?'

'Yes,' I replied, as I frigged his standing prick, 'I would like to see you putting this to Laura.'

He laughed. 'You want to punish her and get pleasure at the same time; but see, here is the means of doing that; she meant this for you,' and he opened a locker and took out a small pliant birch-rod, carefully tied with green ribbon. 'Take it to your cabin and be ready when I call you. Mate Yeats has charge of the deck, but I guess he and Laura will be flirting together, How shall we get her down?'

'Leave that to me, I'll manage to have her here shortly, and then pretend to go on deck myself.'

I found more difficulty then I expected in getting her away from Mr Yeats, whom she evidently treated as an accepted lover. However, I prevailed on her to go down for a book of poems we had been talking about.

I followed and went softly to my own cabin, leaving the door open. I soon heard Laura saying to the captain in a low voice: 'Let me go, uncle, I can't stay now.'

'Why not?' Yeats will have plenty of you by and by. He told me this morning that you had accepted him, and asked my leave to marry you when we called at Port Royal in Jamaica.'

'Well, and what did you say in reply?'

'I told him he might marry you as soon as he liked on one condition.'

'What is that?' she asked.

'Only that he must consent to share you with me, and promise never to turn troublesome or grow jealous.'

'Oh, uncle, how could you? That will certainly turn him against me altogether.'

'Not a bit of it, Mat and I understand each other. We have been always free together. He has many a time watched me fucking his own sister, and once he got so excited, he fucked her himself before me; so you need not fear that he will draw off on that account. Anyway, let us have one more fuck; give my old fellow a suck first just to put him into good humour.'

'There now, it is fine and stiff. Fuck me now and let me go.'

'Here goes, then. I'll lean back and you can mount across me, that's right; how hot your cunt feels. Now stoop down and kiss me,' he said as he pulled up her clothes over her back. 'If Queenie was here now, she would have a grand sight – a magnificent white arse cocked up and a find brown cunt below, plugged with a rampant prick; Queenie, Queenie – come here.'

I quickly made my appearance and closed the door.

Laura turned her face towards me as I entered, smiled at me, and said: 'Queenie, it is your turn, now, to look on,' and then boldly asked, 'How do you like my bottom?'

'It is beautiful, white, plump and dimpled,' I said, laughing. 'All it wants is to be reddened a little – to make it blush for its impudence, you know, a slight touching up with this,' holding up the birch, 'would make it all right; may I try it, Laura?'

'You may, if you do it moderately.'

'Hold her, captain, I owe her something,' I cried, as I gave her bottom some smart cuts with the birch.

She writhed and bounced over the captain as she felt the stings of the rod on her soft creamy bottom.

'That's right, Queenie, that is the way to put life into her cunt; you can't think how it makes her pobble my prick; punish her well, every whack on her arse adds heat and vigour to her cunt.'

'Oh, Queenie, be merciful – that's enough – I can't bear more – indeed I can't – stop – I say, stop – you have cut my bottom to pieces, you cruel girl.'

The spirit of lust and cruelty got possession of me. I scarcely heeded her cries, and continued administering the most cutting strokes I could deliver, making the pliant ends of the birch reach the tender insides of her thighs and delicate borders of her cunt.

There was mercy in this through, for it not only hastened the consummation, but heightened the enjoyment at the last. Her excitement was now intense, and she so bounced against the captain, and compressed his prick with such force in her cunt, that she caused an immediate overflow of spending on both sides, and the frothy sperm ran down over his buttocks and bottom.

The captain commended her fortitude, and giving her a warm kiss, thanked her for the pleasure she had afforded him, pleasure which had been so much increased through her pains.

I took her in my arms as she shook down her clothes over her smarting bottom, and begged her to forgive me this whipping, which I really could not help – her bottom looked so enticing for the rod – and promised we would be friends forever more. 'Well, then I forgive you, and indeed, I must say that the pleasure at the end more than counterbalanced the suffering which led to it, as you will someday experience yourself.'

CHAPTER SIX

The Captain's Yarn

The next time I was alone with Captain St John, I asked him to tell me how he became so intimate with Mr Yeats, and what he meant by telling Laura that he had fucked his sister in his presence.

'Well, Queenie, I must of course obey your command. I knew Mat's father well; he and his family sailed in my ship when they first came to the island. Mat was then a lad of fourteen, and his sister, Bessy, was one year younger.

'Some time afterwards I had the good fortune to extricate Mat from a very ugly scrape. He had been drinking with a lot of wild young fellows, when nothing would satisfy them but to break into the governor's grounds and to rob his conservatory. The governor detected them, and he and his servants tried to capture them. There was a severe struggle, and one of the servants was killed. Mat was stunned by a blow, and taken prisoner, but the rest, who were the really guilty parties, escaped.

'The governor declared that he would have Mat tried for murder; but by great exertion and special inducement, I got him to pardon Mat and permit the affair to be hushed up. This made the whole family attached to me, and I passed the greater part of my time on shore with them. Mat specially became my most devoted ally. He never left my side, and at length he prevailed on his father to let him go to sea with me. He was entered in the ship's books as my apprentice, and he has sailed with me ever since. He passed all his examinations very creditably, and is now full mate, with the promise of a ship the next trip.

'We lived together, drank together, sported together and, like most sailors, had our favourite girls in every port. There was a pretty little black-eyed girl called Susan, living in Bridgetown, Barbados, whom I was fond of and used to visit regularly when I was in that port. Mat accompanied me the first time I went to her after he came on board. Although then eighteen, he had never yet fucked a girl; so I told him he ought to begin with her, and try his prentice prick in her cunt. But he was modest and begged me to show him the way, so to please him, I mounted Susan in such a manner that he could see the whole operation. When he saw me fairly at work, it was laughable the state of excitement he got into. His face flushed, his eyes sparkled, his hands trembled, he came close to us, and eagerly watching my prick as it darted in and out, pushed his hand in between us and felt the lips of her cunt stretched around my tool. He hardly gave me time to get off before he was on her, with his virgin prick deep in the hot recess which I had moistened and prepared for his entrance. He quickly discharged and then almost immediately commenced a second course, to Susan's intense gratification. I also shared in their fun and fingered their privates while they fucked.

'After this, we always had the same girl, one after the other, and used to toss for first turn. We often talked of these things when at sea, and several times when we were in bed, we examined and frigged each other's pricks.

'He got so that he hardly ever looked at a girl without thinking of her cunt and wondering what it was like. He said that even when kissing his sister, Bessy, he could not help thinking of her cunt, and that at one time he saw it and kissed it. I asked him to tell me how it happened.

'He said they were riding together in a thickly wooded place, when her mare put her foot into a hole, stumbled, and threw his sister head foremost into some thick bushes. He ran to lift her up and found her caught in the branches, all her clothes over her head, and her legs kicking in the air, and through the opening in her drawers he saw a pair of hairy lips pouting out and beautifully red inside. When raising her up he could not avoid pressing his face between her thighs and kissing her cunt.

' "Oh, it was so soft and warm," he said, "and had such a delicious smell; I just held her in my arms, while I took one long luscious kiss and then set her on her feet."

'She was not much hurt and was able to ride home.

'I asked what was the colour of the hair on her cunt. He said it was of a rich golden hue, and that while the skin around was of a clear pearly white, the insides of the lips were as red as crimson.

' "Why, Mat, you have given a most enticing description of your sister's cunt, enough to make one long to see it for oneself."

' "And why not, old fellow. I don't begrudge your looking at it, and fucking it too, if you can, provided you are careful to do her no harm; but I know I can trust you in that matter, for you have shown me that it is quite possible to enjoy a girl, yet avoid doing her any injury.'

'Bessy sometimes came on board to see her brother, and bring him presents of fruit and home luxuries. On one of these occasions we had been all drinking grog together, and Bessy herself, having imbibed a tolerable share, was inclined to be merry. Mat suddenly lifted her up, popped her down on my knee, and said, 'Put your arms around him, Bessy, I know you are very fond of him and he deserves it; now give him a kiss like a good girl, it would please me as well as him.' She threw her arms round my neck, and held up her sweet little mouth for a kiss.

'Mat kissed her too, and at the same time pressed one of his knees in between hers, and lifting her skirts, pushed my hand under her petticoats. She did not recognise my hand at first, but thought it was Mat's knee that was pressing up between her thighs. So she leaned back while I went on kissing her, and being excited by the drink she had taken, readily opened her thighs to let her brother's knee press up higher.

'I supported her with my arm around her waist, while my hand slowly worked its way up between her legs outside her drawers until I reached the opening, and then in the soft warm nook at the bottom of her belly, I found the sweet sanctuary I was in search of; my fingers at once spread over the swelling mound, so richly covered with silken hair; then pushing down my middle finger, I pressed into the moist chink, while with the others, I squeezed the fat lips on either side.

' "Oh, my, what are you doing? – take your hand away – captain, let me up – Don't – I'll cry."

' "Bessy, behave, Captain St John won't harm you, let him keep his hand there; you are bound to obey your brother," and he forced open her thighs which she was trying to keep closed.

'She lay back sobbing, and still trying to keep her legs together but in such a way as convinced both her brother and myself, that she was only waiting for a sufficient display of force on our part to satisfy her conscience that she only yielded to compulsion; something like what that poet fellow, we were reading the other evening, said:

> A little still she strove, and much repented;
> And whispering: 'I'll ne'er consent – consented.

'So Mat with a twinkle in his eye, vociferated, "If you don't stop this nonsense, I'll put up your petticoats, and then we shall both see what you keep so religiously covered up from all the world."

' "Oh, Mat, for shame. Why do you treat me so. Captain St John has a wife, let him go to her if he wants this kind of thing."

' "Yes, but she is old, ugly and sick; she may be dead now, for all we know to the contrary; so don't bother about her."

'Then without further parley, he boldly lifted her dress, which was half up already, until we caught a glimpse of the bright hair over her cunt as it gleamed through the open slit of her drawers.

'Don't, Mat; let down my clothes. Oh, I shall die of shame. Captain St John, I thought you were fond of me. If you were, you would not allow him to expose me so."

' "It is just because I am fond of you that I have been longing to see and feel your sweet cunt, and it is indeed very lovely, beyond the power of words to express. Cease struggling, there's a love; lean back; open your legs – more – still more, there's a pet."

' "Well, I suppose you must have your way, for I am tired; I can't fight against you both," and she lay passive in our hands. Mat then placed her head in his lap, and watched me as I unfastened her drawers, pulled them off her legs, and drew up her shift; then – oh, what a scene of loveliness was disclosed to our enraptured eyes. The rich creamy white of her smooth round belly was delicious to look upon, set off as it was by the warm glow of golden hair on the mound which marked its junction with her two voluptuous thighs and clothed the valley between. Pushing in between these fleshy columns, I spread them open as wide as I could. Then it was that we got a full view of all the beauties of her cunt, glistening with the soft dews of love as she became conscious that we were regaling our eyes with the naked loveliness of its long-concealed charms.

'As I observed how Mat gloated over his sister's maiden sweets, the thought passed through my mind, it will not be long, my boy, before you seek a closer acquaintance with these hidden charms now so temptingly opened to your view.

' "Now, St John," exclaimed Mat, "did I not give you a true description of this sweet nest and its surroundings?"

' "Indeed Mat, the reality far exceeds your account, favourable as it was, for, in my opinion, no description could do full justice to its fascinating powers."

'I bent forward to the lovely shrine, kissed its pouting lips, and rolled my tongue in its fragrant recess.

'Mat meanwhile unbuttoned his trousers, drew out his prick, and placed it leaning on his sister's cheek.

'I was not slow in following his example, and put the head of my pego between the moist lips of her love-chink.

' "Oh, captain, take it out, I can't let you do that."

' "Be quiet, Bessy, he is only making his prick kiss your cunt."

' "No, he is pushing it in – don't, captain – pray – don't – Oh, Oh, its hurting me – what are you doing with it?"

' "Fucking you, darling Bessy, with your brother's consent, for he knows I won't harm you; fucking you – driving my prick, this way, in and out of your cunt; each time, sending my prick home, and making my balls smack against your bottom."

'Meanwhile, Mat, inflamed by the sight, pressed her face to his prick and pushed its head against her mouth. He then placed one of her hands on its shaft; her fingers at once closed around it to his great delight, and, led on by natural instinct, she frigged it up and down.

'I could no longer retain my seed, so remembering my promise to Mat, I hastily withdrew my tool from the inner passage where the risk was, and laid it along the chink of her cunt, and burying its head amid the hair, I poured a hot but harmless stream over her belly; at the same moment, the pent-up juices of her brother's reservoir, spurted into her mouth, and ran in warm gushes down her throat.

After this, we had many pleasant scenes with Bessy. Once the ice was broken, she seemed to plunge in with all her heart, and sported with her brother and me with the utmost freedom. Still they both refrained from the greatest favour of all. She did not object to letting him see, play with, or even suck her cunt, and evidently enjoyed playing with his prick and making him spend in her mouth – indeed that was the way she gave him relief when he became over-excited from watching and handling us as we fucked – but as yet he had not attempted to put his prick into her cunt, nor did she seem to desire it.

'She now sometimes brought her maid with her, not without design, I thought, for she was young and pretty, and Bessy often said she pitied her brother, unmatched as he was. However that might be, Mat soon managed to gain the maid's consent, and after watching me fuck his sister, he used to run off and cool himself in her willing receiver. At last he coaxed her to come into the saloon, and made free with her there before his sister. Bessy had now become so familiar with the ways of

love that she readily joined in the sport; so she and I together held
down the maid, while Mat pulled up her clothes, got between her legs
and openly rammed his prick into her cunt.

'Then Mat and I stripped her naked, and after that Bessy, and
finally ourselves. We spread carpets and rugs on the floor, and rolled
about so that bottoms and faces were continually coming into new
and interesting positions. Mat proposed, the cunning fellow, to tie
bandages over their eyes that they might not see what we were doing
and then he whispered to me to fuck the maid by way of change. And
I need not tell you, Queenie, that there is no novelty which a man so
thoroughly appreciates, as the novelty of a fresh cunt, so I quite
approved of his notion, and getting on top of her, I soon found my
way into her soft recess.

'Mat, however, had his own object in view, for throwing himself on
his sister, he eagerly kissed and sucked her cunt, and then turning, he
drove his prick into it without scruple or delay.

'She must have felt some difference in his style of fucking from mine
for, putting up her hand, she hastily removed the bandage from her
eyes and seeing her brother on top of her cried,

' "Oh, Mat, stop – do you know what you are doing – fucking your
own sister."

' "Why not, Bessy, I have kissed your cunt and watched it so many
times filled with St John's prick; and I have so shared in your delights as
often as he fucked you that I could stand it no longer, and I felt that I
must fuck you myself, even though you are my own sister. And let me
tell you, I find your cunt all the nicer," he said as he panted over her –
fucking – fucking. She made no reply, but I observed that she pressed
him more lovingly to her breast as she moved up in ready response to
meet the quick prods of his excited prick.

'I quite shared in their transport, and only wondered how they had
refrained from it so long; so leaning towards them, with my prick still in
the maid's cunt, I kissed her and said, 'Bessy, my love, confess, that you
enjoy being fucked by Mat all the more because he is your brother.'

' "Yes, I must say it is exceptionally good, being fucked by one's
brother. Mat has a fine tool, and he knows how to use it," and heaving
up her bottom, she clasped him tightly in her arms.

' "Don't hurry, Mat," I said. "This is our second or third bout; take it
quietly – we'll enjoy it all the better." And I thrust my tongue into
Bessy's mouth; while still working my prick slowly in the maid's cunt.

' "All right, old fellow," he replied, putting his hand over my bottom,
as we lay alongside of one another, and catching my balls, he pressed
them so luxuriously in his fingers that, convulsed with pleasure, they

ejected their contents and my prick poured the bubbling fluid into the open cunt so ready to receive it and pay it back with interest.

'We sailed in a few days, and the next time I saw Bessy she was the wife of a rich old planter named Hobbs, in fact none other than the lady whom you know as Lizzy, and whom your father fucks whenever he gets the opportunity.

'There, Queenie, you can now understand my extraordinary intimacy with Mat Yeats; and how there was but little danger of my doing Laura any harm with him, when I attached to his marrying her the condition of his afterwards sharing with me. And now, my pet, having not only answered your question, but spun you a regular love yarn, let me claim my reward, in the enjoyment of another fuck.'

CHAPTER SEVEN

Laura's Narrative

Although much occupied with preparations for her approaching marriage, Laura found time to remind me of our promise of mutual confidence, and said that if I gave her an account of my introduction to the enjoyments of love, she would oblige me in like manner. So I told her of Dick's boyish attempts, and final success; and described what I had seen in the punishment house, both with respect to old Snigger and the girls, and my father and Mrs Hobbs, Mat Yeats's sister.

Laura had heard something of this before and was very much amused. I then called on her to fulfil her part of the agreement, and she responded thus:

'Like you, Queenie, I was enlightened at an early age. My mother, who was Captain St John's sister, was married to a doctor. She died when I was a child about nine years old, and he married again. We then lived in a very small house, and for want of accommodation, my bed was placed at the foot of theirs, with only a curtain between. When laying awake at night, I often felt their bed shake in a funny way, and sometimes I heard them whispering to one another such expressions as: "You may do it now – take it in your hand – put it in yourself – open your thighs – lift your legs – keep your hand on it – press it between your fingers"; then there would be a rustling, shaking, panting and father would snort, and cry, "Oh, Oh," and she would say, "Can't you do it quietly, you'll wake the child."

I also heard father making her say: 'Prick, cunt, fuck, and telling her to pinch his arse and frig his prick, and asking her to let him fuck her bottom.

'I did not know the meaning of all those terms then, but I had an inkling of what they referred to and, eagerly listening to every stir and noticing every word, I longed above all things to see what they were doing; but as this amatory intercourse generally took place just after they went to bed, when all was dark, for a long time I could see nothing. However, one light summer morning, I happened to be awake when they commenced their play; I heard him say, "Lift your bottom that I may see your cunt, while you suck my prick."

'In the most stealthy manner, I slightly drew the curtain to one side. The view that then greeted my eager eyes almost took away my breath.

'My stepmother was on her knees, straddling across my father, and her great white bottom was raised up in the most impudent manner right before his face. She was stooping forward, resting her elbows, and holding in her hand a long fleshy thing that was standing up out of a thick bush of black hair at the bottom of his belly. This long thing, the first of its kind I had ever seen, at once arrested by attention; and it seemed to have some peculiar fascinating power, for I could not take my eyes from it. I noticed that it had a large glossy head of purplish colour, which she kissed and rubbed to her nose and cheeks, while she moved her hand up and down on its body; then she took a good portion into her mouth and sucked it with apparent gusto.

' "Thanks for sucking my prick so nicely," he said (then I knew what the word "prick" meant). "Now, let your cunt down on my mouth and I'll have a suck too." (Then I knew what the word "cunt" meant.) And I put my hand on my own little nick, and wondered would it ever be as large and hairy as that of my stepmother. My father held the cheek of her bottom on either side while he sucked her cunt, and kept jerking up his prick, which she still held in her hand, kissing and frigging it all the while.

'Then moving from under her he cried: "Now for a fuck," and telling her to remain on her hands and knees while he fucked her in the rear, he knelt behind her bottom, he pushed her legs apart, drew open the lips of her cunt and peeped into its capacious mouth, now watering as if hungry for something to eat.

'He then took his prick in his hand, and pushing in the head, drove it all the way up. Then he put his arms round her hips and heaved his bottom backwards and forwards, making his tool pass quickly in and out through the hairy lips. That showed me what fucking was, and pushing my finger into my own little chink, I felt about for a place into which a prick might enter, and down at the end I found that there was a small passage, but when I tried to push in my finger, it hurt me too much to go on. However, mama was not hurt, for she kept pushing her bottom back and saying, 'That's the way, push it in strong; give me plenty of it, Harry, I like it so much when you fuck me from behind; it is so pleasant to feel your belly rubbing against my bottom, while you hold me tightly round the loins, and press my cunt with your fingers.'

'Then they both panted and grunted, and he almost roared with delight as, pressing her down flat, he hammered at her bottom, with his prick buried in her cunt.

'I clenched my teeth, pinched my cunt, and pushed in my finger in spite of the pain, and I do verily believe that, although so young, I obtained at that time my first emission.

'I often watched them fucking after this, and soon became familiar with many of the modes and expressions of venereal play. I also regularly frigged my little cranny while I listened to them, and succeeded in forcing up my finger as far as it would go. But in course of time, my stepmother was confined, and I was moved to another room. This was a benefit to me, for I was injuring my health by constant frigging, which I need not tell you is very injurious to a young girl.

'Nothing of particular note occurred again until I was nearly fifteen years old, and the hair was beginning to sprout on my mons. I attended school regularly, and having a great love of learning, I worked hard at my lessons and tried in every way to improve myself.

About this time, a new French master, named Louis Martel, was appointed. He was young and handsome, and of course all the girls fell in love with him at once; but he took no particular notice of anyone, for he was naturally shy and reserved in his manner. He applied himself steadily to his duties, and seemed to think of nothing else. I was one of the most diligent and attentive of his pupils, and on that account he thought more of me, and tried to get me on. I responded by increased efforts, and feeling grateful for his kindness, I tried to please him in every way I could. In short, I began to like him very much, and after a while he seemed to reciprocate my feelings, for he used to hold my hand with a lingering pressure and lean over me when directing me in my lessons.

I remarked that the prominence at the fork of this trousers seemed always to grow larger when he was talking to me, and especially when he was leaning over me. I once pressed my elbow on it, and felt it bound at my touch; that touch acted like an electric spark on my nerves and fired a whole train of amorous emotions; my mind became filled with the idea of his prick, my imagination painted it on every object on which I looked; I dreamed of it at night, and often awoke, fancying I had Louis in my arms, and his prick in my cunt. I now regarded that little rosy chink with increased interest, and used to study its appearance, with a glass placed for the purpose between my legs, wondering what Louis would think of it and wondering whether he would like to put his prick into it and fuck it. 'Oh, if I could only let him see it,' I said to myself, :it would warm his blood, and banish all his reserve.'

'About this time, the school got a holiday, and it was arranged that we should all go to a neighbouring mango grove and look for fruit. We wandered about, and only got further and further from the rest, but that did not distress either of us very much.

'We did not find much fruit, however, and Mr Martel was chiefly occupied in helping me through the bushes and across the ditches while we went on laughing and chatting together. At last we came to a fruit-bearing tree with large low-spreading branches.

' "Oh, here is a tree very easy to climb, and there is plenty of fruit a little way up," I said, putting my foot on one of the lowest branches. "I will pluck the mangoes, and you can pick them up and put them into the basket as I drop them down."

' "Very well," he said, "only take care you don't fall."

'He stood below me as I climbed up over his head. I saw he was watching me eagerly, and the thought flashed through my mind, here is an opportunity for bestowing on him a few glimpses of my secret charms. So I climbed from branch to branch, separating my legs as widely as I could. I had no drawers on, the weather being very hot, and as my frock was short, he must have had a full view of my bottom and thighs and the rosy chink between them, just beginning to be fringed with hair. Glancing down I saw that his face was flushed, and his eyes unusually bright, as he gazed intently up.

' "It is more difficult to get at the fruit than I expected," I said. "I must go further out on this branch."

' "Take care, Laura, that bough is very slight, it will hardly bear your weight."

' "Just as he spoke, there was a squeak and a crash, and the bough and I came down together; but Louis caught me in his arms before I reached the ground; indeed, he was so directly under my clothes that they passed over his head and my bottom plumped right on his turned-up face. This I learned afterwards, for in the course of the fall, my head struck against one of the branches, and I was quite stunned by the blow.

' "When I came to myself, I was lying stretched on the grass with Mr Martel kneeling at my side holding my hands. He looked excited and his face was red, so I fancied he had been investigating more closely my secrets as I lay almost in a faint, and blushed at the thought.

' "Oh, Miss Laura, I am so glad to see you looking like yourself again; I hope you are not hurt much."

' "Not much," I said, trying to rise, "But I fear I have sprained my knee, for it pains me when I lean on it."

' "Let me see if it is swollen."

' "Yes, do," I said, and I raised my dress a little.

He put his hand on my knee and felt it all round.

' "It seems uninjured, but feels hot, may I change it a little for you while you rest?"

' "Thank you," I replied, leaning back, and lifting up my leg. He rubbed about my knee and the under part of my thigh, gradually pushing his hand up higher and higher; at last he brushed against the hair-covered mons, as if by accident, and finding I did not appear angry, he proceeded boldly to put his hand on it, and began to feel the lips and clitoris.

' "Mr Martel take your hand away and let me up."

' "My sweet Laura, let me tell you how much I love and admire you," he said, putting his hand gently on my breast, and keeping me down, 'and this dear little nest, so mossy and warm, is delightfully soft and inviting; let me peep at it again – just a moment," and lifting my frock, he peered up between my legs.

' "Oh, no, Louis," I said, closing my eyes, "don't look at me there, it makes me feel so ashamed."

' "You need not be at all ashamed of it, Laura, for it is the most beautiful little cunt that any man ever looked at," he said raising my dress and opening my thighs.

' "Oh, Louis, how you tickle me with your moustache. Why do you like kissing me there?"

' "Because it is a lovely little cunt, just made to be kissed and sucked, and then to have something nice put into it that will fill it with the most exquisite delight; do you know what I mean?"

' "No, Louis, what could be put into it that would make it feel as nice as you say?"

' "This, my love," placing my hand on his stiff prick, which he had drawn out of its hiding place.

' "I am ashamed to look at it, but I will hold it in my hand just to please you. Yes, and move it up and down, do you like that?"

' "I do, darling, you are giving me more pleasure than I can tell you.

Do you know what men call this?"

' "No, what name to they give it?"

' "They call it prick – say prick, my love."

' "Prick; has every man a prick like yours, Louis?"

' "Yes, every man, though some are large and some are small, but they all like to do the one thing with their pricks.'

' "What's that?" I asked with a laugh.

' "To put them into the cunts of as many girls as ever they can."

' "Oh, my, how funny, and do the girls let them?"

' "Of course they do, why that is what a cunt is made for. This soft moist passage is the place for the prick to enter and pass up; and oh, Laura, it is the pleasantest feeling in the world, and the doing is called fucking. Let me put in my prick and fuck you; there is no one near us, and you will like it so much."

' "Oh, no, Louis, I can't let you put it in now, I would be afraid; perhaps I may let you another time."

'But Louis was too wise to lose the present opportunity and, without asking further leave, he got between my legs, raised them up, and pushed the head of his prick between the lips of my cunt. I thought that having gone so far, the best thing was to facilitate the entrance of his prick as much as I could.

'Louis' prick was of goodly size, and its large round head stuck just inside the opening; but as I was most anxious to get it in, I twisted about and pushed against him, heedless of the pain. In the midst of his efforts to force a passage, his seed burst from him, which, though it checked him for a moment, yet served to lubricate the way and, as his prick still retained its vigour, at the next push he was able to drive home, to my great and entire satisfaction.

'Then, as he commenced that in-and-out movement so dear to us women, he asked me to tell him how I liked the feel of his prick in my cunt fucking me.

' "It is very pleasant, Louis; I cannot tell you how much I enjoy the motion of your prick in and out – that way, between the lips of my cunt ;it makes my nerves vibrate to my heart."

'I did enjoy that, my first fuck, more than I can say; and I need not tell you, Queenie, for you know as well as I, that the sensation of feeling a prick for the first time filling up the whole of one's cunt and distending each throbbing fold inside, is simply indescribable; and then the frantic hug during the last quick prods, and the rush of seed at the end – Oh, it must be felt to be understood.

'Then we lay side by side to rest awhile after our joint exertions, our hands, however, still busy – his fondling my cunt and mine playing with his prick and balls. But as his tool stiffened up again and regained its power, he grew more enterprising, and making me lie back, he pulled all my clothes up to my waist, then he stretched himself between my thighs and sucked my cunt and bottom, after which I sucked his prick and tickled his bottom with my finger. Then nothing would do him but to see me piddle, and he played with my cunt and watched it while I did so. He said he liked to feel my warm piss flow through his fingers.

'In these and suchlike sports, we passed a most delightful hour; during which Louis showed himself to be an ardent and accomplished votary of the Paphian goddess, and initiated me into the various modes of enjoying her favours, and celebrating her rites.

'We then prepared to seek the rest of the party, but my knee turned out to have been more hurt than we at first supposed, and Louis had to carry me a long way. He declared, however, with his national gallantry, that he scarcely felt the weight of his burden, now that he knew the treasure it contained.

'I responded with a loving hug and kiss, as I clung to him with my arms round his neck.

'I was laid up for the week following and was unable to attend school but as Louis called to see me every day, and generally managed to pass an hour with me alone as I reclined on a seat in the garden among the trees, I had no cause to complain.

'One of my class-fellows too, who always professed a great liking for me, passed all her spare time with me. She was a girl with an unusually fair complexion, red hair and deep blue eyes, and apparently considered by our seniors a very model of propriety, but we young people, who knew her better, called her Madam Sly.

'She had quickly noticed my intimacy with Mr Martel, which seemed to interest her greatly, and finding it pleased me, she made him the favourite subject of her conversation. She also contrived generally to meet him either coming or going, though she prudently kept away during our interviews. On one occasion, however, she stole so quietly upon us that she witnessed without our knowledge or consent a very decided love-scene. I had as usual opened his trousers down the front, unfastened his suspenders, and taking possession of his upstanding prick, I fondled and kissed it, and took its glowing head into my mouth, while I tickled his balls and bottom. Louis in the meantime had got his hands between my thighs and was pleasantly titillating the sensitive opening there. Then placing me on my knees on the seat, he uncovered my bottom and thrust in his prick from behind.

'We were both in full enjoyment of our fuck. Louis, panting with pleasure as he gave long deliberate strokes and watched his blunt tool delving in my garden of love, while I expressed the intensity of my satisfaction by various mutterings, and spurred him on by repeating all the amorous words I could think of, when Sly, no longer able to restrain her excited feelings, and perhaps jealous of my sole possession of such great pleasure, suddenly rushed up behind us. Louis started, drew out his prick just as it was beginning to spout forth its liquid sweets, and left my hungry cunt gaping and disappointed at the loss of its favourite morsel; but on ascertaining who the intruder was, his alarm was changed into joy, and he exclaimed, "Aho, Madam Sly, since you have caught us in the act, you must join us both for our sakes and your own."

'To my surprise she offered little or no resistance, but allowed him to kiss her, thrust his hand under her petticoats, raise them up, expose her cunt to view, lay her on her back, and place himself between her legs.

' "Look at Sly's cunt, Laura," he said, pointing to a pair of very fat projecting lips thickly covered with curly red hair. His eyes sparkled as he stooped over this new-found treasure, so temptingly displayed in all its novelty and freshness.

' "You are not jealous, my love; there – put your old friend into Sly's cunt yourself,' and he put my hand on his prick, now bounding with the anticipated pleasure of a new treat. I could not help joining Louis in his admiration of her glowing charms, so, wisely making the best of the situation, I promptly complied, and placing the head of his prick between the open lips, I looked on with curiosity, for her moist chink seemed actually to be smoking with the heat of desire as Louis pushed on with renovated force. But to their mutual disappointment he stuck fast in the entrance.

' "Push harder," I said, grasping his balls.

'She closed her eyes, and seizing the hem of her dress between her teeth, she bit it viciously in her efforts to prevent herself crying out with the pain caused by his energetic attempts to drive in his prick.

' "Draw back, for a moment," I said with prurient warmth, "and I will wet it in my mouth."

' "Oh, don't take it out, my Louis," she panted, clutching him in her arms. "I can bear the pain – there – push – I feel that it is getting in," and she gave a tremendous heave against him; with that the barrier gave way, and his prick rushed up the channel and in an instant was buried out of view. A deep-breathed, "O–h–h" of intense satisfaction burst from them both, as their object was achieved, and the longing hungry cunt received for the first time that delicious morsel which kind nature had provided for its special use and delectation.

'Although deprived myself of the actual pleasure, I fully shared in their excitement, and felt amply repaid by the peculiar enjoyment I found in watching the prick between the lips of her cunt; they seemed to cling round his weapon as he drove it home, and protruded with most lascivious suction as he drew back to make a fresh charge forward; while her soft creamy buttocks opened out and closed up in the most voluptuous manner as she heaved, responsive to this thrusts, and his pendant balls plumped against her bottom at every stroke.

'Louis had discharged almost immediately after the first entrance of his prick into her heated receptacle, but having rested a few moments while his prick lay amidst its throbbing folds, he was soon able to answer her love-twitchings by the renewed action of his pleasure-giving tool.

'Louis's new-found treasure soon led him to forget the old. After his enjoyment of the treat so freely accorded him by Sly's insidious love, I quickly perceived a change in his conduct towards me. He sought my company less, and plainly showed that he did not find in my arms the same satisfaction he used to do.

'I thus learned from bitter experience the fickleness of men, and that a new cunt, simply because it is new, will often attract them from that which gave them the fullest satisfaction before. However, I was too much of a philosopher to repine; having tasted the sweets of love, I felt I must go on, so I determined to look out for its continued gratification elsewhere.

'There were plenty of young fellows, as good-looking as Louis, who I knew would rejoice in my favours if I only gave them opportunity and encouragement. One in particular, named Bertie, who often met me at a dancing academy, seemed to suit my purpose; he was young and handsome, and had the manners of a gentleman – a point I was particularly concerned about. I found him to possess a manly, enterprising spirit, and I think he must have seen me to be kindly disposed, and ready to meet his most ardent advances.

'Accordingly, one evening at a ball, after dancing with me several times, he led me into the lobby and we sat down to rest in a retired part of the stairs away from the crowd. Putting his arm around me, he kissed me warmly, and taking my hand, he placed it on his prick outside his trousers and said, "My sweet Laura, I cannot tell how it is, but whenever I am near you, and above all when I touch you, and hold your dear hand, this part of me swells up and stiffens, so that I become quite uncomfortable and don't know what to do with it. You are kind and indulgent, can you tell me how to relieve it?"

' "Why do you ask me, I am not a doctor. If you want medical advice go to my father, he might be able to help you." He commenced fumbling at my dress. 'No, I do assure you, there is nothing in my pocket but my handkerchief; well, you may try if you wish to much – oh, but that is not my pocket, that is the opening of my dress – no, sir, I cannot let you put your hand underneath."

' "Dearest Laura, that is where the remedy I want is to be found; isn't there a soft mouth somewhere up here? Let me just touch its sweet lips. Ah, here it is, Oh, how nice. How deliciously soft, but how hot it feels. Why Laura, I declare you are spending. Get up and come in here for a moment,' and he drew me towards an open door close by.

' "Oh, no, we shall be missed, and somebody will come in on us."

' "Don't be afraid, I have the use of this room for tonight, and we will remain only for a few moments."

'He closed and fastened the door, and pulled me towards a bed, which I could see by the light of the lamp outside the window. He placed me sitting on it, and then tried to push me back, at the same time putting my hand on his standing prick.

' "Feel how hot it is; and have pity on it, for it's just ready to burst, and this sweet cunt is the only thing that can give it relief. Let me put it in, you will find it so jolly."

' "No, I can't let you put it in, it would hurt me, and do me harm besides."

' "It shan't hurt you, and I won't let it do you harm – that's a sweet girl – open your thighs – wide – wider still;" and drawing me to the edge, he lifted up my legs, and coming between them, he placed the head of his prick in the slit of my cunt, then resting his hands on my shoulders, he began to shove.

'His prick was large, much larger than Louis's. And as I opposed its entrance in every way I could, for the purpose of making him think that he was the first to force the passage, he found considerable difficulty in getting in.

' "How uncommonly tight you are, Laura, help me or I shall never be able to break through your virgin fence."

'To confirm that notion, I cried, "Oh, take it out, it's hurting me, I can't bear it," and I tried to move from under him.

My resistance, as I intended, only increased his ardour, for holding me firmly with his hands, he pushed on with the greatest determination; and very soon I felt the dear thing making its way in and rushing up the passage, distending all its folds and causing every nerve to fill with rapture.

'My opposition had served its turn, and now I strained myself open, that I might receive all that he was able to give.

' "Now, my sweet Laura, you will have no more pain. Oh, is that not good? Oh, oh, Laura – it's coming – press me in your arms – Oh, oh.'

'I received his discharge into my longing cunt with the utmost satisfaction and, regardless of the consequences, I held him in my encircling arms until his prick had drained out the last drops of its sweets far up in the soft entrails of my belly.

'I could not help it, though I knew the risk I was running – for, as you know well, Queenie, one loses nearly half the pleasure when the prick is suddenly pulled out of the cunt just at the moment when you want it to be driven home, and to feel it in all its length and breadth filling up the cavity of delight.

'So I hugged him and made my cunt suck his prick, and jerked my bottom up and down until I got him into humour again; then, to encourage him I cried: "Now, Bertie, now Bertie, fuck me again – Oh, yes, I will say cunt and prick and bottom and arse and anything else you like; yets I like to feel your prick fucking me!" And then, he poked and I heaved, and we both panted together as the old-fashioned move progressed, until the culminating point was reached and we spent, fast and locked in each other's arms.

'When we stood up, I observed how very much my dress was tumbled and disarranged, and said, "See how you have tumbled my dress, how can I enter the room again in this state."

' "Don't think of going back at all," he replied. "I will tell madame that you are tired, and are going home."

'Without waiting for an answer, he ran off, and soon returned carrying my wraps and a bottle of champagne. In my warm and excited state, the wine was peculiarly welcome, and between us the contents of the bottle quickly disappeared. I was, as you may suppose, quite uplifted, and felt I had the heart for any fate, and so I stepped boldly out into the dark under escort of my dancing acquaintance.

CHAPTER EIGHT

Laura's Narrative Concluded

'We were soon joined by another spark who rejoiced in the suggestive name of Toplady, but was familiarly known as Topsy; he and Bertie were boon companions, and were known to have shared in many a wild adventure. At any other time, I would have been slow to trust myself to their questionable guardianship, but now, being both excited and bewildered by the wine I had drunk, I scarcely knew what I was doing. So when Bertie held me while Topsy kissed me and then ran his hand up under my petticoats and explored all my cunt and bottom, I offered no resistance, observing which, he boldly pulled up my clothes, pushed his prick against my cunt, and wanted to fuck me then and there; but Bertie checked him, saying: "Stop a moment, Topsy, we shall find a more convenient place than this." Then taking me by the arm, one on each side, they hurried me along, until we came to a gloomy looking house in the outskirts of the town. I did not like the appearance of the place, and begged them to take me home as they had promised. 'Not yet awhile, darling, said Bertie. "The ball won't be over for another hour; we can safely enjoy ourselves here without fear of molestation, and then I will bring you safely home."

'He then took me up in his strong arms and carried me up the steps into the hall, where Topsy struck a match, lighted a candle, and led the way up a ruinous staircase until we reached the door of a room containing several broad couches round the walls. Topsy next lighted some candles on a large table in the centre of the room, while Bertie laid me on one of the couches and, drawing up my clothes, said: "Now Topsy, here is a treat you may thank me for, give up your low tastes and enjoy for once in your life a good honest fuck, and remember you have a lady in your hands, and not one of the common sort you are accustomed to. Look here, this is a cunt fit for an emperor. See these full lips, how they push out, so thick and round and hairy, and the notch between so red and moist and fragrant.'

'Topsy replied, "Very true, it is grand," and he plunged his head between my thighs and titillated my cunt with his tongue, winding it round and pushing it up the passage; then he grasped the cheeks of my bottom-hole, poking in his tongue as far as he could, and stirring up within me the most libidinous sensations.

'Meanwhile Bertie had placed my hand on his prick. I liked the touch of its warm animated substance, and drawing it towards my mouth, I took it in and sucked its head.

'Topsy raised himself and said: "I have an idea, Bertie. Lie on your back with Laura over you and your prick in her cunt, then let me mount on top of you both, and get in where I can."

'Bertie laughed. "All right, I know what you want; let us gratify him, Laura. You will have a double treat, and I will take care that he does not hurt you."

'Between them, they stripped me almost naked, which did not please me, but when Bertie lay back on the couch with his prick standing up in fine erection, I willingly got over him, and with my own hand, helped by Topsy, quickly placed the distended limb in the gap prepared for its reception. As I pressed down, it passed sweetly up and filled my belly with luxurious warmth; but when I proceeded to obey the impulse of pleasure and heave up and down over him, he checked me and said, "Softly, sweet Laura, wait till Topsy gets in too, and then we shall all work together."

'Meanwhile, Topsy was busy anointing my cunt and bottom. I, in my innocence, still thought his only desire was to enter my cunt alongside of Bertie; but having grasped me firmly by the hips, before I knew what I was about, he suddenly forced his tool into my well-greased bottom-hole, and began to fuck me there with all his might. The first entrance of his big-headed tool in so narrow a passage hurt me considerably, but no sooner was that effected and the whole prick inside, than the pulsation of pleasure commenced. The action of the two pricks so close to one another was in fact delightfully lascivious; every time Bertie heaved up and smacked his belly against mine, I got a shake on my rump as Topsy darted his slippery engine into my bottom.

'No description, however, could give you any adequate idea of the extraordinary pleasure I then felt and enjoyed. But in the height of our amorous furore we heard steps on the stairs, and before we could disengage ourselves, two half-naked men, and two girls in a similar state of dishabille burst into the room.

'Taking in the situation at a glance, they called to Bertie and Topsy not to mind, but to go on with their sport, and all four gathered round us. The men poked their pricks, which were on the stand and sticking out, up to my face, while the girls began to finger the two pricks inserted in my cunt and bottom. We did not heed them after the first start, and I was in such an exaggerated state of grand feeling and excited lust that I actually seized the two pricks with avidity, and holding one in each hand, put them to my lips.

'What mad fools we become under the influence of drink, and what unaccountable and freakish things we are impelled to do when stimulated by venereal excitement; here were two common-looking fellows, whom I would scarcely have spoken to, much less have touched, at any other time, presenting their fiery red-headed tools reeking, no doubt, fresh from the cunts of these two girls, without causing me any repugnance, nay, rather gratifying my senses of taste, touch and smell. I took them alternately into my mouth, while I frigged them with my hands in time with the motion of the two pricks, which now seemed bent on knocking my bottom and cunt into one by their mighty prods.

'The two girls were all this time slapping and pinching us and frigging their own cunts as if bereft of their senses. Then, as the fun waxed furious, we all gave tongue together, and amid a perfect storm of exclamations in which the words, prick, cunt, fuck, arse, frigging, sucking, pissing were terms most easily distinguished, the flood-gates of pleasure were burst open, and torrents of spunk flowed on every side.

'After resting a short interval, it was voted that one of the girls should have her arse whipped to reanimate the rest. On our promising to be merciful, and that she should be well-rewarded for her pains, one of them consented to be tied down with her naked arse well turned up. To prepare her for the ordeal she was primed with a good allowance of the rum which was liberally served round, and which made us all madder then ever.

'While I was being fucked by each of the men in succession, the others punished her bottom with their straps until she yelled aloud. Altogether such a scene of fucking, frigging, singing and shouting went on as was almost indescribable. In the midst of the uproar, one of the men, in a drunken frolic, with a match he had struck to light his pipe, singed the hair on the cunt of the girl who was tied down. She at first screamed in pain and anger, but quickly stopping her outcry, she called him by some term of endearment and told him to put his prick in her mouth as she wished to suck it. He, foolish man, did so, but as soon as she got it well into her mouth, she closed her teeth on it which such fierce revenge that she bit it nearly through.

'The wretched man roared with pain, and tried to draw it back, but she only bit all the harder.

'The uproar was at its highest when, just as I was trying to separate them, a party of watchmen burst open the door, and at once took them all prisoners. The men, who were very drunk, were marched off to the lock-up, while we women were told to clap on our duds and make ourselves scarce.

This denouement overwhelmed me with shame and confusion. I hurried on my clothes as fast as I could, but the sergeant, observing from my dress that I was different from the others, offered to see me home. As soon as he understood who I was, and how I came to be there, he became wonderfully attentive and assisted me in every way he could. As he led me through the dark lanes, he supported me with one arm and held my hand with the other. Finding that I walked heavily, and seemed hardly able to drag my legs after me, he asked, when we had travelled half the distance, whether I would like to rest a little. I said I would for I felt thoroughly exhausted.

' "Well, it so happens, here is a most convenient place for resting," and he lifted me over a stile into a yard where some dried grass was piled; upon this he placed me, and sitting down at my side with his arm round my waist, he muttered, "Dear young lady, I feel a great pity for you. I am sure you were deceived into joining the company in that house of ill-repute, and I am very thankful to have been able to render you my humble services, but don't you think I am worthy of some reward?"

' "I do indeed, sergeant, tell me what I can do to show you how grateful I am."

' "If you will put your arm round me and let me kiss your sweet lips it will more than repay me for anything I have done."

' "Well, sergeant, I can't refuse you; besides I am quite in your power. You may kiss me if you like, but – oh – I did not give you leave to put your hand there. That was not part of your request."

' "No, my dear, but the glimpse I have already had of your ripe young charms has excited my desire for something more – so you cannot, will not refuse me."

'He had meantime pushed his hand up to my cunt, and was busy pressing it and exploring it with his fingers; then, leaning me backwards, he separated my thighs with his knees, and opening his trousers at the same time, he released his prick and place my hand on it. I could not see it, but it felt unusually large and strong, and held up its big round head with great life and vigour.

'I had been fucked that night no less than nine times, and by four different pricks, and now this, one of the finest of the lot, stirred up my lustful desires as strongly as ever.

' "Well, my dear, what do you think of it? Is it not as well able to give you pleasure as any one of those you so favoured tonight?"

' "Oh, sergeant, don't refer to that again, I am a most unfortunate girl – everyone seems to have their will of me, whether I like it or not."

' "But, dear lady, I mean to make you like it – yes, frig it a little first – Oh, how nice, would you mind taking it in your mouth for a moment?"

'He pushed it up to my lips. I took in the head; it was very large and indeed quite filled my mouth.

' "That's good, now my dear, lie back, spread your soft thighs,' he said, as lying upon me he inserted his prick, 'there – how easily it slips in and passes up, oh, isn't that nice?"

'His prick filled my cunt as he drove it home and pressed it in between my outstretched thighs. The sergeant was an old and experienced hand, he fucked steadily, and with a great deliberation so as to make every stroke tell, and as he was the last who had his will of my poor person that memorable night, so he gave me the best and highest satisfaction of all. But when he was done, I was so entirely worn out and exhausted, I was unable to stand and he had to carry me home.

'Next day he called to enquire for me, and warned me privately that the man who was so cruelly bitten had to be taken to the hospital and was in a dangerous state; that, in consequence, he was certain there would be an investigation; he therefore advised me, if I wished to avoid having to appear as witness, to get out of the way as speedily as possible.

'This caused me to accept at once an invitation from my uncle to visit him and take charge of his sick wife, and as I set out without delay, I escaped the grievous annoyance of a public exposure. It was during this visit that both my father and my aunt died, and I was left altogether to the care and protection of my uncle; and thus it comes to pass that you find me here on the good ship *Cammarrilla*.'

'Why, Laura, you have a most charming way of telling a story, and you have excited my fanny beyond measure; you have fairly set it on fire, would you mind putting your hand on it, dear, and assuaging its burning heat with your finger? And meanwhile tell me what you have already hinted at – the way Captain St John managed to overcome your maidenly scruples, and obtain the enjoyment of your favours.'

'Well, Queenie, my love, lift your leg that I may watch your pussy while I stir her up, and you can perform the same kind office for me while I go on with my story – yes, now then. You know how amorously disposed the worthy captain is, and will understand how, while I attended his wife, he was continually making attempts to induce me to allow him the freedom he desired. But although I liked the thing well enough and really longed for a good fuck, yet I rather shrank from him as being the brother of my mother; I therefore avoided being alone with him and always kept the door of my room locked at night. However, he persuaded me on one occasion to join a boating party, under his care and management, to visit a small island about ten miles distant which was famous for its shells.

'The weather was fine when we started, and the sea calm, but it soon roughened and became very stormy so the captain decided on returning and steered amid a heavy sea for the nearest port. It was late in the evening before we reached the harbour for which we were making and which was on the opposite side of the island from where we set out.

'I was half-dead from fear and seasickness, and besides I was wet through, so the captain gave up all thought of taking me home and brought me to a small hotel whose landlady he was acquainted with. He ordered supper and tried to cheer me up, but I felt very sick and preferred going to bed. A little room was opened off the private sitting-room we had engaged and was accordingly prepared for me and I gladly took off my wet things and turned in.

'After supper uncle ordered coffee, and bringing me some, he found me shivering as if I had the ague.

' "Why dear, how your teeth chatter, you must have got a terrible chill – we must bring you something to warm your heart, and set your blood in circulation."

'So he went out and mixed a stiff tumbler of hot punch and brought it to me. I took it readily, for I felt a chill all over me, but it was stronger that I expected and made my brain swim. I was sitting up in the bed supported by his arm and feeling light-headed. I said with a hysterical laugh: "Oh, uncle, I am quite drunk, what shall I do?"

' "Do nothing, my pet, at least just now. Rest your head here on my bosom, and the effect will soon pass away."

'He drew me close as I leaned against him, and began squeezing and moulding my breast; but I was too much upset to mind him, until I felt his hand inside my dress, pushing down over my belly. I then caught it with mine and said, "Oh, uncle, how can you? You forget that I am your niece. Oh, take your hand – indeed it is not right."

' "You need not mind me, Laura, I am old enough to be your father and the fact of your being my niece only gives me a right to pet and fondle you – there now – let go my hand, I only want to pet you here for a moment – it will do you good – so – there's a good girl."

'He had succeeded in pushing his hand down to my cunt and was working two of his fingers between the lips.

' "Oh, uncle, I am ready to faint, lay me back."

'He laid me down, still keeping his hand, however, between my thighs, then he kissed me and said, "My sweet Laura, I am fonder of you than of anyone else in the world; your aunt, as you know, is dying. I never intend to marry again, but I will adopt you and treat you as my daughter; and as you have shown this loving confidence in me, I will settle her fortune on you.

'All this time he had skilfully frigged my cunt, and I felt a pleasing warmth stealing over me, and a hot glow pervading my quim and the region around. I accordingly permitted him to spread my thighs more open and made but slight resistance as he uncovered them and kissed my cunt. My excitement increased, and my hand, which was next him, involuntarily stretched out as if seeking for something. He saw it, and with a smile, placed it on his prick. My fingers closed round it and I slipped its soft skin up and down, and played with the tips of my fingers over its head and around its indented neck. The way to enjoyment was now open; so hastily divesting himself of his coat, trousers and boots he drew me to the side of the bed with my bottom projecting over the edge, then, after regarding for a moment with evident satisfaction the rosy clink lying bare before him, he separated the lips, and inserting the head of his prick, pushed it quickly up. When he felt the whole of it enclosed in my warm quivering flesh, he leaned over me, pressed me in his arms, and commenced that grand movement which, though old as Mother Eve, is ever new and ever pleasing to her daughters while youth and health remain. Suffice it to say, he fucked me to his fullest satisfaction, and then he left me to recover my strength by sleep.

'When I awoke in the morning, as in your case, I found myself in his arms, and the prick whose penetrating power I had so fully experienced the previous evening I felt poking its head with renewed vigour against my thighs. So I turned and took it in my hand while he threw the bedclothes down and, pulling up my shift, examined me all over. Of course, as is the custom with all men, he praised my cunt, then he asked me to lie over him with my cunt on his mouth and suck his prick. I readily complied, and turning my bottom to his face, I rolled gently from side to side as I bobbed my head up and down on his prick so as to make it fuck my mouth, and I soon felt that contraction of the balls which precedes emission and a hot stream of spunk burst into my mouth and flowed in successive gushes down my throat.

'Such then, my dear Queenie, was the commencement of my queer connection with my Uncle St John – half daughter and whole mistress. It has been, I must say, a very advantageous and enjoyable connection for me, but it is not one which I would wish to prolong. I have, therefore, determined to break it off, if I can do so without offending him, for I love and admire him very much, and your arrival and my marriage with Mat Yeats will, I think, afford me the opportunity I desire; but time will show.'

CHAPTER NINE

The Wedding Voyage

On arrival at Port Royal, we learned that the American War of Independence had broken out and the captain found orders awaiting him from the owners containing instructions to sail for Trinidad with the new governor, Sir Charles Stanhope, and to provide accommodation on board the ship for his family, consisting of his wife, the Hon. Lady Stanhope, their daughter and their attendants.

We had some delay, however, for the governor required a few days to make preparations for his leave; so the captain decided that Laura's marriage should take place in the interval before sailing.

Accordingly, we all went on shore, and she and Mat Yeats were duly spliced, the captain and I being the legal witnesses.

Our party was increased by an old friend of the captain's, whom he called Johnny and who was accompanied by a young coloured lady, full of life and fun. I don't know her real name, but they called her Miss Betty.

After a grand feed and plenty of champagne, we drove to a country village, where rooms had been engaged for the night.

Mat and his bride were put into a carriage, and as they drove off with blinds down, we threw old shoes and handfuls of seed after them, and wished them a happy fruitful conjunction.

We soon followed in an inside vehicle, called a buggy, with a black driver on the box. I sat by the side of Johnny with the captain as my *vis-à-vis*; he had his arm around Betty and his jovial face in close proximity to her blooming cheek.

Altogether, we were a very merry party. The occasion, the exhilarating character of the day, and above all, the wine we had taken combined to elevate our spirits and excite our amorous emotions and desires.

Our first difficulty was how to stow away our legs; the captain would have it, that, contrary to the usual custom the natural way was for the gentleman to place his legs between those of the lady opposite to him. We objected, but as Johnny declared that the vehicle was the captain's ship for the time being, we were bound to obey his commands. In the little scuffle that ensued, Betty was discovered to have blue garters. Johnny praised their beauty and said that he was sure mine were equally pretty, and that I ought to favour the company with a view.

The captain applauded his proposal, and kept my legs asunder, while he tried to pull up my coat, to the great amusement of our black driver, who looked over his shoulder, and grinned from ear to ear.

Miss Betty, who fully entered into the fun, exclaimed, 'Queenie's garters are pink, I know, but she has something higher up of a richer colour, and more worthy of your inspection.'

'Speak for yourself, Miss Slyboots,' I replied, 'what is the colour of your own?'

'Hi,' cried the captain, placing his knees under my thighs, and tilting me backwards, while Johnny peered up between my legs; 'that's the way – run the possum to his hole.'

'Ha, ha,' laughed Betty, who was bent on mischief, 'it is all very well to talk of the possum's hole, but I see no signs of the creature himself.'

'You shall not have that long to wait, Miss Betty, for here is one possum,' drawing out his tool, in full erection, 'and I dare say Johnny can favour us with another.'

Johnny needed no pressing. The buttons of his trousers were hastily unfastened, and out sprang a noble prick, full nine inches long, lifting its glowing head in proud erection.

'There, I told you so,' cried the captain, 'look at it, Queenie. Put your dainty little hand on it – oh – ah – it is so nice,'

Meanwhile Betty directed her attention to the captain's affair, to his great delight. She opened his clothes down the front, so as to be able to pull out his balls with it, then thrusting her hand in underneath, she pushed on until she reached his bottom with her finger, while she frigged in the most delicate and skilful manner his throbbing, bounding prick.

His hands, you may be sure, were equally busy with her fat bottom, and moist gaping cunt.

Johnny and I were carrying on a similar game; he titillated my cunt into such a mad state of excitement that I willingly acceded to his request to sit with my naked bottom on his lap, and allow his prick to poke up between the lips of my cunt.

It was well we were on a quiet country road out of the way of observation, or some of us might have come to grief, for our intense excitement made us rather forgetful of the requirements of society, at least in public. However, on this occasion we only met a few black people and deemed ourselves tolerably safe.

So I slid over Johnny, making my buttocks rub with delicious friction against the hairy surface of his belly; then lifting my dress in front that the captain and Betty might see what we were doing, I raised myself sufficiently high to put the firm head of the tool in the furrow where I intended it to work, and pressing down, soon placed it out of view.

'Bravo,' shouted the captain. 'Queenie has, as usual, taken the lead. Let us follow in her wake, and lifting Betty's leg over his, he told her to hoist her stern while he plugged the leak she had there with his oakum rammer.

Miss Betty, being evidently used to the sport, did not hesitate to obey, and uncovering her broad luxurious backside she held her bottom over his lap, while he with skilful fingers fixed the head of his eager prick at the inner opening of her cunt; then she pressed down, and with a rollicking laugh exclaimed, 'I have the possum now. Oh, how he pokes his head and dances in his hole.'

Both men discharged immediately, as might be expected, but as they found the situation so agreeable, they begged us to remain seated as we were.

Our black driver too enjoyed the sport immensely, and looking back he displayed no end of white teeth while he chuckled and rolled about as if ready to fall off his box. In the midst of his contortions, his black tool started out through his pantaloons, which did not seem to be much encumbered with buttons.

'Hello,' cried the captain when he observed it. 'Face about, Pompey, and let the ladies see that bald-headed piccanniny you are nursing there in front.'

Pompey slung himself around and said, 'Good massa, and gentle missy, sense dis nigga de flash am too strong for dee spirit in dis chile,' and with a wide grin he projected the shining head of his enormous prick right into the midst of us. Betty caught it in her hand, and as I was nearest, she pushed it against my mouth.

I confess that I have always had a special penchant for a black prick, so I readily took its sleek round head between my lips and ran my fingers up and down over the satin skin that covered its muscular column.

The view of Pompey's prick entering my mouth reanimated all the rest. The captain's face reddened with delight as Betty worked herself up and down over his lap, making his tool pass rapidly in and out of her slippery sheath and crying out at each downward thump: 'Fuck, fuck, fuck.'

I screwed my bottom between Johnny's thighs and just as I felt his swelling prick inundate the regions below, a gush of glutenous sperm darted into my mouth from the end of Pompey's noble tool. I swallowd every drop while I squeezed his balls with my hand, and compressed my lips round its indented neck as, with rapid jerks, spurt after spurt flowed down my throat.

I received his emission with more than my usual relish, not only because of the great excitement of the moment, but because I found as I had observed before, that the semen of the negro has a more pungent taste and a more aromatic flavour than that of the white man.

Meanwhile the captain's eyes seemed actually starting out of his head with the intensity of his pleasure as he cried: 'Lift a moment, Miss Betty – let me finish in the rear.'

She raised herself while he quickly transferred his moist tool from her cunt to her bottom-hole.

A flush of delight then came over her face as she pressed down and the soft round head passed into her vitals, while the delicate skin of her other entrance rubbed against the grizzled hair that clustered round the root of his manly tool.

It would occupy too much space to describe all that went on in that conveyance, for the whole drive was one continued scene of licentious larking and unrestrained enjoyment.

When we reached the inn, we found that Mat and his wife were in their bedroom with the door fastened, so the captain, after listening a moment outside, cried through the keyhole, 'Go it, Mat! How are you getting on Laura?'

'Oh, uncle, I am nearly dead, Mat is murdering me with his – '

'Don't mind her St John she has her bottom over my face, while she is sucking the very life-blood out of my tool.'

'Well, don't kill yourselves quite, or, if you do, make short of it, for we want our supper.'

We soon gathered round an excellent spread and, while the waiters remained, behaved ourselves with as much propriety as we could, though a good deal of fingering and peeping passed on the sly.

The landlord, Mr Toots, was a fine-looking mulatto and seemed greatly amused at our party and never spoke to any of us without a broad grin on his face.

I think he must have heard something from the driver, for he watched us all evening and seemed resolved some way or other to join our sport. His portly wife, too, seemed animated with a similar spirit and ogled the captain or Johnny whenever she brought in a fresh supply of liquor.

We could only obtain three bedrooms and the parlour, which was the only public accommodation afforded by the small inn. So it was arranged that Betty and I should have one room between us, the captain and Johnny the other, while the third was left to the bride and bridegroom.

After a nightcap of grog all around, we retired to our respective apartments.

Betty and I found that our room was between that occupied by the landlord and his wife on the one side and Laura's on the other, and the partitions being thin, we heard many curious noises and mutterings on both sides, but I was so tired and so muddled with drink that I could not remain awake. The last thing I was conscious of was Betty fumbling between my thighs.

I must have been some hours asleep when I felt her hand still playing about my cunt. She had uncovered me, and having drawn me to the side of the bed, had lifted my legs and was busy exploring all between them.

'Oh, Betty, let me sleep. There's a good girl,' and I put down my hand to push away her fingers.

She caught it and held it to one side.

'Why, Betty, what a strong hand you have. What is that you are rubbing between my lips? Is it a dildo, Betty? Where did you get it? Push it in dear: how well you do it. I could almost fancy it was a prick fucking me.'

Here I heard a chuckle that was not quite of a feminine character and putting my other hand suddenly down I felt the warm prick of a very hairy main prodding my cunt and distending its folds to an extraordinary degree.

'Who are you?' I asked, raising my hand to feel his face. The first thing I touched was a smooth round chin with a big tuft of hair in the middle which I knew was not possessed by either the captain or Johnny.

'Get away,' I cried, 'whoever you are I won't let you,' and I tried to slip from under him, but he only seized me firmly by the hips and fucked away as if his life depended on his ramming his great prick into my cunt to the fullest extent possible. His balls banged against my bottom while the room shook with the concussion of his blows. Then a torrent of hot spunk filled my cunt and effectively stopped all further complaints on my part. I even returned his kiss as he lay panting on my bosom.

After discharging, his prick remained soaking in my cunt without any perceptible diminution while our tongues touched and enfolded one another. He did not long continue quiet, however, for moved by the convulsive throbs of the folds of my cunt he placed his hands under me and grasping the cheeks of my bottom he began to shove again. I spread my thighs and jerked my cunt to meet every thrust while I spurred him on by hammering his backside with my heels.

But alas, for earthly bliss, just as the hot pleasure was speeding on to complete enjoyment, we were both startled by an apparition rising up suddenly behind him in the shape of a tall woman in a white dress and nightcap with her long hair streaming over her shoulders.

'Toots, you vagabond,' she screamed, with her eyes ablaze, 'is it here I find you? Not content with your lawful wife, you grope all the maids and even assault the ladies who come to our house. Get out of here, you lascivious beast,' and setting down the lamp she carried, she threw herself on her husband, and with her arms round his loins tried to pull him off.

But Toots held on like grim death, and seemed resolved that come what may, he would finish the job.

Her outcry, however, brought other actors on the scene; the captain and Johnny followed by Betty each, with a candle in hand, rushed into the room.

'Hallo, Hallo,' cried the captain, 'what's the row? Fight fair boys, two against one won't do,' and dragging off Mrs Toots he tumbled with her on the floor. In the struggle somehow her petticoats were tossed up and the jolly captain found himself between her legs. The result of such a position naturally followed and, to use his own expression, 'before one could say Jack Robinson', his ready prick had plunged into her open cunt.

'Toots, Toots, you cowardly villain, will you stay there and see your wife ravaged before your face?'

Toots turned his head and with a sideways leer, said, 'Serve you right, my love,' and quietly renewed his fucking operation.

Meanwhile Betty, ready to burst her sides laughing, threw herself face downwards on my bed and whispered in my ear, 'How did it all happen, dear Queenie? You at least have no cause for dissatisfaction.' And I felt her fingers feeling around the big prick which was plunging in and out through the widely opened lips of my cunt.

Johnny, after surveying the scene for a moment thought he could not do better than follow suit by availing himself of the favourable position of Betty's turned-up bottom, so lifting her shift, he uncovered the two glossy brown cheeks of her dimpled posteriors and poking his prick through a huge tuft of tangled black hair, penetrated her well-moistened recess.

The captain, who was revelling in the enjoyment of a new cunt, even so well-used an affair as that possessed by Mrs Toots, was delighted with the additional incentive afforded by the view of Johnny's unexpected attack on Betty's quivering bum, and renewed his exertions with increased vigour.

Then we all had a few hours' rest and after breakfast we returned to Port Royal, and so ended Laura's wedding trip.

CHAPTER TEN

The Governor and his Family

As the captain expected to return to Jamaica after a few weeks, he kindly told Mat that he may take a run on shore during that time with his wife and that he would help the second mate to perform his duties during his absence. He also placed in his hands most honourably the dowry he had promised Laura.

We set sail for Trinidad with the governor and his suite on board.

Sir Charles was an elderly man of the fine old English type, his manner was bland and courteous and from the first he was most particular in his attention to me.

This seemed to arouse all the ire of his proud and jealous wife. She was positively rude in her conduct towards me and made it her habit whenever she saw us conversing together to swoop down like a bird of prey and carry off her meek old husband in the midst of a storm of reproaches to him and angry glances at poor innocent me.

The captain had given up his cabin to the governor and had taken Mat's, while the governor's daughter, Blanche, was located in the one next to mine at the opposite side of the saloon. She was several years my senior and being filled with grand notions of her birth and station was cold and stand-offish in manner so that we had not much intercourse together. She assumed the role of a prude, but there was something in her eye that told a different tale, and set me on the watch to ascertain whether my suspicions were correct.

She had an English maid, but she was so grievously afflicted by seasickness that she required more attendance than her mistress.

The governor had his own valet, an Italian named Sporio, but he seemed to consider it his principal duty to wait upon the ladies and especially the younger.

They all suffered at first from the usual seasickness, but the governor, being the first to recover, gladly availed himself of the opportunity to ingratiate himself with me, and in consequence of her ladyship's ill-usage I was more disposed to encourage his advances than I otherwise would have been. The captain also, who enjoyed the joke, to spite the old lady facilitated the enterprise in every way he could.

So it came to pass that one calm evening after sunset we were seated together on the poop; his lady was as yet not able to favour us with her benign presence and his daughter had gone below to preserve her complexion.

The old governor was in high glee; he tucked a rug around me to protect me from the dew which was falling heavily, and after sundry warm speeches and loving pressures, he ventured a kiss.

Emboldened by finding that I did not oppose him, he leaned more against me, and stealing his arm round me said, 'My sweet Queenie, you are one of the most loveable girls I ever met. It is such a joy to sit by you and hold you in my arms, even for a minute.'

'Oh,' I replied, laughing, 'you say that to every girl you meet but what would my lady do if she found you here?'

'Don't mind her, the old witch, she can't trouble us now at all events. Let me, my sweet pet – I will be so fond of you and will give you anything you like or would ask for.'

He kept pressing me back, and trying to get his hand under my petticoats.

'Oh, Sir Charles, this is too bad. I did not think you would attempt that. I like you very much but I can't let you do that.'

But the old fellow was too experienced in the ways of women to mind my affected opposition and after much struggling he succeeded in forcing his hand between my thighs.

'How firm and plump your thighs are, and this mossy nest, oh how soft and warm it is. Queenie, you are a delicious girl – open your legs – let me between them – there now – don't be alarmed. I only want to see you more easily.'

'O Fie, Sir Charles, take your hand off, how can you be so rude.' He had pulled me forward and leaning over me held me down by his weight, while he groped my cunt with his fingers. 'Pray don't, you frighten me – here on the open deck, too.'

I had felt him opening up his dress and slyly taking out his prick.

'Oh, my, what are you doing? Don't put that there – you will ruin me – what a lot of fumbling – there, it is in now – take care – do it easy – the captain will see you.'

With much difficulty he had at last got in his prick. It did not seem very large or very strong, so to facilitate its progress, I spread myself more and heaved up gently against him.

'My darling, you have a sweet little quim. It holds me like a glove – move forward a little so that I may get more closely in; you must help me. That's the way. I am not so active as I once was. Do you like it now? Does my old tool give you any pleasure?'

To humour him, I replied, 'Yes, Sir Charles, but don't leave it in too long, it might harm me, perhaps.'

After a few gasps and with a spasmodic groan he spent; then, while lying palpitating on my bosom, he asked, 'Did I hurt you much, my love, I felt it hard to get in.'

'Yes,' I said, 'at first you did hurt me very much, but when you did get in it felt very nice.'

'You are a dear innocent girl' – much he knew – 'I will be so fond of you and I will teach you all about it. Would you like me to fuck you again? Say the work fuck, my love.'

'Fuck; you may fuck me again if you wish.'

'Say, with your prick in my cunt.'

'Well, to please you, with your prick in my cunt. Will that do?'

'Yes, let me kiss you for being so good, now I will put my hands under you and press the fat cheeks of your lovely bottom and do put your hand down and hold my prick as it passes in and out of your cunt.'

I took hold of his prick. It felt soft and flabby, but still able to slip in and out. I put my other hand down, and gently pressed and moved his balls.

The old fellow was delighted, and regaining something of his youthful ardour, he fucked with all his might.

'Thanks darling, you have quite warmed my old blood and made me feel myself a young man once more.'

Soon afterwards I learned something of Miss Blanche's doings that placed us on a more even balance. My maid, Zilla, kept me informed of all that was going on in the forecastle. She described her numerous flirtations there, and knowing the gratification it would cause me, told me how she had permitted both the boatswain and the carpenter to enjoy her, each deeming himself to be the sole possessor of her favours, until they mutually discovered one another by both coming to her one night at the same time; when, like sensible men, in place of quarrelling over her they agreed to have her in common, which gave them all the more satisfaction as they could enjoy fucking her turn about or both have her at the same time, which Zilla pronounced to be the best plan of all.

The latest of her conquests was Sporio, the governor's valet. She said he was awfully spoony on her and used to call her *Carrissima mia nigra*.

She taxed him with his devotion to Miss Blanche. He declared that she bored him; that she had seduced him when he was a mere lad, but that she was so exceedingly kind to him that he was loth to break his connection with her; that although so proud to all the world, she actually fawned on him; and that she had requested the boss to allow him to teach her Italian in her own cabin, under plea of being more free from interruption there than in the saloon; but that he did not like going to her for she did nothing but frig and suck his prick.

When I repeated all this to the captain, he laughed until the tears rolled down his cheeks. 'Ha ha, ho ho, only think of our stately flamingo cuddling the tool of that olive-tinted rascal; that would be a sight worth seeing; and now that I think of it, there is no reason why we should not see it. Queenie, my lass, we will circumnavigate them. The panels between these cabins can be loosened. Stay here on deck and remain on guard; while the coast is clear below, and I will go in and try what I can do.'

Accordingly, after some time, he came up to my usual nook on the port quarter, and with a merry twinkle in his eye, said, 'All right, you may set the watch as soon as you please, and be sure to keep your weather eyes open. Remove the loose moulding from the left-hand panel at the end of our berth – you can then slide it to one side far enough to command the whole of the flamingo's nest and all her vagaries, and don't forget to note down everything in your log for me. She will soon be under way now, for I was hardly done, when she came down, and I heard her telling the Olive to bring the Italian dictionary after tiffin.'

So I went below, and passing up the saloon, I observed that Miss Stanhope's door was closed. I entered my own cabin and having carefully shut the door and darkened the port, I softly moved the panel and applied my eye to the small aperture indicated by the captain.

The view that met my delighted gaze was even more lubricious than I anticipated. Sporio was reclining on a sofa, holding in his hand a book out of which he was reading in a low voice.

He trousers were all open in the front and his shirt tucked up under his waistcoat. Miss Stanhope was seated by his side on a low stool with her head leaning against him and both hands on his dark-coloured prick. She kissed it and gently moved its head about her face, all the while gently frigging it with her fingers.

It was a finely proportioned prick, seamed with blue veins, and holding its head in proud erection, as if conscious of being just such a plaything as any lady of warm temperament would like to fondle and put in her pocket of delight. The book he was reading was Boccaccio's *Decameron* in Italian; she repeated after him as he translated sentence by sentence, occasionally stopping him to ask questions.

The part they were engaged on was novel ten, of the third day, where the innocent Alibech is instructed by the hermit Rusticus in the pious work of putting the devil into hell, and is induced to believe that the sturdy prick of the holy man, the view of which has excited her astonishment, was the devil sent to buffet and torment him. 'How happy I am,' she exclaimed, 'that I have there no such devil to torment me.'

'Oh, but you have much more than the devil in that same place, for you have in that same spot the hell in which he ought to be thrust,' and he pressed with lewd fingers the as yet unentered sanctuary of love. 'Permit me, my child, to plunge him into this place of darkness, where he ought to be put, and we shall gain all the delights of heaven.'

She accordingly, most innocently and as she believed most piously, permitted him to perform the meritorious act on her willingly subjected body.

The hermit, having placed her in the most convenient position, and opened the shaded portals of her lovely abyss, proceeded to drive the devil in, greatly to his own satisfaction, but with no small pain to the poor novice, who, afflicted by his forcible entrance into her delicate recess, cried out with the pain and said, 'Oh, *padre mio*, how wicked this devil must be' – sensing him draw the devil from that hot and insatiable abyss – 'even in hell he causes so much trouble.'

But very soon she found that the prolonged movement of the devil inside caused such delightful sensations, that she begged the good hermit to persevere in his pious efforts.

Blanche seemed greatly amused at the eagerness of the innocent Alibech and said, 'But I don't wonder at her, if Rusticus had as grand a devil as this fellow of yours, Sporio mio, which looks so ready for the warm nook that is waiting for him. Why it is even shedding tears at the thought,' she added as she sipped off a pearly drop that glistened on its summit.

'So be it, Carma mia, how shall I put it in?'

'Lie along the couch. I will mount over you and put it in myself and you can look whether I guide the devil aright.'

She fastened up her skirts, and jumping on the couch straddled over him, holding up her shift as she bent forward and watched the purple-headed demon while she directed him to the clover entrance of his den; when she had him safely housed she laid hold on a projection over her and allowed the motion of the ship acting on the muscles of her thighs to produce the exciting friction he required.

Her extreme coolness showed what an adept she was in obtaining and prolonging the fullest enjoyment of her pleasures. She continued this mode of operation until she had completely pumped him dry; leaning back his head, he drew up his arms and yawned.

'My Sporio is easily tired today, he must be going too much after new loves. Do you find your dark beauty as attractive as ever, or perhaps it is her *petite* mistress who is inspiring you with tender passion, is it so?'

'Why no, she has given me no opportunity; but now that you suggest the notion, I will seek for some means of approach, for she is without a doubt a charming little piece.'

'Ah, vous êtes mechant, *mio Sporio*, you only say that to tease me. I can't imagine what you all see to admire in that chit of a girl. She would fain look like an angel, while she only simpers like a fool.'

When I related all this to the captain, he rubbed his hands together in glee and declared he must manage somehow or other to witness with me one of those Italian lessons.

As a special reward for telling him all that passed between Sporio and the Flamingo, and also for describing how I helped the old governor to accomplish his desired fuck, he made me lean back with my cunt fully exposed to the light of the lamp, and then kneeling between my wide-spread thighs, he gave me a most delicious tongue frig and just as I was going to spend, he arose and buried his fiery-headed prick among the folds of my throbbing cunt, and then finished by entering the more narrow passage which lay so invitingly near and from my position peculiarly open to his attack.

Sporio soon found that his best way of approaching me was through Zilla and he therefore made her large presents and promised her everything in his power to bestow if she would use her influence with me in his favour.

She readily undertook to plead for him, not for the sake of the reward, but from her own natural love for any kind of *amour*.

She began by telling me how greatly he admired me, and she endeavoured to inflame my fancy by describing his insinuating manner and especially the peculiarly skilful way in which he used his fine tool. 'He has such a coaxing eye and such a warm soft hand, the very touch of it makes one thrill, and then his prick – oh missy, it would do you good to feel how firm and strong and at the same time how soft and smooth it is, and while he holds you with a grip like iron, he moves his hand like a cat's paw over your cunt, and with delicate fingers tenderly open the soft yielding lips, and then so deftly introduces the luscious head of his pleasure-giving instrument, and oh! the vigorous spring of his active loins, as at every plunge, he fucks – fucks – fucks; until your whole inside seems to rush forward to give it a melting reception. Oh, missy! only try him, and you will find I have told you but half the truth.'

All this time Zilla had been most skilfully frigging my clitoris; and titillating with the nervous tips of her knowing fingers the entrance of my glowing recess.

'Why, Zilla, you are a famous advocate! You must have been trained in the very courts of Cupid! But suppose I consent, how do you propose to bring it about?'

'Well, missy, that is the difficulty, for if Miss S had any inkling of it, she would just go on fire and set the ship in a blaze; but I have a notion, and if you won't be angry with me, I will just mention it for your consideration.'

'Go ahead, Zilla, I won't be angry, what's your notion?'

'To meet him at night in the saloon after they all turn in; and that might be safely effected in this way: the captain is always casting sheep's eyes at me, and I know well what he wants, so my notion is that if I were to gratify him with your consent, he would willingly connive at Sporio's remaining in the saloon at that late hour, and you could meet him then without fear of any disagreeable interruption.'

'Well, Zilla, your notion is clever enough, and would most likely accomplish the object you have in view; but what an insatiable girl you are! I do believe you would not object to having the whole ship's crew from the cabin-boy up, and perhaps you have, for all I know, and indeed you might for all I care, provided you keep yourself from harm.'

Zilla laughed and her eyes sparkled as she replied, 'Ah, missy, there is safety in a multitude; and after all, we can all tell of the pleasure of variety.'

'Well, that will do for the present, I will think the matter over, and let you know.'

CHAPTER ELEVEN

Sporio's Success

After Zilla left, I pondered over her proposal. I had no objection to an intrigue with the valet, personally, for he was a well-made and, I might add, an exceedingly well-mannered fellow; but the fact of his being an object of such peculiar regard to the disdainful Blanche was, in itself, a powerful inducement to me to grant him my favours. In short, my desire was not so much to obtain pleasure myself, as to have an opportunity of paying her some return for her unceasing haughtiness to me; and this seemed a favourable opening for the purpose.

But before committing myself further, I thought it better to consult my friend and ally Captain St John. I told him how warmly Zilla had pressed the valet's suit, though I did not mention her suggestion respecting himself, but I praised her wit, her good nature, and her amorous disposition, and observed that I had no doubt he had marked these traits himself, he was so good a judge of female character.

I saw that the mention of Zilla was pleasing to him and made him more inclined to look with favour on my commencing an intrigue with the valet.

'Well,' he said, stroking his beard, 'I'll not cross your fancy for the Olive, he is young and lusty, and no doubt well able to give you pleasure; but won't you find it hard to manage?'

I then told him of Zilla's plan for him to come to the saloon after they had all turned in and the doors were closed for the night, and I added, 'I would not be at all surprised if Zilla herself came with him, and you, dear old boy, might have a quiet little lark with her at the same time.'

This last decided the matter. He was now more anxious than Sporio himself, and directed me to get Zilla to prepare matters for that very evening, and to charge her to come herself.

I quickly informed Zilla of the result of my interview with the captain. She was rejoiced, and ran off to tell Sporio. The latter soon showed by his change of manner that he felt himself in a different position as regards me. He never passed me without a respectful salute, accompanied by an expressive glance of his dark eyes which I now observed were remarkably clear and intelligent. He even brought me a cup of tea before dinner, and made some remarks in Italian.

I smiled, and shook my head.

'Ah, I did forget me; my language, *la signorina* does not understand.'

'No, I wish I did, for I believe it is a very beautiful language.'

'It is most beautiful and expressive; if the honour was granted me, I would be happy to teach *la damigella*.'

'Why not, but we shall not have many opportunities for we are getting near our destination, so when you next find me alone you may begin. I have, I think, the work of a famous author – Boccaccio. I would like to know something of his writings.'

'Certainly, I shall be too happy; perhaps tonight, the *signorina* might make the opportunity?' and he gave me an enquiring look.

I nodded, and said, 'If the weather keeps fine.' He gave a smile of pleased apprehension, and passed on.

Zilla attended me as usual that evening in my cabin. She was a little more dressy in her appearance, and a good deal more fidgety in her manner than was her habit. Several times she expressed impatience at the old lady and her daughter remaining so long in the saloon. At last they retired and the captain was left alone, poring over his charts and log book.

Zilla peeped out, and seeing him thus engaged, stepped softly up to him and asked when he expected to reach Trinidad.

'Tomorrow afternoon,' he replied, and then asked her would she like to see on the chart the exact spot where they then were.

She said she would, and went close up to him.

'Here is Trinidad, and we are about fifty leagues to the north, just here,' he said pointing to the place with his compasses.

As she stooped over the chart to see better, he put his arm around her, and drawing her down, said, 'Sit here on my knee, my pretty, and I will show you Port o' Spain, where I hope to anchor tomorrow evening.'

With a little coaxing he got her fairly on his knee, and then demanded payment of a kiss.

'What rough creatures you sailors are!' she said, wiping her mouth, and pretending he had scratched her with his board; then he kissed her again to make her well.

'There – that will do – let me go – Miss Queenie wants to get an Italian lesson from Sporio; shall I tell him he may come?'

'Will you promise to return to me, if I let you go?'

'Yes, if you will be quiet and good.'

She then hurried off, and quickly returned with Sporio, whom she had found waiting near at hand.

Meanwhile the captain had gathered up his charts and carried them to his own cabin, and as she passed the door, he said: 'Come here, Zilla, leave them to themselves and we shall be more comfortable in here,' and putting his arm round her, he drew her in.

The captain had left his lamp burning at the farther end of the saloon, and I went and sat down by it as Sporio came up.

'In obedience to my queen, I have brought Boccaccio. Will *mia regina* receive me not merely as a teacher but as a humble, loyal and devoted subject?'

His manner and address surprised me not a little, and made me conclude that whatever he might be, he was no ordinary valet, and succeeding events proved that my conclusion was correct; so I replied: 'Very well, Sporio, I accept your devotion; sit here at my side and read a little of your Italian, I want to hear how it sounds.'

Opening the book, he said, 'This is a collection of short stories or novels of different degrees of merit and interest told successively by a party of friends; shall I begin with the first, or will you make a selection?'

'I would rather leave the selection to you; choose something funny and amusing.'

'Dioneus is about the funniest of the party, and one of the best of his stories is that where he tells how a pious hermit instructs an innocent novice in the ways of love.'

'Oh, I know that story,' I said, laughing, 'it is very funny; does Dioneus tell any other stories as funny as that?'

'Yes, there is something of the same character,' and he turned to novel ten of the ninth day.

After reading a portion, he translated as follows: 'There lived once at Barletta a learned doctor named Barolo who helped his small income by attending the fairs of Puglia; in the course of his travelling, he became very intimate with a peddler named Pietro di Tresanti. They often travelled together, and Barola, in token of kindness and friendship, always called him "Comrade Peter", and whenever he came to Barletta, he invited him to sleep at his poor dwelling, and gave him the best cheer in his power. Peter, however, was still poorer, having only a little cabin in the village of Tresanti; which was merely big enough for himself, his young and handsome wife, and his ass; nevertheless when Barola came to Tresanti he brought him to his cabin and received and honoured him in the best manner he could, out of gratitude for the treatment he had met with at Barletta. But when bedtime arrived, Peter could not accommodate Barola in the manner he could wish, for he had but one little bed for himself and his wife; therefore Barola was obliged to sleep on some straw near to his mare, who was lodged in a little stable with the ass. Peter's wife, knowing the hospitable reception which the doctor gave her husband when he went to Barletta, was desirous of going to sleep with a female neighbour, in order that he might have her half of the bed. The doctor would not suffer this, but said to her: "My good Dame Gammata, be not troubled on my account, for I am very well off; I can when I please turn this mare into a beautiful girl, and be happy with her; and when I wish to go, I can transform her into a mare; therefore I never separate myself from her."

'The young wife was greatly astonished at this, but believing it implicitly, related it to her husband, saying: "If he is so much your friend as you tell me, why do you not make him teach you this enchantment, in order that you might make a mare of me, and carry on your business with the ass and the mare, by which means we should gain double, and when we came home, you could turn me into a woman again, as I am."

Peter, who in these matters was as simple as his wife, agreed to her proposition, and began with the best grace he could put on to solicit his friend to teach him the secret.

'Barola, who was very crafty, in order to make him all the more eager, endeavoured to dissuade him from such nonsense; but Peter would not be refused. He therefore said, "Since you will have it so, we must rise tomorrow before daybreak, and I will show you how it is done! But the most difficult part of this thing is the putting on the tail, as you will see."

'Peter and his wife having scarcely slept during the night, and being so anxious about this affair, rose while it was yet dark, and called Barolo, who got up and came in his shirt to their chamber. He began by saying: "I know no one in the world for whom I would do this but you, and I do it solely to please you, and because you so much desire it; but you must strictly follow my directions, however strange they may appear, if you wish the incantation to succeed."

'They eagerly promised to obey all his commands, and do everything he bade them. Barolo then placed a candle in the hands of Peter, and said: "Notice well what I do, and remember what I say; but have a care, as you love yourself, that whatever you see, you utter not a single word, or you will spoil the whole; and pray that the tail may be well put on."

'After this Barolo made Gammata strip herself stark naked, and go down upon all fours after the manner of a mare. He then began with his hands to rub her face and head, saying: "This will be a find mare's head," and touching her hair, "This will be a fine mare's mane";

examining her arms and legs, "These will be fine limbs for a mare," next, with lingering fingers, he felt her soft voluptuous breasts, and finding them full and round, he said, "These will make a good mare's chest"; then he passed his hands over her smooth belly, using like words, then down her fleshy thighs which he caused her to spread open as much as she could, and coming close up behind, he began to examine with curious touches and prying looks her buttocks and all the secret parts adjoining.

'Meanwhile Peter, rather impatient at the slow progress of the charm, held the candle and looked on curiously while Barolo moved his roving fingers over that rich valley, the abode of love and pleasure, which lies between those voluptuous orbs, and which was divided down the middle by a furrow having round swelling lips of a glowing pink inside, and whose edges even now glistened with the dew of passionate desire.

'Peter was not altogether satisfied at this close investigation of his wife's secrets, especially as she did not at all object to it herself, but he was afraid to speak lest he should break the spell.

'Now nothing remained but to put on the tail, the most important part of the undertaking, for it would be the completion of the charm and the accomplishment of the doctor's design. But Gammata had nothing in that quarter which could be used for transformation into a tail, so Barolo had to supply the deficiency himself – but I am almost ashamed to proceed unless my queen commands me –'

I hung my head to hide my blushes as I whispered: 'Go on.'

Laying the book on my lap he slipped off his seat, and knelt on the floor, leaning forward against my knees, and thus gently forcing them apart. I felt his hand stealing up the calf of my leg as he continued, 'Barolo raised his shirt, and taking hold of that staff of love which distinguished him as a man, he planted it, O, my queen, to Peter's great amazement, in that sweet furrow of his wife which lay near the spot whence the tail should spring, a lovely, warm and juicy furrow, like the one you have here, O, my love; open, dear – open these voluptuous thighs, which stand like twin pillars guarding the portals of bliss. O, my beloved! How good and kind you are! Lean back a little; suffer me to raise this envious veil; oh, what beauties burst upon my view! what intoxicating fragrance exhales from this balmy mouth – so mossy and so sweet! Let me kiss its luscious lips; and suck this rosebud clitoris which so temptingly uprears its tiny head! Oh, sweet chink of love; wrinkle of desire and furrow of delight! who can resist thy power or worst thee in the fight! *Carissima mia*, thy cunt is heaven to me – O, let me enter in.'

Embracing me with one arm, he leaned over me, while with his other hand he directed the loving head of his eager prick.

He rubbed its soft point up and down that most sensitive furrow. He stopped at the entrance, and oh! he knew where to find it. He pushed; it entered; and the dear thing passed up like a living creature. I felt its head penetrating my vitals and pressing into my womb. When he had driven it in as far as possible, and the whole length of his prick lay buried in my belly, and his balls pressed against my bottom, he exclaimed, 'Oh, my Beloved, my long-felt desire is more than gratified, I hold my queen in my arms, my prick revels in her cunt, my balls rub against her bottom, and as I kiss her sweet lips, I fuck – fuck – fuck,' and at every repetition of the word, he drove home his prick with increased energy, and made his firm stones bang against my upturned rump.

I have had larger pricks in my cunt before, but I never was more firmly embraced yet at the same time handled as tenderly as a babe by its nurse. I felt as if I had nothing to do but spread myself open and receive all I could of his pleasure-giving tool.

We both groaned together when the moment of transport arrived; and, clasped in each other's arms, we lay in that sweet calm which succeeds fully gratified enjoyment. Opening my eyes, I caught his bright glance of triumphant love as he enquired, 'Is my queen satisfied with the devotion of her slave?'

With a smile and a hug, I whispered, '*Mio Sporio*, fuck me again, and yet again – fuck – fuck – fuck – fuck,' heaving up my rump and compressing his prick in the hot folds of my cunt.

A depth of love gleamed in his dark eyes as he responded, '*Mia carissima*, I have enjoyed many women, but my queen has given me more rapture than any other; I have sported with many and various cunts, but that of my queen is *facile princeps*, the very abode of bliss and acme of delight.'

Then as he leisurely recommenced his thrilling movements, he said: 'While thus pleasantly engaged, it may be well they my queen should be made acquainted with the true quality of the man whom she so highly honours. Though now in the humble position of a valet, I am the younger son of a noble Florentine family. When my elder brother inherited the family title and estate, I was a boy of twelve years old. He treated me harshly and made my life so miserable that I ran away from home, and went to sea. I joined a vessel that traded with the Spanish island of Cuba. After making several voyages, I fell among a set of freebooters. In an affray with the Guarda Costas, some of the latter were killed. A price was then set on our heads by the government. I fled to Jamaica to get under British protection, and after some time, being in great distress, I gladly accepted the situation I now hold under governor Stanhope. He knows something of my antecedents, and has been very kind and indulgent, allowing me much time for study and self-improvement; which has been of great service to me. Since I left home, I have mastered the Spanish language, and attained a fair proficiency in English, as you probably have observed.'

Here we were interrupted by the sudden heeling over of the ship on one side, and a frightful roar overhead as of a mighty tempest. The captain rushed half-dressed out of his cabin, ran to the barometer, and exclaiming that a hurricane had burst upon us, ran up the companion-way closely followed by Sporio.

CHAPTER TWELVE

The Capture by Pirates

A terrific storm had indeed arisen with scarcely any previous warning, as is usual in the Tropics. When the captain came on deck he found everything in confusion. All hands were piped up; but before it was possible to take in sail, the fore top-mast and jib-boom were carried away, and the ship, encumbered by the wreckage, became the sport of winds and waves.

Sporio offered his help and soon proved himself to be a smart and skilful seaman. After great exertions the wreckage was cleared away and the ship got under some control, but so great was the violence of the storm, that we were compelled to let the ship drive before it under a treble-reefed spanker and foresail.

Meanwhile in the cabin all was terror and confusion. Lady Stanhope and her daughter caught hold of one another and shrieked. The sea poured down the open hatches. The smashing of glass and crockery added to the din. The lights were out, we were up to our knees in water; and everything that could move was knocking and plunging about.

At last the ship righted herself a little, and, with Zilla's help, I got the lamps relighted, and the place into some kind of order.

Sporio and the captain visited us occasionally, and assured us there was no further cause for alarm, as the worst was over, and they were now busy putting the ship to rights.

Next afternoon the storm ceased almost as suddenly as it began; but when our position could be ascertained, it was found that we had been driven far out of our course, and that we were not far from the coast of Mexico.

The sea gradually went down, and every effort was now being made to get the ship into sailing trim again. In this service, Sporio turned out to be a valuable aid. The captain was delighted with him, and with the governor's permission appointed him mate – his jury-mate, as he called him – for the time being.

But now came a sad and sorrowful turn in my ever-changing life.

During the calm of that night, when most of the crew were taking a little rest after their violent and long-continued exertion, we were boarded by two large boats crammed with armed pirates. They had observed the crippled condition of the ship, and stole upon us in the dark without being noticed until just alongside.

The captain and the watch on deck made the best fight they could, but were quickly overpowered by numbers, and my gallant friend, so kind, so genial and so true, was slain bravely defending his ship and doing all in his power to protect those entrusted to his charge. Alas! alas! such is life.

The pirate chief, whom they called Don Pedro, soon made his way into the after cabin, accompanied by his two lieutenants.

Then commenced such a scene of outrage, lust and violence, as is difficult to describe.

Don Pedro had already made himself acquainted with the number and quality of the women on board, and also with the rank and office of Governor Stanhope. He addressed him in a kind of Spanish patois, mixed up with Yankee oaths and slang phrases, to the effect that he was his prisoner, and that he would keep him under strict guard until a full and sufficient ransom was paid by the British government; that he regarded the ladies as his proper spoil, but that their lives would be spared if they were obedient and submissive to him and his mates. 'But remember,' he shouted, turning to us with a dreadful look and a fearful curse, '*Mesdames*, if you oppose me, or offer any resistance, I will shoot you through the head, and pitch you out of the cabin windows,' and by way of emphasis he fired off his pistol close to our faces as we sat crouching together.

He then bound the old governor to his seat, and directed his lieutenants to drag out Lady Stanhope and strip her naked.

She cried and entreated, but it was all of no avail; they never stopped until they had stripped off every stitch except her stockings, and placed her standing in the midst with her hands tied over her head, and the cord fastened to a ring in the beam above.

Don Pedro surveyed her with the cool air of a connoisseur, and with a Spanish oath pronounced her a fairer bit of mutton than might have been expected.

And indeed, I was surprised myself; I knew her to be fair and fat, but I had no idea that she had such a smooth white skin. Her belly was round and full, a little protruding perhaps, but it was set off by an unusually large tuft of jet black hair that filled up all the space between its lower part and the adjoining thighs; but what especially attracted my attention were the two half-globes behind; not only were they extremely full and beautifully shaped, but they had a more dazzling whiteness than any buttocks I had ever seen.

The next order given was to strip her daughter in like manner. Poor Blanche, sobbing bitterly and shivering with fright, clung to me; our common misfortune having drawn us together, and dissipated her foolish pride, she cried most piteously, 'Oh, Queenie, can't you save me? Oh! what shall I do?'

I tried to comfort her by saying, 'We have nothing to do but to submit as best we can, and hope for better things.'

As they were dragging her away, one of the men, whom I heard called Carlo, stooped close to my ear and whispered in good English: 'Offer no opposition – be courageous, trust and wait,' and giving me a significant look, added 'Sporio.'

My heart bounded at the word. 'Sporio will save us,' I said to myself, 'I will be courageous, trust, and wait.'

Blanche resisted more than her mother, and when they attempted to remove her chemise and drawers, she screeched and kicked with all her might.

Don Pedro grinned in satanic pleasure, and told them to throw her on her back on the table, and hold her legs asunder, while he fucked her in the presence of her father and mother; but first, let the old fellow enjoy a good view of his daughter's cunt and ass; I suppose he has not looked upon those precious secrets since she was a baby.

They took her up bodily and carried her over to him, and held her up, so that he could not help looking at the rich hairy gap that extended down between her widespread thighs. But to say the truth, he did not seem to regard it as any great punishment to be forced to gaze on his daughter's nakedness.

'Make him kiss it, boys, rub his old nose into his daughter's private scent-bottle.' They pressed her cunt and bottom to his face, and rubbed it up and down over his mouth and nose.

I hope I don't wrong him, but I saw him smack his lips when they let her down, as if the taste and smell were both pleasant and exciting.

'Lay her down on the table again, and now bring forward that little half-breed' (poor me), 'and let us see what she is like when peeled.'

When they put their hands on me, I said, 'Please don't, let me do it myself.' And Carlo nodded approvingly, as I quietly divested myself of all my usual coverings. Then Don Pedro, beckoning me to him, said: 'Good, my little dame, you are now the best; now find my pego and bring it into view.'

I understood him tolerably well, for I had learned something of the mongrel jargon he spoke from two runaway slaves that were found by Captain St John in an open boat off the island of Cuba and brought by him to my father, who treated them well and placed them among his negroes. They were great friends of Zilla's, and we picked up from them a smattering of Spanish as it was then spoken in the Indies.

So I at once obeyed, and knowing something of his dress, I unbound the rich shawl round his waist, and opening his tight-fitting breeches, I groped for his prick, and soon drew it out together with the wrinkled bag that held his large firm stones.

Pirate though he was, he had a fine handsome tool, and his cods were large and round like a stallion's.

He was evidently pleased at the way I regarded his affair, especially when I frigged it softly up and down; but I quite won his heart when I pressed its smooth glossy head to my lips, and allowed its point to pass into my mouth.

After enjoying this little by-play for a moment, he got up and went to the table where the other two were holding Blanche still struggling on her back. She was keeping one hand pressed firmly on her cunt, while she kicked violently with her feet, and bit and scratched any part of them that came within her reach.

Don Pedro laughed at the frantic exhibition she was making of herself, and seizing her hand he pulled it roughly off her cunt, whereupon she drew it back and fetched him such a box on the ear that the smack sounded through the cabin.

The two lieutenants, though somewhat alarmed, could not refrain from laughing; while he, stunned at first by the affront, grinned most maliciously, and ordered them to turn her over.

He then smacked her bare bottom with the full force of his muscular arm until he made it all over as red as a cherry.

Then drawing apart the lips of her cunt now of the brightest crimson inside, he plunged his fiery-headed prick into its soft recesses, and proceeded to fuck with great skill and tremendous vigour.

This mode of treatment soon caused her to cease struggling and submit quietly to what was now clearly and palpably inevitable; besides, the very excited state of her bottom must have rendered the action of his prick in her cunt agreeable.

As soon as he had discharged, he drew out his inflamed tool, and sitting down to rest, he called one of the others, named Federigo, and told him to go at her now, as he knew he had a special fancy for a buttered bun (i.e. a cunt just wetted by another's spunk).

Federigo needed no second invitation, but at once took his chief's place, and plunged into Blanche's well moistened gap. I expected she would cry out, but not a bit of it; she seemed to relish the second turn more than the first; and, what appeared to me still more strange, her mother, who at first had kept her head turned away, now watched with growing interest the rapid jerks of Federigo's rump as he drove his eager prick in and out of her daughter's highly excited cunt.

Meanwhile Don Pedro directed me to pull out the governor's affair, and frig it into life. I obeyed at once, and as I knelt before him, petting and kissing the dear old prick with which I was already familiar, he told me to cock my rump, and then motioned to Carlo to take me in the rear, if he liked.

Carlo came with alacrity and knelt behind me, and putting his arms round under my belly leaned over my back, and poking his stiff prick up between my thighs, whispered in my ear, 'I won't, unless you give your kind permission.'

'You may,' I answered, 'for I like you, Carlo,' on which the old governor smiled at me, and being soothed by my attention to himself, said, 'You are a brave sensible girl, Queenie. You understand that when our kismet comes we must bend before it whether we like it or not, and true philosophy teaches us to try and make the best even of adversity itself.'

His stiffening tool however plainly showed that his kismet had not deprived him of the capacity for amorous enjoyment. It literally bounded in my hands as he watched Carlo pushing his prick into me from behind and with firm but gentle strokes reach the desired goal, just as Federigo with a shout poured his boiling sperm into Blanche's overflowing cunt.

Meanwhile Lady Stanhope was standing with her hands tied over her head, and although evidently tired of that constrained position was intently watching all that was going on.

As soon as I stood up, she appealed to me to get her released.

'Tell him,' she said, 'I will be quiet and obedient, too, for I see that no good can be gained by resisting.'

I at once begged Don Pedro to have her hands untied, and promised that she would comply with his desires as far as possible.

'Well, we will give her a chance,' and he told Carlo to cut the cords binding her hands. Then turning to me, he desired me to order Blanche to stand on the locker over her father with her legs on each side of him and her cunt on his mouth.

With great difficulty, I got her to obey this unnatural command, and indeed she only complied when her father himself told her it was wiser to obey as their lives were in peril.

I don't think he felt any great disinclination himself, for as soon as I had got her into the required position, he began to lick with evident gusto all within the savoury chink.

Don Pedro observed it too, and cried, 'So far, so good,' and turning to me, said: 'Now, get the mother to stand up too, and frig her daughter, while the father licks her cunt; so we shall complete the family circle.'

Seeing that her ladyship hesitated, he pounded on the table with the butt of his pistol and so terrified her that she jumped upon the locker at once, and putting one hand on her daughter's buttocks, she frigged with the other the upper parts of her cunt, the chink below being filled with her father's tongue.

He next told Federigo to stand on the locker at the other side, and present his prick for Blanche to suck. She threw back her head in disgust, but the old gentleman said, 'Suck it, Blanche; anything to satisfy them.'

She then bent her graceful neck and took the pirate's prick into her dainty mouth just as it was, and quickly relishing the taste, rolled her tongue round its swelling head.

Then Don Pedro mounted on the other side, and embracing what he called Lady Stanhope's splendid arse, managed after a few attempts to force his well-greased tool up into her entrails as she stooped forward frigging her daughter's cunt.

I then, at a nod from him, resumed my former place between the governor's knees, sucking his prick and tickling his stones, while Carlo again entered my love regions from behind.

The thought now occurred to me as I looked up what a remarkable *tableau vivant* we formed. I was struck with the subdued earnestness combined with the most intense action that seemed to permeate each member of the group. Oh, for some artistic eye to discern and cunning hand to portray the scene of impassioned lust and most refined lechery; but there was no one besides the actors in that dimly lighted cabin to witness how that fine old English gentleman, impelled by relentless fate, relished the sapid flavour of his daughter's cunt, while her own mother, driven by the same necessity, with active fingers drew forth its bubbling sweets; she herself enjoyed at the same time the embrace of a lusty pirate, whose prick was buried in her vitals just under her husband's nose; and above his venerable head, his daughter received between her dainty lips the spending prick of another of the band, while his own organ of delight delivered its diminished stream, though with equal pleasure, into the mouth of a sympathising friend.

But this spending, as everybody knows, is rather exhausting work, therefore when the last throb was felt, and the last gush of melting love was poured forth, we gladly changed the *tableau*, and threw ourselves into various attitudes of repose.

Meantime, I untied the weary hands of the old governor and Don Pedro dispatched Carlo for a supply of the best liquor to be found in the captured ship.

Here it may be well to pause and, in order to make what follows more intelligible, narrate the events which had previously occurred in other parts of the ship, as I learned them afterwards.

As soon as the pirates had obtained complete possession of the ship after the brief struggle on deck, they bound securely every man of the crew and locked them into the forecastle.

Sporio, as being only a servant, and because he might be of use in directing their search and providing refreshments, was left at large. He quickly recognised Carlo as an old and favourite messmate, and having taken him down into the hold under pretence of showing him where the governor's plate chest was stowed away, he made himself known to him.

His old friend was delighted to meet him again and said he never should have known him now that he had grown his beard.

In the course of their hurried conversation, Carlo happened to remark that his present life was very distasteful to him. Sporio at once replied that now a grand opportunity of complete deliverance was presented such as might never occur again; that if he joined him in effecting the rescue of the governor, he would be certain not only to obtain a free pardon, but also to be very handsomely rewarded. By these and similar arguments, he induced him to promise his hearty coopera-tion, but on condition that the lives of the pirates should be spared. Sporio then explained his plan, which was to supply them freely with drugged spirits, and then, leaving them bound in their own boats, to make all sail for Trinidad; that he was able to do this, for he had charge of the governor's medicine chest, in which were large quantities of laudanum, morphia and other narcotics. He then gave him the message for me, and begged him to have a care that we receive no real injury.

This all occurred in a very brief space of time and immediately before Carlo entered the after cabin with Don Pedro. In the meantime, the pirate crew pounced upon Zilla and the English maid; the latter, who resisted, was very severely mauled, dragged about, and really hurt;

whereas Zilla, who both from necessity and inclination let them have their will of her, escaped comparatively unharmed.

They stripped her, they felt her, they gazed at her turned up and turned down; they sucked her cunt, and they sucked her bottom, above and below, one after the other and sometimes three or four together; for her part she played with their pricks, petted their stones and tickled their bottoms; she frigged them and sucked them until they one and all declared her to be the randiest and most gamesome little devil they had ever met.

She certainly did display the most wonderful powers of endurance. She told me that after the twenty-fifth fuck she gave up counting, and that for more than two hours her hands, mouth and cunt were never without a prick. My belief, from observation, is that if a woman will only submit quietly and keep her temper and humour the men she can stand almost any amount of fucking without serious injury.

All this time, Sporio had been most liberally supplying them with the strongest rum and other spirits, all well charged with narcotic drugs, and so, by degrees, from the effects of drinking and fucking, they one by one dropped off and fell into a dull and heavy slumber.

Now let us return to the after cabin: Don Pedro, as we have seen, feeling not a little exhausted after his exertions, told Carlo to find out from the governor's servant where he kept his master's store of spirits, and to bring in a good allowance of the best.

Carlo obeyed with great readiness, and soon returned with Sporio, carrying a case of choice rum, 'the finest Old Tom', he said, and proceeded to draw the corks while Sporio provided drinking vessels. As the latter set a cup before me, he whispered: 'Don't drink, only pretend, to make them take the more.' They pressed us to join, and we all sipped a little while we kept their glasses filled, for though I did not know the reason, I saw that both Carlo and Sporio were trying to force drink on them. But indeed they did not require much forcing, and very quickly the drugs began to take effect; they nodded their heads and soon fell into a heavy stupid sleep.

Now came the time for action: their weapons were carefully removed, and then Don Pedro and Federigo were gagged and tied up in the strongest manner, while we poor women, trembling with eagerness and excitement, were joyfully putting on our cloths after having been stripped for the past two hours.

Then Sporio and Carlo went to look after the other pirates; they found that all between decks were asleep, and that Zilla had cautiously put away all their weapons, but there was still the watch on deck and also a couple of men in each of the boats. They had all taken a share, however, with the exception of one man who refused to take any in the most determined manner – he said he had killed a comrade in a drunken fit, and though acquitted by his fellows he had sworn to his patron saint not to touch spirits for a year.

Zilla was in despair, but Sporio suggested taking him a cup of coffee well dosed with morphia.

She lost no time, and was quickly at his side putting forth all her wheedling powers; she wanted to be with him, she said, and had brought him that cup of coffee as a mark of her special favour; who could resist her? The coffee was drunk, and the certain effect speedily followed.

So with respect to all the others, in turn they each succumbed to the influence of the potent drug; then having been securely bound they were lowered into their boats and laid along under the thwarts, without weapons, and with only two oars for each boat, lest they might afterwards pursue the ship. Then they were cut adrift and left to their own resources. Our own men had of course been released as soon as it was possible to do so with safety, and they now, under the direction of Sporio, bent every available sail and soon left the pirates far astern.

Sporio, with the consent of all, assumed the command of the ship, with Carlo as his mate, and steered for Trinidad. He was now the hero of the day. The governor was profuse in this thanks, and we all hailed him as our deliverer and lauded his coolness and his skill.

But poor Lady Stanhope was taken very ill. She had long suffered from heart disease, and the excitement and terror of that night proved too much for her, and notwithstanding that her daughter and I attended her most assiduously, aided by Sporio's medical resources, she passed away, and the next day her remains were solemnly committed to the deep.

This sad event threw Blanche and me more together and cemented our newly formed friendship. The old governor, too, in spite of his sorrow seemed relieved, and joined his daughter in requesting me to make their house my home during my stay on the island. He said he would write to my father to allow me to remain with him as companion to his daughter, and that he would look after my education himself.

His invitation was acceptable to me for many reasons and I gladly consented to stay at Government House until a reply had been received from my father.

We saw no more pirates, and after a quick and pleasant sail cast anchor at Port of Spain where, thankful for our miraculous escape, we gladly prepared to enjoy once again the comfort and security of our freedom.

❧❦

Part Two

SAFE HAVEN WITH
THE GOVERNOR

CHAPTER ONE

My Adopted Father and Protector

Passing over for the present the events immediately succeeding our landing, behold me, settled in Government House, the favoured guest of the respected governor, and the chosen companion of his only daughter.

My rooms are luxuriously fitted out in the cheeriest part of the building; I have almost a little suite to myself: a comfortable bed-chamber, with a commodious bathroom adjoining, and the snuggest possible little boudoir opening through a verandah on to a portion of the grounds especially set apart for my enjoyment and supervision.

For attendants, I have my own maid Zilla and an intelligent black boy, called Davy, to work in the grounds and run errands.

The old gentleman himself pays me every attention and visits me often on the sly; in public he is most circumspect, yet always exceedingly kind and indulgent.

I have grown very fond of him, and do everything in my power to please and gratify him.

Blanche and I are very good friends; we read and work together and receive joint instruction from various masters.

I am not sure whether she is fully aware of the connection between her father and me, but if she is, she takes no notice of it, wisely judging that it is at all events better for her than if he married again. In due course, letters were received from my father, thanking the governor for his attention to me and gladly consenting to our present arrangements.

Carlo obtained from the English government the pardon he sought, together with a substantial reward; and being found efficient as a seaman and a navigator, he was appointed captain of the good old ship *Cammarilla*.

Good tidings also awaited our Sporio: the governor heard from the British envoy to the court of Tuscany, not only confirming the account he had given of his family, but announcing that his brothers were dead, and that he was now the sole heir to the title and estates of the Lambertini.

Sporio, now Count Lambertini, heard himself from the family lawyer, informing him of the same event and placing a large sum of money at his disposal.

One of his first acts, was to offer me his hand and fortune; but I was not then inclined to marry, for having youth, position and independent means I loved my present freedom too well; besides, I thought that among the proud nobles of Italy, the irregularity of my birth would surely be cast in my teeth; so I declined his generous offer in the kindest manner and with many expressions of esteem and affection; at the same time I advised him to turn his thoughts to Blanche, who was more suited to him by birth and connection, and I know loved him very dearly.

He took my advice and having proposed for Miss Stanhope was accepted by both father and daughter and after a marriage celebrated with musical *éclat*, Blanche set sail for Italy as the Countess Lambertini.

Having thus satisfactorily disposed of our chief *dramatis personae*, let me return to my humble self, and my protector, the old governor, Sir Charles Stanhope.

To arrest scandal he went through some legal procedure adopting me as his child; and having made a settlement he prevailed on me to assume his name. In consequence, I was everywhere well received, had great court paid to me and no end of suitors.

But now I must explain our private arrangements. He had a concealed entrance to my rooms of which even the servants were ignorant. In my bathroom was a press for hanging towels; it had a movable back, which also formed the back of a similar press in the room at the other side, which was furnished as a spare room but was never occupied.

His practice was to retire early in the night, pleading in excuse his advancing years, for though not yet sixty, and hale and hearty for that, yet his grey hair made him look much older.

My boudoir was my favourite place for working and reading, and I avowedly devoted my evenings to study. So when the house was quiet, and my doors and windows well secured, the governor was able without attracting notice to visit his fair Rosamund, as he loved to call me.

Then in the full light of brilliant lamps I would strip for him, and take out and fondle into life his soft and attenuated prick, while I read aloud some luscious work or related some amorous tale. But nothing so thoroughly pleased and excited him as hearing me describe my own fucking adventures; and he was always begging me to get myself fucked as often as possible, and as soon after as I could, even while my cunt was still saturated with the spunk which had been poured into it, to give him the fullest details; then he would examine my inflamed quim, sniff up the salty odour and lick its moistened lips.

On one typical occasion, the governor was lying on a wide comfortable sofa opposite a large mirror; I was leaning back by his side in such a position as to afford him a full view in the glass of my cunt and bottom. I petted and frigged his slowly stiffening prick, and he titillated my excited orifice, watching its appearance in the glass, while he asked me for the latest news.

'Well, Queenie, my pet, have you anything to tell me tonight? Did you succeed with James our English coachman? He seems a safe kind of man, and amorously disposed. I was glad to see you coming in this evening from the stables.'

'I did, my Charlie' (his pet name in private); 'don't you feel and see how moist my cunt is? I have not even wiped it since; smell it, dear.'

'Yes, my love, it is in a delicious state. It is very moist, and the hot smell from it is most fragrant and exciting. Now tell me everything that happened; don't miss one word.'

'Well, I went out to ask after my mare which was so frisky in the morning that I could scarcely mount her. James met me in the stable, and as I passed him on my way into the loose box to pat the mare on her neck as usual, he put his hand on my shoulder to keep me back saying, "Take care, Miss Stanhope, she is not just now in a humour to be trusted," and in some way he made her plunge. I naturally started back, and he caught me in his arms. "Oh, Miss Queenie, you were near being hurt, and I should have been so sorry, for we are all so fond of you," and he pressed me to his breast. "Dearest lady, who could help loving you! how glad I am to save you from harm," he said, as he drew me towards a sheltered corner. I thanked him for his care and attention and said: "Now, let me go, James, I am in no danger here!" He put his face close to mine, and whispered: "Oh, might I make so bold – just one – darling Miss Queenie."

' "Well, as a reward – here – take one – now, that will do – let me go – you will make me fall – Oh, James! what are you doing? Don't push your knee between mine – don't attempt to raise my clothes – what do you mean by unbuttoning my dress? O stop! I did not give you leave to put your hand there – Oh, James! how your fingers tickle me! Oh! how big you are! it will kill me – Oh! it is in! how nice it feels! how well you do it! press up to my heart. Yes, James, I will say it if you wish, I like you to fuck me. Yes, it is a strong, large prick. Yes, you may pinch my bottom and put your finger in while you fuck, fuck, fuck," I cried, as I felt his great tool poking my cunt while I lay under him on a heap of hay in the corner; he drove it home with such energy and force that his hard balls banged against my bottom as with a suppressed shout he flooded my cunt with boiling spunk.'

By this time, I had Charlie's prick in fine erection and he cried: 'Get over me, my love, lay your sweet arse on my face; I will suck your delicious quim while you draw from my prick its milky juice.'

I presented to him my arse, as he wished me to call my bottom, while he licked and sucked both the apertures in my furrow of delight, I received in my mouth the discharge of his seed, and frigged his bottom-hole with my finger.

Then we took some refreshment which I always had ready, and he returned to his own apartments, for he seldom cared for more than one emission at a time. Next evening he came as usual, and asked had I anything new to tell him.

'Well, Charlie, you know I am always on the lookout for any love adventure that I think will give you pleasure. You spoke the other day about Dr Prickett, and asked me to give him some encouragement. Well, he called again this afternoon, and by my direction was shown into my boudoir. The blinds were down, and I was reclining on the couch, complaining of a headache and pain in my chest. He examined my chest with his stethoscope; while doing so I allowed him to get a good view, and feel too, of my swelling bubbies. His eye sparkled as he gently pressed one of my nipples in his trembling fingers. Then putting his hand down, he said he wanted to feel the region around my liver. "But I can't through all this dress; may I put my hand underneath?"

' "You may, over my chemise," I replied, leaning back.

'He bent forward, and as if by accident, passed his hand up, not over, but under my chemise.

' "Oh, doctor! I said *over* my chemise, and I feel you hand on my bare skin."

' "Well, dear Miss Queenie, what difference does it make. It is after all a professional hand, and we medicos are accustomed to have no secrets kept from us." All the while his hand was roaming over the lower parts of my belly, and at last I felt his fingers passing down my thighs and pressing the lips of my cunt.

' "Oh, doctor! that's not where my liver is at all."

' "True, but it is very intimately connected with it. When the liver is inactive there is always sympathetic disturbance here. Do you ever feel any unusual heat here, or anything like obstruction in the passage?" and he pushed his finger boldly into the entrance of my easily excited cunt. Then, rapidly changing his hands, he put the other which had been in his pocket on my cunt, and began to rub the clitoris and nymphae.

' "No, doctor, there is nothing wrong with me there indeed – Oh!

what are you doing? you will drive me wild! you are making me so hot. Do I want anything there? – I do – Ah, you have made me so foolish, I really do not know what I am saying or doing. What do I want, ah, you know yourself. A prick? well, a prick, if you like. Yes, of course I know you have a prick; how could you be a prickett if you hadn't? I said, laughing at my wretched witticism. Put my hand on it? well, I will to please you. Yes it is a fair specimen of the manly organ – both stiff and long. Do ladies like that kind of prick? You know that better than I do. Would my cunt? Yes, doctor, for however you have managed, you have set it on fire and made it glow like a furnace. I am sure you have put something into it, it burns so."

' "Nonsense, child, it is the sight and feel of my prick which has made you long for a fuck; now confess, isn't that it?"

'All this time, he was most skilfully manipulating my cunt, making every nerve in and around it tingle with pleasure.

' "Yes, I am longing for a fuck – you have made me, whatever you have done; come, hurry – put it in, or you will drive me distracted," I cried, spreading my thighs, and pushing up my cunt naked and open before his face.

' "There – in with it – Hah! I have it at last – now fuck away; how grand your prick feels! it quite fills up my cunt; you doctors are great fellows, and can do just what you please with us poor women." Then pushing my hand between our bellies, I felt the root of his prick and squeezed his balls, while I threw up my legs and hammered his bottom with my heels, to force him further into my cunt, now in a state of the most ravenous excitement. He held me with a grip like iron, while he fucked away, and then with a frantic yell of delight, he poured into my cunt a torrent of his boiling injection.'

Meanwhile the dear old governor fairly quivered with emotion, as he poured his scanty discharge over my breast, where I was frigging his prick with my bubbies pressed against its sides.

He next prevailed on me to favour him with an actual fucking exhibition, while he lay concealed in my room, and Davy, my black errand boy and gardener, was fixed on as the medium.

Though called a boy, Davy was a well-grown lad of eighteen, and not at all bad-looking.

'But what if Davy should prove unwilling?' I asked.

'Oh,' he replied, 'don't trouble yourself about that; you will find him only too willing, if a woman, and that woman a lady, happens to throw herself in his way.'

'But if so,' I added, 'are we safe in trusting him?'

'You can make him safe by gaining his affection, and young fellows of his class are often more trustworthy than those from whom you might expect better things; but to make assurance doubly sure, you may threaten my displeasure; the fear of that would, I think, be sufficient to shut his mouth.'

So I consented, and arranged with the governor for him to be hiding in my room about the middle of next day; the time when I usually took my bath and he his siesta. And through the open door, he might hear and see all that passed.

The next morning, having warned Zilla to allow no one to disturb me during my after-bath sleep, I directed Davy to gather a nice bunch of flowers and bring them to my boudoir.

Meanwhile the governor entered by the secret door, and was duly ensconced behind my bedroom door.

Soon afterwards Davy appeared, his ebony face beaming and all his ivory flashing by way of contrast, while he held a glowing bouquet in his hand. He found me loosely dressed and lying on a sofa. I said, 'Oh, Davy, I am so glad you have come as I cannot sleep for these horrid flies; lay down the bouquet on the table, take my fan there, and like a good fellow keep them off while I try to get a little rest, for I am tired and sleepy.'

Davy took the fan and kneeling on a stool at my side, with the quiet noiseless movement of his race, discharged the office thus imposed on him. While I, overpowered with heat, lay tossing about and affording him sundry peeps at my fair arms and bosom. 'Oh, Davy, I am so hot that I cannot rest, could you unfasten my belt for me? it is hooked behind,' I said, turning over on my side. With deft and ready fingers he did what I required.

'Why Davy, one would think you were trained as a lady's maid,' I said, turning on my back and raising one of my knees.

He grinned and said with inborn gallantry that I made him very happy, and asked, could he do anything else to give me more ease. I smiled up at him, and said: 'Davy, you are a good attentive boy, and you see how much I trust you in having you by me while I sleep.' Closing my eyes, I continued: 'Yes, there is one thing more I think you could do for me, and which I am too lazy to do for myself, and that is, to unbuckle my garters; they feel very tight now that I am so warm.' Davy almost bounded at the word, and quick as thought, his trembling hands were fumbling about my knees, while I pretended to be more than half asleep and totally regardless of his manoeuvres. My garters were fastened above my knees, and the heat, I suppose, had caused my thighs to swell, for he seemed to find considerable difficulty in opening the buckles; at last, and with some effort and much lifting of my skirt to see what he was doing and perhaps something more besides, he succeeded with the leg that was raised, but the other he had to lift himself to facilitate the operation. He stooped a good deal, and in raising my leg managed to separate my thighs. I was conscious that he was most intently gazing up, but I lay quite motionless, as if overpowered with sleep. Meanwhile, having removed the garters, he continued touching and softly pressing my thighs, first on the outsides and then on the inner parts, gradually lifting my dress more and more. He now bent forward until his head was almost between my thighs, and I heard him sniffing, as if he was perceiving and enjoying that subtle perfume which exhales from the cunt of every healthy woman – no matter how cleanly she is in her habits, or how particular she may be to keep her private parts nice and sweet. I could almost hear his heart beating as his trembling fingers approached the hairy chink which was now the great object of his desire and which lay so temptingly within easy reach. At last his fingers touched the outer edges of the lips; as he perceived no shrinking from his touch, he let his hand rest lightly on the soft pouting ridges, and looking up he attentively scanned the features of my face.

At first, a slight twitching at the corners of my mouth seemed to alarm him; but I quickly brought the refractory muscles under command and the symptoms of heavy sleep prevailed; so he ventured again to investigate the object of his special interest and desire. He softly pushed his fingers in between the lips, and at the same time in the gentlest manner spread my thighs a little further apart. His head bent forward as if irresistibly drawn towards the magic spot. His breath stirred the hairs that grew around it. He kissed the lips. His protruded tongue entered and played around the soft recess.

My nerves began to tingle and my clitoris to swell. To remain quiet longer was impossible – I stirred; he started up, looked caught, and seemed covered with confusion. To reassure him, I said in my blandest tones, 'Oh, Davy! I have had such a pleasant dream, I thought I was once more a child, bathing with my nurse, and that she was kissing me all over'; then glancing down, I continued: 'But Davy I am sure you must have been looking at me, and touching me somewhere; did you mistake me for your sweetheart?'

'No, missy, Davy hab no sweetheart, he lub nobody but missy herself. Oh, missy! when I take off your two garters, I force to look up, and I did see something; de bery opening ob heaven did shine out between your lubly thighs. Oh, missy! it too much for poor Davy; if you no let him see dat heaven again, he die, dat sure.'

'Ah, Davy, I fear you are a foolish boy; however, I would not wish you to die; yet if I let you look again, you might boast of it to somebody, and that would grieve me and make me sorry for being so kind to you and trusting you so much.'

'Sweet missy, you may trust Davy, he die sooner than make you sorry.'

'Well, then, Davy, to show you how much I trust you, you may take one peep, but only one, mind you.'

In a moment my dress was lifted up, my thighs widely separated, and Davy's head and shoulders between them. He darted on my cunt like some famished animal on its prey. He kissed its lips, and rubbed his nose in the chink between; then thrusting in his tongue he licked all the inside, and up the passage as far as he could reach.

This tasting of love, as pleasing to me as it was ravishing to him, only whetted his appetite and increased his excitement.

He looked up again, and now his eyes seemed actually ablaze with amorous fire as he exclaimed, 'Oh, missy! you have sweet cunt, as juicy as a melon and hot like a baked yam. It surely long for um friend. Oh, look at um here! Darling missy, don't be angry wid poor Davy,' he pleaded as he pulled out a fine black tool of goodly size, with a full dark-coloured top, stiff and erect; and, pushing it towards me, he said, 'Feel um, missy,' emboldened by the look of interest with which he saw that I regarded it.

It throbbed as I felt it with my hand, and when my fingers closed around it, it gave a bound as if electrified by their touch.

He now leaned over me, and with a most entreating look, said, 'Darling missy, won't you let him in? he will fill you all up wid lub and delight.'

'Well, Davy, I can hardly refuse you now, as I have let you go so far; but first see that the door into the verandah is bolted securely; you need not mind my bedroom door, no one can enter by that; and now let down your pantaloons, or take them off altogether, that will be better, it is so warm. Now tuck your shirt well up, that will keep you cool.'

He obeyed with the utmost alacrity, and presented to view fine muscular legs and shapely buttocks as he stooped over me and gently drew me across the couch. I twisted my body into such a position as would afford my dear old Charlie the fullest and most exciting view of the whole transaction. I smiled towards him, as I could just distinguish his face through the slightly open door.

The room inside had been darkened for our purpose, but I could see that he was nodding approval, and rubbing up his tool with his hands.

Meanwhile Davy, having raised up my thighs, had inserted the point of his weapon in the open sheath prepared for its reception and, led on by natural instinct, was working it forward and back with both skill and effect.

Each time he drove it home, he grunted: 'Oh, missy! Oh!! and as the feeling of pleasure grew more intense, the loudness of his tones increased until, with his eyeballs almost starting out of his head, he shouted: 'O – ah! Ah – O!' and I felt a torrent of hot sperm discharged with unusual vigour into my throbbing and swimming receptacle.

Davy desired a repetition, and was quite ready for it, too, and so was I, but my thoughts turned to my dear old Charlie. So I checked him, and said: 'Not now, Davy, some other time. I will call you again; you must really put on your things now, and be off to your work; it would never do, you know, for anyone to find you here in my boudoir.'

He reluctantly obeyed, and getting into his trousers set himself to rights. I then let him kiss me, and promised to receive him soon again, on which, after a loving hug, he hastily withdrew.

I bolted the door after him, and turned to meet Charlie, who now entered, radiant with smiles and holding his prick in a state of unusual stiffness in his hand. Folding me in his arms, he thanked me for the great pleasure I had afforded him, and commended what he called my extraordinary cleverness in conducting the affair in such a natural and satisfactory manner.

I said: 'I am glad you liked it, Charlie, and I may tell you that the thought that you were looking on and enjoying it too increased my own pleasure tenfold; and I am now ready, as you see, to give this poor fellow a specially warm and lubricious reception. Look how red and swollen the lips are! and see what a lot of white oily spunk is trickling down the furrow! now pop him in, and he will feel the welcome I have ready for him.'

He then revelled as usual in my excited and well-moistened cunt; and after a most enjoyable fuck, accompanied by expressions of fondest endearment, took his departure.

CHAPTER TWO

The Training of Susy

About this time Zilla, who rendered me willing and valuable aid in my efforts to please the old governor, received into her charge a pretty young girl to train as lady's maid. She was the orphan daughter of a soldier, Susy by name and just fifteen years of age. The governor was greatly pleased when he heard of it and said it would be such a treat to see her in the bath with me and hear us talk together, and 'my

Queenie knows the kind of talk that will please her old Charlie best'.

I planned the matter with Zilla, who was to be her initiator in the first instance and who promised carefully to report progress to me. She therefore brought her to her own room, and they slept together the first night. Next morning when Zilla attended me as usual she told me she had no difficulty in obtaining Susy's fullest confidence; that she had a charming little cunt with smooth lips and just a suspicion of light silky hair at that part of the projection where the slit begins; that the little rosy clitoris was very sensitive and easily excited, and that altogether, from her disposition and previous learning, she was fitted and prepared in no ordinary degree for all kinds of amorous sports and enjoyments.

Zilla also found out that although Susy had not as yet been regularly fucked, she was perfectly familiar with the act and knew the names of all the parts employed – and liked to talk about them too; that she had seen her mother fucked by other men besides her own husband; and that one of the officers had frequently petted and looked at her cunny as a child, and taught her to frig and suck his prick. I said I would like her to attend me when taking my midday bath, and went on, 'You may tell her, Zilla, as if from yourself, you know, that the more free and unconstrained she is with me, the better I will like her, and that nothing would please me more than to hear from herself a full and minute account of all she has ever seen and heard of these interesting matters for I am exceedingly curious about such subjects.'

The old governor was delighted when I told him all this, especially when he heard that Susy had a smooth little fat cunt with scarcely any hair on it. 'How I shall enjoy,' he said, 'seeing her naked with you in the bath!'

So on the following day, I had him snugly ensconced in the towel press, seated on a chair and able through a slit in the door to see and hear all that passed in the bathroom.

Susy was in attendance, and as she assisted me in taking off my dress, I said, 'Now, Susy, you may as well strip too, for the bath is large and I like to have someone to bathe with me.'

I was soon *puris naturatibus*, but I observed that she hesitated about pulling off her shift.

'Why Susy!' I said, laughing, 'You don't mind my seeing you naked, I hope; it is natural enough to be ashamed before men, but it is excess of modesty for women to mind one another, for I expect we are all furnished pretty much after the same fashion. That's right,' I continued, as she drew her shirt over her head, 'and certainly,' I said, drawing her towards me and putting one hand on her bottom and the other on her smooth plump little cunny, 'you have no reason to hesitate, for you seem very nicely furnished for so young a girl; come: let us compare together.' Of course, my object was to make the girl display her young charms in the fullest manner, and to lead her on to lascivious talk so as to give more gratification to my dear old Charlie, who was, I knew, at that very moment, rubbing up his old cock as he feasted his eyes on her budding cunt of fourteen summers.

I drew her forward to face the press, and passing my hand over her pretty rising mound asked, 'Is it long, dear, since these silky hairs began to sprout?'

'No, missy, it is only within the last month that I observed any hair to be growing on me there.'

'These fat round lips are very soft, and this funny little lump between, how it slips about, do you often pet it with your finger?'

'Sometimes, miss,' she said, as she laughed and blushed.

I laughed too, and as I frigged her, said: 'Susy, you and I will be good friends, I think. And now, let me assure you that the more confidence you have in me, the better I will like you; and besides, I know very well what girls are, and that no matter how demure they are before men, when they are among themselves, they delight in unrestrained liberty, both of speech and action. And moreover, I don't think the worse of a girl, provided it be done wisely and discreetly. Now tell me, dear, was this pretty little chink ever touched by a man?' I asked, still continuing the frigging, so that she twisted and started as often as I pressed the sensitive top of her tiny clitoris.

'Yes, miss, Oh!'

'By more than one?'

'Yes miss.'

'Often?'

'Yes miss.'

'Ah! I thought so and I like you all the better. Now let us take our bath, and we can finish our talk afterwards.' We then stepped in and enjoyed the refreshing effects of the cool water while we dipped and splashed about.

Susy grew more familiar as we played and toyed together, and became quite affectionate as she dried me afterwards.

Before we put on our things again, I said, 'Sit down here with me awhile, Susy; lean back and open your thighs, you have a charming little loose chink and I want to get a good view of it; now tell me, who touched it first, and how he did it; but first tell me, do you know any name for it?'

'I do, miss, but I am ashamed to say it.'

'Why need you be ashamed? is it cunt?'

'It is, miss.'

'Well, say it.'

'Cunt.'

'And before you proceed, what is a cunt for?'

'Oh, it is for – for – '

'Out with it.'

'Well, it is for fucking.'

'With what?'

'La, miss, you want me to say everything.'

'Of course I do.'

'Well then, fucked by a prick.'

'Good girl, now go on.'

'Well, miss, the first man who touched my cunt was captain Joyce. My mother was her washerwoman and she used to send me to carry home his clothes. He always got me to put them away for him in his drawers. He knew the time of my coming and generally had cakes and something nice for me to eat. One day he kissed me and called me his pretty little maid. He quickly saw that I felt flattered, for at that time I thought it a great thing to be kissed by an officer. Then he got me to sit on his knee and tickled me, first under my arms then between my thighs; at last he got his hand upon my cunt, and after awhile he prevailed on me to lie back, open my legs and let him look at it; and what do you think, nothing would satisfy him but to kiss and lick the inside with his tongue! was not that horrible?'

'Not at all, dear Susy, it is quite a natural thing for a man to kiss and suck the cunt of a nice girl like you; why I have known even women to kiss each other's cunts; but go on, what did he do? did he show you his prick at all?'

'Indeed he did, he coaxed me even to unbutton his trousers, and take it out with my own hand, and then he showed me how to frig it up and down, and got me to kiss it and suck its head; one day he stripped me stark naked, and placed me across his lap with my bottom to his belly, and he pressed his standing prick along my slit in front, while I frigged it with one hand, and stirred his balls with the other, and soon a lot of hot milk spurted out of it all over my belly.'

'Did he every try to get it into your cunt?'

'Yes, often, but I was quite too small, though he hurt me a good deal.'

'Did you ever see anyone fucked, Susy?'

'Oh, dear yes, I saw my mother often fucked, and indeed most of the women in the barracks.'

'I am so glad; tell me everything and all about it; but, I declare Susy, I do believe you are spending – stay let me taste it'; and putting my hands under her plump little bottom, and my face between her widely spread thighs, I rubbed my nose in the sweet savoury chink, and lapped up the hot rich juice that exuded from its excited depths.

'Dear miss, how pleasant that it,' she said, wriggling about, 'how kind and good you are! I never felt anything so nice; let me kiss and suck your sweet cunt in return.'

'Here then, Susy, I will hold it open for you while you suck it, and slip the tip of your finger into my bottom, I love to be tickled there at the same time, yes, that is very pleasant.'

I lay back, so that Charlie might have a good side view of my cunt while Susy sucked it, and as she leaned forward, her own pretty little bum with its round hole just over the rosy chink of her cunt was turned to him too.

'O! Susy dear! I am spending now, suck it, love, suck my cunt,' and putting down my hands, I pressed her head between the wide-spread thighs as I felt the sweet suction of her lips on the clitoris and the point of her tongue darting into the sensitive orifice beneath.

'That is a good girl, you gave me great pleasure, Susy; I must see that you are nicely fucked some of these days; how would you like to feel a good prick going into this little chink?'

'It would feel very nice, I am sure, but would you really like to see me fucked, miss?'

'That depends upon whom you were fucked by; how would you like to be fucked by the governor?'

'La, miss, sure he would not care to fuck a girl like me.'

'Why not, Susy, you could give him as much pleasure as the finest lady in the land.'

'Oh, but isn't he too old? He might not care for that sort of thing now.'

'Ah, he is not so old as he looks! What's more, I have reason to know,' I said smilingly, 'that he enjoys a fuck now as much as ever he did in his life.'

She opened her eyes and looked at me in an earnest and excited manner.

'What I mean, Susy, is he has no wife now, and you know, a man needs a woman at times, and I am sure you are just the one he would like to have; and if you are inclined to gratify him, I would not in the least object, for I am very fond of him and like to have him pleased, and then he would be very good to you, and might be of service to your mother, too.'

'Well, miss, I will let him, as it pleases you – if he cares for it himself; but how and when can it be done?'

'Oh! I will manage that. He will be taking supper with me tonight; you and Zilla will be there to open oysters for us, and then perhaps we shall all have some fun together; in the meantime, if you care for it, you may have a little play with Davy in the garden.'

She blushed crimson, and said, 'Why miss, you don't think that I play with Davy?'

'No, but he plays with you, and is not that much the same thing. Ah you little rogue! you little thought that I saw him kiss you this very morning, and, if I mistake not, run his hand up to where your little fanny hides herself.'

'Oh, my, miss! what sharp eyes you have! it was a great piece of impudence in him, but he shan't do it again; if he does, I will give him such a slap as he won't forget in a hurry.'

'Oh, well, don't be cruel, Davy is a merry boy and full of fun; I don't think he means any harm; now go, I am not angry, as you see.'

I was quickly in dear old Charlie's arms; oh! how he fondled and praised me. Love's vocabulary was exhausted in the effort to find sufficient terms of endearment and delight.

We had a delicious fuck. And here, let me say a word in explanation. After an unusually wide experience in the matters, I prefer the embraces of an elderly man, provided he has not enfeebled by early excess or self-abuse. As a rule young men are too hasty and precipitate, and their only thought seems to be self gratification. Whereas, an elderly man is usually more deliberate in his action and more anxious that the woman he is with should fully participate in the pleasure, so that she might more lovingly respond to his emotion; as Byron tunefully expresses it:

> All who joy would win, must share it –
> Happiness was born a twin.

An elderly man also is generally more fond and tender in his love and far less exacting in his demands.

But another and deeper reason for this partiality arose from the different way in which the act itself is regarded by the two sexes. Man, who is perhaps by nature and training more selfish, generally looks for pleasure irrespective of the female who supplies it, anyone in fact that suits his purpose will do. It is not so with woman, at least not generally, and I know my own sex well; their chief and highest gratification arises from their capacity to import enjoyment to the man they love, and hence they seldom care for the venereal connection except with one whom they esteem and love. Of course, I don't refer here to those who from unfortunate necessity are obliged to grant favours to anyone who will pay for them; for such as they the poet speaks when he declares:

> Let all mankind this certain maxim hold,
> Marry who will, our sex is to be sold.
> With empty hands not tassels you can lure,
> But fulsome love for gain we can endure;
> For gold we love the impotent and old.
> And heave, and pant, and kiss, and cling for gold.

I refer only to those who bestow their favour freely, without that wretched greed for money or costly presents which degrades so many. And with respect to such, I consider that even Byron slanders us when he reproduces the French maxim:

> In her first passion, woman loves her lover,
> In all the others, all she loves is love.

Now my dear old Charlie, though not perhaps the object of my first passion, had really gained possession of my heart's best affection, and I therefore enjoyed and reciprocated his embrace with a warmth I experienced with no other man.

I found him always kind, gentle and considerate, and, what would have been a special charm in the eyes of many, he was absolutely free from all tinge of the green-eyed monster, jealousy.

On the contrary, instead of restricting me in dispensing my favours, he was continually urging me to form fresh connections and seek out-of-the-way adventures.

Provided I kept his secret inviolate, and that he occupied the first place in my affections, he rather rejoiced in the number and variety of my lovers; in fact there was not an aide de camp or officer in attendance whom he did not suggest as a likely subject for an amorous intrigue; but more of this anon. Now, as he lay soaking in my arms, he asked me to tell him more about Susy and Davy. 'But, how quick the fellow was in making up to her!'

'It turns out,' I said, 'that they are old friends. His father has charge of the barracks garden, and Davy worked there with him, and often brought Susy in to get fruit. So this morning he went out to renew her acquaintance. He seemed delighted to meet her again, and drawing her under the shade of wide-spreading banana trees, he took her in his arms, felt her young breasts, and then suddenly stooping ran his hand up her petticoat. I saw it all, for I was watching through the jalousies, and although she pretended to me that she was very angry, she certainly showed no displeasure at the time, so far as I could observe, for she remained quiet, and even opened her thighs to give him more room; what more might have happened I would not venture to say had not Zilla come into the garden to call her; when she heard Zilla's voice, she jumped and ran to meet her.'

'What fun it would be, if we could watch them together! Could you manage it, Queenie?'

'Well, I might; the kiosk at the end of the grounds commands the whole guarden. I pass much of my time there reading in the upper room. If we could get there without being seen by them, we might watch all their manoeuvres and see everything they did through the jalousies. But perhaps the better plan would be to take Davy into my confidence, and let him know beforehand that I was looking on and that he was giving me pleasure, as well as getting it himself. You might, without his knowledge, enter the grounds by the wicket gate close to the kiosk, and be there before me.'

'That is a capital notion, Queenie; arrange with him for tomorrow forenoon, and I will come around after dispatching my letters and telling them inside that I am going for a walk; but what would you think of calling him in now, settling with him, and giving him a little sport as a reward? The very thought of it is stirring me up, and making me disposed for a second turn.'

'Very well,' I replied, 'Go in there and conceal yourself while I call him in; I dare say he won't be slow in availing himself of the opportunity.'

So leaving the governor to settle himself again behind the door in my darkened room, I stepped into the garden and called Davy.

After a moment, he showed himself at the farther end, looking flustered and hurriedly getting his dress into order, while at the same time I caught a glimpse of Susy's skirt as she hastily disappeared through a side door.

'I want a bunch of geraniums to take with me in the carriage. Davy gather some please, and bring them into my room.'

He quickly followed me with the flowers in his hand. As I took them from him, I said, 'I am sorry to have disturbed you just now, Davy, what were you and Susy about?'

'Oh, missy, I was talking to her and she wanted to kiss me,' he said grinning.

'Very good, and you, Joseph-like, ran away from her?'

'No, no, miss, Davy nebba run from a petticoat.'

'I believe you, Davy, you are too fond of what is under the petticoat; forgive me for having called you away from it.'

'Ah! missy, I have been just longing for you to call me again as you promised; Oh, missy, may I now, just one leetle feel?'

'Well, Davy, if I let you for a moment, will you be very good and do everything I ask you?'

'Dat I will, everything.'

He went on his knees, and I quickly felt one of his black paws roving over my bottom, and the other exploring my well-moistened cunt.

'Oh, how soft!' he muttered, smacking his large fleshy lips, 'it all melting wid lub; let me look.' I helped him to raise my dress. 'Oh! it hab bright colour – red as de rose; and a lubly smell, like one pinky; let me kiss um – oo–oo–ah; and suck um; it hab sweet juice like one sowsap.'

'Now, Davy, stand up before me while I sit on the sofa so; I want to see what you are like,' I said, drawing out his black tool, 'why, it is all hot and moist, what were you doing with it?'

'Oh, missy, don't you know? Susy was kissing it.'

'Then it must have been with the mouth between her legs; I know by the smell it has; you may as well tell me honestly; I won't be angry with you.'

'Well, missy, I won't tell you one lie, I had just given her one little poke, and was going to begin the second time, when you called me. I felt angry then, but I glad now.'

'Has Susy a nice cunt? Did you ever fuck it before?'

'No, missy, but I kissed it. It is very nice, and you can see it all very plain, for it hab scarcely any cubbering, and it bery smooth to suck; but oh missy, I nebba see cunny so nice, and soft, and beautiful as yours; may I get in and hab one little fuck?'

'Yes, Davy, but listen first. I want to see you fuck Susy. To enable me to do so, you will have to bring her into the lower part of the kiosk in the garden, and lay her down on the matting in the corner, with her clothes well thrown up, you know, so that when I look down through the floor of the room above I may see all that you do. I will be there tomorrow forenoon and Susy will be sent into the garden while she thinks I am out riding. And if you do it well, and have plenty of talk too, I will give you a reward soon. Do you understand?'

Davy grinned with satisfaction. 'Good missy, Davy will do all he can to please.'

I then leaned back, spread my thighs, and let him push in his engine of love, turning him so that Charlie might have a view of it as it glided in and out between the clinging lips of my cunt.

'Now Davy, my boy, push home; what do black people say you are doing now?'

'I braggin, missy.'

'And what name have they for the tool itself.'

'Tommy, miss.'

'And what do they call the woman's thing?'

'The hole in her crack.'

'And what is your tommy doing now?'

'He just going to puke. Oh! oh!!'

'Let him puke away then.'

Davy now pounded away with all his might, and just as the seed was gushing from him, he let out a tremendous rouser, which so tickled the governor's fancy that he fairly laughed out, but Davy was in such a commotion that he did not observe it.

I then sent him out and gratified my Charlie with another inspection, but would not let him emit; I wanted to save his force for the evening.

After dinner the governor came openly into my part of the grounds and strolled about with me until suppertime; then we entered my boudoir where the lights were burning, and the windows carefully closed. Zilla and Susy were in attendance, and we had a good deal of chaffing with them while they were opening the oysters. The governor insisted on their taking some champagne to refresh them after their exertions, and we soon all grew very merry. The governor began to kiss and tickle them, they retaliated, and Zilla even pulled his beard; in return, he ran his hand up her petticoat and seized the hair of her cunt. She pretended to be angry, and squealed out; Susy came to the rescue, and in the mêlée was tumbled on the floor with her clothes tossed up.

Zilla laughed, and cried: 'Oh, for shame, Susy, you have shown the governor everything you have between your legs.'

Susy struggled to get up, but I held her down, saying, 'Don't mind, Susy, you are just as nice there as any of us; we'll have a peep at Zilla herself by and by.'

Meantime the governor pounced on her, and getting his head between her legs began to kiss her smooth little cunt.

Then, at a nod from me, Zilla unfastened his braces, while I unbuttoned his trousers in front, and drawing out his prick and balls, cried: 'Now then, governor, you are cleared for action; engage under the old flag that for forty years has braved the battle and the breezes.' Susy struck her colours to keep up the metaphor as the governor ranged alongside, and with open arms and legs received him in to her sally-port.

Zilla knelt in front, and holding up her dress, gratified him with a view and feel of her luscious thick-lipped savoury cunt, while I guided his not over-stiff affair into Susy's tender recess, letting it slip in and out through my fingers as I slapped and pinched his bottom to stimulate his efforts.

He ran the usual race of pleasure, and with loud and repeated grunts testified his satisfaction at reaching the desired goal.

Then when he had put himself to rights, he kissed me, and said, 'Darling Queenie, you and your charming maids have given me very great pleasure, I look forward to many happy reunions here; meanwhile, let me remind them, I rely implicitly on their secrecy and discretion, and they shall not repent of pleasing me.'

He then took his departure and we finished the supper by ourselves, and laid our plans for future joy.

CHAPTER THREE

Susy's Account of her Experiences of Barrack Life

The kiosk referred to in the last chapter was a light ornamental structure built in the Turkish style, consisting of two storeys and commanding a beautiful and extensive view of the government grounds and also a large portion of the island. The lower part was used for keeping garden tools and implements and rolls of matting for covering young trees and plants. The upper part was luxuriously furnished with loungers and easy-chairs; and the windows were protected with outside shutters and jalousies. It was sheltered by a fine old tamarind tree, and was a cool and delightful retreat in the hot sultry weather that prevailed.

I passed much of my time there, and often received Charlie, and other privileged guests. For through living in the house as the governor's daughter I acted in all respects as my own mistress.

The next forenoon, I started to pay some visits, but soon re-entered the grounds by the wicket gate of which I kept the key, leaving the door unfastened after me. Then having given some directions to Davy that would keep him for a time at the further end of the grounds, I returned to the kiosk.

The governor soon joined me, and after a few warm caresses, and a sight and kiss of my cunt, which latter salute he never omitted, he cautiously raised one of the loose boards of the floor.

Then he arranged the rugs and matting so that we could recline at our ease and at the same time see and hear all that passed in the place below.

We had scarcely made all comfortable, when we heard Davy's voice.

'Come in here, Susy, my lub, dis nice cool place. Missy is out, and de garden door locked, so dere is nobody to bodder nor disturb us; sit down on dis nice clean matting, and we will take our fill ob lub and delight.'

He then threw off his jacket, and helped Susy to remove everything but her handkerchief and shirt; then, making her lean back, he spread her legs wide open, and pushed a roll of matting under her bottom, which caused her fair smooth little cunny to stand out and project in a most lascivious manner.

The governor watched it eagerly, while I petted his slowly stiffening tool, and with loving touch sustained its drooping head.

Davy threw a knowing glance upward, and went on, 'Do you mind, Susy, the night when you and I were hiding in the cupboard, and we saw Sergeant Tompson on top of your mammy; and she clutched and hugged him as he darted his great tool in and out of her hairy crack; and how I wondered at your liking to look at dat secret place where you did gib your first squeak?'

Susy, who was evidently enjoying Davy's lustful toyings, and whose wanton fingers were at the same time busy manipulating his fine standing prick, replied, 'Why should I not look at it, when she let me see it so often before; shall I tell you how I saw it first?'

'Do, Susy, my lub, dere is nothing I would so much like to hear.'

'Well, one night my dad and Corporal Simms agreed to exchange wives, and all went to bed together; they had all been drinking, and I suppose that would be their excuse; however, when they came to the bed, I was in it fast asleep. Mother said something about not disturbing the child, but they all laughed, and dad said: "She's now a well-grown girl, and her time for being fucked will soon come, so she may as well have her first lesson now." Whereupon they took me up and stripped me naked like themselves. When they all got on the bed, dad rammed his prick into Mrs Simms' cunt, while the corporal hoisted mother's legs, and slapping her behind, said: "Look here, Susy, when will you have a cunt like this?" and he drew open a pair of great hairy lips, showing a long red chink extending from the furry mound of her belly down to her bottom. And not content with my looking at it, he took my hand and rubbed my fingers up and down in that moist furrow.

' "Now, Susy, I'm going to fuck your mother, and if I can knock as fine a child as you out of her, I'll be proud – here, hold my prick, and put it in." I felt excited, and not a little curious to see how it was done, so I placed the red swollen nob at the end of his prick in the hot crevice of mother's cunt, and felt the whole prick as it slipped through my fingers and passed up into her belly until the balls pressed hard upon her bottom.

'Mother only laughed, and said, "In for a penny, in for a pound." And drawing me up, she made me lie with my bottom by her face, and my cunt turned up, so that the corporal could lick and suck it while he fucked her. This seemed to afford him great delight, for he sucked my cunt with such force that he almost sent me wild; while mother bit my bottom as she shook under the impetus of his heavy prods, I could distinctly hear the sound made by his prick as it rushed in and out between the unctuous lips of her receptacle.

'Dad, who was lying on Mrs Simms stretched alongside, though in the contrary direction, and hammering at her cunt with his muscular backside, now turned his flushed face towards us, and seeing how I was placed, panted out: "Ho! they have got little Susy between them; how the corporal sucks her cunny while he fucks her mother; put your hand here, child, and you will feel your father at the same sort of work."

'He then raised himself to let me see the whole of his large prick, as he drew it out of the hairy sheath into which it had been plunged. Child though I was, I was quite familiar with all these things; I liked the look of it, it seemed so strong and full of life and had such a bright ruddy colour. So I willingly put my hand on it and held it firmly as he drove it again into the pouting mouth that seemed to devour it with such relish and satisfaction. It slipped easily through my fingers for it was greasy with moisture and glowing with heat.'

'Well, Susy, dey war queer women dat libbid in dat barrack room; but sogers' wives and sogers themselves seem to lib for nutting else dan shagging and drinking. You hab oder funny tings to tell, I know, but you see dis here chap won't wait; see how he nods his head; he smell a rat in dis here little hole, and he long to poke in his nose; now open wide and push up to him – ugh! how he runs up – there – all inside – ugh! he out again – up once more – ugh! hold im – Susy – hold im – he going to turn sick – shall I take him out?'

'Davy, you're an ass – you black fellows can never fuck like other people – you make such an awful splutter and commotion – can't you be decent, and don't be letting all the world know what you are doing.'

The old governor shook with fun and enjoyment. He whispered to me, 'Queenie, your plan has turned out a great success. That Davy of ours is quite a genius in his way. Susy and he are well matched and improve one another by their contrast; I owe them something for they have given me a glorious cockstand. Get over me, my pet, and put this shameless fellow out of sight.'

He then carefully closed the aperture in the floor, and gave himself up to the enjoyment of his own sensations.

'How uncommonly tight you are, Queenie! after all the fucking you have had, you have the most wonderful power of contraction I ever met with in any woman; I feel not only a strong suction at the entrance but a powerful grip the further I push in; how do you manage it?'

'Oh! it is just a knack I have learned. Do you like that?'

'Yes, it is very delicious – I feel as if my whole soul were in my prick, and as if, at the point of it, it formed a junction with your own – Oh! oh! I can't help groaning out – I hope they won't hear me. But I think they are talking again – let us listen.'

He then put up his again shrunken tool, and having softly removed the covering from the opening, we reclined as before.

'Davy, what's that queer muttering I heard?'

'Parrots, Susy, de parrots in de tamarind tree, dey are trying to copy us,' he said with a grin, 'but dey cannot get beyond de sound.'

'It seemed to me, more overhead; what's upstairs, Davy?'

'On it is dere Missy Queenie sits and reads in de heat ob de day. Dat is de way up, but she out now, and she always keeps de door locked.' Susy got up and tried the door, but fortunately we had bolted it inside; so finding it fastened, she returned to the side of Davy, and amused herself playing with his prick and balls.

Davy again glanced up, as he said, 'Go on, Susy, tell us something more of what you seen in dat barrack room – warn't dere a girl, called Nelly Sykes, just about your age?'

'Oh, yes, Nell and I were great friends, it was from her I learned almost everything, for she was older, and had seen more than me; her mother had the far end of the room, which was always thought the best part. You know, it was a long room with six windows, and the six married woman on the strength were all lodged there, but it was curtained off, so that each couple had a window and the space about it to themselves. The fun of it was that the men coming in from guard, often under drink, were continually making mistakes and getting into the wrong beds. Most of the women thought little of this and after having the full benefit of the men while they were fresh would then ramble about until they found their husbands and lug them back to their own compartments.

'But there was one, a Mrs Morgan, who pretended to be very particular, and she was always trying to set us all right, but everybody disliked her, for she was a great scold. She often kicked up a row at night, when the wrong man got into her bed; but the men all declared that she never discovered the mistake until she had been well fucked and got from them all they were able to give; then she would shout: "Morgan! Morgan! come to your own bed; here is somebody else got in by mistake"; and if he did not at once respond, she would jump up and go round the room in search, waking everybody and scolding all round.

' "Mrs, Sykes! I do wonder at you! what do you mean by keeping that rapscallion of mine, you ought to know better."

' "How can I help him, Mrs Morgan, when he won't go; and you're worse yourself, for you have had my man with you this last quarter of an hour, and were quiet enough until now; out with you, and don't be ballyraggin in that fashion."

' "Nell and I used to enjoy all this amazingly. We often followed the men when they came in, and crept under the curtains after they got into bed. We would then get close up alongside, and listen to every sound and word. Sometimes we even ventured to push our hands between the sheets and feel them fucking; when they were at all muddled or much excited they never minded us, and many a good feel we had of their slimy pricks as they passed in and out of the wide hairy gaps of the women.

'When Nell and I were by ourselves, we could talk of nothing else: "What a queer thing fucking is, Susy!" she would say, "it is such slobbery work, it must make them feel very nasty."

' "It can't be very nasty, when they are all so fond of it. Did you mind how Mrs Morgan hugged the corporal last night, and pushed up to him, though she knew right well, I am sure, it wasn't Morgan himself; and then without saying a word how she got over him and gave him her cunt to lick; how would you like to be licked there, Susy?"

' "I am sure it must feel very nice; did anybody ever lick yours, Nelly?"

She laughed: "Well, let me look at your little fanny, and I will tell you."

' "Oh! I don't object in the least if you care to see it," and I held up my frock; "but you must show me yours at the same time."

' "Well, lean back and let me kiss your smooth little slit, and you can kiss mine afterwards if you like."

'She then got her head in between my thighs, and holding open the lips, she sucked my clitoris, and tickled it so with her tongue that she almost made me spend in her mouth.

'Then she lay back, and poked out her mossy chink for me to tickle and kiss. It had lots of short curly hair about it, and the clitoris was very big, and it grew bigger as I rubbed it and pushed my fingers into the opening below.

' "Now Nelly, tell me who has been kissing it, and making the passage so wide and roomy."

' "Shall I tell you how it all commenced."

' "Yes do, that is what I mean."

' "Here goes then: do you mind the night when my dad was carried in tipsy, and was confined in the guard-room?'

' "I do well."

' "That night, I want to Sergeant Luby, into his room, to ask him to get father off; he's colour sergeant, you know, and has great influence with the captain. He put his arm around me, and said, 'You are a good girl, Nelly, for being so fond of your father; but what will you do for me, if I get him off?'

' "What would you like me to do, sergeant?" I asked.

' "I would like you to give me twenty kisses.'

' "That I will, as many as you like,' I said, holding up my mouth, and throwing my arms around his neck.

' "Oh, but anybody may kiss your mouth, I want you to kiss me where you kiss nobody else.'

' "How could I kiss you except with my mouth?'

' "Have you not another little mouth lower down? that's the mouth I want you to kiss me with.'

' "His meaning now dawned on me, and I hung my head.

' "Let me see where it is, and I will show you well it can kiss,' and he pressed his hand on the bottom of my belly, and began to pull up my dress.

' "Oh, sergeant, mother is crying in the room; get my dad out, and send him to her, and then I will let you.'

' "I was knowing enough, you see to secure my bargain first.

' "Well, my little pet, that's fair; but if I go and get him out, will you stay here, and wait until I return?'

' "I will, sergeant, but don't be long.'

'Just let me feel it for a moment, and then I will go.' He quickly got his hand on my cunt, and began to pinch the lips, and rub his fingers in the slit. After a moment, he rose hastily and went to his press, and taking out a book placed it in my hands, saying: 'Here's something that will amuse you while I am away,' and he went off smelling his fingers as he left me.

' "That was the funny book; it was full of coloured pictures of naked men and naked woman; and the men had the finest pricks ever seen, and the women the biggest cunts. They were sucking and frigging and fucking in every way that could be imagined. The sight of them made my blood boil. I raised my dress and rubbed my cunt in the vain attempt to relieve the intolerable itching I felt there. So absorbed was I with the pictures and my own sensations, that I never noticed the return of the sergeant until he was close-up; when he burst out laughing observing my excitement, and the manner in which I was trying to alleviate it. 'Bravo! little woman – you have the right stuff in you – but I will show you a trick worth two of that.' He then took me in his arms, and kissing me, said: 'But first I must tell you that your dad is free. I had him safely taken to your mother, for he was not able to go himself. Now let me see the little mouth we were talking of before I went out.'

' "Of course, I had to yield to his wishes now, so I let him place me lying across his bed on my back, and naked from my waist down. He then knelt on the floor, and shoving his hands under my bottom began to kiss and lick my cunt. 'There – my little pet, I have taught you a new way of kissing, how do you like it?'

' "It is very pleasant, but now you have got the twenty kisses you asked for, won't you let me go?'

' "I will, Nelly, but first I want to show you something. You seemed to like looking at the pictures; now look at the reality,' and he pulled out his fine standing prick. I sat up to look at it as he asked me. 'Put your hand on it, dear; you are a clever good-natured girl.' How well these men know our love of flattery. He saw that I liked his praise, and taking my hand, he placed it on the nervous shaft of his animated prick. 'You have delicate fingers like a lady, and they feel soft and tender to the touch; now move it up and down – this way – put your other hand down here; these two round things are the stones which hold the seed, the stuff, you know, of which children are made. Did you ever see it Nelly?'

' "No, sergeant.'

' "Would you wish to see what it is like?'

' "I would, sergeant.'

' "Well, close your fingers firmly round, now gently push back this loose skin all the way; see how that makes the head get redder and stand up more erect! go on that way – softly up and down – now hold your hand – Oh! oh! there it comes!' and such a lot of thick white stuff like starch spouted out and ran down the sides.

' "The sergeant gasped and lay back, and his prick became quite soft and much smaller. After resting awhile, he sat up, and pulling me across his lap made me rub my bottom and cunt against his prick. 'That will bring him to life again,' and sure enough, I felt it grow quite hard between my thighs. Then lifting me up, he placed its top between the lips of my slit. 'Now push down; once you get it in, it will feel so nice.'

' "I like the touch of it in that most sensitive spot, and so pressed down as he asked me, but the moment it began to enter, I felt a terrible smart. 'Oh! Oh! it is hurting me. Oh! I can't bear it.' But he only put his strong hands on my shoulders and forced me down. The cruel wretch, only thinking of his own pleasure, was altogether heedless of my cries of pain; in fact, judging from the fire in his eye, I do believe he enjoyed it all the more for my anguish. Be that as it may, the whole of his great tool passed up into my belly, and the lips of my cunt rested on the hair which clustered round the roots of his prick.

' "I almost fainted at first but in a few moments, when he began to move it softly again, a most heavenly feeling succeeded and I hugged and kissed him in the greatest delight. I have been with him often since, and that is why you find me so wide and roomy."

'Such was Nelly's account of how she was first sucked and fucked. And now, Davy, I must be off; it would not do for Miss Queenie to find me idling with you when she returned. So for the present, goodbye.'

CHAPTER FOUR

Dick's Letters

It will no doubt gratify my readers to hear something of my old friend Dick. During this period, I received several letters from him acquainting me with the progress he made in his studies and describing various love adventures, which he narrated in glowing terms and with great particularity of detail.

I will therefore interrupt the course of my story by introducing a brief account of these proceedings, not however in the disconnected way in which he wrote them but placed together in the form of a continuous narrative.

After arranging his college matters, he went about looking for suitable lodgings. The ones he selected were kept by a widow named Mrs Bond, and what chiefly influenced him in making the selection, was, as he told me, that the hall door was opened by a pretty clean-looking girl called Polly, with a bright smiling face, and about seventeen years of age.

So finding the situation good, the rooms comfortable, the rent moderate, the landlady agreeable and, above all, that Polly was to wait upon him, he at once agreed to the terms and had his traps brought from the hotel.

He soon learned also that Mrs Bond had two daughters: the elder, Mary, was a quiet ladylike girl who played and sang well, and was nineteen years of age; the younger, Jemima, more generally called Jim, was a lassie of thirteen, still attending school, but when at home, full of fun and up to every kind of lark. Dick, being large hearted and ambitious of making wide conquests, determined on going in for the whole three, and even the mother herself, who was of the fat, fair and forty school, was not excluded from the range of his far-reaching desires. He therefore laid himself out to please them all by every means in his power. In doing so he tried to adapt himself to the tastes and ideas of each; to the widow, he was affable and good, and all that was proper and becoming; he sang and played with Mary, listened to her music and praised her performance; he romped with Jim, and filled her pocket with goodies and sweets; while on Polly, he lavished his warmest look and most insinuating speeches, backed up with a crafty presents now and again.

But for some time Polly, who had a great idea of the proprieties of life, resisted all his overtures and kept him at arm's length.

He then bethought himself of his medical resources. He knew that there were certain drugs which exercised powerful action on the genital organs. He therefore searched the college library, and through his knowledge of Latin ascertained from the learned works stored up there the names and qualities of the drugs he was in search of, while his position as a student enabled him to obtain the drugs themselves.

Thus armed, he commenced a series of cunning assaults on the innocence of the unsuspecting Polly. Now Polly herself, it must be admitted, rather laid herself open to these attempts; for she had the common but evil habit of sipping and tasting the wine and sweets which Dick kept in his cupboard. He found this out, and gladly utilised the knowledge for his purpose, but although he commenced dosing his wine bottle and jam mug, it was but for some time without any apparent effect, for though the wine and jam certainly suffered in his absence, she still resisted his advances and seemed proof against all his allurements.

Yet he persevered, and one evening, when Mrs Bond and her daughters were out taking tea with a neighbour, he determined on making a more decided attempt. He usually took a tumbler of rum toddy after his late dinner, and when Polly brought in the hot water, he mixed a glass for her, which he pressed her to accept; I need not say, it was both strong and well-dosed. Polly had been that day more jovially inclined than usual, and Dick had made her a nice present; she did not like to refuse. She took the glass and began to sip it, still standing however at a respectful distance.

After a little chaffing about her sweethearts, and her own good looks, Dick prevailed on her to sit by him on the sofa. The toddy now began to tell: her eyes brightened, her bosom rose and fell, as if some tumultuous emotion was stirring her within, and Dick perceived that the crisis of victory was approaching; his hand went around her waist and he pressed her in his arms.

He kissed her cheek, he kissed her lips. She feebly struggled to free herself from his encircling grasp. Her imagination became inflamed as his toyings became bolder. First the treasures of her virgin bosom were explored and brought to light. As he waxed warmer she grew more languid and yielding. She vainly strove to stay the rapid progress of his roving hand as he lifted her snowy smock and exposed to view her beautifully rounded fleshy thighs and the rich tuft of auburn hair which nestled in the voluptuous angle at their junction.

With muttered entreaties, she begged him not to take advantage of her weakness, but the feeble lamb might as well ask pity from its devourer; not that Dick felt at all like a devourer, he was conscious only of being impetuously driven on by his all-subduing passion. He pushed her back by his weight, and gently but firmly separated her closely pressed thighs. Then he got the first view of her charm of delight. The pouting lips seemed throbbing with desire. As he parted the soft, moist folds with his fingers, they felt hotter than those of any cunt he had ever touched. He pressed his middle finger up the tight-fitting passage, and he felt a kind of living suction inside, as if some vital force was acting on the incoming digit. She gasped, while warm tears trickled down her blushing cheeks. He kissed them off, and while doing so released his fiery charger, and placed his ruddy crest within the projecting ridges of her cunt, now burning for enjoyment of the unknown but much desired pleasure.

He plunged in, not without difficulty to himself and pain to her; but she was so terribly excited, and so eager for the coming joy, that she heaved madly against him; and between the two opposing forces his stiff prick rushed at one bound into the soft warm bed so ready for its reception. A shiver of delight passed through her languid frame. Her overstrained muscles relaxed their tension, and all the feeling of her body seemed centred in the region of love as she breathed out, 'Oh, Mr

Dick! it is too much, you have your will of me at last! Oh, yes, I will be good to you, it is delicious, oh!'

Dick quickly spent, and after reposing for a few moments in her now loving arms, recommenced his cunt-stirring, soul-thrilling movements and in the midst of warm moist kisses and gentle love-murmurs finished his second course.

From that evening, Polly was all his own, and at night when everyone had retired, and all the house was still, she used to creep into his room and pass the happy hours in his fond embrace.

Under Dick's tuition, she acquired a practical acquaintance with the various ways of fucking, and all the favourite modes of producing sexual excitement. She seemed to take special delight in using lascivious terms and expressions; she talked freely of his prick, bollocks and spunk; to please him she held open her cunt for his inspection, then squatting down, she willingly piddled before him, and said: 'Now you must piddle for me, and I'll hold the chamber and let you piddle through my fingers; then she sucked his prick; in short, she made use of every device to inflame his passion and gratify his lust.

Dick had soon to discontinue his stimulating drugs, for he felt that otherwise he would be consumed in the volcano he had himself ignited and stirred up.

Moreover, Dick loved variety and desired fresh conquests. He therefore put forth all his powers of persuasion to induce Polly to aid him in his efforts to gain the favours of the two sisters.

Polly was not naturally of a jealous disposition, and being very much under his influence, and exceedingly fond of the sport herself, she readily entered into his view.

Fortune too favoured him in a most unexpected manner, Jim hurt her leg climbing a tree, and a tumour formed on the inside of her thigh. Mrs Bond consulted Dick, and allowed him to examine Jim in her presence. He lanced the tumour and ordered a poultice, and said she would require both rest and care.

The tumour was very near her little cunny and although her mother tried to keep it covered, Dick managed to get a good peep at the smooth little chink while he pretended not to see it at all.

The poultice was to be changed every day, and the tumour reopened; so each morning, Dick, with the mother's help, performed the operation. After a few times, the mother, observing how delicately he discharged his duty, uncovered her without scruple before him, and Jim opened her legs to give him more room to examine her. But one morning Mrs Bond had to go out, and she sent Polly to tell Dick to visit her daughter as usual.

Jim always enjoyed his visits, and liked to feel his hand moving about her as he was so skilful and tender in his touches; and though he often pressed the poultice to the ridges of her modest little slit, she was quite unconscious of his object, and much enjoyed his caressing touch.

So, on this occasion, her face lighted up with pleasure when she saw him enter her room. She lay back and held up her clothes while he examined her, and when he asked her to open her legs more, she spread them out as widely as she could.

Dick now feasted his eyes on her budding charms as he gave directions to Polly about preparing the poultice. He gently passed his hand over the fat smooth lips, and with the tip of his finger rubbed lightly up and down the warm cleft.

She felt the thrilling effect of his knowing touches, and with a flushing face, said: 'That is very nice, Mr Dick; it quite removes the pain.'

'Yes, dear, that is what I am trying to do, the nerves here are very sensitive and this friction stills the pain.'

When Polly came with the poultice, she was not a little surprised to see Jim lying back with her thighs wide apart, her eyes closed and her face flushed with pleasure, while Dick leaned over her with one hand under her bottom and the other busily engaged in frigging the rosy slit of her projecting cunt.

'See, Polly, I have almost cured Miss Jemima by rubbing this sweet little mouth; she quite enjoys my touching her here, don't you, Jim?'

'Yes, Mr Dick, it feels very nice, and has quite lulled the pain!'

'It is such a pretty little mouth, too; I would so like to kiss it; might I, Jim?'

'Oh, no, Mr Dick, you surely would not kiss me there – nobody would do that.'

'Yes, there is somebody that would, and somebody that will,' and raising her plump little bottom with his hand, he pressed his mouth between the pouting lips and took a long sucking kiss. Jim's face glowed with pleasurable excitement, and turning to Polly, she asked: 'Did you ever know such a thing?'

'Yes indeed, Miss Jemima, I have heard it said that when men are very fond of us they like to kiss us there.'

Meanwhile Dick sucked her clitoris, and frigged her with his tongue and he soon felt the thrill of pleasure agitate her frame.

She breathed fast and hard, and then lay back with her eyes closed.

When she recovered, he kissed her mouth and said, 'You are a sweet little pet, Jim, and as I have relieved the pain, I will put on the poultice and leave you to rest.'

She smiled and said: 'Thanks, Mr Dick, you have given me great ease, and you are very kind.'

Dick then motioned Polly to accompany him, and when they were out of hearing, she laughed and said: 'You are a terrible man, Mr Dick, you seem to get your own way with us all.'

'Well, I have made a fair beginning,' he said, 'and I must leave the rest in your hands. She will be sure to question you, and you know to lead her on – return to her now, and tell me about all that passes.'

When Polly and I were next alone, she told me that when she went back to Jim, she at once began: 'Well, Polly, isn't Dicksie' (a pet name they had for me among themselves) 'a funny man! I can't to think what made him kiss me between my legs but, do you know, it felt so very nice I don't think I could refuse him if he asked me again.'

'Of course you would not, he is very fond of you and that's why he kissed you there.'

'But, Polly, it made me feel so hot and the heat is there still.'

'Let me see,' said Polly, and she lifted her skirt. Jim leaned back and opened her thighs and Polly softly and tenderly frigged the little love slit, and went on: 'This is the part of us women that men are always thinking of, and longing to see and feel, and do something else to, too.'

'Why what else could they do?'

'Do you know what they have themselves?'

'No, Polly, how could I?'

'Ah you do, every girl knows; you have surely seen little boys' cocks?'

'Oh, yes, is that what you mean? I thought you meant something big.'

'And so I do; when little boys grow they become big cocks.'

'And what have the big cocks got to do with us, that's what I want to know?'

'Just this: they are made to go into us here, and that's why this little crevice is like a mouth, and when you grow older hair will come there like a man's moustache.'

'How funny! I never thought of that; you are older than I, have you a moustache there? Show it to me, Polly, there's a good girl.' Polly allowed her to lift her dress as she stood by her side; the Jim put one hand behind her bottom and drew her nearer, while she pushed the other between her legs to open them, and exclaimed: 'Oh, my! so you have! and so bushy and soft! and such thick lips! and so hot inside! and so large! I declare, two – three fingers go in easily; was a big cock ever pushed into you, Polly?'

'Ah, Miss Jim, that's not fair, what would you think of me if I told you?' 'I would think you the kindest and best natured girl in the world;

tell me, Polly, you may trust me, and I will be so very fond of you.'

'Well, miss, I may as well confess that I have enjoyed that pleasure, and you'll not find many girls of my age that haven't; and whether they have or not, or whatever they may say, they all wish for it; even you, Miss Jemima, young as you are, seem quite ready; see how far I can push my finger into this soft opening and it does not appear to hurt you.'

'It does hurt a little, Polly, but still I like it; you may go; on that's nice – would a big cock feel nicer than that?'

'Twenty times nicer, dear, it is so smooth and soft and has such a pretty round head and slips in and out so deliciously that it would make you just tremble with delight; oh, if it was here in place of my finger, how pleased you would be.'

'I think I would Polly; has Dicksie one of these nice big cocks?' she asked with a knowing look.

Polly blushed and turned away her face: 'Ah! Miss Jemima, how curious you are: of course he has, but he does not call it by that name.'

'How does he call it? I am so fond of you Polly for telling me these things, and I want to know everything; what does he call it, Polly?'

'He calls it his prick, miss; I am sure he would like very well to show it to you, and let you feel it too, if you ask him.'

'I would not ask him for the world; prick . . . prick, I remember seeing that word chalked on a gate. But I did not know what it meant, and there was another word just below which seemed to belong to it – cunt; what does that mean?'

'Why, that's the name of this little mouth here.'

'Is that what Dicksie calls it?'

'Yes, dear, the very thing, but now I must go, I have told you enough for this time.'

Dick praised Polly's tact and cleverness, and having satisfied her with an extra-loving embrace said: 'Now, Polly, all we need is an opportunity to complete the work you have helped to commence.'

That opportunity soon occurred. Mrs Bond was again invited out to tea, and as Jim was unable to accompany her mother and sister, she obtained leave to ask Dick to come and sit with her in the evening. Dick readily accepted the invitation, and made himself as agreeable as he could. When Polly had removed the tea things, Jim asked her to remain and keep them company. Then came that happy 'tide in the affairs of men, which, taken at the flood, leads on to fortune'.

Jim and Dick reclined together on the sofa, while Polly sat on a stool before them. Dick remarked that Jim must now be almost quite well, as he had not to lance her for several days but 'let me see again to make sure', and he raised her dress to look.

'I am ashamed, Mr Dick, at your seeing me so often uncovered.'

'You need not feel ashamed, for you are beautifully made; and this is the sweetest little mouth I ever saw or kissed,' and slipping off the sofa he pushed in between her legs and frigged her with his tongue. Her excitement was now evident, for she spread her thighs and pushed forward her cunt.

Dick felt that she was now ready for the climax itself; so he looked up and asked if she liked the feel of his tongue in her love-chink – 'this dew little cunt, I mean'.

Jim blushed, and murmured that nothing could be nicer.

'Oh, yes, there is something that would be nicer, is there not, Polly?'

'Indeed there is, Miss Jim, let me show it to you,' and opening his trousers at the front, she drew out his fine standing prick.

'Look at it, dear, put your hand on it – feel how firm and stiff it is!' Jim smiled, and looked at it with admiring eyes; she let Polly close her fingers around it, and under her direction, she frigged it up and down. 'Now, dear, lean back and push your bottom to the edge, and Dicksie will rub the nice soft head of his prick between the lips of your longing cunt, and then you will know what pleasure means – so – isn't that nice?' and holding the prick in her hand, she rubbed its head up and down in the moist furrow. 'Now let him push it in; it will feel so good!'

'Oh! Polly, it is hurting me – take it out – take it out.'

'No, I won't; you can bear it until it gets in, then it will hurt you no more – that's a brave girl – push, heave – there, it is in! now fuck away.' Polly rubbed her cunt on Dick's bottom, and joined in every push, and getting greatly excited as she felt the last quick probes, cried: 'Prick! cunt! bollocks! fuck, fuck!'

How Dick proceeded with the others, and his final success, must be left for the following chapter. Suffice it to say that these letters were all read to the old governor, and were a source of the greatest delight to him. He sent many kind messages to Dick, and a special promise that if he came to Trinidad after he had completed his college course he would obtain for him a government appointment and otherwise forward him in his profession.

CHAPTER FIVE

Mary

Dick had less difficulty with Mary than he anticipated. She drank in his flattery with avidity, and seemed pleased with his attentions. They often sang together, and when he accompanied her in a duet, his arm would naturally stretch across her shoulders as he held the chair on which she sat. After a while, as they became more familiar, his hand would as naturally steal around her waist.

Again, when he stooped to turn the music, their cheeks could not avoid touching and then their lips. Not wishing to frighten her by a too rapid advance, he remained satisfied for a short time with such chaste salutes, though gradually increasing them in warmth and frequency, and occasionally indulging in soft pressures of the lovely breasts, swelling out in ripe and most inviting luxuriance.

They now passed much of their time alone together; her mother regarded Dick as an eligible suitor and thought that if their liking for one another ripened into love, he might not be a bad match for her daughter, and therefore she rather encouraged and promoted their increasing intimacy.

The accomplishment of this design was further facilitated by Mary's love for classical studies. Dick placed in her hands a literal translation of Ovid's works, which gratified her poetic taste while it stimulated her amorous inclinations. She seemed greatly interested in the account given by Ovid of Jupiter's *amours*, and put many questions to Dick respecting Europa, Leda, Danae and others. He told her how Jupiter loved the beautiful Europa, and assuming the shape of a bull, coaxed her to mount on his back, and then carried her off to Crete, where she became his mistress and had many children by him. How when Danae was shut up in a brazen tower, Jupiter got access to her by means of a shower of gold, and when she had spread her knees fill to her lap with the glittering treasure he availed himself of her position to attain the object of his desires. Mary blushed, but evidently understood what was meant, and did not object to listening.

He accordingly though he might now venture a little further in his account of Jupiter's *amour* with Leda. He described how when she was bathing naked in a river, Jupiter came to her as a beautiful swan chased by an eagle; how she naturally opened her arms to give him protection, and when he found himself pressed against her soft bosom, and between her lovely thighs, he was able, even though a swan, to give her a taste of the sweet joys of love and fill her with happiness and delight; somewhere here you know,' he said, slipping his hand suddenly up between the yielding thighs of the half-bewildered Mary.

'Oh, Dick, don't you tickle me too much, don't lean against me so hard, don't my love. Oh!' she panted, as Dick pressed her in his arms, called her his darling, and drew her on to his lap.

'Oh, Dick! what do you want? what is your hand doing there? I can't let you do that, don't you know it is not right? Oh! how you tickle me, what would mamma say if she knew that you had your hand there?'

'Why, what could she say? she was often tickled there herself; how could she have had you if someone had not played with her there, and put something into this sweet little mouth, you know what I mean.'

'No, Dick, Oh! I can't sit quiet! you tickle me so! How could I know what you mean!'

'Well, Mary, let me enlighten you, put your hand here my darling.' Having already unbuttoned the front of his trousers, he drew her hesitating hand towards the opening, and pushing it in, placed it on his bounding prick standing up with uncapped head inside.

'Oh, Dick, for shame! I won't put my fingers around it; I can't move it up and down; oh, Dick! oh! what are you doing? don't press me back – don't spread my thighs, you mustn't see it, you mustn't kiss it – how can you! oh, your tongue is sending me distracted!'

'What a lovely cunt you have, Mary! how red it is between these fat lips! how soft it feels! and its scent is most delicious; how nice to kiss it, and smell it; and lick it and suck it! and this dear little round bottom-hole, I must kiss it too. Lift your legs more, that I may the better see all your lovely white arse. Now let me pop my poor fellow into this sweet mouth and give you a practical lesson in the Art of Love.'

Dick now had her lying on her back across a broad sofa; her bottom on the edge, her thighs drawn up, and at their greatest stretch. This position, of course, caused her cunt to appear like a hungry mouth gaping widely before him.

He placed the firm head of his excited prick in the rosy chink under the clitoris, and rubbing it up and down in that luxurious and highly sensitive hallow, he asked her if she liked the feel of his prick in the mouth of her cunt, and whether he might push it in?

'O yes, Dick, it feels very nice, you may push it in, but won't you do it very gently, my love?'

Dick held open the lips with his fingers, stooped over her, and began to push.

'Oh! it is taking my breath! Oh! it is tearing me up! oh my! it is smarting terribly! Oh, it is in! I feel it – oh I feel it – ever so far up my belly! Is this fucking?'

'Yes, isn't it good? Do you like me to fuck you?'

'Yes, you fuck me so nicely. I like to say fuck, when I know it pleases you; and I feel your long prick stirring up my cunt; as it is now – fucking – fucking – fucking. O yes I knew these words before, but I never used them until now.'

When they had finished fucking, and while Dick was lying on her belly with his prick, pleasantly so, soaking in her cunt, she whispered: 'I will tell you a secret – I saw you fucking Polly yesterday evening in the garden; you did not think I heard you telling her to follow you there; but I did, and I followed too; and she unbuttoned your trousers, the shameless girl, and took out your prick. Then she kissed and sucked it, while you, bad man, kept fingering her cunt and bottom.

Then you placed her on her back and rammed your prick into her cunt, while she kicked about her legs, and called out: 'Fuck me, fuck me, fill my cunt with your prick, the balls against my arse, fuck – fuck – fuck.'

I fell in love with your prick then, and envied Polly the great pleasure she enjoyed when you pushed it up into her belly.

Stand up now that I may see it again, balls and all, and after I have frigged and kissed it, you may put it into my cunt and fuck me again if you wish.'

Dick declared that of all the randy girls he ever saw, he never met the equal of quiet, demure, modest-looking Mary Bond.

He had no sooner finished one fuck, than she wanted another, and she was always suggesting some new plan for varying the enjoyment or intensifying the pleasure. She loved to look at erotic pictures, of which Dick had a store, and was always trying to imitate the attitudes and adapt the positions therein depicted.

She told him that for years she had been conscious of great irritation in her cunt; that she often frigged it while watching its reflection in the glass; and that she never met any young man without casting a sly glance at the lump in his trousers and wondering what his prick would be like when it was stiff and standing up.

She had also a particular fancy for looking at and playing with the cunts of other girls. She assured him that there was scarcely a young lady of her acquaintance whose cunt she had not seen and handled, and that she liked even to kiss and suck them.

Dick asked if she generally found it easy to prevail on them to allow her to take these freedoms?

She replied, that of course most girls more readily yielded their hidden charms to the enterprises of the other sex, and were more inclined to trust them, too; yet, as they all liked the thing itself, she usually found that, by gaining their confidence and by skilful allusion and suggestion exciting their imagination and provoking their desires, she could mostly get them to meet her halfway; especially as they knew that with her they ran no risk of a big belly; and as she was always ready to gratify them with a similar inspection of her own belongings, she seldom experienced much difficulty. Dick told her how delighted he would be if he could witness one of these inspections without being seen himself.

She promised to gratify him if she could. So one day she told him that a young lady, Miss Madge Stevens, whose cunt she had often seen and petted, was to visit her next morning; and as she always brought her special visitors to her own room, she would hide him there first if he could spare the time.

He said he would arrange that, and promised to be there at the time she fixed. So accordingly, remaining at home next day under plea of a headache, he quietly stole upstairs to Mary's room, and by her direction, concealed himself under the dressing table; in the cover of which a slit was made to enable him to look out and see as well as hear all that passed.

Soon afterwards, Mary and Madge entered the room together, with their arms round one another.

'Come sit with me on the bed, Madge, I have not seen nor petted your little fanny for nearly a fortnight; how is it getting on?'

'First rate,' replied Madge, 'how is your own?'

'Just as troublesome as ever; it is for all the world like a bird in a nest opening its mouth every moment expecting some titbit to be popped into it!'

Madge laughed, 'I suppose that most girls, who know what the titbit is like are in the same sort of expectation and desire; and true for you, Mary, your cunt is in a most excited condition; oh my! how hot it feels! and how red it looks. I am certain you have had a fuck lately; now tell me all about it like a darling; ah! you are laughing! you can't deny it, you may trust me, dear.'

'Well, lie back first and perhaps I will tell you; draw up your thighs, and poke your bottom out that I may see it all, as I like a good sucking and kissing.'

The bed was opposite the table and window, so Dick had a magnificent view of Madge's splendid arse, with its great fat cheeks bulging out on either side, and a most delicious hairy randy-looking cunt gaping in the hollow between.

Mary pulled open the lips with her fingers as widely as she could, showing the rich carmine of its interior folds all glistening with the dews of love. Then drawing up her own dress behind, so as to indulge Dick with a view of her own naked posterior, which she knew he greatly admired, she kneeled on the floor and plunged her face between Madge's wide-spread thighs, and kissed her cunt with such vehemence that she caused that voluptuous young lady to exclaim in a loud voice, 'Oh! Mary you drive me wild! you make me long for a prick! have you not got one? how I wish you were a man! I would tell you to stick in your prick and poke it up to the last inch'.

'Hush Madge if anyone heard you, what would they think?'

'What would they think? they could only think that we were a pair of love-stricken maids that were ripe and longing to be fucked, just like their mothers before them. But, Mary, in sober earnest, I never did feel in such humour as now! where is that dildo you were talking of? Fetch it, my dear, anything at all in the shape of a prick to give one some relief.'

Dick had already given Mary one of those precious instruments, and when he had to save his own over-taxed energies, he enjoyed watching her endeavours to satisfy her cunt with that inanimate substitute for the living tool. Not that I mean to repudiate or make light of the dildo. It has its own peculiar excellences and good qualities. It is more under command, and does not need the coaxing and the humouring which the living article sometimes requires. We can make it move fast or slow, just as we like, and it will retain its stiffness as long as we desire. It will discharge too at the precise moment when we can meet it with our own. But, at the best, it is still only a poor substitute for the living, throbbing organ of bliss wielded by a man we like, thrust into our quivering cunts by successive heaves and driven home by the mighty push of a vigorous backside.

But to return. Mary said: 'Well, remain as you are while I unlock my drawer and take it out of its hiding place.'

As she turned around, she glanced towards the dressing table, and catching Dick's eye peeping out through the slit, she smiled and put her finger on her lip to warn him to keep quiet.

Then quickly returning she reoccupied her former place between Madge's wide-spread thighs and holding up the dildo, cried: 'Is not this a pretty plaything for two innocent maids like you and me, Madge, to amuse ourselves with! Now I will give you a taste of its performance, but I must stiffen it first,' she said, blowing into the tube and then screwing up the nozzle.

'Let me feel it in my hand,' said Madge, taking it up and rubbing its smooth red head to her lips; 'and, Mary is this an exact resemblance of a man's prick? I did not think it was quite so large, but you can tell me about it, I am sure.'

'Don't be too inquisitive, Madge; one thing at least you may depend on, it is intended to be an exact resemblance, and as to its size, you can best judge of that when you have it in your cunt; now open it as much as you can; once we get the head in, the rest will be all plain sailing.'

She spread open the lips of the randy-looking cunt, and standing so as not to interrupt Dick's view, took the dildo again, and having moistened its tops pushed it against the tender opening.

'Oh! Mary! Oh! it does feel very big, ah! you have got it in, that is a relief – how well you work it – yes, I like that – Oh! it is beginning to feel very nice, go on push it in further – move it faster, harder.' Mary worked the dildo with one hand, while she frigged her own cunt with the other, panting at the same time, 'I am fucking you, Madge, and frigging myself. Oh! Prick – cunt – bottom – piss – fuck – fuck,' and throwing herself forward on Madge she hammered her own cunt on the butt of the dildo, while they both squirmed about in all the voluptuous wriggles of full enjoyment.

Dick described this scene as having a most overpowering effect upon him. It made his prick stand like a bar of iron, while his spunk seemed actually boiling his cods; his heart beat audibly, and his breath came fast and hard. Yet the fear of frightening Madge and offending Mary caused him to use every effort to restrain himself; but at last he could endure it no longer; the view of Mary's splendid arse bounding between Madge's voluptuous thighs fairly conquered him. So slipping out from under the table he crept upon his hands and knees behind Mary, and seizing her round the thighs began to kiss the soft cheeks of her bottom. Mary seemed almost to have expected his approach, for she did not start, nor utter any cry, but quietly spread her legs further apart and bent her bottom more to his face.

Under any circumstances Dick could not fail to have been moved by this extraordinary sight, but in his present excited state, it appeared absolutely celestial. He could just distinguish the fat lips of her cunt spread out on the end of the dildo, close to the little round hole of her arse, with its delicate pink edge wrinkled up, and fringed by fine silky hair and flanked on either side by the resplendent semi-orbs of her glorious bottom, lasciviously quivering with amorous excitement.

He applied his mouth without hesitation to the sweet little orifice, sucked it with vigour, and thrust in his tongue.

This was a treat he had not given her before, and she enjoyed it immensely. She pressed her bottom on his face, and relaxed the constricting muscle, to allow his tongue to penetrate more deeply into that highly sensitive entrance.

It prepared her too for his next move when, raising her up, he softly pushed her forward over Madge so as to cover her face with Mary's bosom, then drawing the dildo out of her cunt, he replaced it with his inflamed tool and slowly worked it in and out.

At first Madge did not perceive the difference, but after a few strokes the delicious friction of the living instrument on the fleshy ridges of her cunt stirred up every lustful emotion, and forced her to exclaim: 'Oh! hold me, press me – I feel as if I were in heaven, my cunt is just bathed in rapture – oh! keep on, don't stop, sweet dildo, precious tool, fuck me, fuck me, fuck me, let fly now – I'm off!' and Madge sank back in love's delicious swoon.

Meanwhile Dick pressed his belly against the fat cheeks of Mary's arse, and squeezing her in his strong arms moved her body from side to side as he plunged energetically in and out of Madge's hot receptacle and uttered groans of prolonged delight as he inundated Madge's cunt with his boiling spunk.

Mary looked over her shoulder and whispered, 'Oh, Dick! what have you done! do go back to your hiding place, like a dear fellow.'

But Dick was not yet satisfied; finding that his prick still retained a fair allowance of stiffness, he drew it out of Madge's dripping cunt, and placing its well-moistened head to Mary's little pink arsehole, with one push he drove it up to the hilt. Mary groaned, but it was a groan of extra delight.

'Oh, my bottom! Oh, my bottom! Yes, push – yes, my arse – Oh! I can't keep still – fuck – fuck my arse – I can't help it,' and tightening her arsehole, she closed it like a fiery ring of pleasure round Dick's tool as it slipped rapidly in and out.

'What are you saying, Mary? Who is fucking your arse?' and looking up, Madge blushed crimson as she saw Dick stooping over Mary, his face flushed and his eyes starting out of his head, while his thrusts made them all shake together.

Just then, a loud knocking at the door made them all jump. Dick, without saying a word, rushed back to his shelter, Madge smoothed down the bed and threw herself into a chair, while Mary fumbled at the door to give them time. When she did open the door her mother, who was standing outside, asked: 'What on earth are you two girls about?

Making such a noise! and your door locked and your faces like scarlet and your dresses all tumbled!' and she glanced from one to the other. 'What I wanted was to ask whether you know anything of Mr Dick? A messenger has come from the hospital for him, and he is not in either of his rooms, though I thought he had not left the house.'

'How are we to know? You don't expect to find him here, I hope, mamma.'

'I don't know as to that, my dear,' she replied laughing, 'for when two such skittish girls as you and Madge Stevens get together, if you have not a young man with you, I am quite sure you would be wishing for him, or perhaps even trying in some way or other to make up for the deficiency. What sort of a thing is that?' she said, with a twinkling eye, and a knowing look, as she pointed to the dildo lying on the floor at the bedside where Dick had thrown it, and forgotten to put it away.

'Oh! mamma,' groaned out Mary, covering her face with her hands, 'how horrible! what ill luck brought you in?'

'Ah well, dear,' said Mrs Bond mildly, not wishing to make her presence disagreeable, you need not mind me so much; don't I know very well that it is not at all unnatural to like this sort of thing, and most girls have an itching for it, more or less, whatever they may say; and indeed, if they only amused themselves with such innocent playthings as this' – taking up the dildo – 'it might be much better for them. But which of you was trying it, may I ask?' As she spoke, she passed it through her fingers with a loving kind of touch, while her eyes glistened with amorous excitement.

Mary made no answer, but she and Madge looked at one another, and seeing the turn that matters were taking, they broke out into an uncontrollable fit of laughter; the events which followed, however, require a chapter to themselves.

CHAPTER SIX

Mrs Bond

Mrs Bond, as already described, was fat, fair and forty; but she was something more, for not only had she a very imposing presence, and a remarkably find physique, but she was possessed of one of the hottest, randiest and most insatiable cunts that ever poor widow was plagued with; but, at the same time, she was clever enough to maintain a character of the greatest decorum and respectability.

On this occasion, she felt that having caught the girls *in flagrante delicto*, she might safely indulge her favourite passion; besides, she had been listening for some time at the door, and had heard sufficient to agitate very keenly her prurient inclinations.

So, sitting down on the bed, she joined in the laughter, and invited the girls to sit by her side. Then, placing her hand with lascivious pressure on Madge's soft thigh, she said: 'You really must give me a lesson in the use of this clever invention. I need it to make up for pleasures that have been taken from me, while you employ it in anticipation of pleasures you hope to enjoy in the future; and which, if report is to be relied on, you at least, Madge, will soon have to the utmost of your desire. Jack seems well supplied – eh Madge! – and I am certain that you are equally well prepared to give him every satisfaction. Let me feel how you are furnished up here. You know I have had great experience in these matters,' and stooping forward she ran her hand up under Madge's petticoats.

'Oh! Mrs Bond, how can you!'

'What a luxuriant crop you have! This is a larger bush than mine though I am twice your age; and such a pair of luscious lips! how they will suck in Jack's tool, and cling around it with loving delight! Oh, Madge, I envy you your first fuck; but very likely you have tasted that pleasure already – eh, Madge? – you are quite as roomy here as I am.'

'Oh, Mrs Bond! how you talk!'

'Why not, dear, I was myself fucked many a time before I was married, and my good man was never the worse for it; of course, I was not fool enough to tell him, though he got the benefit of it, all the same, for I knew beforehand what would gratify him much better than if I had been a poor innocent unsophisticated girl. And now, as I want you both to be quite at your ease, I will, if you wish, give you a full account of how and when I was first fucked.'

'Do, dear Mrs Bond, it will be delightful.'

'Very well, but let us place ourselves in position; I can talk more freely when I am looking at a cunt, and when somebody is petting mine. Tuck up, Madge, and let me see it, and place your hand here.'

'Oh, Mrs Bond, what nice soft silky hair you have; and the mouth feels as hot as fire! May I see it?'

'Yes, dear, if you wish,' and pulling up her petticoats she displayed a pair of fleshy thighs, and between them a cunt of extraordinary luxuriance and extent, its great lips pouting out in the most wanton manner as if ready for any kind of prick.

'Oh, Mrs Bond, what a grand affair you have! Mary, did you ever see such a glorious love-chink?' and drawing the lips apart with her fingers, she exhibited its glowing interior.

Mary looked at her mother's cunt at first with a sly kind of interest mingled with feelings of shame at its exposure to the prying eyes of Dick, who, she knew well, was then regarding it with most lustful desires. But when Madge went on manipulating it, rubbing the large distended clitoris, pressing together, then opening wide, the fat pouting lips, her libidinous propensities overpowered her natural disinclination to make free with her mother's cunt, and with a sudden dash, she placed herself on her knees between her mother's widespread thighs, and having regarded for a moment the mysterious portals through which she had passed into life, she pressed her lips on the secret spot, drew the soft clitoris into her mouth, and probed with her penetrating tongue the hot folds of the passage inside.

Mrs Bond laughed with pleasure, as she pushed her tingling cunt against her daughter's mouth, and said: 'Why, Mary, Mary, are you sucking your mother's cunt? I must see that your own sweet little pussy is soon gratified in the way it likes best. I have no doubt that if Mr Dick was here, he would be quite ready to repay it for the pleasure you are giving me; and I would place his prick myself in its mouth and hold his balls and tickle his bottom while he fucked you. And now that I think of it, when I finish my story, we will search for him, for I am sure he is in the house, and if he gives me his promise to marry you, he may enjoy you at once, and we will all be happy to assist at the demolition of your maidenhead – that is, if you have not given it to him already, which I am strongly inclined to believe.'

Mary kept her head down, and said nothing, so turning to Madge, Mrs Bond asked: 'What's your opinion, Madge, don't you think that Mr Dick, who often passes whole evenings alone with her, has already explored her maiden secrets, and made her acquainted with the power of his pleasure-giving tool?'

'Indeed, it is highly probable; and as I was saying to her before you came in, in spite of her innocent looks, I am sure she has been often fucked, and could tell us all particulars of Mr Dick's prick and balls and everything, if she pleased. But in the meantime, don't forget the story you have promised us.'

'Well, my dears, let me say, by way of preface, that I am a great admirer of what the Americans call going the whole hog, that is, if I go in for a thing at all, I go in for it altogether; I mean what I say, and say what I mean. I am not ashamed to call a cunt, a cunt; and a prick, a prick. I enjoy fucking, and I like to talk of it. I delight in frigging and being frigged; and I find great pleasure in looking at and petting a nice cunt, like yours, Madge, and to have my own cunt at the same time caressed and sucked by my darling child is heaven itself.' Here she laid her hand most lovingly on the back of Mary's head as she licked between the fat unctuous lips and darted her tongue into the recess.

'I sometimes think,' she continued, 'I must have been born with an itching cunt, at least, I don't remember any time when it did not. When I was quite a child, I used to play with two young cousins, and their little pricks were objects of great admiration and wonder to me. I loved to fiddle with them and suck them in my mouth, and was always gratified when they repaid the compliment by inspecting and kissing my little nest, as they called it. I had a governess, and used to tease her with all sorts of queer questions: what was a virgin? what was a eunuch? why was it wicked for a man to lie with a woman? and what harm could it do her? Her attempts to evade my questions only made me all the more curious. As I grew older, nature made me feel that my little slit was evidently so formed that something might enter it, and whatever that something was, I felt sure it would be a source of great pleasure and enjoyment. And I determined that if any opportunity ever presented itself, I would not fail to make the most of it. Well, my dears, the opportunity came in the shape of a slave boy, named Dindee. My uncle had a plantation in the hills about six miles from Kingston, where we lived, and I sometimes rode on my donkey to visit him. On such occasions I was always attended by Dindee, as the donkey was his special charge.

'We usually took a short cut across the wild part of the country through which a small stream flowed rapidly down. One very hot day, we were passing near a deep pool in a retired part of the river. Dindee asked permission to take a dip to cool himself; so I dismounted a little way off and told him I would mind the donkey while he was bathing. I soon heard Dindee splashing about in the water and the temptation arose in my mind to creep among some bushes that lined the bank and watch him as he sported naked in the water. The shrubs were pretty thick and enabled me to come quite close to the edge which overhung the water some four or five feet. I was delighted with the view of his black shining body and queer-looking tool lolloping from side to side as he rolled about enjoying the refreshing coolness of the stream. He was sixteen years old, and had an unusually large prick for so young a lad. He touched it occasionally with his hand and shook it up and down. Oh! I said to myself, that is the very thing I want for my little slit. How nice it would feel going in! and putting down my hand, I squeezed the lips and rubbed the clitoris. His further proceedings were still more attractive, for leaning against the bank right opposite my hiding-place, he commenced frigging his prick in the most deliberate manner, drawing down the skin from its large round head, and making it stand up firm and erect; then placing his hands on each side of it he jerked his bottom so as to make his prick pass in and out through his palms, just as if he was fucking a cunt.

'In my eagerness to see all I could, I incautiously stretched too far over the brink, and to my terror and dismay, the bough on which I was leaning gave way, and I tumbled head-foremost into the water. I gave a cry as I sank below the furnace, but in a moment I felt myself borne up by the arms of Dindee, taken to the other side and drawn up the sloping bank.

'Beyond a good fright, and a thorough wetting, I was uninjured, so, looking at Dindee's rueful countenance, I burst out laughing, as I said: "Dindee, what shall we do? I am wet to the skin."

' "Missy must take off her wet things or she will catch cold; leave them here and I will dry them on the rocks." And he turned as if to go away.

' "Stay Dindee, I want you to help me; I am so drenched, that I never could get them off by myself."

'I turned my back to him, and after a deal of tugging and twisting, we got them all off except my stockings and shirt. I then sat down while he spread them on the rocks to dry. Shivering with cold, I called Dindee again: "Dindee, you must help me off with these also, they make me quite chilly. Thanks. Now come and give me a good rubbing, as if you were shampooing me."

'I stood with my back towards him, while he rubbed my arms and legs. I knew by his quick breathing that he was growing very excited. I pushed my bottom up to him, and felt his stiff prick poking against me. He put his hand on my buttocks, and rubbed the cheeks; then passing it between my thighs, rubbed softly up and down. The side of his hand touched the lips of my cunt; I opened my thighs a little and he touched my cunt again, and yet again, each time pressing more firmly against the lips. He passed his other hand round in front and placed it on my mons, just beginning to be overspread with silky down. One finger slipped in between the lips. "Oh! Dindee, that tickles me."

'The other hand passed swiftly round, and with both together, he pressed my bottom into him. I felt the head of his prick poking stiffly between my thighs, and rubbing up against the lips of my cunt. He opened the lips with his fingers, and rubbed the head of his prick in the moist chink.

'He little knew how my cunt tingled as he said, "Darling, missy, stoop a little."

' "What do you want to do, Dindee?" I asked, stooping as he wished me to, and twisting my bottom about.

' "To fuck, darling missy, to fuck this lubly cunt."

' "Oh! Dindee! how it smarts! Oh, how strong you are! hold me – I cannot stand against you." He leaned forward, and let me down on my hands and knees, and grasping me firmly by the hips he pressed hard against me from behind. My cunt opened, and, oh girls! the dear soft thing I had been longing for passed up into my belly. It seemed to reach my very heart and filled me with supreme delight.

'How delicious is the first fuck! To feel the dear prick passing in and out through the clinging lips, rubbing every sensitive ridge, opening every voluptuous crease, and then, after a few vigorous strokes, pouring into you a hot flood of living spunk.

'The joy I felt in giving down my own share of love's essence was so great that I fell prone on my belly, with Dindee over me, pressing on my bottom, and his prick still soaking in my cunt.

'Oh, Mrs Bond! I'm coming too,' cried Madge; 'rub your finger in the entrance. Oh! I'm coming. I'm coming.'

'Straddle over my face then, Madge, put your cunt on my mouth and let me taste your spending.'

Mary too resolved to share in the common ecstasy as she gazed with pleasure at the voluptuous prospect Madge presented with her mother's mouth buried in her cunt. So, pulling up her skirts behind, she turned her naked arse in all its attractive beauty towards the table, while she frigged herself with her finger and lapped up the rich streams which now began to flow from her mother's fountain of delight.

Dick described this scene as being the most exciting spectacle he had ever witnessed, and though he had spent twice but a short time before, his prick bounded up like steel, and he felt consumed with vehement desire. He had a shrewd suspicion, which he afterwards found was correct, that Mrs Bond was perfectly aware of his presence, and was in fact only endeavouring to draw him out from his hiding place.

She was naturally of a prying disposition, especially in such matters, and by listening at doors and spying through peep-holes, she had made herself acquainted with all that was going on between Dick and her daughter; and had been for some time planning how she could turn her knowledge to account, not only in compelling Dick to marry her daughter, but in gratifying herself by a participation in their joy.

On this occasion she felt certain he was in the room, and her sagacious eyes at once fixed on the dressing-table as the only shelter that could afford him a sufficient hiding place.

She accordingly arranged the little scene on the bed and told her exciting story, both with the intention of drawing him out and then profiting by his excitement to make him give the promise she required and obtain for herself the gratification she desired.

She did not succeed however as she expected, for Dick, wishing to hear more of her extraordinary confession, by a great effort restrained himself.

Among her other distinguishing qualities, Mrs Bond never allowed that she was beaten. Apparent failure only nerved her for renewed and stronger effort.

So after resting a few moments on the bed, she sat up and said: 'My dears, we all want something to give us fresh spirit; run Mary to the pantry and fetch a little of my French liqueur.'

Mary soon returned with a decanter and glasses. The effect of the strong and highly spiced stimulant was soon apparent; Mrs Bond tumbled the two girls on the bed, tossed up their clothes, smacked their bottoms and kissed their cunts. They retaliated in like manner upon her, to her evident satisfaction.

'Now Mary,' she cried, 'I must have a good look at your own pussy; lie across the bed with your head resting on the edge, and I will straddle over you and suck your cunt, while you watch Madge giving me a taste of the dildo.'

Mary placed herself in the desired position, and her mother, after fastening up her skirts, stooped over her and buried her face between her upraised thighs. Her object evidently was to favour Dick with a full view of her splendid posteriors bulging out like two creamy globes on either side of the furrow where nestled her moist cunt and inviting arsehole.

Madge also tucked up her dress at Mrs Bond's request, and then with Mary's help worked the dildo in her salacious cunt.

Mrs Bond was one of those whose pleasure is intensified by the consciousness that all the secrets of their cunt and bottom are open for inspection. So she exclaimed, 'Dear girls, that is most delicious, are you both watching?'

'O yes, dear Mrs Bond, we see all your fine bottom, and your beautiful cunt sucking in the dildo – how I wish it were a real prick! Could you go on with your story now, or shall we wait until you spend?'

'Oh! I can tell it now, if you wish; keep the dildo where it is, and only stir it a little now and then.'

Here, as luck would have it, some stray hair or fly so tickled Dick's nose that, in spite of all his repressive efforts, he delivered a tremendous sneeze. Mrs Bond jumped from the bed, ran to the table, thrust her hand under the cover and caught hold of the first thing that met her touch, which was nothing other than Dick's rampant tool.

'Hallo! what have we here? Murder! Thieves!' and tightening her grasp on the exposed limb she tugged with such force that Dick was compelled to crawl forth, trying to look droll, with his finger in his mouth.

'Oh! Mr Dick! what a shocking fellow you are! prying into the secrets of us poor women. What shall we do with him, girls?'

'Tie him to the bedpost,' said Madge, laughing, 'and lather his breech, and let Mary be the executioner, for I guess she is more to blame than he is.'

'Capital, the very thing Madge, you are worthy of your salt. Come here, my young man, and don't stand there in that barefaced manner before these innocent girls. Face about, sir, we will make you barebottomed as well as barefaced,' she said, tucking up his shirt behind, while the girls tied his hands firmly with towels to the bedpost.

'Now, Madge, off to the garden, and fetch a bundle of good stout twigs, and do you Mary go to the house closet for some strong cord to tie them up.'

Having thus got rid of the girls, she turned to Dick.

'Now sir, I want your serious answer, by a strange stroke of luck you have got behind the scenes; now I want you to assure me that you intend to act honourably by my daughter Mary. If you give me your faithful word then you shall be welcome, not only to enjoy her anew, but to share in all our private amusements.'

(This was a trying question, and very craftily put. According to my notions, Dick answered wisely and well. He had found an agreeable, clever, well-educated girl, devotedly attached to him and of a temperament warm and lascivious as his own; and that knowledge, which might have repelled others, he wisely judged, only secured for him that very freedom without which marriage would have been to him insufferable; hence his reply.)

'Well, dear Mrs Bond, my answer is ready. I love Mary. She is just the girl to my taste. As soon as I have a home to take her to, I will make her my lawful wife.'

'All right, I always knew you were a gentleman; now we will try to gratify you as much as we can,' and she placed her hand lovingly on his still erect prick, and pressing up to him, gently frigged it.

Dick looked up at his hands, and said, 'My hands are tied, or I would return your kind caresses.'

She at once reached up and untied the knot; in doing so, her fine swelling bosom was brought close to his face, he kissed the voluptuous globes, and at once placed his hands on her bottom and cunt. She leaned back on the bed, her thighs expanded, he slipped in between; his projecting prick poked against her open cunt; he pushed it, it entered; he passed up; his balls pressed against her bottom; he placed his hands under her thighs, and raised them up; she crossed her legs over his back. They heard steps approaching; he stopped heaving. 'It is only the girls,' she muttered, 'don't mind them; fuck away, give me all you can, quick.'

Mary entered and could hardly believe her eyes when she saw Dick on top of her mother, and the sight did not please her. Dick looked around and smiled, while Mrs Bond said, 'Mary approach. Dick has given me his promise to marry you, and this is his reward.' Mary still looked doubtful. When Madge returned with the twigs and heard the last words, she rushed into the room with a merry shout: 'Hold him, Mrs Bond, Hold him – now's your chance, Mary – punish him – punish the wretch; after promising to marry you, the very first thing he does is to fuck your mother! – did anyone ever see the like?'

She hastily tied up the twigs, put them into Mary's hand and pushed her towards Dick's naked bum, which presented itself in the most suggestive manner as he heaved gently up and down.

He looked smilingly at her, and said, 'Do it Mary, I deserve a whipping.' But Mary had evidently no heart for the office, and she applied the twigs in the softest way to the buttocks of her lover.

Observing which, Madge pulled the bundle of twigs impatiently out of her hand saying: 'You are no good; give it to me, I'll punish him,' and she laid on Dick's arse with such a will that she made him jump again, to Mrs Bond's manifest delight.

Dick fucked as he had never fucked before. 'Oh! Madge, have you no mercy? Stop you vixen!' and he discharged with fury into Mrs Bond's fully gratified receiver.

After a few moments of rest, during which they all arranged their tumbled dress, Mrs Bond said, 'Now, my children, we must separate for the present; but as Madge has promised to remain for the day, we hope that you, Dick, will join our party this evening.'

'Thanks, Mrs Bond, I will be most happy,' replied Dick; while Madge added: 'And then, Mrs Bond, you will favour us with the continuation of your interesting story.'

CHAPTER SEVEN

Mrs Bond's Story

On his way to the hospital after accepting Mrs Bond's invitation for the evening, Dick bethought him – to use his own words – how strangely Fortune in her blindness totes her gifts to us mortals! While she ignores some, she heaps on other more than they know what to do with. Many a poor devil goes moping about looking for someone to take pity on his loneliness, and cheer him up with a bit of cunt; while I, perhaps not half so worthy, feel overborne by *l'embarras des richesses!* Now there is Polly, who must not be forgotten; merry little Jim, she will not be overlooked; Mary, my sweet fiancée, ever ready and exacting too; and now, the circle is enlarged not only by Madge but by Mrs Bond, the weightiest of them all. I am nearly used up as it is, and if I encounter these three tonight on my own, I guess that by tomorrow morning, I shall be like what Polly calls a ha'p'orth of soap after a week's washing. I must get someone to share the burden with me. The friend who sprang to mind was Jack Price, who, he had just learned, was engaged to marry Madge Stevens. We have had many a spree together, he went on to himself, and it was only the other day that, in a fit of great cordiality, we promised one another that if ever we married we would sometimes swap wives for the sake of a little variety; and if wives, why not sweethearts?

So he looked up Jack, and soon found that, so far as he was concerned, there would be no objection; it was, in fact, just the thing to please him, and he was all expectation and desire.

It only remained to win over Mrs Bond – which might involve some difficulty as she was so very particular about her reputation.

At first when Dick broached the subject to her, she did not at all relish the idea of entrusting the secrets of their private sports to one who was a comparative stranger; but when Dick undertook to answer for his fidelity, and said he had already sworn him to secrecy, and especially when he dilated on his manly capacity and virile powers, she readily gave her consent.

It was then arranged by Mrs Bond, who wanted to pay off the girls for their treatment of herself, that Jack was to lie in hiding until they were in full swing then to be called forth by herself.

Mrs Bond had a private sitting-room, which she called her 'sanctum' and in which sscene of their orgies that night, and she said he could conceal himself there if she could smuggle him into the house without the knowledge of the girls.

Dick suggested leaving the hall door open at tea-time, when Jack could slip into his rooms unobserved, then by watching his opportunity he might himself conduct him to the sanctum.

So it was finally settled; Polly was allowed out for the evening, and Jim, as usual, went early to bed.

Jack succeeded in getting in without notice, and was soon concealed under a sofa, while the girls were upstairs dressing, or rather undressing, themselves – for the very lightest costume was to be the order for the night.

Passing over the merry jokes and light freedoms that diversified the supper, and the plentiful libations that followed (the hidden one not being neglected), we come to the real business of the night.

When they had betaken themselves to the sanctum, they found the rooms so warm that with one consent they threw off all remaining covering. Then Mrs Bond, with one of the girls on either side of her, reclined on the old-fashioned sofa (under which Jack lay concealed) and invited Dick to lie across on their bare thighs. Dick highly approved of the plan, for he could thus lay his face close to Madge's fragrant slit, and by turning in his foot, he could nestle his toes between the soft lips of Mary's sweet recess, while his bottom rested in Mrs Bond's luxurious lap, and her experienced fingers played with their accustomed skill around his prick and balls.

Dick told me that no one every touched him so pleasantly as she did; she was perfect mistress of the art. She knew, what all women seem to know, that the virile organism is a highly sensitive apparatus and needs delicate handling. She did not rub nor frig, but she applied such soft and ever shifting touches that for a lengthened period she sustained the prick in the highest stage of exaltation, without extracting one drop of its brimming seed.

'Now for the story,' cried Madge, as she spread her legs to enjoy more of Dick's gratifying titillation; 'we are all longing to hear how you and Dindee got on together.'

'Well, my dears, I can't tell you how fond I grew of Dindee's black prick. I used to pet it and frig it and kiss it at every opportunity. He sometimes climbed up to my window and entered my bedroom at night, and then we would both strip naked and play all sorts of antics. His favourite way of fucking was from behind; he said he liked to rub his belly on my bottom the way dogs and horses did. I did not dislike it either, so to please him, I generally went on my hands and knees, and he held me around the hips, and tickled my clitoris while he fucked. However when I found out how he acquired the taste, I turned from him in disgust and never let him come near me again.

'It happened this way. One evening when I was alone, I went out to the stable to look for Dindee. Intending to surprise him, I softly approached the open door, and looked in. I saw Dindee in the far corner, as I thought grooming the donkey, and I was just going to call him, when something in his manner stopped me and caused me to look with more attention. And oh! girls, what do you think he was doing? He was fucking my donkey; and she seemed used to it, for she stood perfectly still, and stooped her haunches with her hind legs spread apart and her tail twisted to one side, and his long black prick rushed in and out of the slit at her bottom.

'I turned and went away in disgust, and soon afterwards got my father to part with him, for I abhorred the notion of being co-partner with a beast.

'But though I gave Dindee up I had no intention of giving up my favourite pastime. Indeed I could not if I would; for my cunt had grown quite imperious in its demands; it was always craving for a prick. I tried in every way to appease it; I bathed it; I injected hot water; I used candles and various substitutes. I certainly had nothing half so good as this dildo, but if I had, it would not have satisfied me; nothing but the living, bounding prick would do for my longing, hungry cunt.

'So I cast about for someone to fill his place. At last, I bethought me of our family physician. He was married, it was true, but that did not stop me; in fact, it added zest to the enterprise.

'He had shown me in many little ways that he was quite ready to make free with me, and you know how quick a girl is in such matters, so I felt certain there would be no hesitation on his part to go as far as I would allow him.

'I therefore called boldly at his house, and told his servant that I wanted to consult her master. I was shown into the surgery, as I intended, and soon after, Dr Bolus came in smiling.

' "What does the fair Sophia want with me today?" he asked, as he motioned me to an easy-chair with a very sloping back and low wide cushioned arms.

' "Doctor, I am not well, and I suffer from constant irritation."

' "Is it in the bowels," he said, putting his hand on my stomach, "or lower?" sliding his hand down.

I blushed, and nodded assent.

' "Will you let me examine you and then I shall know what is wrong and be better able to prescribe?"

' "Could you not prescribe without examining me?"

' "Of course I could' – Oh, the knowing fellow – 'but it will be far more satisfactory to us both to ascertain by inspection what is really the matter. There now, lean back, that's a good sensible girl – open your legs, let me uncover you just for a moment."

'He lifted my dress, at the same time drawing me forward to the edge of the chair. "Let me spread your thighs more open," he said, lifting my legs over the arms. He then went down on his knees, with his face close to my cunt, and felt all around it, and opened the lips with his fingers.

'Yes, the vulva is a good deal excited, but there is nothing abnormal about it; the nymphae are somewhat inflamed, and the vagina is in a very heated and sensitive condition. Have you been doing anything to it?"

' "Yes, I syringed it with an ivory syringe which mother has."

' "Ah! I thought so, but that is not suited to you, it is too hard for the very excited state of your organ; you require a syringe of a peculiar construction" (clever dog) "not only smooth, but soft and flexible. I have one just the right size, and if you will allow me, I will apply it myself."

' "Very well, doctor, if you promise not to hurt me." He went to a press and took out a mahogany case, which he brought over and opened before me; it contained some black-looking tubes of different sizes. He laid the case on the floor, and again knelt between my thighs. He threw my dress higher up so as to cover my face, which I did not object to. I then felt him trying the tubes in my cunt, beginning with the smallest. He asked each time how I liked it, and whether he was hurting me? I said, "No, on the contrary, you are giving me great relief." "Just so," he replied, as he put in one that had a peculiar soft pleasant feel. Ah girls! there is no mistaking the real thing. Do you guess what he was doing?'

'Yes, Mrs Bond, he must have been trying the natural tube.'

'So he was, my dears, and doing it so skilfully that I could not help panting out, "Oh, doctor! that is nice – push it in further – I want more of it, Oh, doctor! that is very good – don't take it out – press against me – Oh! Oh!! that will do."

'When I sat up, the doctor was still panting after his exertions, his face was beaming, and his eyes twinkled as he said, "You are a famous patient; what I have done will, I think, be of great use to you, and when you need my services, come again; you know my consulting days are Tuesday and Fridays, but whenever I am at home when you call, I shall always be at your command.' Then he kissed me, and I went away.

'Well, my dears, you won't be surprised to hear that it was not long before I paid the doctor another visit; and let me tell you, there was nothing singular in my going to him, for he was a well-known ladies doctor; and many came from great distances to consult him, especially in cases of disappointment at not having a family, and if report is to be relied on, he not only prepared them for their husbands, but often took the place of the husband himself. And I am sure many came to him with that notion.

'Well, be that as it may, I willingly submitted as he placed me in position as before; and when he had excited me by skilful rubbing, and by various touches and pressures, he said, "You are making very satisfactory progress, my dear, and now, as I have the tube which suits you in my pocket, if you will lean back more at your ease, I will introduce it, and administer the usual injection."

' "Very good, doctor, am I right now?" I asked, pushing up my cunt; "no wonder you carry that tube always in your pocket, for I guess you find that it is in great request among the ladies."

'He looked up at my face, and catching the merry twinkle in my eye, he perceived at once that I understood the true character of his instrument.

' "Ah!" he said, his face relaxing into a genial smile, "there is no use attempting to humbug you, you are too cute and too clever. I knew from the first what you wanted; and after all, it is the only thing that can give you real relief. I am therefore glad that you approve of its exhibition."

' "Well, why don't you exhibit it now; I know it by feel, let me know it by sight also."

' "You are a charming girl, Sophy! If my wife were only like you, I would never think of any other woman in the world." As his said this he rose from his knees, opened his trousers in front, took out his prick and stood at my side.

'I sat up and took the dear thing into my hands. Oh! how nice and attractive it looked! A black tool may be all very well as a novelty now and then, but to a refined taste there is nothing like the white. Now, the doctor had one of remarkable freshness and purity of colour. My eyes gloated over it – my mouth watered to suck its rosy head – my cunt throbbed to feel it encircled in its soft embrace – its smooth loose skin was of such a clear milky whiteness, its head was so large, round and glossy. I pressed it to my lips – I rubbed it to my nose – I sniffed with delight that subtle odour which always pervades the prick of a healthy vigorous man. A little pearly drop glistened at the tiny slit-like opening. I licked it up, it had a spicy flavour, and its taste made my cunt glow.

'The doctor put his hands on my head, and played with my ears and chin: "My darling, you handle my prick most deliciously, I love to feel your delicate fingers playing with my balls – that is delicious – you are too kind." I had pushed in my hand, and inserting my forefinger in his bottom, I stirred it gently around. "Would you like me to spend in your mouth, dear? I cannot keep it in much longer."

' "You may – I would like it – you can put it in my cunt afterwards," I replied, taking out his prick for a moment. I quickly replaced it, taking as much as I could in my mouth, and sucking as hard as I was able, while I stirred up his balls with one hand, and tickled his bottom with the other.

'Oh! darling Sophy, there, Oh! Oh!' He stooped over me, and groaned with delight, while the hot bubbling drops of spunk spurted into my mouth, and flowed down my throat.

'He brought me a glass of wine, and told me to remain as I was, while he sat on the floor to rest between my legs, his head supported by my thigh, as he kissed and frigged my cunt.

'He questioned me as to when and how I had first fucked. I hesitated a little, but thinking it wiser to trust him altogether, as I had trusted him too much already, I told him all about Dindee and his black prick; but said I liked a fair while tool such as he had far better.

'He laughed and said he had never met a girl that pleased him so much; and that my talking so freely was an especial charm, for nothing enhanced the enjoyment of the act itself so much as the preliminary feeling and looking and talking about it and kindred matters.

' "Now let me put this pillow under your bottom to elevate the shrine of love, and enable me to pay my devotions with more ease and effect."

'He then watched his prick glide into the sanctuary, and when it reached the innermost retreat, and we were closely pressed together, he leaned over me and placed his hand under the back of my head, further to excite what he called the cerebellum, or lesser brain, which is the seat of animal desire.

' "Now, my dear, concentrate all your mind on the sensations in your cunt, as I slowly draw out my prick. Now the head is just at the entrance, between the two little clinging nymphae. Now as I slowly drive it in again, I make the ridge on the glans rub against every fold and furrow of your vagina. How do you like it?'

' "Oh, doctor! it is maddening! – Oh! you know how to fuck – press me in your arms – hold my head up to take your tongue into my mouth – Ah! fuck, fuck, fuck."

'We panted with effort and emotion, and both cunt and mouths became vocal with soft slurping sucking sounds, attended by a rubbing accompaniment, as our bodies bounded together in all the heat of amorous encounter.

'Just as my cunt had drunk up his hot sperm and he sank with a long drawn sigh upon my breast, I caught his eye, and asked, "What would your wife say, if she saw us now?"

' "She would say: You old sinner!" exclaimed a voice, to our consternation, from behind the opening door. "Have I caught you at last! You cannot taunt me about young Lyons now; you must forever hold your tongue – come in, Mr Lyons, and see how your employer practices surgery with ladies when he gets them by themselves.' And his assistant, a good-looking young fellow with ruddy face and merry eye, peeped into the room.

'Oh, my dear, stop your foolishness; you may do with Mr Lyons just as you please; don't barge at me, and you can have him as often as you like. Lyons! come in, you are a right good fellow. I have for some time regarded you as a son, but I suppose I must for the future look at you in some other light. As she does not even veil her desire for you – and for the sake of peace – you can have her with all my heart; only let there be no more hugger-mugger, or concealment, let everything be done openly; come and watch us – then, it is only fair that we in our turn should have the satisfaction of witnessing your performance together."

'I never admired anything so much as the doctor's clever way of getting out of his difficulty, and completely turning the tables on his wife. She seemed scarcely to relish his proposal, however, as she had nothing to say; she folded her hands and sat down on a sofa. So he went up to her, just as he was, with his trousers still open, and giving her a kiss, said: 'Now, like a wise old girl submit cheerily, and then we shall be quits – come here, Lyons – I am sure you know these quarters pretty well already,' and, inclining her back, and drawing up her skirts, he added: 'Look at this fine randy fat cunt,' and pushing her legs apart and opening the lips, said: 'This is for my special use, but I am no dog in a manger. I here constitute you my partner in the fucking line, as well as in all my other business; and if that is not true liberty, equality and fraternity there are no such things in the world."

'Here Lyons looked amused, and muttered some kind of thanks, while he evidently regarded the randy fat cunt with admiration and desire, for he stooped and pressed his mouth on the open lips.

' "Now, Sophy, my love," cried the doctor, "come here, and prepare this bashful young man for his work; unbutton him, and take out his prick – there's a dear!"

'You will agree with me, I think, that under the circumstances, any display of modesty on my part would have been unnecessary and out of place, so, discarding it for the time, I unbuttoned his trousers, pulled up his shirt, and soon brought to light a fine young healthy prick in full erection.

' "Kiss it, Sophy." I pressed my lips to its soft head, then let it slip in and gave it one little suck.

'The doctors's wife, now more at her ease since her husband was presiding, threw a handkerchief over her face and resigned herself to the job appointed her; and when she felt young Lyons between her thighs, she drew up her legs and spread herself as open as she could. The action showed how eager she was for the dearly loved fuck.

'She reminded me of a randy cat, cocking up her end, and poking it out to make the way plain and easy for her favourite tom.

'The doctor held open the lips of his wife's cunt while I, kneeling behind Mr Lyons and holding his prick in both hands, pushed in the head; as it passed out of view, I grasped his balls, and quietly squeezed them as he went about ramming his prick in and out. Some women don't care to handle a man's balls – I do, and I find it the best way to stimulate and increase his efforts.

'What do you say, friend Dick, do you like having your scrotum petted, and your testicles gently pressed and stirred about?'

'Oh! Mrs Bond, it is delicious, but I am on the point of discharging, let me in somewhere or I shall burst.'

'Yes, you are in first-rate condition; look here, girls, here is a prick for you, which of you will enjoy it first.'

'Dear Mrs Bond, you ought to have the first of it yourself, for it is your beautiful story and delicate handling that have brought it into such fine condition; come Mary, we will amuse ourselves on the floor, while Dick fucks your mother. I am just in humour for a little tribadism; get over me, my dear, and place your cunt on my mouth, and let us have as sweet a fuck together.'

She laid herself down on the soft carpet before the sofa, with her legs stretched wide apart, while Mary, straddling over her, rubbed her cunt on her mouth and presented her magnificent arse in full view of Dick and her mother, and of Jack too, who was impatiently peeping out from under the sofa.

'Good, my daughter! Sappho and Telesilla never presented a more attractive combination. If Jack Price could only see you now he would not know which to fuck. Jack, appear!'

In a moment Jack was on top of them. They started with surprise and alarm, and tried to get up, but he held them firmly as they were. He was quite naked like themselves, and his fine prick, which had been on the stand for the last hour, poked fiercely at Mary's bottom.

'Put him in, Madge, put him in,' laughed Mrs Bond.

'No, I won't, you mustn't fuck Mary. She doesn't want you.'

'Yes, I do,' cried Mary, who having caught Dick's eye quickly understood how matters were and pushed her bottom up towards him.

'No, Mary, he shan't; if he does, he shall never fuck me again!'

'Don't be cross, Madge, what harm will it do you? – there – let him in – you will enjoy him all the more afterwards,' and putting down her mouth she thrust her tongue into Madge's cunt and produced such a titillation, that in her excitement, Madge actually held her lover's prick to Mary's lascivious slit, and watched it rush eagerly in.

Meantime, Dick had mounted Mrs Bond, and that salacious dame, as soon as she felt the full length of his prick enclosed in the folds of her heated cunt, embraced him so firmly with her arms and legs that he found himself unable to stir.

'Keep quiet, dear, for a moment or two, while we watch that interesting trio. See how your friend Jack fucks! – he is a powerful man indeed, and has a noble tool; doesn't Mary enjoy it! see how she wriggles her bottom! and look at the face of Madge below, how she watches the great prick as it glides in and through those soft furry lips! There, she is actually kissing and licking his balls, while she pinches the clitoris and lips; and look at Mary, how she plies her busy tongue both in cunt and bottom! Now, Dick, fuck away as hard as you like, poke my cunt well – send home your prick,' and clutching his buttocks, she drove her nails into those soft cheeks of his backside, while he deluged her cunt with an overflow of boiling spunk.

During the rest which followed, Mrs Bond gratified her lecherous taste by a minute inspection of Jack's formidable tool and magnificent stones. She handled them with delight, and sucked his prick still moist with the juice of her daughter's cunt.

Madge, feeling somewhat ashamed of her little spurt of jealousy, now called on her lover to favour Mrs Bond with a practical proof of his ability, while she spread herself more conveniently for Dick, who, cojointly with Mary, was examining and petting her wanton recess. Jack was willing enough, for he greatly admired Mrs Bond for her spirit and dash; and soon found that she more than made up for her want of youth by her greater experience and fertility of invention. So gently turning her up across the end of the sofa, he plunged into her region of delight, just as Dick was similarly occupied with Madge at the other end, while Mary, not willing to be left out, formed herself into a connecting link by going between and holding each prick as it worked in and out of the cunts of her mother and Madge.

They quickly spent, and then they all lay on the floor in one commingled mass of arms and legs, cunts, pricks, bottoms and faces, all rubbing up together.

When they were a little rested, Mrs Bond proposed a general spongification; and then, after they had taken some light refreshment, she arranged the following *tableau* as a parting scene.

She set Mary, who was the strongest, on her hands and knees on the floor then she turned up Madge reversed on her back, with her head resting on Mary's bottom, so that, while Dick on his knees fucked his own sweetheart from behind, he was able to kiss Madge and take her tongue into his mouth; Jack at the other end pressed in between Madge's up-turned thighs, and entered her open cunt, and leaning forward sucked the nipple of her breast.

Thus each girl had the enjoyment of being fucked by one man and caressed by another at the same time; while the lascivious touches and wanton pinches of Mrs Bond's busy fingers added piquancy to the whole.

This concluded a night of rare and unmitigated pleasure, character-ised, it is true, by extreme licentiousness, and unnatural obscenity.

Dick's letters were a source of great enjoyment to us all. The arrival of the fortnightly mail which brought them was looked forward to with pleasant anticipation; and the governor was sure to find his way into my boudoir that evening.

He loved to lie at his ease toying with my cunt and bottom, while I read Dick's exciting descriptions, written indeed for this very purpose; for when he heard that his letters were so highly appreciated by the governor, he redoubled his efforts to please, and filled them with lewd expressions and ideas.

He sometimes favoured us with pen-and-ink sketches of a very humorous character, and sent also some excellent copies of the lascivious drawing found on the walls of Pompeii, lately exposed to view. These latter were sent from Rome to a young Italian who was studying medicine in the same college as Dick.

He generally accompanied the drawing with some such description as the following:

In number 1, you have Marpesia, Queen of the Amazons. She has been taken prisoner by the Fauns with whom the Amazons waged frequent war with varying success. She is young, lusty and well-made.

The leader of the Fauns has determined to enjoy her after a peculiar fashion. She is bound, as you see, to the back of a trusty member of his troop. One of her captured attendants is forced to stoop with her hands and feet tied together. The Faun with Marpesia on his back rams his great prick into the attendant's cunt from behind, while his captain, sitting before her, sticks his rampant tool into Marpesia in front. But you observe he leaves all the work to be done by his lieutenant, who, as he fucks the attendant, works Marpesia's cunt most luxuriously up and down on his leader's tool.

Marpesia has her finger raised as if she was saying: 'Ah! you have me now, and can drive your goatish prick into my poor cunt to your full satisfaction, but wait till the Amazons catch you and maybe they will make you spend to some purpose.

In number 2, the Faun varies his enjoyment. He wants to have his prick rubbed up, so he has Marpesia suspended over him, with her legs and arms tied to a bough of a tree in such a posture that her breasts rest on his belly, then he nestles his languid prick between her soft swelling bubbies, and makes his lieutenant stand between her thighs and fuck her while thus suspended. The shoves of the lieutenant, as he drives his prick in and out of Marpesia's cunt, make her breasts rub back and forth on his leader's belly, thus imparting the most stimulating friction to his lethargic tool.

In number 3, you find matters reversed. The Amazons now have the upper hand. They have surprised the Fauns in a night attack, and have captured a large number. Marpesia, who has regained her liberty, now takes her revenge and her gratification at the same time. She has them securely fastened down on their backs, on logs of wood, so that she and her feminine troop can stride over them, and gorge to satiety their fasting cunts with their subjugated pricks. Behold Marpesia herself, in grand muscular proportion and beauty, astride over the chief. She has stuffed his pliant tool into her lascivious gap, and sustaining herself by the branch of a tree overhead, works her body up and down until she pumps out all the seminal juice left in the poor wretch's cods.

She has exhausted several in the same way; one of her attendants tries a poor fellow whom she has just left, but she finds his tool so limp and powerless, so completely sucked dry, that he cannot get it into her receptacle, so raising her disappointed cunt, she contemptuously discharges over the useless prick a hissing stream of ejected piss.

In number 4, we have a front view of this famous queen: her breasts are proportionally small, but her arms, thighs and legs are in the highest development of muscular strength and beauty.

She is seated on a gigantic Faun with his great tool stuffed into her lecherous receiver; the protruding lips of her hairy cunt grasp it firmly at the root, while her nimble fingers churn his reluctant cods.

With her other hand she frigs the inflamed prick of another of these deformities, whose hands are fastened behind his back.

'Spend, you ugly beast!' she cries, as with energetic hold and rapid motion she works his tired machine.

Then the scene changes, peace has been proclaimed between the Amazons and their Sylvan neighbours. To keep up their unnatural tribe, the Amazons are allowed occasionally to wander in the woods, with a view to meeting the Fauns and obtaining the service of their virile powers.

In number 5, you have, accordingly, Marpesia herself embraced by three fine specimens of these horned and goat-legged monsters. One encircles her with his left arm and elevates her thigh with his right, while he plunges his vigorous prick into the luscious cavity of her hungry cunt. Another presents his bursting tool to her open mouth; with lecherous lips, she sucks its throbbing head, and draws streams of frothy love from the fount within. The third kissed her ruddy cheek and feels her bottom with searching fingers while she frigs his sturdy prick. Her warm and nervous grasp soon makes the hot spunk shoot in milky jets from its glowing tip. Just as her mouth and cunt are each liberally treated with an overflow of the same fecundating fluid.

At last the time drew near for Dick to pay us his promised visit. He had successfully passed his final examination, and was now duly qualified to act as a medical practitioner.

The governor directed him to bring his certificate and testimonials with him, in order that he might be able to fulfil his promise of obtaining for him a suitable and lucrative appointment.

He also told him to propose to Mrs Bond a move to Trinidad, where she could procure an excellent residence near Government House and, by his influence, an unfailing supply of good lodgers.

Although this was stated with apparent indifference, I saw plainly enough that the account Dick had given of Mrs Bond and her interesting family had, in the highest degree, excited the desire of the governor to obtain the enjoyment of a closer acquaintance with that salacious lady.

I foresaw indeed that such acquaintance would assuredly lead to a lessening of my influence over him; but he was growing old, and I might at any time, have to look for some more permanent position, so I did not feel greatly alarmed. Besides, having my old friend Dick, even though married, near me again would be a source of very great gratification and support, Mrs Bond readily accepted the governor's invitation and in due time arrived on the island with all her belongings.

The result I anticipated was quickly verified; and the coming of Mrs Bond and her party gave rise to many new and interesting complications, which will form the subject of succeeding chapters.

CHAPTER EIGHT

Dick's Poetry

The selection and arrangement of Mrs Bond's future residence was entrusted to the governor and myself.

To account for the interest he took in the matter, it was given out that she had been the wife of an old friend of his to whom he had promised when dying that he would look after and protect his widow and orphans.

It so happened that there was a suitable and commodious house, not far from the government grounds, at that time untenanted. The governor at once engaged it for his friend's widow, and set about having it furnished and fitted up, not forgetting a special boudoir or sanctum for Mrs Bond's own use.

In the midst of our preparations, another batch of letters came to hand, telling us that they were just about embarking and containing Dick's certificate and testimonials for the governor and also some papers for myself.

Dick had a taste for scribbling what he called poetry, and as it may gratify my readers, I transcribe for them the specimen which I received on this occasion. It shows, I think, some talent, but I am not sure that it is mythologically correct.

Venus and the Centaur

Arms! and the thing, I sing – half-man, half-horse;
Impelled by fate, a sort of equine cross,
Whose front developed half in human mould,
But left the other half as it was foal'd.
Unique was he; no other of his form
Was there to gambol 'mid the Aegean storm;
And all too proud the common herd to seek
While owning human faculty to speak
He lived alone till passion claimed its sway:
'Twas rutting season, and the month of May.

Wandering forlorn in this unpleasant guise
In vain each nymph, incontinent, he tries;
No sooner does the monster breathe of love,
Than shrieks of laughter echo through the grove;
'A hideous beast like thee!' young Lesbia cries;
And straight each wanton from his presence flies;
'We'll none of thee,' the sylvan nymphs declare.
' 'Tis pity Pegasus is not a mare.'
Despairing tears his human cheeks bedewed,
Condemned to solitude, unloved, unwed;
Sought he a mate throughout the whole of earth,
His importunities but moved their mirth.
At length a settled gloom upon him falls,
And on Love's Goddess in despair he calls;
Scarce had his prayer re-echo'd through the wood.
Than lovely Venus in his presence stood.
Her beauteous form in all its naked grace,
And wreathing smiles illuminate her face.
Her faultless limbs no envious drap'ry hides –

A living model which all art derides.
To her the Centaur his petition made,
And in his misery invoked her aid.
The Goddess smiled and heaved a gentle sigh,
Then to the Centaur blushing made reply:

'Oh! noble Centaur, whose peculiar race
To form of stallion add the human grace;
And hast thou, piteous being! felt the dart
Of my unsparing offspring in thy heart?
Alas poor Centaur! could not Cupid spare,
Malicious boy! but plant his arrow there;
For those delights which gentle lovers prize,
Thou art not fitted, Centaur, in the eyes
Of those fair maids who thus thy form deride;
Nature has laws by which we must abide.'

Thus spake the Goddess, and her beauty's charm
To his nature sounded the alarm;
Her naked shape and the secrets thus reveal'd
To his fierce instincts all at once appeal'd.
Extreme desires assail his wanton heart,
And tingling fires through all his body dart,
Fancy runs riot as he views her form,
Her charming naked parts, and glances warm.

To her the Centaur, as he seized her hand:
'Art thou Love's Goddess, and my pains withstand;
Can'st thou not quench the burning fires within?
To Venus all divine, no love is sin.'
Thus spoke the Centaur, while her roving eyes
Observed his weapon of portentous size;
A lively red suffused her damask cheeks,
And her clasped hands her strong emotion speaks.
Not such as won her, when the shipling boy,
She first embraced and taught him to enjoy
Within her circling arms the pruient bliss:
His latest spasms dying in a kiss.
'Twas not Adonis now, the Goddess fired,
To more substantial joys her mind aspired;
Effective means to stir such wanton hearts
Had he possessed of such stupendous parts.

Now beat his pulses with inflamed desire,

His stallion nature owns the mystic fire,
His crimson cheeks betray his burning lust,
The Goddess saw it, gently sighed and blushed.
Intense emotions struggle in his breast,
And his rude weapon shows its ruddy crest;
Its swollen veins and long, distended length
With frequent jerks proclaim its stallion strength.

The wanton Goddess feels the lustful fire,
And all aflame, now pants with warm desire,
His trembling hands rove o'er her glowing charms,
And wild with joy he clasps her in his arms.
Her eyes askance devour the bestial brand,
Impulsively she takes it in her hand.
With gentle pressures she his lust requites,
And firmer grasps afford him new delights.
The throbbing weapon raised on high its crest,
While Venus kneeling pressed it to her breast.

Now too excited long to brook delay
The snorting monster urged the prurient play:
So Venus forward on the bank reclined,
While the Centaur, rampant, mounted her behind,
With furious thrusts his untaught falchion plies,
Beats round the bush, and entrance vainly tries.
But sacred pity acts in godlike minds:
Plants the fierce point between her lily thighs,
And lust-distended, twixt the lips it lies,
With poignant throbs all swollen and impressed,
While Venus labours to engulf the rest.
Constrained by that firm grasp and guided true
The stiffened gristle disappears from view.
Propelled by lustful force within its slips,
And stretches wide the love-moist roseate lips –
Ah! thus forever love will have its way:
So Venus cries, enraptured with the play;
Not less, the Centaur madd'ning impulse feels,
And beats the verdure with his horny heels –
While roars expressive of his joy are forced
From his hoarse throat, and in the woods are lost –
Divine sensations now he feels, and new,
Convulsive pressures prove her pleasures too,
While tingling raptures fill the Centaur's veins,

And each convulsion fresh insertion gains,
Till gorged at length with monster such as this,
The fainting Goddess owns the melting bliss.

With furious thrusts the Centaur's throbbing shaft
In Venus' cunt lies buried to the haft,
Thrust upon thrust the greedy monster dealt,
While hot with lust the enraptured Goddess knelt.
His joy increased till nature could not more,
And his big globes were banging at the door,
So close the pressure, despite her pains,
The quick'ning pleasure bubbles in his veins.
Too short! too warm! the luscious struggle ends,
And with a howl the clinging Centaur spends.
As spouted forth when sweet Narcissus died,
From Mother Earth the clear cerulean tide:
So now behold the swollen limb distend
And spout the exquisite essence from its end –
With furious pressures and impulsive thrust
He shoots the torrents of his heated lust,
While pent-up nature makes prodigious throes,
And the thick juice in rich profusion flows.

The Goddess feels this inundation pour,
And sinks exhausted on the verdant floor:
Her flooded cunt the fierce coition owns
While sobs of pleasure mingle with his groans.
And sated thus, his passion finds relief:
His dripping weapon slips from out the sheath.

The Goddess rises from the reeking ground,
And startled wood nymphs, trembling, gather round.
Convinced at last he has some power to please,
They watch his wanton gambols at their ease,
Not one so coy she will not gladly share
His wondrous gifts, and own their pleasures rare;
In fact, the monster, thus in great request,
Soon trotted off to take some timely rest.
'Tis thus that fashion, once set in and strong,
Obtains, and rules by force the mouthy throng;
And many a rude exterior hides a charm
Which, once 'tis tasted, use conceals the harm.

CHAPTER NINE

The Widow's Crafty Scheme

The governor and I were waiting on the shore ready to welcome Mrs Bond's party on their arrival.

Mrs Bond was younger and more fresh looking than I expected. She had the sprightly vivacious manner of a Frenchwoman, and all the ease and accomplishment of a well-bred lady.

Mary, I did not fancy so much: she was pretty, but there was something reserved and sly in her look and demeanour which rather repelled me; but Jim, with her merry open face, and warm impetuous little ways, was altogether to my taste, and we quickly became close friends. Dick I thought wonderfully improved; he had grown more manly in appearance, and his handsome bronzed face was set off by a full dark-coloured moustache. He met me with the greatest *empressement*, and his salute was something more than brotherly.

The governor's interest secured for him the appointment he desired, and when he had obtained apartments in a neighbouring lodging house, he entered into his duties with zeal and ability. Mrs Bond quickly made herself at home, and the governor, I need not say, was a frequent visitor at her house and was soon fully initiated in all the mysteries of her sanctum.

From the first she brought all her seductive arts to bear upon him, and knowing that he had been made acquainted, through Dick, with all her secret tastes, habits and capabilities, she permitted him to take her in his arms, and after a little coy remonstrance, push his roving hand up between her easily separated thighs and explore with lecherous fingers the secret charms of her ripe and unctuous quim.

Then having carefully secured the door, she allowed him to raise her petticoats and lay bare the hidden beauties that clustered round the junction of her large fleshy thighs; then she even reclined back and spread herself open to afford him the fullest gratification by a near inspection of the gradually swelling mound and full voluptuous lips of her well-garnished cunt.

While he stooped over her, she unbuttoned his trousers, pulled up his shirt, and drew forth his soft and attenuated tool.

'Let me fondle it a moment, my dear sir, it has plenty of life in it yet, it only needs a little attention to flatter and excite it.'

She took it coaxingly in her well-practiced hand and with a stimulating touch passed her fingers gently up and down its shaft and over its pendant head. Then, leaning towards it, she took it into her warmmouth and played around its top and neck with her pliant tongue, while with soft suction she compressed her lips as she moved her head back and forward over it. At last, yielding to her skilful treatment, it slowly filled up and attained a certain degree of firmness and erection.

Still nursing it with her stimulating touches, she looked up, and with a smile, said, 'It is in fair condition now; would you like me to call in Mary? She is young, fresh and beautifully made; in fact, she has one of the most satisfying cunts that ever man entered and I am sure she will think herself happy in being able to minister to your pleasure.'

The governor's face quite brightened as he replied that while nothing could exceed the ripeness and the beauty of her own lovely charms, yet as she had kindly suggested the idea, it would certainly intensify his enjoyment to include her fair and accomplished daughter.

Mrs Bond thoroughly understood the old governor, and with a wily craft impressed a lascivious kiss on the sensitive end of his half erect tool and said: 'Cheer up, you dear old prick, I bring you a fresh young cunt that will fill you with new vigour and delight.'

She got up and went out, soon returning leading her daughter Mary by the hand.

The governor rose to meet her and taking her in his arms said, 'Allow me to congratulate you, sweet Mary, on the bloom of your lovely cheeks and the sparkle of your bright eyes.' Mary looked shy and turned away her blushing face.

'Don't be over modest, my child, the governor has been very good to us, and we must do what we can to show our gratitude in pleasing him by every means in our power; and that reminds me, I intended correcting you for being too lazy this morning. I will do it now, and that will make us all easy together,' and sitting down, she made her daughter bend over her knees, and then proceeded to pull up her skirts.

'Oh, mamma! don't uncover me before Sir Charles. Ah, don't! you will let him see – all – every – Oh, my! what a shame! Don't look, Sir Charles.'

'I will uncover you before Sir Charles, just to punish you all the more; and if he cares to look, he shall see all you have to show. Now, you lazy girl, take that and that – and that,' each time giving her a smack on the bare bottom with the palm of her hand. 'I will make this saucy bum blush, like your rosy face.

'Look, governor, do you see how red her bottom is getting? How she pokes it out! and wriggles it from side to side, the impudent hussy! Yes, I will smack you in here too, open your legs, miss.'

'Oh, mamma! Oh, mamma! don't let Sir Charles see my – '

'Your cunt, you mean, yes he shall see your cunt and everything about it; just to punish you; lift your bottom and spread your thighs more – that's the way. Look, governor, at these two pretty fat lips. I will pull them open for you – see this clitoris, how stiffly it stands out! and this deep chink, how red and moist it is! I declare the impudent girl is spending; look at this white juice oozing out! how hot and randy she is! Now, Sir Charles, where's your prick – I will hold her while you stick it in – get down there between her legs – so – let me guide it for you – now push there, how nicely it slips in! Now work away while I keep my hand on your cods and tickle your bottom.'

'Oh, mamma – let me up – what are you and Sir Charles doing to me?'

'Fucking you, my dear, don't you feel his nice prick rubbing in your cunt, and his hairy balls smacking against your bottom? Tell him, Mary, how you like it.'

'Dear Sir Charles, your fucking gives me a very pleasant feeling in my cunt. I hope you are enjoying it yourself. Do you like looking at my bottom? Can you see it while you fuck?'

'Yes, darling Mary, I don't know when I enjoyed a fuck so much, and your talking about it so freely makes it still more enjoyable. You have a most delicious cunt; it holds my prick like a hand; and you have the sweetest roundest and plumpest little arse that ever lady carried behind her. But I must withdraw now, as I am going to spend,' and he pulled out his prick.

'Pop it in here,' said Mrs Bond, drawing it under the cheeks of Mary's bottom and presenting the little brown hole in the most easy and inviting position.

'Shall I Mary? shall I fuck your arse?'

'Yes, Sir Charles, fuck my arse, if you like.'

The governor pushed at the narrow entrance and the well-moistened head of his prick slipped into her bottom, passed up, and discharged amid her entrails the few drops of spunk it was able to deliver.

Mary then ran, poured water into a basin and returned, bringing her own sponge, then carefully washed, wiped and then petted and kissed the drooping article which the governor dignified with the name of prick.

I was not present at this first step in their wily plot, but was informed of what took place afterwards, when all was settled and we had fallen into the positions which stern fate apparently had allotted to us. Mrs Bond was as ambitious as she was clever, and at once on her arrival she perceived that the amorous tastes and weaknesses of the old governor presented an opportunity of making her daughter Mary so attractive and so essential to his pleasure that he might be induced to take her as his second wife.

The engagement with Dick, she treated very lightly, as she knew that she had brought it on herself, and that he probably would not regret being released from the promise which had been exacted from him; while my connection gave her no concern whatsoever.

I soon perceived the old man's infatuation. He was perpetually at Mrs Bond's; and when with me, which was more seldom than formerly, he could talk of nothing but Mary – her beauty, her accomplishments and her charms.

So I said to him one day when he was returning my caresses in a languid manner, 'My dear old Charley, I see how the wind blows; you like Mary, you want Mary – why don't you marry her, and you will have the full command of a find young girl, and her accomplished mother into the bargain?'

Well, I might, except on your account, and also that she is engaged to our friend Dick.'

'As for me,' I replied, 'don't let that be an obstacle. Thanks to your liberality, and my father's kindness, I am independent; and my affection for you will under any circumstances remain the same; and as for Dick, I don't think he cares much for Mary after all; it would not break his heart. He would like to see her the wife of his friend and patron, Sir Charles.'

To make a long story short, it was soon understood, and acquiesced in by us all, that Mary was to be the second Lady Stanhope; and Dick, being thus set free, reminded me of the old passion he had always nursed in his heart of hearts, and asked me to become his wife.

I consented on the condition that I was to retain the command of my own money, and that we should both be absolutely free to enjoy ourselves just as we had when in possession of our unmarried liberty.

This arrangement smoothed away every difficulty, and restored confidence and kindly feeling amongst us all.

Dick and I were invited to join the parties in the sanctum; and Mary and her mother often came to my boudoir to meet the governor and Dick, who continued the best of friends.

On such occasions Mrs Bond was always called by general consent to preside.

She naturally made the governor the great object of her attention, and left Dick and me to follow our own devices and join in as we liked; which plan suited all parties very well.

I will describe one of these scenes as a specimen. Having settled the old governor in a most voluptuous position on the couch, his bottom resting on soft cushions, his back supported by sloping pillows and his thighs wide apart, Mrs Bond would kneel at his side and stoop forward so as to elevate her naked posterior beauties, of which she was justly proud, in front of a large mirror in full view of the reclining governor. Then in the most skilful manner, she would take in hand and delicately frig his prick, which though only partially erect was fully sensitive to the delicious touch of her pliant and mobile fingers. Her other hand meanwhile would stealthily pass under his thigh, and with cunning play, titillate him behind.

By their direction, Mary would kneel at the other side with her fair white bottom turned towards his face, so that he could feast his eyes or amuse his fingers either with her delicate little nether entrance, or the thick hairy lips of her luscious quim; and sometimes, at a hint from her mother, she would vary her position by straddling over his breast and pushing her bottom to his face, that he might kiss and smell the fragrant apertures there; all the time, however, keeping her open mouth over his prick, so that her mother might pop in its head when she wished to vary the sensation.

She soon discovered how fond the governor was of listening to randy talk and the special delight he found in hearing women freely use all those wanton terms and expressions which are suggestive of lecherous thought and practice.

She accordingly gratified him and intensified his excitement by carrying on with Mary a most lascivious and suggestive conversation; occasionally having recourse to Dick or me for the sake of variety.

'Fucking, mamma! Fucking; there is no more delightful feeling than that of a nice prick being pushed up into one's cunt, rubbing against its sensitive creases and filling it to capacity.'

'Do you like the feel of Sir Charles's prick fucking your cunt?'

'I do greatly, especially when you put it in, mamma, and hold it by the root, which makes it stronger; and then I feel your fingers playing about my clitoris and the lips of my cunt.'

'Where do you feel his cods rubbing when he fucks you lying on your back with your legs raised up?'

'I feel his colds rubbing against the whole of my bottom – well, my arse, if he likes me to say it. Do you like looking at my naked arse, Sir Charles?'

'I do, darling Mary, I enjoy greatly looking at your naked arse; it is so soft and round, and of such a creamy whiteness; push it up nearer, and I will kiss it for you.'

'What to you do, Mary, just before you get into bed?'

'I take out the pot, mamma, and piss into it; and sometimes I watch my cunt while it pisses. I suppose most people piss before going to bed. Don't you? Sir Charles wished to see me piss the other night. I pissed through his fingers, and then he kissed my cunt before I wiped it and while the drops of piss still hung about his hands; then I made him piss for me, and I held his prick as I watched the amber stream shoot out of the little slit at the top, then I sucked it, and got some of the piss into my mouth, I think.'

Dick and I laughed; we were highly amused at the wily craft of the mother, and the unblushing effrontery of the daughter.

Meanwhile, we carried on our own little play of kissing and sucking, and petting and fucking. We had enjoyed a nice fuck on a couch parallel with and close to that on which the governor was lying – so near, in fact, that by stretching out his arm he was able to place his lecherous hand on Dick's fine sturdy prick as he worked it slowly and deliberately in my cunt. And for a moment Mrs Bond and Mary had paused to watch us also.

Dick was now resting with his head on the pillow, while I straddled over him holding his softened tool in my hands, rubbing and pressing it against the warm lips of my still excited cunt. Mrs Bond, who studied the governor's prick as a doctor does the pulse of his patient, perceived that further stimulation was needed; so, winking at Mary she asked, 'Did Sir Charles ever get anyone to fuck you while he looked on?'

'He did, mamma; I did not quite like it, but you know, I would do anything to please him. He brought the coachman into his room, and having told him he wanted him to fuck one of the maids before him, he blindfolded him perfectly. Then he placed him on the bed on his back and desired him to get his prick in order for the girl he was about to bring in.

When all was ready, he came for me, stripped me naked, led me in and directed me to get on the bed and straddle down over the coachman's face that he might first gratify and excite himself by kissing my cunt and sucking my arsehole.

Of course, I liked that very well, especially as the governor was pleased and kept on fingering me all the while.

I was therefore quite ready when Sir Charles told me to squat down on the man's prick while he stuffed it into my cunt. Then I worked away like a postilion up and down while Sir Charles held his prick to my mouth and asked me to frig and suck it and tickle his bottom until he spent.

'How did you like it yourself, Sir Charles.'

'Oh! it was grand! do you remember how I held you by the shoulders, as I drove my prick through your fingers in and out of your mouth, as if it were a cunt. And the best of it was, the coachman had not the least idea whose cunt it was that gave him such delight, but thought and still thinks that it was one of the maids.'

The coachman, however, was none other than my old friend James, and he told me on one occasion when he was indulging in that second bout, which women so love and appreciate, that he knew perfectly well who the lady was that the lecherous old governor wished him to believe was one of the maids. But that he thought it wiser to keep his knowledge to himself, especially as he expected her to be his future mistress. 'But oh! Miss Queenie, that's where you ought to be – we all love you, but no one cares for Miss Mary, she is too haughty and conceited.'

Another device of that most lubricious dame was very successful, and is therefore worthy of special record. She obtained a broad shallow basket, purposely made with an open bottom. This was secured like the scale of a balance to a rope that passed through a pulley overhead, so that it could be hauled up and down. In this basket Mary was placed quite naked, with the plump white cheeks of her arse protruding through the open bottom; which position caused her cunt to stand out with a moist luxurious and exciting prominence from the furrow between her smooth round buttocks.

Of all the varied postures to which prurient fancy has subjected the female form, this is the best I have ever seen for displaying in full perfection both the exterior and interior beauties of a woman's cunt.

In most cases, no matter how they spread their thighs, the nymphae or inner lips remain closed; but by this arrangement the pressure of the body so forces out the cunt that those little shell-like wings (*ailerons*, as the French call them) are drawn widely apart, and thus afford a most ravishing view of the crimson depths between them.

Mary having seated herself in this basket so ingeniously contrived by her mother was hoisted about four feet from the floor,.

The old governor stretched himself underneath on his back with his lustful eyes fastened on the interior charms of Mary's cunt, so invitingly opened out above his head; while her experienced mother frigged up his prick into some degree of life and stiffness.

Then Dick or I would lower the basket gently down, so that, under Mrs Bond's management, the ripe ruddy lips of Mary's cunt would just alight on and enclose the head of the prick which was so skilfully sustained by her mother's hand.

Then, as the rope was further slacked off, the weight of her body would cause the hot moist lips to swallow up the whole of that luscious morsel. But as soon as we perceived the soft lips pressed hard on the hair at its roots, we would draw her suddenly up, and expose the governor's tool standing up red and smoking after its sweet immersion; then quickly down again; then up, until the pleasing friction set them both wild with excitement.

Mary being so much younger and more vigorous, always felt it more keenly. She used to lean over the side of the basket, and looking down on the ruddy tool standing up beneath her, would complain of its having been too quickly withdrawn from her throbbing cunt, and crying, 'Queenie, let me have the dear thing again, drive it up fast, make it fuck me harder – quicker,' and stretching down her arms, she would pinch her own bottom, and try to catch hold of the slippery tool; and knowing how it gratified him, she would go rattling on: 'Oh, my cunt! Oh, dear prick! Fuck me, governor – fuck my cunt – push up your prick – fuck, fuck, fuck.'

Then the governor, twisting about with pleasurable emotion, would direct Mrs Bond to squat down with her bottom on his face, in order that he might suck her cunt while he fucked her daughter.

Mrs Bond would then place her cunt on his open mouth as soon as she felt his pliant tongue licking up and sucking out the juice exuding from it, she would take the basket in her hands, and so press it down and work it from side to side as to make his prick wriggle about in Mary's belly in the most luxurious and exciting manner, and thus bring on a grand and abundant discharge.

CHAPTER TEN

Davy's Rape

On another day, after we had been reading a stirring account of a successful rape, we all agreed that it must be a most interesting and exciting thing to witness the violent defloration of a young girl with well-developed charms.

'How delightful it would be,' said the governor, 'to watch her struggling in the arms of a big lusty fellow, flinging about her legs and twisting her rump as she felt his great tool bobbing at the mouth of her cunt, and trying to force an entrance; and when at last he succeeded in getting in, and commenced shoving it up, to hear her screech and yell, and give him all manner of abuse, until she felt it all inside, and began to find out that being fucked was not such a terrible thing after all; and then, like most girls, trying to hide her satisfaction under the appearance of only giving way to unavoidable necessity. Oh! it would be grand!' he said, smacking his lecherous lips. 'Could it be arranged, Queenie? With your resources and well-known tact, you might effect it, if anyone could.'

'I will try,' I replied, 'I am very sure that if Davy thought he could gratify me by performing in that manner, he would not hesitate to do all that lay in his power. I will according consult him and let you all know the result.'

When I proposed the matter to Davy, assuring him at the same time that I fully relied on his cleverness and affection, his eyes danced with delight as he answered, 'Ah, Missa Queenie, you allays bery good to Davy, and he lub you very much. It can be done, and it must be done as you wish; let dis chile alone for dat. I know one young missy, dey call her Juliar, who passed by de ground ebery day going to and coming from school. She fine big girl too, and as she walks along, her two fat cheeks behind wag from side to side. I allays look after her and thinks to myself: what grand arse you hab Miss Juliar! if de mouth between your legs stick out in front like de bottom behind, you fine piece for de fuck.'

'Well, Davy, you have a great eye for girls; and when you see their bottom wag that way, does it make your prick get up? come here and let me try what it is like now.'

Davy bounded to where I was sitting on a chair, and standing before me, placed his hands on my shoulders while I opened his pantaloons myself, thrust in my hand and found a fine black tool, nine inches long, standing in proud erection. I drew it out, and pulling down the skin from its dark-coloured head, pressed my lips on its velvet tip. It had more of its peculiar perfume than usual, which in my then excited state, gratified my wanton taste and made my cunt tingle with lecherous emotion.

'Now Davy, tell me truly how you were using this great prick last. Whose cunt were you prodding with it? – I will give it a little suck while you are telling me.'

'Well, missy, Davy will tell you de whole truth: Gobernor send me last evening with bunch of camelias to Miss Mary. Polly open de door and take me into de kitchen. She make me good strong coffee – Oh! it did warm me up and make my prick stand like anything. She soon notice, take him out and pet um wid her lily-white hand. Den she say: "Davy, I hab one great secret; you, good sensible boy; Miss Mary will soon be mistress of Government House. She like you, Davy, and intend to make you head-gardener, and gib you de front lodge."

' "Bery good, but what about Miss Queenie?'

' "Nebba mind her, she go marry Dr Dick; but now, listen to me, Davy, you like to please me, don't you?" – Here, she let me take one kiss – "Well, to get me, you must gib Miss Mary a taste ob this first" – frigging my prick gently up and down – "She tired of nursing and coaxing de Gobernor's old cock, and she dying for one good fuck. She make me promise to put her in de way; and so I tink ob you Davy, dis here big fellow – " drawing back the skin from de bursting head – "is well able to gib her satisfaction and it will be de making ob your fortune, let me tell you."

' "But, Polly, me no lub Miss Mary, no ways; me lub your leetle finger more nor her whole body – Ah! let me," I said, trying to push my hand under her petticoat.

' "Not now, Davy, no matter what part ob me you lub, you can't had it till you please Miss Mary first."

' "Well, let me please her soon, that I way hab you; can I go and please her now?"

' "Don't be such a hurry, Davy; hurry spoils eberyting – Can you stay here tonight?"

' "I can stay until twelve, will dat do?"

' "Yes, dat will do bery well. Now attend; do you see dat ere door? dat de door ob my room. Come in and I will show you where de bed is – here in de left-hand corner. I will be going to bed soon, and I want you to wait outside while I am undressing, and when you see dat de light in de kitchen has been quenched, den open de door softly, cross over to my room, and go up to de bed; and remember, no matter wat you tink, you must make believe dat it is me, and nobody else, and allays say Polly, whenever you speak. Be wise, do your best, and you won't be sorry; now off wid you, and I won't keep you long," and she pushed me out and shut de door.

'I had to wait longer than I liked, but at last de light was quenched, and I went softly to de door. It was on de latch, I opened it and went in. I undressed by de fire, and den went to Polly's door, which was partly open. I passed in, and up to de side ob de bed; I heard somebody breathing, so I said, "Polly my lub, I'm Davy, let me in," and I lifted de bedclothes and slipped in. A pair ob warm arms took hold ob me and pressed me against two delicious bubbies. Den a soft hand found its way to my prick, felt it all over, as if calculating its length and thickness, it den passed on to de balls, moved dem about, and held dem, as if to find out how much dey weighed. Den both hands were at my prick, one holding de root, while de oder passed lightly up and down de shaft.

' "Stop, Polly, my lub, or you'll make me spend. Shall I get on top of you and fuck you?"

' "Not yet," she answered in a low hoarse whisper, "let us have a little play first – bring your prick nearer till I kiss it," I straddled over her breasts, rubbing my balls on her bubbies, as I pushed de head ob my prick towards her mouth. She took it in between her lips, and made her tongue play around it, at de same time clutching my bottom wid her hands until she had me just mad.

' "Oh, Polly! I'm just busting – may I put it in your cunt."

' "Cannot you keep it a little longer – you have not petted my cunt yet."

'I knew what she wanted, so I said: "Let me face about den and I will lean over you and kiss it."

' "Do, Davy, dat will be bery nice."

'I turned around, still straddling over her, and bent down my head towards her cunt, as I did so, she raised her knees and spread her thighs. My mouth den rested on de hottest cunt I ever touched; it seemed burning like one furnace, and de juice dat was bubbling out was as thick as molasses. But de clitoris filled up my mouth, it was stiff too, like a small prick.

'As I sucked she kept hoisting up her cunt and twisting her bottom about, while she grunted: "Good, Davy – you suck my cunt nicely – push in your tongue – squeeze my bottom – that is nice – now turn and give me a good fuck – a good long fuck; I turned about and lay upon her belly. Her two hands held my prick to de mouth ob her cunt. She said: "Push, Davy." I shoved; my prick made one bound and plunged into de tank ob lub. Oh! it war hot like boiling water, and sucked um in like one whirlpool. Her legs crossed on my back, and her hands pressed my shoulders. "Push, Davy, push – farder in – farder still – Oh! now! another big push!" I pull him out until only him nose remain between de lips; den I shove hard. With one spring ob her rump she bounded up to meet me; our two bellies came smack, my balls banged her arse, her whole inside felt alive; hands, feet, mouth, breasts, bottom, cunt, all seemed to catch hold ob me, "Fuck, Davy, fuck," she cried at ebery bound; if she habn't held me so tight wid her legs and arms, she would have pitched me off.

' "Fuck, Davy, fuck; fill my cunt; pinch my arse; fuck, Davy, fuck – den such a flood. I nebba spent like dat afore. I taught my bery soul was leaving me and all going into her cunt. I just rolled ober on one side like one dead, and every little sense I had flew away.

'After a while, I came to myself, somebody was at my prick a-kissing and a-kissing it; some oder body was raising my head and holding a cup to my lips; it had hot coffee like what she gib me before. I felt good when I drank it, my heart warmed and my prick stoop up.

'Dey two laughed. I heard Polly say: "He all right again; get ober him now."

'De one dat held me straddled me, and stuffing my prick into her cunt, sat down upon me.

'I den catch de one dat had de cup, and say: "Dear Polly, let me kiss your pussy-cat." De oder whispered: "Yes, Polly, do." Polly spread her thighs ober my face, and put her lubly cunt to my mouth. Oh, it was nice! Dey ten took hold ab one anoder, while de one below worked up and down, crying: "Fuck, Davy, fuck." Dey now gave up shamming, for Polly said: "Hasn't Davy a fine prick, Miss Mary?"

' "Yes, Davy gib grand fuck; he hab balls like a stallion, rump like a bull and prick like one donkey. You are de only man, Davy, I would trust in dis matter; now promise me faithfully to keep my secret, and mind you don't tell Miss Queenie, above all; and I will take good care of you, and let you fuck me as often as you please."

'I muttered something dat I s'pose she took for a promise, but indeed I promised nutting, and I soon left dem for I was tired out. Now Miss Queenie, I hab told you eberyting, won't you let me gib you one nice fuck before de spunk spurt out. Lean ober de arm ob de sofa and let me see all de booties ob your lubly arse and mossy quim, wid its sweet red chink.'

I placed myself as Davy wished, and greatly enjoyed the feel of his soft paws grasping the cheeks of my bottom and drawing them open as he kissed and sucked the sensitive apertures there. And when he had produced by that most effective means the highest degree of wanton excitement in my cunt, he plunged his great tool into the hot recess, and begged me to tell him how I liked all that he did to me.

'I like to have you look at my bottom, Davy, and press it with your hands. I like to feel the play of your tongue in my bottom-hole, and the feel of your warm breath blowing about the hair of my cunt, as you suck the clitoris; and now I delight to feel your great prick ramming my cunt and your belly smacking my arse; fuck, Davy, fuck, as they said to you; put your arms around my hips – press my cunt with your fingers; Oh! that is nice – fuck, Davy, fuck, fuck.

'Now that you have cooled down, Davy, tell me what you think as to the rape of Miss Julia. You know it must be managed somehow in the open space under the kiosk so that I may see all that you do.'

'Davy think to manage it dis way; wheneber she see me, she allays beg one flower; now I will watch at de gate tomorrow, and when she pass, will invite her into de garden to choose for herself, den I will show her de kiss, bring her underneath, and den we shall soon get a view ab all dat she so carefully hide under her petticoat. So, if you are dere about three o'clock in de afternoon, you and me see some sport.'

'Very well, Davy, I'll be there but I don't wish you to hurt her, you know. I only want to see how you can manage to fuck her against her will, and what she will do in her attempts to keep you off.'

'Nebba fear I'll not hurt her more than I can help, ob dat you may be sure; but you won't mind if she squeaks a little and kicks her legs about.'

'O no, I expect that,' I said laughing.

The governor and the whole party were delighted when I told them of my arrangement with Davy. So the next afternoon, having employed Davy in the farthest part of the ground, I got them all together in the kiosk without his knowledge. Then I called him and said I was ready and would be on the lookout.

With Dick's help, we prepared three good slits in the flooring through which we could see all that passed underneath while we reclined at our ease on the soft rugs and carpets.

While waiting for Davy's appearance we diverted ourselves with a few small exhibitions of our own. The governor, seconded by Dick, requested us three ladies to lie in a row with our bare bottoms turned up for their admiration and inspection; and after we had been handled, viewed and turned about to their satisfaction their two pricks came in for their share of attention; the governor's limp as usual, while Dick's affair, which I now regarded as my peculiar property, was in good working trim. Mrs Bond, following out her plan, devoted herself chiefly to the old governor; but Mary seemed more occupied with watching for Davy and painting in her mind the expected treat of seeing his fine prick engaged in amorous play.

Knowing all I did, I regarded her with much amusement, and being anxious to ascertain the actual state of her feelings, I put my hand on her cunt as she lay at my side. She was pleased at this mark of attention, and opened her thighs to give me more room. I confess that, as a rule, I don't particularly admire a woman's private parts, I suppose, from being so familiar with my own; however, when much excited, I have at times enjoyed petting, and even kissing another woman's cunt. But on this occasion, there was something in the touch of Mary's love chink that made me feel as if I had put my hand on an electric box. It seemed actually throbbing with amorous fire. The lips were exceedingly full, prominent and open; the clitoris protruded boldly out from between them and felt very large, strong and wonderfully hot; it slipped about under my fingers as if endowed with life. I felt irresistibly drawn towards it, and bent down my face. She turned on her back and spread her thighs as I passed between them and stooped to kiss her hot recess. Drawing open the lips I buried my mouth in the moist charm. As soon as she felt my tongue playing the clitoris and penetrating the passage, she muttered: 'Oh, Queenie! you are very good – I cannot tell you how much I am enjoying that. It is better even than a fuck. Oh, – Oh! Queenie, I'm spending – Oh! Oh!!' and a hot gush of the sweetest and most lascivious spunk I ever tasted filled my mouth. I really at first thought she was pissing but the thick unctuous flavour testified as to its true character.

She had scarcely recovered from the languor caused by this emission, when we heard steps approaching the kiosk.

Davy quickly made his appearance below, dragging with him a good-looking creole girl, nearly white, and about fourteen years old. As he drew her in through the door, we heard her say in an angry voice, 'What are you hauling me in here for? Stop, you ugly black nigger, you shan't pull up my clothes – stop – I tell you.' But Davy, holding her firmly with his left arm around her waist, drew up her frock boldly with his right.

'I will, missy, I see your white stockings, and your lubly smooth thighs, and your round fat bottom.'

'Let me go – how dare you expose me so – you nasty wretch, take your hand off me or I'll bite and scratch you. Oh! stop, I tell you, you shan't put your hand there.'

'You may kick and bite and scratch, and do anything else dat you like, but I will put my hand on your bottom in spite of you; aye, and in here too, between your thighs – on your little fat cunt; and I'll push my finger in between these hairy lips – Oh! it is so nice and soft – Oh! isn't dat good.'

'You abominable beast – take your hand out, your finger is hurting me – stop – do you want to kill me?'

'No, missy, I lub you too well to kill you; I only want to feel your cunt, and den put my prick into it and fuck you.'

'But you shan't – I'll die first – Oh! I'll screech, if you attempt to lay me back.'

'Screech away; for back you go.'

'You shan't put in – Oh! you are hurting my hand.'

'Well, take your hand out of the way.'

Davy forced her down on some matting, and having dragged her legs forward, the whole of her body as far as her waist, was now completely uncovered.

She plunged violently, jerking her supple body from side to side, thereby affording us most luscious peeps at the interior charms of her maiden cleft: its pouting lips looked beautifully round and fair and its inner folds were of a glowing red.

Her frantic struggles gradually decreased in violence as he forced himself in between her thighs. His vigorous prick, sticking out before him like a thing instinct with life, poked its glossy head against the lips of her cunt, as if eager to find an entrance. No girl endowed with ordinary feeling can be altogether insensible to such an appeal, although, for appearance sake, she may prolong her resistance; notwithstanding the throbbing she felt in the region of bliss, still she endeavoured, with the one hand not held by Davy, both to cover her cunt and push away his prick. But he soon contrived to seize this hand also, and then her last resource was gone and she seemed to lie at his mercy. Besides, she was getting tired and worn out by her long continued struggles, so with a sorrowful moan she threw her head back, as if resigned to her fate.

Davy did not lose a moment in directing the point of his tool to the critical spot between the lips and with a vigorous plunge drove it in about an inch. The smart occasioned by its entrance recalled Julia to life. She screamed out: 'Oh! oh! Davy, you are murdering me.' Davy heedless of her cries thrust again. She yelled: 'Take your horrid thing out of me – Oh! it cuts like a knife.'

But Davy gripped her more tightly around the loins, and heaving his great muscular arse, with successive prods forced his rampant prick up her maiden sheath.

Then doubling up her legs under his arms, he rested for a moment on her knees, and pressed his balls with all his force on her up-turned bottom, while with a grin of intense satisfaction, he grunted out, 'Now Miss Juliar you hab your belly full up with prick; how you like um? dis leetle cunt stretch bery wide, and dese here bollocks rub sweetly on your lubly bottom. Now for the fuck,' he said, slowly drawing out his prick all red and glowing from her newly opened cunt, and quickly driving it up again, continued: 'Now, Juliar, ain't dat good? fuck, oh! fuck, fuck; fuck' – at each word passing his slippery prick in and out of her cunt.

Somehow, Julia had grown very quiet, and if she moved at all it was only a slight upward heave of her body as she felt the prick rushing through the clinging lips of her cunt. After a few rapid strokes, Davy threw himself forward and, clasping her in his arms, lay motionless on her body. When he had rested thus for a moment, he drew out his now pendant tool and slowly raised himself on his feet.

She never moved, however, but lay back in a kind of faint; observing which, Davy knelt between her thighs and gratified his eyes with a minute inspection of her cunt and bottom.

Then lifting her up in his arms, with her head down, he carried her round and round with her bare legs brandishing in the air.

This was evidently done for my special gratification, and it did afford us a very favourable and a most exciting view of her cunt and all its surroundings, its open mouth, all red and inflamed after the forcible entrance of Davy's prick, being thus displayed to us in the most attractive manner as its ruddy lips were either closed up or drawn asunder by the motion of her legs.

'Let me down, Davy; let me down – there's a good fellow, and I won't scold you any more.'

'Will you be good and obedient?'

'I will.'

'Well, say cunt.'

No answer.

'Say prick.'

No answer.

'Will you let me fuck you again?'

No answer.

So stooping down his head, he first kissed her cunt and then gave her a smart bite on her bottom.

'Oh! stop; I will – there – let me down.'

Davy placed her carefully on the matting, and sitting down by her side, supported her with his arm.

Her whole tone and manner were now quite altered from what they were a short time before, and it occurred to me as I watched them, what an extraordinary change is usually effected in most girls by a reall ygood fuck. Before it they will treat a man's advances with scorn, and even repel him with violence and abuse, but if he only has the resolution to go on, and the power to effect his object – for that is the main point – the most violent opposition will soon cease, and soft compliance takes its place.

So it was with Julia; she now looked the very pictures of meekness, and smiled when Davy told her how much he admired her, and that she had the sweetest and most delicious cunt he had ever fucked.

'But Davy, now that you have done all that you wanted, won't you love me, dear, and never grow tired of me, nor give me up for somebody else.'

'Sweet Juliar, nebba fear, while you are good and do all you are asked to do, Davy will nebba tire ob you, nor gib you up; and now tell Davy, like a good girl, dat you like looking at and petting his prick. Say datmy Juliar.'

'Dear Davy, let me look at and pet your nice prick.'

She took it in her hands, and smiled as it stiffened up while she frigged it up and down.

'Would you like me to kiss your prick, Davy?' she asked, looking most coaxingly at him.

'Yes, dear, dear,' he said, lying back and spreading his legs. Still holding his prick in her hands she rubbed its big head to her nose and lips. Meaning to give her a hint, he said, 'You hab sweet cunt, Juliar, it had bery good taste; when I suck it, did my tongue rubbing in it make it feel nice?'

'Oh, yes, Davy, when you sucked my cunt it was very pleasant, but I did not like you to bite my bottom.'

'I only did dat,' he replied, laughing, 'to make you speak; you can punish me now if you like, by giving my prick a good nip in your mouth.'

'I would be very sorry to hurt it, Davy, but I will take it into my mouth and suck it like a cow's tit.'

She went on her knees and stopped over his prick to suck it, while he uncovered all her white bottom and grasped her cunt with his fingers.

'Davy it makes me feel ashamed to have you looking up that way at my naked bottom.'

'Den you needn't my lub; anybody would like to look at your beautiful round white bottom, and dis fat hairy-lipped cunt underneath, and dis pretty little hole in de middle ob de furrow dat run up between dese smooth cheeks. Throw your leg ober me now and let down your bottom on my face and I'll suck it while you play wid my bollocks and prick.'

While this scene was being enacted below, we all lay on the floor intently peeping down.

The governor and Dick varied their enjoyment by keeping their hands on our cunts; I favoured the latter by similar attention, while the ever watchful widow carefully manipulated the prick of the former, Mary's regards seemed all concentrated on what Davy was doing with the now pacified and compliant Julia.

Turning towards me she whispered, 'Hasn't Davy a fine prick, Queenie? and how well he uses it! That boy is quite a treasure, I wish we had him up here.' Then looking up, she asked, 'Governor, would not you like to see Davy on top of one of us? What fun it would be to have him here with us.'

'It would no doubt be great fun; but I think Davy would run some risk of being spoiled among you all; what do you say, Queenie? we all rely on your judgement and taste.'

'I don't think we would spoil him, if we went the right way about it,' I replied. 'And as Mary seems to have set her heart on having him here' (I gave a malicious wink to the governor), 'if you leave the matter in my hands, I think I shall be able to get up such a lovely performance as will gratify all parties, and prevent our Davy being spoiled.'

It was then agreed that we should all meet in the kiosk at the same hour on the following day.

CHAPTER ELEVEN

Another Turn of Fortune's Wheel

The day fixed for Mary's nuptials was drawing near, her dresses were ready and the wedding-cake ordered. Mrs Bond, inflated with a sense of her own importance, fussed about everything, while her eye beamed with delight as she anticipated the approaching triumph of her schemes. But a sudden turn of fortune's wheel dashed the cup of joy from her eager hands even as she raised it to her lips, and overwhelmed her with disappointment and regret.

The very night after our meeting in the kiosk mentioned in the last chapter, the old governor was seized with a fit when undressing for bed; he lingered for a few hours and then unconsciously passed away.

This sad event of course upset all our plans, and destroyed the fine prospects of Mary and her mother.

I did not very much sympathise with them in their trouble, for they had shown utter disregard for the feelings of others.

But for the poor old governor I felt real sorrow, and readily assumed the deep mourning that was becoming in his adopted child.

As soon as we decently could, Dick, and I were privately married. He was by this time established in a very good practice, and was able to take a pleasant residence furnished with every comfort and convenience.

We found our previous arrangement worked admirably; and as we were both resolute in expelling the demon jealously from our doors, all went on smoothly. Dick, of course, slept with me and fucked me to his heart's content; and when he desired a little change – and where is the man that does not – he frankly told me, and I never objected; not only that, I even provided him with the means of enjoying it, and he reciprocated by doing the same kind turn for me.

What was the result? He loved and admired me all the more, and ever returned to my arms with renewed zest and intensified enjoyment. We were really happy, for we had no secret from one another, no suspicious feelings, no heart burnings, we mutually shared each other's joys and contributed to each other's pleasure. My intercourse with Mrs

Bond and Mary gradually lessened, but my affection for Jemima increased, and she passed much of her time with me. On the evening of her first visit to us after our marriage, when the servants had ceased their attendance and we could bolt the doors and feel ourselves free from prying eyes or interruption, we commenced our love sports.

Dick smiled knowingly at Jim as he passed his hand under my petticoats, and I at once responded by unbuttoning his trousers and drawing out his rosy-headed tool, saying at the same time to her: 'You see, darling Jim we make no stranger of you – you have seen this dear fellow before, and felt it too in your sweet little cunt; now, I want to place it there again myself, and to watch it fucking you. Come here, my pet – sit beside me, lean back; what a delightful little cockle-shell you have! stay I must kiss it first.'

Jim spread her legs and pushed up her pretty round bottom as I knelt on the floor and with my fingers separated the hairy lips of her cunt; then I applied my mouth and tongue with thrilling effect to the dear little orifice of love.

Oh! how she panted and twisted about her rump! and how she grunted with satisfaction as she pushed her cunt against my mouth.

'Queenie, you are a darling,' cried Dick, 'and I love you more and more every day.'

Then, coming behind me, he threw up my dress and pressing the cheeks of my bottom, asked: 'What is she doing to you Jim that makes you wriggle your arse in that fashion?'

'Oh, Dick, your wife is sucking my cunt! she is frigging it delightfully with her tongue; she is making me mad for a fuck.'

'And you shall have it too, my sweet Jim, the next turn; for the present, I am deep in the folds of her own randy cunt.'

'Oh, yes, I feel every push you give her. Fuck her well – ram home your prick – press against her arse. Oh! that was a grant stroke! you must let me get behind you someday and watch you fucking; and I will hold your prick and poke it into her cunt and stir your balls, and pinch your arse, and frig your arsehole with my finger – I know, you like me to call bottom, arse, and to talk of your arsehole, and to speak of pissing and fucking, and all that.'

This kind of wanton talk, as usual, stirred up my naturally hot and lascivious temperament. I rolled her soft, thick, luscious clitoris in my mouth, while I relished with intense delight the long, steady strokes of Dick's vigorous prick in my throbbing, palpitating cunt. It felt so different from the feeble, flabby affair to which I had lately been accustomed. Indeed, I often found it hard to tell whether a prick was in my cunt at all or not. But Dick's fine manly tool made its presence felt and no mistake. Its big sturdy head pressed hard on the mouth of my womb seven or eight inches up from the outer lips while the projecting ridge of the glans rubbed with firm delicious friction against the sensitive creases of my vagina. And just a Jim's warm essence filled my mouth, Dick's spouting sperm met my own dissolving flow and we all sank together in that enjoyable languor which usually follows fully gratified desire.

After resting a while, Jim and I commenced playing with his prick and balls, while he tickled our cunts and bottoms. When we got his prick into fair working order again and Jim had given it a good suck, she looked up and said, 'Now, Queenie, I want to place this in your cunt myself, and see it fucking you; so pull up your clothes as high as you can, lean back, spread your thighs and lift yourself while I put this pillow under your bottom; that's the way – look Dick, how your wife's cunt opens its mouth for your prick! see how red it is inside; and look at this big fat clitoris! how it pokes out its rosy head! I am going to suck it first, before I put in your prick, and you can either watch me or play with my bottom, as you please.'

The next moment, I felt her warm mouth buried in my cunt, my whole clitoris drawn within her sucking lips and her tongue pushing here and there, poking into every crevice. Not content with that, the little wanton, having moistened her finger in my cunt, thrust it up my bottom, and in the most lubricious manner stirred it round and round inside, saying as she did so, 'I am frigging your arse, Queenie; do you feel my finger in your arse! And, oh! Dick has his finger in mine – but, Dick, you must not fuck me this time – come here, kneel on this cushion. Oh, but your prick is fine and strong; wait now – let me first rub its head up and down in this nice soft furrow – now, that's the spot – push – how it rushes in! now pull it out. Oh, how wet it is! and so red and hot! and how nice it smells!' And she licked it with her tongue: 'Now drive it up again – how your balls bang her arse! Now, another stroke, how she heaves up to meet you! Oh, what a smack that was! What a grand thing fucking is! Fuck – fuck – fuck! There, now do you feel me! I have got a finger in each of your arses! Fuck – cunt – prick – bollocks – arse – pissing – fuck – fuck – fuck.'

When Dick, urged to wild delirium by her wanton cries, made his final thrust, she threw herself on his back and rubbed her excited cunt as hard as she could against the quivering cheeks of his bottom.

Here, I must retrace the steps of my story for a little space. A short time before my marriage with Dick, I attained the legal age of twenty-one; and was then able to carry out my father's intention of conferring the gift of freedom on the faithful and devoted Zilla. She asked me at the same time to sanction with my presence her marriage with Davy who, on the break up of the governor's establishment, had set up for himself as market gardener, with a snug little cottage of his own.

I readily complied, and gave her a liberal present as a wedding gift. They were both very grateful, and begged me to favour them by assisting at the consummation also. They evidently meant this as a compliment and also as a proof of the continuance of their confidence and affection.

So after the ceremony was duly performed, I returned to the cottage, and went with them into their bedroom, where they both at once began to strip off their light clothing, and were soon in a fit condition for the work they intended. Without more ado, Zilla threw herself on the bed on her back, and spreading her thighs, she asked me to hold Davy's prick and put it into her cunt myself. Davy grinned with delight as he looked down on the rosy chink of his wife's quim as it lay so invitingly open before him and at the same time felt my hands, as in days of yore, fondling his prick and skinning its swollen head.

As I drew him up to her, she raised her body so as to display the whole of her lascivious bottom in all its attractive proportions.

Davy ran his hands over the voluptuous cheeks, and then pinched her excited clitoris, as I placed the head of his prick at the entrance of her longing cunt.

'Now take your time,' I said, 'and you will enjoy it all the more.' But they were too excited to heed me; for just as Davy pushed, she heaved, and the whole prick disappeared in a moment amid the hot folds that closed around it with such eagerness and delight. I kept one hand on her mount that I might press her clitoris between my fingers and, passing my other hand around his bottom, I squeezed his balls from behind while I watched with great interest their pushing thighs and amorous grunts which indicated the excess of mutual enjoyment to which the deepest instinct of their natures had brought them. They then commenced a second course.

Afterwards, while resting in each other's arms, Davy's scarcely diminished prick soaking in Zilla's snug recess, they looked up at me, and with a happy contented smile, Zilla said, 'Davy is a good boy, I am very fond of him; but, Missa Queenie, if you have at any time a fancy for him, and he himself be willing, as I am sure he always will be, you are heartily welcome to the services of the best of all tools; for though I might be jealous with respect to others, I never will regarding you.'

'Very well, Zilla,' I replied laughing, 'perhaps someday I may put your good nature to the test in that way; but what do you say yourself,

Davy? you surely won't desire any change when you are so well supplied in your good wife.'

'Ah! Miss Queenie, nobody is always pleasant; she bery wise for she know well dat when she let me go to you I come back to her wid new delight, and lub her all de more.'

I admired their simple philosophy and felt it was the result of some deliberation, and therefore followed with more satisfaction; and I left them to themselves.

Now to return to our visitors, whom we left so unceremoniously.

Jim had decidedly Sapphic tastes, and declared that while she enjoyed amazingly the prods of a sturdy prick in her cunt, yet her pleasure seemed increased tenfold when she could at the same time pet and suck the cunt of another woman in as randy a state as herself. So to gratify her, I used to lie on my back across the bed with my head resting on the edge; then she would bend over me with her belly resting on my breasts and her open cunt right over my face. Then she would encircle my thighs with her arms, and holding open the lips of my cunt with her hands, would suck the clitoris while she frigged the passage with her fingers.

Meantime I would call my husband: 'Come Dick, you have here, what I know you delight in, a woman's arse in all its naked beauty turned up for your admiration. Look at these great round cheeks, how soft and smooth they are! look at this lovely valley between them, and here in the middle of it, the dainty little bottom-hole, which you say holds a prick tighter than any cunt. Ah! but I am sure the cunt is nicer and sweeter far! Does not this rosy chink look especially inviting? Why, it seems almost to beg for a fuck! See these fat lips, how they pout at the thought of your neglecting them! and this rosebud clitoris, how innocent it looks as with tiny head up-reared it demands attention!'

'Queenie, you are right,' replied my husband, with his usual good sense, 'it is no doubt the natural place, and what is natural is always the most satisfactory; besides when you're after it, my pet, no one would be so churlish as to refuse.'

Then taking his prick in my hands I popped its head into the moist chink where Jim was expecting it. How fondly the firm lips closed around it as he slowly drove it up! up! until the hair at its root pressed strongly against them, and his balls plumped on my face. I felt him give a thrill of pleasure when the whole prick was embedded in Jim's belly and its head poked against her womb.

His tool looked grander than ever when he drew it out, all red and smoking with heat and moisture, while the smell from it was delicious.

Pushing up my mouth, and thrusting out my tongue, I could touch at the same time the soft lips of her cunt and the under side of his slippery prick, while her mount rubbed my chin as she twisted herself about.

All this time she was sucking my clitoris with fury, and frigging with her fingers both my cunt and bottom.

I repaid her by energetic manipulation of her own cunt and bottom until she cried: 'Oh, Queenie, that is delicious! Oh, my cunt! Oh, my bottom! Fuck – fuck – fuck.'

Jim had never seen a black prick, and when I described Zilla's wedding as mentioned above, and expatiated on the wonderful power and efficiency of Davy's black tool she was intensely interested and said how highly she would be gratified if I could manage to prevail on Davy and his wife to share our sports and exhibit their sable charms for our joint entertainment. I promised to pay them an early visit, and sound out their inclinations in the matter.

Davy and Zilla seemed quite flattered at the proposal, and readily entered into my plans. Between us we arranged a little scene in which Davy, or rather Davy's prick, should be the principal performer.

On the night appointed they came at a late hour, as we did not wish our servants to know what was going on.

Davy first appeared upon the stage (that is, my boudoir), while Zilla, Dick and I, the spectators, in a nude condition, looked on through the open door of the room adjoining.

He pulled off his pantaloons, raised his shirt, took his prick in his hand and, slowly frigging it, thus soliloquised: 'So Missa Jim, she want to see a black prick, and take him in her lily hand, and press him to her rosy lips; and then, I guess, she will gib him one little suck, and when she taste him in de mouth above, I tink she will wish to hab him in de mouth below.'

While speaking, Davy kept looking at his prick and drawing the loose skin up and down until he had it standing up in the stiffest erection. Then he walked back and forth, jerking his bottom at each turn, and causing his prick to shoot out its ebony head through his encircling fingers.

'Now, my boy, you be in fine condition for Missa Jim.'

But I wonder what is keeping her so long! praps a-rubbing ob her fair skin after de wash! praps a-combing out de chestnut hairs ob her cunt! or praps she doing a leetle drop ob piss! Ah! Davy would like to see dat nice warm yalla piss a shooting out from de rosy chink ob her lubly cunt. I would like to put my face close up and let her piss away; den I would kiss and suck de wet cunt. And den, when she see de big black prick stick out, praps she say: "Now Davy, as I let you see me piss, and kiss my cunt, you may finish by putting in your prick and fucking – fucking it." But ah! I's tired waiting, and feel sleepy too, so I lie down on dis sofa, and go sleep on my back with my prick bare, so dat if Missa Jim pass dis way she can hab one good look and feel and anything else dat she like.'

Davy lay back, his firm prick still standing up, and putting his arms across his face began to snore.

Jim now entered the boudoir quickly, and rubbing her naked limbs with a towel, as if coming from her bath, said, 'Oh, my! what's that black thing on Queenie's sofa? I do declare, it is a black man fast asleep; and see, his great black tool is standing up all uncovered! What an opportunity for investigating the secrets of a black prick!'

She went close up to the sofa and put her hand gently on the noble limb.

'How fast asleep he seems to be! I fancy, he must have taken too much drink – anyway he has a splendid prick, what length and firmness! and such thickness too!'

She softly encircled it with both her hands, and drew down the yielding skin, as she continued: 'And what a noble head it has! It makes all my cunt tingle merely to look and touch it. I wonder would it awaken him if I kissed it!' She pressed her lips on its pulpy head; her pliant tongue softly playing around it, as her open mouth gradually sucked it in. 'Ah? how soft and nice it feels in my mouth! and this tuft of black woolly hair at its root, how thick and springy! but oh! what cods, he has! so large and firmly gathered up! What a tremendous lot of spunk he would pour into one! – but stay he moves –'

'Oh, ah,' muttered Davy, as if speaking in a dream, 'I must am gone to heaben afore de time; and dis am lubly Wenus a-come to make me happy. She like black prick too, she know how to pet um and suck um. Get across me, Missis Venus – put de black prick into your rosy slit – ha! you understand, I see; de heavenly goddesses no dispised black nigger; dey knows him for a man and a broder. Oh! Ah! how tight. How warm! how hot! Oh, ah! press hard, harder, quicker, squeeze um, hold um,' cried Davy, in his loudest tones, while Jim, with glowing cheeks and flashing eyes, bounded up and down making the prick rush in and out of her well-moistened cunt, with a sucking squash at every plunge, until at last she threw herself forward and clasped him in her arms.

Meantime, we spectators had not been idle; I induced Zilla to lean over a table while she watched the performance of her husband. Then I uncovered the glossy cheeks of her large and beautifully rounded bottom and called Dick's attention to it as I pushed her legs apart and drew open the lips of her cunt so as to show the deep red of its voluptuous interior. Dick came close behind the black bottom, and putting his prick into my hands, said, 'Well, Queenie, I must say you and Zilla are paragon wives. What a different world it would be if all wives had your sense and spirit!'

I liked being commended by my husband, and I knew he was right; for jealousy is a sore evil, it benefits no one, and makes multitudes miserable. I suffered no loss, when I took my husband's prick, which he had promised to use for my special benefit, and with my own hand placed it in the cunt of another man's wife. In fact, I gained instead of losing, for I attached my husband more firmly to myself and took pleasure in witnessing their enjoyment.

As soon as I felt my husband's prick driven up to the roots in Zilla's cunt I went behind and, pressing his bottom with my naked belly, began to push. The table I had provided moved freely on castors, and we three gilded into the room just as Davy, recovered from the effects of his first emission, was standing up, holding Jim in his arms, with his prick still buried in her cunt while she clasped him round the neck and loins with her arms and legs.

They gave a shout of amused delight when they saw us moving up to them as if we three, like themselves, were amalgamated into one body, nobody propelled in successive jerks by the energetic shoves delivered on Zilla's arse by my husband and myself.

Davy lost no time in laying his sweet burden down on the table by the side of his wife, but with her head in the opposite direction. Zilla put her hand approvingly on them, and feeling the root of her husband's prick tightly embraced by the lips of Jim's well-satisfied cunt, said: 'Well, Missa Jim, how do you like my husband's black tool?'

'Oh, Zilla, it is grand. You are very good to lend him to me. I hope you are enjoying Mr Dick's prick yourself, and our dear Queenie is no doubt adding to your pleasure. I wish very much that she had somebody too.'

'Oh! she is very well off!' I said. She loves watching and feeling all your cunts, bottoms and pricks.'

But our sports were brought to an abrupt termination, for just then the night bell sounded with a sudden sharp ring and Dick had nothing for it but hastily to assume some integument, and answer the door himself.

He found several men carrying on a stretcher a body which proved to be that of a Lord Ferrars, a young Englishmen who had visited the islands in his yacht, and when returning on board that night had fallen off the pier, hurt his head and been nearly drowned; and his men thought the best thing they could do was to carry him at once to the house of the nearest doctor.

Dick had met this Lord Ferrars before, and rather liked him.

So when he had examined him, bound up his head and found nothing else much amiss with him, he dismissed his attendants and delivered him into my care.

We placed him in bed in the best spare room, gave him a composing draught and made him all snug for the night. Next morning he was much better, and able to get up after breakfast. He was very grateful for my husband's attention, seemed to like amazingly his present quarters, and gladly consented to remain with us until quite convalescent.

He proved to be a choice specimen of a young English nobleman, most accomplished and agreeable; and, making himself thoroughly at home, he entered readily into all our amusements and pursuits.

From the first, he paid me the most marked attention, which Dick observing, he said to me: 'Why, old lass, you have gained another admirer, and if you care to have him, I don't object – for Ferrars is a right good fellow, albeit rather fond of the ladies.'

This kind treatment of my husband made all pleasant, but events arose out of it which neither of us calculated on and which changed the whole tenor of my afterlife.

Part Three

MY LIFE OF FREE ENJOYMENT
AND ECSTATIC LOVE

CHAPTER ONE

Lord Ferrars

The assiduous attention which my husband paid to his professional duties kept him much from home, and therefore the entertainment of Lord Ferrars chiefly devolved on me. Jim had returned to her mother for a time, and his lordship and I were thus left very much to ourselves. He did not seem to regret this much, for he evidently spared himself no pains to make his company agreeable and his person acceptable to me. He even neglected his yacht that he might more entirely devote himself to the enjoyment of my society.

My husband watched the progress of events with increasing interest. The idea of jealousy never entered his mind, nor had I the slightest thought of concealing anything from him. In fact, he often asked me at night, when fondly playing with my cunt or when lying on my breast after one of his delightful fucks, whether his lordship had yet made any advance or attempted any freedom? From some time, I had to say: 'No, with the exception of holding my hand and pressing it whenever he can.'

'Ah, he is only waiting for a good opportunity,' he would reply, 'or perhaps, he is wishing to ingratiate himself more in your goodwill, and thus render his conquest more secure; I expect you will soon have something funny to tell me, and what a grand fuck we shall then have together when he has oiled the way and you are telling me all the details.'

Accordingly I never declined to walk with Lord Ferrars alone, but on the contrary offered him every facility. Still, from some unaccountable reason, he held back. Perhaps, it was my apparent, innocence and confiding simplicity that retrained him; or rather it might have been owing to that peculiar quality in our nature which prevents our grasping at once any object of desire that appears easy of attainment, whereas opposition or difficulties in the way only serve to arouse our energies and excite our ardour to obtain speedy possession.

However, one day he asked me to join him in exploring the rocky summit of a neighbouring height. We drove as far as we could by road, and then proceeded on foot to climb the steep ascent. Of course, in the more difficult places, his lordship had to show his gallantry by affording me his ready help. And he often found it necessary to put his arm round my waist; and once, when pushing me up a steep rock, he found it needful to place his hands on my bottom. He kept them there as long as he could, and even managed to press his fingers into the furrow between my well-rounded buttocks. And I have no doubt he easily distinguished through my light dress the swelling fullness of the lips which pouted in the luxurious hollows.

I voluntarily delayed my ascent, and separated my thighs that we might both get the full benefit of his electrifying touch.

When we sat down afterwards to rest on a grassy slope in a sheltered nook, he reclined at my feet; and putting his hand on my ankle, he praised my agility and said he could not help observing what a remarkably fine instep I had. I only laughed, and stretching out my foot said I saw nothing remarkable about it. He moved his hand a little higher up, and said, with a most insinuating smile, 'I am discovering fresh beauties! What a splendid calf you have, Mrs Harpur! you ought to be a first-rate dancer, and I am sure you enjoy it very much.'

'Yes, I am very fond of dancing, especially when I have an agreeable partner.'

'How I would enjoy being that partner, for I love to have my hand on you – you are so exquisitely formed; this leg is the very perfection of beauty – it might serve as a sculptor's model.'

While saying this, his hand was playing about my knee; at last he touched my thigh above the stocking.

'Stay, my lord, are you not making a little too free?'

His hand kept pushing on and it fell hot and tremulous.

'Oh, stop – you are waxing too warm – I do like you very much, but you know, my lord, I cannot permit such a liberty as that,' and I tried to get up. He placed his right arm round my waist, and in a moment his left hand was on my cunt. It thrilled at his touch, yet to maintain appearance I said, 'My lord, take your hand away, you forget that I belong to another.'

'I don't forget it, sweet Queenie, but after the wealth of love you lavish on my friend Dick, he surely will not miss a small favour bestowed on me. Besides you are just made for love – no one can come near you without getting under its influence – extend a little of your wonted kindness to me, if only for a moment – open your lovely thighs, my sweet pet – there – I knew you would be too good to refuse. How deliciously you are made! What a delightful softness! What a ravishing warmth! Lean back a little – so.'

'Oh! my lord, you frighten me – I have yielded too much – it may be very pleasant to you, but it will be ruination to me.'

'No, darling Queenie, you shall never regret your kindness to me. I will be minister to your pleasure, and at the same time will be so careful of your good name that no one shall ever suspect that anything has occurred between us.'

'Oh! how lovely you are! What a heavenly cunt! I have looked at and handled many a cunt in my day, but I never saw one as attractive as yours, Queenie; its full pouting lips push out in such an inviting manner that they seem to beg for something soft and nice to put between them. Now, I have just what they want – see here – let me introduce this poor fellow to your kind notice – put your hand upon him, Queenie, there, how proud he looks now – see how he thrusts up his rosy head between your white fingers – now place him yourself in your sweet cunt – there – ah my love, he seems to know the way; how sweetly he passes in! Oh! Queenie, how hot your cunt feels! Tell me, does it enjoy my prick? Tell me if you like to feel it fucking you.'

'Oh! yes, I like it now – your prick does its duty well; I like to feel it fucking my cunt; do I move up to your satisfaction?'

'You do, my sweet little wagtail – you move your bottom in the most charming manner; go on talking – I love to hear you speak of your cunt and bottom, and of my prick, and to talk of fucking; but please drop the lord and call me Freddy.'

'Then push, Freddy, push home your prick – fuck my cunt, squeeze my bottom,' I replied, shoving up my cunt to meet every thrust of his prick.

He evidently had great experience in fucking. I never knew anyone fuck with such scientific deliberation. He made every stroke tell to the uttermost. He would slowly draw out his prick until the tip of the glans only rested between the lips, and then with equal deliberation drive it slowly back, making its ridge press firmly against the upper creases of my vagina as it passed into my cunt. Then when the whole length was enclosed, and my belly seemed full of it, he would gently work it about from side to side causing the big round head to rub deliciously on the sensitive mouth of my womb. In my ecstasy, I cried, 'Oh, Freddy, my darling, that is nice! Fuck me, my love, fuck me – push in your prick as far as you can into my cunt – press your hands on my bottom – Oh! how nice! Fuck; fuck.'

Painting with effort and emotion, he grunted, 'Now, Queenie, now – hold me in your arms put both hands on my bottom – squeeze the cheeks of my arse! Oh, my love, say with me: prick; cunt; arse; pissing; fucking; prick; cunt; arse: fuck; fuck.'

We both groaned with excess of pleasure, and my cunt tingled round his palpitating tool as the life flood darted from the opposite sources of delight in reciprocating streams of unctuous spunk.

He lay back to recover breath and rest himself after his exertion; but when he saw me wiping my wet receiver with my handkerchief, he asked me to perform the same kind office for him. I willingly complied, and kneeling at his side took his soft and moistened prick into my hands and tenderly wiped it all round; then stooping forward I pressed my lips on its flowing tip.

This position elevated my posteriors, and he proceeded at once to avail himself of it. Throwing my dress over my back, he moved me towards him until my naked bum was almost opposite his face. Then, spreading my thighs, he opened the lips of my quim with his fingers, played about the clitoris, and having moistened his finger in my cunt, pushed it into my bottom-hole. I rather enjoyed this display of my posterior charms. Few women object to showing their bottom to men whom they like as they always calculate on the exciting effect of the inspection of this interesting feature. They know well that the bottom-hole is situated so close to the opening of the cunt that it is scarcely possible to look at one without seeing the other, but they consider that the fact of their being placed side by side in the region consecrated to voluptuous enjoyment is a clear intimation that nature intended them to share in those attentions which usually precede and lead up to the grand consummation itself.

So while I fondled his prick and moulded his balls, he played with the crannies and fissures of my bottom.

Then getting me to straddle directly over him, he made me stoop until my cunt rested on his mouth. All the lustful feelings of my nature now became strongly excited as I felt his warm breath blowing aside the hairs of my cunt, and his pliant tongue winding round my clitoris, playing between my nymphae and exploring the secret passage inside. But when he went on to the nether entrance, and I felt the titillation of his tongue amid its sensitive creases, the sluices of pleasure burst open and I became conscious of that melting sensation which we women call spending but which is very different from the spouting flood which issues from the male organ.

'Oh, Freddy!' I cried, twisting my rump, and expanding the wrinkles on my bottom-hole to let his tongue further in, 'that is delightful! Oh! I'm coming! Freddy! I'm coming!' Taking the head and shoulders of his prick into my mouth, I sucked with all my force, twining my tongue around its indented neck and all the while, moulding his balls with one hand and frigging his arsehole with the other. The usual effect quickly followed. He began to heave his loins up and down, driving his prick in and out of my mouth as if he were fucking it. His prick grew larger, stronger, and hotter; and just as I felt his open mouth in my cunt sipping up the pleasure drops that trickled down its excited folds, a torrent of hot spunk, luscious and sweet, burst into my mouth and flowed down my throat.

I sank down upon his body, and still pressing my tingling cunt on his hairy chin, muttered: 'Oh! my Freddy, that was delightful! how my bottom and cunt thrilled while you sucked them! But what a torrent of hot spunk your prick shot into my mouth! What great bollocks you have, Freddy! And how hard they grew when your prick swelled up in my mouth and tried to force itself down my throat.'

The ice was now thoroughly broken; and what between my husband at night and Lord Ferrars by day, I had as much fucking as any woman could possibly desire.

Dick seemed to love me better than ever; and no loving couple on their honeymoon ever enjoyed each other more fully than we did. Like the old governor, he seemed to have a special fancy for having me immediately after being fucked by another.

He said my cunt then felt hotter, and my whole body more springy; that I sucked on his prick with more gusto, and fucked with more animation than at other times.

Indeed I was conscious of it myself, for the feel of a different prick in my cunt just after being fucked by another was to me specially enjoyable, and I could not help showing my pleasure by increased activity in heaving up my rump, pressing and hugging with my hands and arms, and using with more unction and freedom those amorous expressions and bawdy terms which I knew from long experience were the surest provocatives of sexual delight.

My husband would sometimes send me into Lord Ferrars in the early morning before any one was stirring, with express injunctions to hurry back to him as soon as his lordship had discharged in my cunt; and so entirely did he rise above the usual popular prejudice in these matters, that if the morning was dark he would even follow me to the door, and stand there wrapped in his dressing gown to enjoy hearing his wife fucked by another man. On such occasions, I would leave the door open and contrive to make my lord talk of everything so that Dick might know all that was going on and follow each step of the pleasurable race. But on one of these occasions an event happened which we did not expect.

On coming to the bedside, I slipped my hand under the clothes and felt about for his lordship's prick, saying: 'Are you awake, Freddy? where is your prick? I can only find your bollocks.

'Here it is, my pet, I have it tucked up in my shirt to keep it safe for you.' And throwing down the bedclothes, he added, 'Get up – lie on your back, and turn up your sweet little arse; that's the way I like best to fuck you – my prick gets further into your cunt, and my bollocks press more luxuriously on your arsehole.'

Then, getting between my thighs, with my doubled-up knees under his arms, he pressed the length of his prick along the slit of my cunt, telling me to put down my hand and pet it for a moment before he popped it in. So taking it in my hand I rubbed it between the lips and over the clitoris, as I said, 'How strong and big your prick feels tonight, Freddy; I am sure you were just longing for a fuck! and very likely dreaming about it when I came to you, were you not?'

'Well, I was, and a queer dream I had.'

'Tell it to me, dear, I love queer dreams.'

'I dreamt, Queenie, that your husband was lying in bed on his back, that you were straddling over him with your bottom towards his face and his prick was in your cunt; that I happened to come in, and you both called me to watch you fucking; that I went up, and you at once caught hold of my prick and put it in your mouth; and that as you rose up and down over him causing his prick to slip in and out of your cunt, you moved your head over mine, making it pass in and out through your lips. But the funniest part was that my prick seemed to grow longer and longer as you sucked it, and passed down your throat into your belly, where it still went on extending, and at last made its way out through your cunt; that then your husband began to laugh, and exclaimed: "I say Ferrars, you have spitted my wife, but you must lose your penis, for I shall have to amputate it to save her life." "No, you shall not," I replied and putting down my hands, I grasped my prick, and was holding it tightly when you came in.'

'That was a funny dream; but I don't think you will ever lose your prick in that way, for even if Dick did find it in my cunt, I am sure he would not be so barbarous as to cut it off. That would be a terrible loss to you;whatever would you do without a prick to fuck with? – I don't think you would live long.' And putting down my hand, I grasped the root of his prick as its well-moistened head worked up and down in my cunt.

'Do you like that?' I asked, turning up my rump until my body was curved like a bow.

'I do, sweet pet,' he said, giving me a prod that made me feel his prick at my backbone, 'and how do you like that?'

'It is exquisite,' I replied wriggling my bottom and squeezing him in my arms.

'Oh, my love, your cunt is perfection – it takes in my prick with such satisfaction and holds it with such tenacious eagerness that it doubles the pleasure of fucking. How I envy Dick having such a cunt always at his command.'

'Well, I am sure you get enough of it; if you had more you would soon grow tired of it.'

'Never, my pet. I could not have too much of it,' he said, moving slowly, and evidently holding himself in check, to prolong his enjoyment; 'but what would my friend Dick say if he knew I was so favoured by his beautiful wife – I suppose he would soon turn me out of doors.'

'I am not so sure of that, Freddy; for, in the first place, he likes you very much; secondly, he has not a spark of jealousy – he has too much good sense for that; and thirdly, he likes me to be happy and enjoy myself, even as I am doing now – Oh! Freddy – now pour it into me – fill my belly with spunk – push against my bottom – fuck – prick – cunt – fuck – fuck – fuck; now let me go – I have already stayed too long and you have had enough for one time – it you want more, come into my bathroom when I am up – so, here's a kiss, and goodbye.'

Dick took me in his arms at the door, and fairly lifted me up, as he hurried me off to bed; one of his hands all the while rummaging my cunt and bottom.

'You did that famously, Queenie,' he said, as he laid me on the bed; 'I listened to every word, and heard every stir – I could even hear the gurgling sound made by your cunt as his prick pushed in and out, and the creak of the bed every time you heaved up your bottom. Ferrars fucks judiciously; he always spares his powder, and rams home his cartridge with great deliberation. I declare, I felt strongly tempted to steal in and place my hand under your bottom and feel your cunt while he was fucking it. Would you have been vexed if I had?'

'Not in the least, dear! Lord Ferrars is a perfect gentleman and a kind true-hearted man and he loves fucking – well, as much as you do yourself. No, I would not object at all, now that your prick is poking my cunt, so delightfully, to having his lordship down there below us and feeling his hands playing about my cunt and bottom; I think I should enjoy your fucking all the more . . . 'Is that you, Dick, tickling my bottom and pinching my cunt? Oh, but there is someone there – go on – it is delicious.'

'Hallo, Ferrars! is that where you are? Hold on, my boy, you shall have her when I am done.'

'Thanks, Dick; I heard you at my door and followed you here; you are a noble-minded fellow, and have the most lovable wife that ever man was blessed with, and you are worthy of her.'

From that time, I often got a rare pounding between the two, and was seldom fucked by one without having the prick of the other in my hand, my mouth, or somewhere else.

CHAPTER TWO

The Middy

Knowing the dangers attending satiety, I invited Jim to come to us again, both for her own gratification, and as a diversion for Lord Ferrars and my husband. But before her arrival, a strange denouement occurred which I will now proceed to relate.

Lord Ferrars was visited almost every day by a very handsome boy, dressed in naval uniform, whom he called his middy. He had beautiful violet eyes, and a profusion of flaxen curls. He generally came in the morning and remained some hours in Lord Ferrars' room, writing his letters and making up his accounts – as he told me. I took a fancy to the boy and often tried to get him to talk with me, but he seemed very shy, and evidently avoided meeting me as much as he could.

Lord Ferrars always spoke most kindly to him, and in every way treated him with marked consideration.

When I questioned him concerning this youth, he told me he had picked him up at an English seaport, and as he could keep accounts, understood the management of a yacht and had a decided taste for the sea, he retained him in his service as an attendant companion.

This explanation did not quite satisfy me, and my curiosity becoming more aroused, I set myself to probe the matter, and find out the true nature of the connection.

Besides, I was piqued at the youth's indifference to myself; it was a new sensation to me to meet one of the other sex who appeared totally unaffected by my charms; and what increased the mystery was that in spite of my admiration of his good looks, there seemed some subtle influence pervading him that repelled us mutually, just as if we were two similar poles of a magnet; and the cause, I determined to find out.

So one day, getting my husband to take Lord Ferrars out of the way about the time when the middy usually called, I opened the door for him myself, brought him into my boudoir and closed and fastened the door.

He seemed surprised, and sat down with great reluctance on the seat I offered him, looking around as if prepared to bolt at the first opportunity.

In order to set him more at his ease, I sat down beside him, and looking kindly at him, said, 'My young friend, I am so pleased with your constant attention to Lord Ferrars that I wish to know something more about yourself. First tell me how old you are, then your name and how you came to meet his lordship.'

'I am seventeen years old, my name is Francis Gripton. My mother kept a lodging house in Southampton, and Lord Ferrars used to stop with her when he remained on shore. He often took me out in his yacht, and finding me useful, he asked me to enter his service.'

'You seem greatly attached to Lord Ferrars.'

His eyes flashed as he quickly replied, 'Why should I not be? He is very good to me, and to my mother also He his constantly sending her presents.'

'I like you all the better for it; we are all fond of him here.'

A look of scorn passed over his beautiful features as he said, 'Yes, but you are a married lady, and have not any right to be thinking of Lord Ferrars; you ought to be fond only of your own husband.'

I was both surprised and amused at the earnestness of the boy, and I thought, more than ever, that there was something underlying this and I must discover what it was. So I said in my kindest manner, 'Why, Francis, you need not be angry; at all events, if you are so much attached to Lord Ferrars, you ought to be pleased at our being fond of him; and we would like to be fond of you too' – and I put my hand on his shoulder.

He drew back with a frightened air, 'Oh, please, don't trouble your head about me; I am not worth thinking about.'

'But you are, Francis, and I like your very much,' and I tried to draw him towards me.

'Please let me go, Mrs Harpur; you remind me of Potiphar's wife,' and he smiled in a curious way. 'I am not, however, going to fly from you like Joseph, but I really have duties which I must attend to.'

He arose as if to go, but I held his arm with my right hand, and passing my left down his front before he suspected my object, I pressed it in between his thighs; as I expected, there was no appearance of what

Shakespeare calls his codpiece there; all was smooth, with the exception of a rounded fullness, which told me how luxuriously the want was supplied by a pair of pouting lips.

'Why, Francis, you have been deceiving us all; you are a girl,' and I put my hand on her breast to make sure.

'Oh! Mrs Harpur, what shall I do? If Lord Ferrars knows that you have found me out, he will be terribly vexed. He will hate me, and perhaps leave me behind when he sails away,' and she burst into tears.

'Ah well, don't cry, dear, I will see that he is not vexed with his little mistress – you are a brave girl – I admire you for your devotion to Lord Ferrars, and if you let me, I will love you as a sister, but you must conceal nothing from me – there must be candour on both sides, and then we shall be the best of friends; and let us begin by being mutually free with each other. Pet my fanny with your pretty little hand,' I said, lifting my dress and spreading my thighs as she pushed her hand up to my region of delight, 'and I will investigate the sweets and capacities of your own little love chink,' proceeding to unbutton her trousers and open them down the front. Inserting my fingers between the moist lips of her fat little slit, I said, 'Of course, you know this is your cunt, and you are familiar, I have no doubt, with all the terms and expressions of love.'

'Yes, I think I know them all pretty well. Lord Ferrars likes me to use them; do you like to hear them too?'

'I do, dear Francis, it not only saves trouble and beating about the bush, but I find, as almost everybody else does, that the free use of bawdy terms has an extraordinary effect in stirring up amorous emotions and creating sexual desire. So, let us talk freely of pricks, and cunts, and fucking, and bottoms, and of arses too. Does Lord Ferrars fuck you often? And how does he like most to do it?'

'Almost every day, and sometimes oftener. In the daytime, he is fond of having me seated on his lap; my trousers, as you perceive, are made to open in such a way that he can get his prick into my cunt without letting them down; but at night, he loves to have me quite naked, and he fucks me in every imaginable way and position, though I think what he likes best – at least, when he is fresh – is to have me lying on him sucking his prick, while my cunt is on his mouth.'

'I know the position well, it is a general favourite. Did you ever suck a woman's cunt, Francis?'

'No, I never had the opportunity though I have often seen pictures of it, but I am quite willing to suck yours, if you like.'

'Well, we shall have a mutual suck by and by; the salty taste of a nice cunt like yours, Francis, is very pleasant. But tell me, would you be very jealous if you saw Lord Ferrars fucking me?'

'No, not now that I know you. He can't marry either of us. I once thought he might have married me' – here, her beautiful eyes became suffused with tears – 'but that,' she added, checking herself, 'was, I suppose, great presumption in me; yet it was a pleasing dream.'

'Would you mind, dear Francis, telling me how his lordship first obtained the enjoyment of your favours.'

'Not in the least, Mrs Harpur, but remember it is in strict confidence. As I told you, his lordship used to lodge in my mother's house when staying at Southampton and I often waited on him. He was very kind and gentle in his manner to me, and gave me nice presents. I liked him. I loved him. I was then only a silly child. I allowed him to hold my hand and kiss me. One evening, we two were alone in the house; when I brought in his tea, he took me in his arms, told me that he loved me, and called me his own Fanny. He kissed me, drew me on to his knee, and put his hand under my neckerchief and felt my breast.

'This did not alarm me, for I thought it was quite *en règle* for a lord to marry a pretty innocent girl such as I was – most of the novels I was in the habit of reading had some such circumstance for their plot; and then, his manner was so seductive, and his touch so delightful, that I felt intoxicated by his love, and unable to oppose him as he went on from liberty to liberty until he had explored my cunt with his fingers and, having pulled up my dress and separated my thighs, was at last gazing on its virgin bloom.

'It was the first time a man had meddled with me there, and I felt as if my whole being was concentrated in that one spot. My cunt thrilled as he rubbed about the clitoris, but when he pushed his fingers up the as-yet-unbroken passage, I started, and exclaimed: "Oh! my lord, what are you doing to me? I never felt like this before," and I wriggled my bottom, while the lower part of my belly and all between my thighs tingled with voluptuous heat mingled with pain.

' "Does my finger hurt you, darling?"

' "It does, my lord, but I like it," spreading my thighs and turning up my bottom to him, "only it makes me feel so queer."

' "Ah, I have something here that will suit it better – look at this little plaything – put your hand on it, darling. Doesn't it feel soft and nice?"

' "It does, my lord."

' "Move it up and down – this way – see, that makes it grow larger. Look, how it holds up its head! Do you know what it is for?"

' "No, my lord; I never saw anything like it before; what is it for?" I asked, blushing.

' "It is just made to go in here where my finger is now."

' "Oh, it could not go in there – it is too big."

' "Yes it could, let me try – lean back more – spread open your thighs as much as you can, and lift your little bottom, that's a dear girl."

'I allowed him to place me as he wished, with my cunt turned up in the boldest manner before him; then he rubbed the head of his prick up and down the slit; you know, Mrs Harpur, what an agreeable tickling sensation that causes, especially when done for the first time, so I could not help laughing as I put down my hand to feel his prick and said, "Oh, my lord! that is nice! you may do anything to me that you like."

' "Well, my darling, I am going to push it in, very gently; it may give you a little pain at first, but once it gets in, you will have nothing but the most delightful pleasure."

'I then felt him spreading open the lips, and pushing the head of his prick against the sensitive opening at the lower end of the slit. Something stopped it there, and he gave a sudden thrust.

' "Oh, my lord, it takes my breath." He thrust again.

' "Oh! it hurts me, but don't mind, go on, oh my! don't stop push. Oh! – it is getting in, I feel it; oh, I feel it, far up, so nice – there, it is all in," as I felt his balls press hard against my bottom.

' "My little pet, you are a brave girl, and bore that splendidly; my prick is altogether inside, and your cunt holds it delightfully; I will now move it in and out, which, you know, is called fucking – tell me if you like fucking?"

' "Oh, I do, I do, my lord, I like your fucking – fuck my cunt with your prick – put your hand under my bottom." I noticed him looking down. "Do you see it, my lord? Do you see your prick going into my cunt? Do you see it fucking?"

' "I do, my love, I am watching my prick passing in and out between the hairy lips, and I can see your rosy clitoris and soft nymphae clinging round it, and pressing it most delightfully. Oh! isn't that nice, tell me how you like it."

' "Yes, my lord, it is delicious – fuck me faster – smack your balls against my bottom, try and get more prick into my cunt. Oh! I don't know what is going to happen. I feel as if I were all cunt, and you were all prick. Oh! there, there, it is over." Then he strained me in his arms. And that was my first fuck.'

'Why, Francis, you have told that in the most charming way: you know what love is – you were born for it. Cupid must have had something to say to the getting of you. You are worth a score of the mawkish, half-dead-and-alive women one meets nowadays. But, let us now have a little taste of tribadism together and first let me have a good view of your little fanny, I am sure her lips must be watering after all this talk,' and I made her lie back. Then lifting her shirt, I uncovered all her smooth white belly. 'Open, love, spread wide open the book of your secret charms. What voluptuous development is here! Lord Ferrars made a wise choice in you, Francis, for here is cunt to perfection, and plenty of it. People say that little women have the largest cunts, but I never saw yours excelled by big or little. Your light hair too enables one to see more of its luxurious shape, and the extreme whiteness of your skin sets off its most lascivious lips which look as if they were just going to speak of pricks and fucking; and this clitoris shines like a piece of sensitive coral, and this crimson furrow seems the very avenue of bliss. And how moist it is! and how extremely hot inside! It makes me wish I were a man and had a prick to satisfy its cravings. However, I will do what I can with my mouth and tongue,' and stooping down, I kissed and sucked the fragrant lips.

'Dear Mrs Harpur, it is your goodness makes you praise my little fanny. I am sure your own is much nicer – won't you get over me and let me have a suck too.'

'I will, my pet, but not just now; I have a plan in my head: let us take a bath together, and when we are quite naked we can enjoy one another with more satisfaction. Go in there; I want to give directions to the servants, so that we may not be disturbed. You can meanwhile undress, and I will be with you in a minute.'

I then ran to the surgery, where, with my usual good fortune, I met Dick and Freddy, who had just come in.

'Hah! my lord, I have found you out; your pretty little page turns out to be a blooming mistress, and I commend your taste, for she is a choice little piece.'

'Well, Queenie, I knew it would happen sooner or later. But how does the little pet bear the discovery herself?'

'Oh, she shed tears enough when I forced her secret, but she brightened up when I promised to love her myself and make all square with you; so you will have to be kind and indulgent; and if you don't object, she will form a very pleasant addition to our social party.'

'That is just what I was planning in my mind, you have only anticipated me, my dear Queenie. I meant to offer her as a titbit to my friend Dick as a small return for his kindness in the matter of his beautiful wife.'

'Right, my lord; and Dick, I promise you a treat, for she has the most charming love-trap I ever saw. She is now in my bathroom undressing. I am going back to her in a few moments, and if you and Freddy care to witness a little love-play between two womenkind, you may betake yourselves to the spying place which you and Dick so cleverly contrived.'

They were both delighted with my plan, and went off to my husband's dressing-room, which opened into my bathroom by a concealed door by means of which anyone in either room could hear and see all that passed in the other.

Meanwhile I gave instructions to the servants not to admit visitors, nor allow us to be disturbed, and then I hastened to rejoin Francis – or Frances as we must now spell it. I found her undressed with the exception of her shirt; she blushed when I helped to draw it over her head, and the lovely girl stood revealed in all her naked charms.

Her shapely limbs, so smooth and glossy, shone like alabaster. Her delicious belly spread itself like a voluptuous plain between her firm strawberry-tipped bubbies and the rising mount sacred to Venus. And the mount itself, covered but not obscured by light silky hair, divided into two remarkably full and sensuous lips which curved down between her swelling thighs, while the inner furrow gleamed as a crimsom streak, the rosy clitoris protruding its tiny head at the upper end.

I noticed these particulars as she stood before me helping me remove my clothes.

When all was ready we entered the bath together; and then commenced a scene of sportive play which must have displayed in fullest perfection whatever beauties or feminine charms we possessed. The invigorating effect of the bath joined with the lascivious ideas produced by the touch and view of our naked bodies threw us both into a state of extreme amorous excitement.

So when we came out and had dried one another, with particular attention to our cunts and bottoms, I took her in my arms and turned her up on the couch. As I stooped over her with my head between her up raised thighs, she pressed me down until my cunt rested on her mouth. Then the mutual suction of our lips and the active penetration of our tongues caused us to turn and twist our bodies in all the circlings of voluptuous enjoyment. We rolled over and over, alternately taking the upper side, all the while tightly enfolded in each other's arms; until at last a copious spend subdued our excitement and cooled us down.

Then as we rested, I placed Frances so that her moist and rosy quim was turned towards the concealed door, and asked her to favour me with a full account of how she came to assume man's attire, and of some adventures which she said she had encountered while endeavouring to conceal her true sex; and I added, 'Call me Queenie, like everybody else.'

CHAPTER THREE

The Middy's Tale

'My dear Mrs Harpur, I will call you Queenie, as you wish me.

'After Lord Ferrars had taught me to know and enjoy the delights of love, I clung to him with all my heart. His image filled my soul, and devotion to him became the guiding principle of my life. How I used to long for the friendly covering of the night, when I could steal unobserved into his room! How fast the happy hours speeded by as I lay encircled in his arms! How my fond and curious hand wondered over his manly frame, and with what delight I handled his noble prick, and conducted it myself to love's retreat! He often lighted a number of candles that he might view me naked. Then with what pleasure I spread my thighs to allow him to see and examine all my hidden charms. How willingly I turned and bent my body to let him view my cunt and bottom in different aspects. I frigged my cunt; I piddled before him, and to please him, called it pissing; I contrived different ways of fucking, and invited him to put his prick into my cunt in the most outlandish positions I could imagine.'

'Did he ever put his prick into your bottom?'

'Oh, dear yes, scores of time; but he liked me always to call it my arse, and to say: fuck my arse.'

'Thus a few weeks passed rapidly away; and then I fancied he was growing tired of me, for he spoke of going to sea. I burst into tears and said he did not love me, otherwise he would not think of going away and leaving me.

'He assured me, he had no intention of leaving me; that his great desire was to have me with him, and that he had been planning how he could get me away without a commotion, and then provide for my security and comfort.

'He told me that he had a lady friend at Brighton, who would take charge of me at first, and in whose house he could see and enjoy me as much as ever; that he was purchasing a new yacht and intended to engage a different crew, who would not recognise me. Then he suggested my assuming man's attire and sailing with him as a middy.

'I hesitated about the male costume, but as, on talking it over, that seemed the only feasible plan, I consented. So Lord Ferrars got his friend Mrs Simpson to write to my mother inviting me to pass some time with her and offering to complete my education and bring me out in good society. She was highly pleased, and thus all was satisfactorily arranged.

'Lord Ferrars started for London, and in due course I arrived at Brighton and was met at the coach office by a smart young lady who introduced herself as Miss Anna Simpson, the youngest daughter of Lord Ferrars' friend. We took a cab and shortly arrived at a quiet house in a retired street where I was cordially received by Mrs Simpson and another young lady.

'I did not fancy them much, for they seemed a good deal over dressed and not very refined in manner; however, they were Lord Ferrars' friends and that was enough for me.

'Mrs Simpson told me she had instructions from his lordship to provide me with a middy's uniform, something like that of the Royal Navy, and everything necessary for a sailor's outfit; and she handed me a letter from him in which he stated that he was detained in London, but would rejoin me at Brighton as soon as possible and meantime to make myself at home, call for all I wanted and enjoy myself in every way I could.

'Anna attended me to my room, and as she was a very merry girl, we had great fun together. She soon made me understand that she knew all about my connection with Lord Ferrars, but, she said, that was nothing uncommon, for nearly all the girls of her acquaintance had some gentleman friend whom they especially liked, and whom they often favoured by yielding to their wishes.

'While saying this, she was trying to get her hand up under my petticoats.

' "Why do you push away my hand?" she asked. "Come dear, don't be over modest – don't I know very well that your little fan is well used to being petted, and looked at, too – there – let see it; now must have a kiss – open your thighs – open more. Oh! how nice you are! no wonder, Lord Ferrars is so fond of you! Do you know," she rattled on, 'we often have gentlemen to supper, and plenty of drink, and then we have no end of fun. They love to tumble us about and see our bubbies, and our cunts and bottoms too; and then, of course, we retaliate by pulling out their lolloping pricks and dangling stones; and then we are sure to fall under them and our cunts get crammed with prick in no time. We expect such a party tonight; will you join us and share in the fun?"

' "Oh, no, Anna, I would be sorry to let any man touch me there expect Lord Ferrars. How could you let any man make free with you in that way except you loved him.'

' "My dear Fanny, what a child you are! Nobody could get on with such a notion as that. In the words of the poet:

> The mouse that always trusts to one poor hole
> Can never be a mouse of any soul.

The way to enjoy life is to be free with everyone who treats you well and pays you well.

' "There are two more of us in this house; we find it convenient to live with Mrs Simpson, for she is respectable, takes good care of us, manages all our business and on the whole treats us fairly and well. We all like her, and call her mother, though none of us are really related to her.

' "You will only be with us for a day or two, but my desire is, don't make yourself singular; enjoy life while you can, and depend upon it, Lord Ferrars won't think the worse of you. He knows this house and the company one may expect to meet in it, for he has been often here himself; and more than once, I have had him for a whole night in my arms, and I can tell you, he was not idle there – now, what do you say to that? – so make your mind easy on his account. Most of the gentlemen about town keep mistresses, and more than that, many of them like, now and then, to exchange with one another for the sake of variety."

'This extraordinary revelation took me all aback. An uneasy sensation crept over me as I, for the first time, realised my position. I threw myself on the bed and sobbed aloud.

'Anna seemed to pity me; she put her arms round me and whispered in my ear: "Don't fret, Fanny, you are a sweet girl – these things are perhaps strange to you, but nobody will harm you; you can do just as you please while you are here.

' "Lord Ferrars warned us to treat you with every consideration, and to make you as happy as we could. He is very fond of you – so dry your tears, and come with me, I will show you some funny scenes that will amuse you and drive away those melancholy thoughts.

' "We have a habit here of bringing our gentlemen visitors to our own rooms where we can have them all to ourselves. But Mrs Simpson has made spying places for viewing all that passes in each apartment. We all know this very well, and none of us minds having prying eyes watching us as we sport with our lovers, exposing our cunts and turning up our bottoms. In fact, I enjoy a good fuck ten times as well when I know that there are wistful eyes watching how I heave my rump, and hold my man as he works up and down, driving his prick into my cunt." But perhaps, dear Queenie, I am only boring you with this long recital, and you don't care to hear a description of what Anna brought me to see.'

'On the contrary, I am deeply interested, in fact, you are giving me such pleasure, darling Frances, that my cunt is just on the flow, and if you care for a suck, now's your time.'

'Here I am, then, dearest Queenie, draw up your legs and let me get my hands under your bottom, so that I can push my mouth well in between the moist lips of your quim.'

As she buried her face between my drawn-up thighs, I so managed that her beautiful arse should be in full view of the aperture in the concealed door. This opening though large was covered by a tall mirror, which could be moved on a sliding frame. As I looked towards it I saw that the glass was being noiselessly pushed to one side, until there was space enough for a large prick with a glowing head to be projected in. It was my husband's prick, but held in the hands of Lord Ferrars.

They told me afterwards, that having taken off their coats and waistcoats on account of the heat, they both stood close together intently watching us through the aperture; that the full exposure of our cunts and bottoms, and above all our wanton talk, had excited them in the highest degree and, as they pressed together, their pricks became so ungovernable that they had to unfasten their trousers; that Lord Ferrars' hands found their way round him in front of Dick where they naturally encountered and took hold of his prick; that as he pressed behind against his naked bottom, while gazing over his shoulder at the exciting scene in the bathroom, his lordship's prick struggled hard to find a lodgement. What happened after that, I cannot say but I fancy he succeeded.

Meanwhile, Frances in the most randy manner wriggled her arse as she drew from me the soft effusion; and at the same instant, I observed a gush of milky fluid spurt from the summit of my husband's pleasure tube, while Lord Ferrars gave a suppressed grunt of satisfaction and delight.

The looking glass was then moved back nearly to its place, and Frances and I settled ourselves on the sofa. I made her lean back with her cunt and bottom well in view; and she put her hand on my cunt as she continued her story.

'Anna first brought me to a closet adjoining a room which she told me was occupied by a girl named Ellen, who was considered the beauty of their party; that a short time before my arrival, her favourite lover, the rich old Marquis of L——, had come to pay her a visit, and had been taken as usual to her room, so we might expect to see them together.

'The peep-hole was over a couch, so that parties could recline as they watched what was going on in the room. Anna and I lay along the couch and she told me to look through; meanwhile, she raised my dress behind that she might rub her belly and cunt against my bottom.'

Here, I could not help smiling as I thought how funny it was that the very same dodge which Frances described was now being practised with regard to herself. She observed the smile, but thought it was caused by what she was doing in my cunt; so giving my clitoris an extra squeeze, she went on.

'Looking in, I perceived that Ellen, with the exception of her silk stockings and laced sandals, was perfectly naked. Her black hair was down and streamed over her polished shoulders; and her beautiful bottom, under which I could just perceive the pouting lips of her cunt, was turned towards me as she stooped forward in the act of sponging with water the languid tool of the most noble marquis who was seated astride a bidet.

'Then she carefully wiped it, and when he stood up, she remained on her knees that she might hold it to her mouth. She first rubbed its head about her face and over her eyes, then she took as much as she could into her mouth while she worked his balls with one hand and tickled his bottom with the other.

'Meantime Anna got her hand on my cunt, and pressed me into her as she kept rubbing her mouth against my bottom.

' "What are they doing? tell me everything you see," she whispered, still frigging my clitoris and pounding my bottom.

' "She is petting the prick of the old Marquis, and trying to put some life into it, but I doubt if she will succeed."

' "She will, for she is quite an adept at that kind of work; she is famous for it and that's why he goes to her. How is she getting on, and what is the prick like now?"

' "It has grown much bigger and stronger. She has taken it out of her mouth and is frigging it with her hands. Now they are going to the bed. There, she has thrown herself on her back and is spreading her thighs before him as he pushes a pillow under her bottom."

Then, we heard her saying: "Now, my lord, here's my cunt, I will hold it open that you may see how red it is inside; and here's my bottom-hole, round and tight; you can have your choice. You prefer the cunt. I think you are wise. Put some spittle on the head of your prick, it will go in easier – now, push – drive it in. Fuck, fuck, my lord," and to stimulate him more, she continued saying with increasing emphasis: "Prick, cunt, arse, fuck, piss, fuck." To which, his lordship responded by various grunts and moans: "Oh–eh–oh – lift your arse – pinch my prick in your cunt, eh–oh."

'Anna's movements now become very energetic. She banged herself against my bottom. She worked her finger in and out of my cunt, and muttered, "O—eugh! if it were a pri–i–c–k!" spinning out the work prick, 'to fuck your cu–n–t; or perhaps you would like it here,' inserting another finger in my bottom-hole, 'to fuck – fuck – fuck your arse; or, best of all, to have both together – two pricks fucking arse and cunt at one and the same time."

' "Oh! Anna! you are sending me mad! there – that will do, you have made me spend twice already.'

' "So I perceive – you have given down a lot. You are the very devil at spending and your little cunt is all in a glow. We may leave this, however, there will be nothing more to see here, at least for the present. Come, I will show you another scene."

'She then took me to the room of a girl named Sarah, whom she described as the fat girl of the house, and said that younger men fancied her, for she was strong and lusty, and was never satisfied unless her men were as lusty as herself.

'We found the same arrangement as before; but this time, she applied her eye to the peeping-place, and I rubbed against her bottom from behind.

' "Keep your finger in my cunt and rub your belly against my bottom, and I will describe for you all that I see: Sarah, I find, has two gallants with her this time, but she is well able to cope with them both. She is now seated on the lap of one; I am not sure whether his prick is in her bottom or her cunt, but it looks too far back for her cunt. She twists about her behind to as so rub her fat buttocks against his belly, while he presses and moulds her voluminous breasts.

'The other cove stands by her side; she has one stout arm round his bottom, with her hand on his bollocks, the other hand holds the root of his prick and directs its head to her mouth. I am sure he is enjoying his share of the transaction, for his face is very red and his eyes look as if ready to start out of his head.

' "Now they are having a wash, and are busy sponging one another. Pinch my clitoris, Fanny, frig – frig my cunt – right.

' "Now one of her men lies along the couch. She straddles over him. She has managed to stuff his prick up her cunt, and now she remains quiet with her great fat arse tuned up as an impudent invite. Her little round pink bottom-hole looks quite ready and prepared for an assault. And she will not be disappointed. The other fellow is getting ready – he has anointed his tool and the wrinkled passage he means to explore. How easily it slips in! How pleasant it must be to feel his belly rubbing against her soft quivering buttocks. But with what energy she now jogs up and down! How they all work together!

' "Oh, it is grand! Frig, Fanny, frig – put your finger in my arse – stir it round and round – push your cunt against my bottom. Oh! – eugh – eugh! it comes – it comes."

'I really felt I had had enough for one bout, and longed for a little rest, but this girl, Anna, seemed insatiable, and hurried me off to another place of observation. This was next the grandest bedroom in the establishment, that of Mrs Simpson herself.

'This lady, who in spite of her vulgarity was much patronised by the aristocracy, laid herself out to humour and gratify all their peculiar whims and fancies. Amongst other modes of pandering to the tastes of the numerous customers, she always had a supply of young girls just entered on their teens, when their cunts were sufficiently developed to take in a good-sized prick but were not yet shaded or obscured by hair.

'In this matter, she had especially in view one of the most refined of her visitors, a distinguished nobleman who had been for many years ambassador to the Sublime Porte at Constantinople.

'He had there made acquaintance with the Circassian ladies, well trained and accomplished in the art of love, though ignorant of everything else. Following the example of the opulent Turks, he secured by purchase a choice harem of these celebrated beauties, who are taught to consider themselves brought into the world for no other purpose than to please man and minister to his delight. These ladies, knowing the gratification it was to their lord to kiss the lips of their quims, made it a regular practice to extract every hair as it grew, so as to render the whole surface as smooth as they could contrive to make it.

'And indeed, Queenie, I too have sometimes thought what a pity it is that our cunts are so covered up. Admittedly, the hair so grows that it never prevents a good prick finding its way in, but for all that, I cannot but think that it would be a more gratifying object to look at, and to handle too, if it were free from the rough and often tangled hair which hides it from view and obscures whatever beauty of form it may possess.'

'Well, my dear, what you say is very just; but you see, nature evidently intended us to go naked; it was in that condition that the first woman was presented to the first man; now if our cunts had no natural covering, the effect of their free exposure would be so exciting to men that they could think of nothing else; so in mercy to them, and to save us from continual worrying, nature has so covered our cunts that although the exact shape is concealed from view in ordinary positions, yet when required for use the way is plain enough, while the slight concealment imparts the additional charm of requiring some effort to gain the soft retreat; at least, that's my notion. But I am anxious to hear what you saw in Mrs Simpson's room, so pray continue your narrative.'

CHAPTER FOUR

The Middy's Tale Continued

'I will, dear Queenie, but I want to piddle very badly – let me do that first, and then I shall be more at my ease to proceed with my stupid narration.'

'Of course, that necessity must be complied with,' I said, 'but why not say piss instead of piddle, it is shorter and simpler. I want to do something in that line myself, so after you have done, I will perform. Here's the poe, but I want you to do it standing – so. I will hold it for you.'

I turned her in such a direction as to afford those who I knew were watching every movement, a good view of the interesting performance, and held the Poe between her legs, but below her knees, saying: 'Now, Frances, piss away.'

She stooped forward a little and immediately a clear amber stream darted from the hair-covered lips of her cunt and with a gurgling rush rattled into the utensil I held to receive it.

This diversion so tickled the fancies of our unseen observers, that they both laughed out. The flow at once stopped. Frances looked aghast. 'Oh! Queenie, what's that? Somebody is watching us; have you peep holes here?'

Observing my smile, she said, looking most reproachful, 'Why did you not tell me? Who is it, Queenie? O tell me, who has been listening?'

She was cut short by the opening of the door, and the sudden entrance of Lord Ferrars and Dick, dressed only in their shirts.

'We have intruded, dearest Queenie, and best loved Frances,' said Lord Ferrars, in his graceful manner, 'not only to answer for ourselves, but to beg your kind permission to take part in this most delightful conference.'

I smiled a welcome, but Frances only threw herself into my arms, and burying her face in my bosom, exclaimed, in a voice broken by sobs: 'Oh, Queenie! – why did you not tell me – they were listening. I have spoken very foolishly and said many things I should never have uttered.'

'Make your mind easy, my sweet little pet,' replied Lord Ferrars, putting his arm around her and drawing her on his knee as he sat down by my side, 'you did not utter one word that could offend me, but a great many that proved how good and trustworthy you are. In very truth, I never loved you more highly than I do at the present moment. And now that our secret is found out, I am all the better pleased. Our noble-hearted friends here will love you and do all they can to make you happy.'

'That we will, dear Frances, and now, let me introduce you to my husband. He has not seen you in your present costume until now, and I perceive he is admiring you all over. Give him you hand, my pet.'

She looked at Lord Ferrars, as if for direction. 'Give it to him,' he said, 'and not only your hand, my love, but with it every other favour it is in your power to bestow, for he is worthy of it – he is my best loved and most trusted friend.'

She laid her hand in a coy manner in my husband's outstretched palm. As he took hold of it, he drew her gently towards him. She gave one wistful glance at Lord Ferrars, and she slipped off his knee and yielded to Dick's embrace. But as his lordship nodded approvingly when he saw his friend's hand gliding towards her secret charms, while at the same instance his roving hand found a resting place between my thighs, she turned to him with a bright expression on her face, and said, 'He tells me to love you, Dr Harpur, and I do, for you have been always good and kind to me. I don't forget how well you prescribed for me when I was sick, nor how gallantly you rescued me from those horrid Spanish sailors.'

He folded her in his arms, as he replied, 'My sweet Frances, I always liked you for my friend's sake, now I love you for your own; and my good wife, as you see, does not object – we are quite in accord in the matters. But don't call me Dr Harpur any more, call me Dick; and now, my pet, we want you to favour us, by continuing your interesting narrative, which we somewhat rudely interrupted.'

'Oh, I cannot before you and Lord Ferrars; he might not like it.'

'On the contrary, dearest Frances, I join heartily with my friend Dick in requesting you to give us a full a narrative as you can of all your adventures. You have already told me many of them, but I would gladly hear them again in a more connected form: and I need hardly say – tell everything that happened to you as fully as possible. I know that you have been forced on several occasions to comply with the wishes of others; but, as I have often said, in place of that making me love you less, I like and enjoy you all the more. Your dear little cunt is so beautifully made that the oftener it is used the more capable it grows of giving the highest delight to everyone who has the happiness of entering it.'

'My lord, you are always generous and good; I will do the best I can to please you and these kind friends; so to continue – Anna told me on the way, that she, being Mrs Simpson's favourite, was the only one beside herself who was permitted to keep the key which opened the doors of these closets; and as Mrs Simpson was especially particular about this one, she warned me to avoid speaking or making any noise whatever.

'As soon as my eyes became accustomed to the opening, which was more carefully hidden than the others, I perceived a fine-looking man negligently reclining on a broad sofa, which was plentifully furnished with the softest cushions. He had nothing on but a silk dressing gown and embroidered slippers.

'Mrs Simpson sat between his widely separated legs. She was fondling his prick with her hands. It seemed of the ordinary size, but was remarkable for the whiteness of its enfolding skin, and the bright carnation tint of its glossy head. It looked soft however, and could not stand without support.

'This want of stiffness she was trying to remedy by her skilful appliances. She did not trust alone to the action of her hands, for she had with her two young girls whom she had trained for this very purpose. One of these she called Haidee, after Byron's favourite; she was a well-formed girl of fourteen, whose cunt was fully developed but as yet unobscured by any trace of hair and thus well suited to please the oriental taste of the ex-ambassador. This girl was now seated in front of them with what little dress she had tucked up about her waist.

'Mrs Simpson, having directed her to lean back and spread her thighs as widely as she could, with her legs resting on the arms of a chair, said, "Look, my lord, at Haidee's pretty little fat cunt, how fresh and fair it is! How voluptuously the soft lips swell out on either side of the glowing chink! and how red and moist the slit appears! Your lordship's prick well enjoy forcing its way in between its clinging folds, I expect, when we have stiffened it up a bit. And here is sweet Flora, who, thought six months younger, possesses a beautifully formed and most luscious little love-trap. Come here my pet, sit on the arm of the sofa that his lordship may fondle and kiss your sweet little quim."

'This young girl, as blooming as Hebe, sprang on the sofa, and presenting her soft and glowing little cunny to his face, asked how his lordship would like to have it, in front or rear?

' "In front at first, my love; sit on the arm of the sofa, and place your legs on my shoulders."

'Then he plunged his face between her thighs and sucked vigorously at the voluptuous furrow, drawing all the soft parts into his open mouth, while she put her hands on his head – playing with the locks of his hair, as he twisted her peach-like bottom in the most lascivious manner – muttering, all the time, "I do love to feel your lordship nibbling at my clitoris, and pushing your tongue up my cunt."

'Mrs Simpson now redoubled her efforts to invigorate his lordship's tool by various skilful touches and light pinches of all the sensitive parts within reach. It gradually stiffened and began to stand erect. She then asked if he would like Haidee to mount across his loins and receive his prick into her cunt, while he still amused himself with the charms of the younger girl. He lazily consented and stretched himself along the sofa, drawing Flora down until her bottom rested on his face.

'Haidee then got over him, and soon, with Mrs Simpson's aid, engulfed his lordship's yielding tool in her lascivious gap; that being accomplished, she placed her hands on Flora's shoulders, and worked her body slowly up and down. Meantime Flora was not idle, for with active loins she rubbed her moist and savoury cunt over and about his lordship's mouth and nose.

' "Now, Haidee," said Mrs Simpson, "tell his lordship, what you feel."

' "I feel – a nice prick stirring about in my cunt; when I sit down, I feel it pushing up – Oh! – that is good; now I rise up, and it slips back. Then I drive it up again, and press hard to get in all I can – there do you like that, my lord? Does this kind of fucking please you?"

' "Yes, Haidee, it is admirable; your cunt seems actually alive; I feel it biting and pinching my prick all round."

' "And Flora, how are you getting on?" asked Mrs Simpson. "Tell his lordship how you like his gamahuching you."

' "Oh, it is delightful. I like so much to feel the hair of your beard, my lord, rubbing my bottom and your tongue moving in my cunt. It feels like a prick – push it further in – oh! that's nice! Yes, gamahuche me, while you fuck Haidee. Now you are turning to my bottom – Oh! that's good I will lean back to give you more room; oh! Haidee, I'm spending – I'm spending."

'And his lordship seemed to be spending too, for he arched his body under Haidee, and drawing Mrs Simpson to his side, he rammed the fingers of one hand into her salacious quim, while with the other he pinched Haidee's quivering arse until he made her bound again with a cry of mingled pain and pleasure.

'We then beat a hasty retreat and returned to my apartment.

'In the evening, we had a quiet dinner together, and Mrs Simpson and the three girls made themselves very agreeable and spoke of the sport and fun they expected at suppertime with their gentlemen friends. I begged to be excused for that night, as I felt tired after my journey and accordingly was allowed to retire to my own room.

'Anna brought me some tea, and a lot of lascivious books and pictures, and as we looked them over, she made every effort to excite me both by touches and wanton suggestions. I did not understand her object at the time, though I thought her manner somewhat peculiar, but after-events proved that she was acting with fixed design, and from mercenary motives.

'She induced me to take a bath before going to bed, and persisted in placing the bath in a position which, she said, kept me out of the draft, but which I thought only exposed me the more; but she was so kind and merry and I let her have her way. She helped to sponge my limbs, and made me turn and bend my body in a variety of postures; and when drying me afterwards, she so tickled me and slapped my bottom as to make me throw my arms and legs about, and display all the secret chinks and crannies of my person.

'Then she brought me what they called a nightcap – a tumbler of hot spiced wine. It warmed me all over, and seemed to have a wonderful effect on the region round my cunt, for it made all its nerves thrill and induced a spasmodic action strongly suggestive of venereal pleasure.

'Before leaving, she told me that her room was next to mine, and if I wanted anything in the night, or felt lonely, I had only to run into her and she would take care of me.

'When she went out, however, I carefully fastened the door, and then, with my brain swimming, tumbled into bed. The last thing I was conscious of was hearing singing and revelry downstairs, but as my door was locked, I felt secure, and turning over quickly fell asleep. My sleep was disturbed and the highly excited state of my cunt naturally caused dreams of a corresponding character.

'As I lay on my back, I saw descending over me the much desired form of my absent love. His roseate limbs seemed floating in celestial light. I stretched up my arms, and said: "O my love, how delightful to have you with me now!" I felt his dear hands groping between the lips of my palpitating cunt. I opened my thighs, and heaved my bottom, as I muttered. "Yes, feel it, my love; feel my cunt, how hot it is! it is longing, for your dear prick – your fingers tickle me very nicely, but it is your prick alone that can satisfy my cunt – won't you put it in?"

'My love laid himself upon me. I could no longer see him, but I felt his arm around me and his warm body pressing me deliciously. He put his prick in my hand. It was large and stiff. Letting the head pass through my fingers, I drew back the soft covering skin. I felt it bound in my hand. "Now, my love, let me put it in." I said, drawing it towards my cunt, "I am longing for it – my cunt burns." I felt the head rub between the moist lips. I felt it press on the heated orifice. I heaved up. It slipped in. "O how good!" I muttered, as it passed up my cunt extending each humid fold and sensitive crease of my vagina.

' "Your prick, my love, is very big tonight! it fills me up more than usual." I muttered, gradually regaining consciousness, but still over-powered by the pleasurable sensations in my cunt. "How well you fuck! How sweetly you drive up your prick! Oh! I am fairly suffocated with rapture," I cried, pushing up my cunt to him as his action became more vehement.

'He rammed home his prick with desperate energy and with a low moaning cry shot forth a torrent of heated spunk. I felt my cunt filled to overflowing. I knew it was bubbing out at the sides. "Oh, what a quantity of spunk you have poured into me! Where did you get it all? My love, how strong and big you are! And how heavy! but how did you get in? and when did you arrive?" My love made no other answer than a gentle movement of his prick in my cunt. I passed my hand over him. He certainly had grown larger and much heavier. His skin did not feel so soft as usual. "Why don't you speak to me, my lord."

'My mind, now fully awakened, became filled with a strange misgiving that grew into certainly as I felt a thick covering of hair on his breast, which I knew Lord Ferrars did not possess.

' "You are not Lord Ferrars, are you? Tell me who are you?"

No answer only a stronger hug, and a shove of his prick in my cunt.

' "Stop – you have no right. Stop, I won't let you.' And making a sudded bound, I sprang from under him, and jumped out of bed. I heard him getting out after me, so I slipped noiselessly to the other side, and gradually crept towards the door. With nervous fingers I unlocked it, and passing out into the passage ran to Anna's door, which I found open. I quickly stepped in, and feeling for the key, turned it in the lock, and then thinking I was tolerably safe, called Anna.

'She answered from her bed, and told me not to be frightened but to come over to her and tell her what was the matter. I moved in the direction of her voice, and found her sitting on the side of her bed. She took me in her arms, and drawing me over her, leaned back, as she said, "You little goose, what are you making all this noise for? You will waken the whole house."

' "Oh, Anna, someone got into my bed – and – and –'

' "Fucked you? – well, what great harm is there in that? What better thing could happen to a girl than to be well fucked?"

' "Oh! but it was not Lord Ferrars at all.'

' "Lord Grandmother, excuse me; would not any other lord do as well, provided he had as good a prick?"

'At that instant, a pair of strong arms seized me round the waist, and the huge prick was again thrust into my cunt. I kicked and plunged, and did all in my power to free myself from his hateful embrace; but Anna held me like a vice, crying, "Fuck her, major, fuck her – don't spare her – give her such a dose of prick as she never got before in her life," and heaving her body, she bumped me up to meet every stroke.

'In spite of all my opposition, my cunt glowed at every lunge, and I began to wish for his discharge, when the wretch suddenly drew out his prick and, plunging it into my bottom, shot his fiery stream into my vitals. This consummation finished me; my muscles relaxed and I fell into a helpless swoon. While in this state, I was put back in bed, and when I recovered consciousness, the daylight was breaking in through the window shutters.

'When Anna came in, I would not speak to her, and threatened to leave the house. But she only smiled and said I ought to thank her in place of being angry, for she had caused me to make a brave plunge, and I would soon be as jovial as any of them.

'Mrs Simpson, however, pretended to view the matter in a more serious light, and apologised for the intrusion, which, she said, arose out of a mistake made by a young officer of the Guards, who had passed the night in her house.

'But I learned afterwards that both she and Anna had been heavily bribed, the one to permit and the other to assist in the outrage. And also that there was a secret passage through a wallpress, by means of which he had entered from Anna's room and had also watched me taking my bath.

'My uniform was brought in during the day and they all made great fun of my awkwardness when I first donned the male attire. One of the girls twisted her handkerchief and stuffed it into my trousers to represent a prick. Another said I was such a pretty boy that as soon as I went out all the girls would be sure to fall in love with me. I have often thought of her words since, and smiled when I found them verified by fact.

'My dear lord arrived in the evening, and we passed such a happy night together. He laughed when I told him of my adventure, and said he would not leave me alone there another night.

'He thought it better to avoid observation on shore, so the next morning I accompanied him on board his new yacht, the *Ariel*, and we soon afterwards set sail. For several days I kept very quiet under plea of seasickness, and only gradually went about the yacht as I became familiar with my dress and learned to assume something of the usual swagger of a young salt.

CHAPTER FIVE

The Middy's Tale Continued

'Lord Ferrars considered that it would be safer for me not to be seen at any English port until I was thoroughly familiar with my new mode of life, so we started for a few weeks cruise in the Mediterranean.

'Before leaving England, he wrote to my mother, telling her all that had happened and promising to take every care of me, provide for me handsomely and bring me back safely to her in due time. Meanwhile, he sent her a liberal present, and said it would be repeated from time to time. My mother took the money, being a sensible woman, made no noise about the matter and only stipulated that I should keep her regularly informed of our whereabouts and how I was getting on.

'My first adventure occurred when the yacht was in the port of Genoa. While lying at anchor there, his lordship received tidings of the illness of a near relative, which obliged him to return to England without delay; so he determined to leave the yacht at her anchorage and make the journey overland, while I remained in charge as his representative.

'We had then a skipper named Captain Jones. He was a good seaman and a careful navigator, but somehow I never liked nor trusted him. I think he suspected me from the first for I observed that he was continually watching me. He was always giving me advice, and offered to teach me navigation, but I avoided all intimacy with him and kept him at a civil distance.

'Before starting, Lord Ferrars engaged a teacher to give me instruction in French and Italian. I was glad of this occupation, and used to go ashore every day to make purchases and attend my master. My custom was to dine at a restaurant and return to the yacht in the evening. One of the men, named Roberts, who was an especial favourite of mine as he had an honest, open face, came to me on shore, and told me privately that he thought it his duty to inform me that Captain Jones, who was purveyor to Lord Ferrars, was carrying on extensive specula-tion, and was besides in the habit of bringing improper characters on board the yacht in my absence.

'When I returned that evening, I looked over Captain Jones' accounts, and finding many proofs of dishonesty, I charged him with speculation, and at the same time gave him strict orders to admit no one on board without my permission.

'I never will forget the villainous look the fellow gave me, when he found that his dishonesty was detected. Revenge gleamed in his eye, and I felt it would not be safe to pass another night on the yacht without sufficient protection. However, as it was then too late to go ashore, I made what preparation I could to secure myself from sudden assault.

'There was a pair of pistols in the cabin, which I sometimes used, practising at a mark; these I took down and carefully loaded. My own dirk, I placed within reach. Then, calling the steward, I told him I should want nothing further for the night, but to be ready to come to me if I needed him. When he went out, I double bolted the door of the saloon leading forwards, and locked the after cabin door leading to the mizen hatch. Then I lighted the cabin lamp, and sat down to write to my absent lord. I finished a long letter to him, and then commenced one to my mother; after a while, I grew very sleepy, and without thinking what I was doing, laid my head on my arm and fell fast asleep.

'I do not know how long I had remained in that state when I was suddenly awakened by being seized from behind, something was thrust into my mouth and a bandage tied over the lower part of my face, effectually preventing my making the slightest noise; my arms were at the same time firmly held behind my back.

'As I turned my head to see the perpetrator of this outrage, the hated voice of Captain Jones hissed in my ear, while his hand pressed in between my legs.

' "Hah, miss, we have found you out, we'll put a stop to your pranks you" (here, he called me some vile names, which I need not repeat). "You indeed, to order us about, and threaten Lord Ferrars on us! And much we care for Lord Ferrars. I have a great mind, before I leave tonight, to scuttle his fine yacht and send his pretty mistress to the bottom. Meanwhile, my lads" (speaking to two of the crew that were acting with him), "search the cabin, break open all the lockers and put together everything you fancy or consider worth taking, while I amuse myself with this lassie, and afterwards you shall have her to fuck or to bugger just as you please."

'My heart sank within me; I was absolutely powerless, and unable to call for help. I felt that nothing could be gained by resistance; that my only chance was to submit and watch for an opportunity to escape.

'Captain Jones proceeded very deliberately to strip me of my clothing, holding my hands firmly all the time. He then tied my wrists with the ends of two short ropes, and with the other end my ankles at the same side. Then he placed me on the table on my back, and spreading open my thighs with his hands, rubbed his ugly face round and over my cunt; muttering as he did so, "Ugh, Miss Gipton, but you have a fine slit of a cunt! What grand fucking you and his lordship must have had in this cabin!' Then he drew open the lips with his fingers and pinched the clitoris. 'By Jove, it is splendid! so red! so hot! so moist! and so savoury!' He then rubbed his nose up and down the furrow, and after sucking the clitoris pushed his tongue up the passage. I had no idea that any man could use his tongue as he did. It felt so strong and entered so far; it was more like a prick than anything else.

'In spite of my anger and vexation, a voluptuous feeling began to pervade my cunt and bottom, and I could not help heaving up my bum as the thought passed through my mind: "I wonder will he go lower down and suck my bottom?" I longed to feel his tongue in my bottom-hole. If I could have spoken, I might has said: "Suck my arse, Captain Jones, and I will forgive you everything."

'He seemed to divine my thoughts, for clutching the cheeks of my bottom with both hands, he clapped his mouth on my arsehole, and after sucking for a moment the wrinkled edges of the orifice, thrust up his tongue amidst its sensitive creases. Oh! it was delicious! For the life of me, I could not help wriggling my bottom about and opening my arsehole to admit more of his pleasure-giving tongue.'

Here, she had to pause; for the pitch of excitement to which we were all raised, both by her free use of these lewd expressions and the wanton play of our fingers, necessitated our seeking some outlet for the pent-up streams that were ready to burst forth.

The two gentlemen had been persistently exercising their ingenuity in titillating our cunts, but when Frances described the pleasurable sensation produced in her arsehole by the entrance of the Captain's tongue, they transferred their attention to our bottoms, and poking their fingers into our arseholes, stirred them about most deliciously.

This very lustful proceeding made us particularly willing to comply with their request for us to lie on our backs, side by side but in opposite directions across the couch on which we were sitting.

It was a low broad sofa, which I had caused to be specially made without a back, and was therefore admirably suited to our purpose.

While they were placing us in the position they desired, that is with our thighs lifted up and pressed down on our flanks, so that our bottoms were fully turned up with cunts stretched open and neither entrances well in view, I said to Frances, 'What a dear lascivious girl you are, Frances! Your wanton talk about your arsehole has driven our men wild! My husband's prick seems just bursting for a fuck. I will put it myself into your cunt, and hold it while operating there, while you can assist Lord Ferrars into mine – not that he needs help, however, for I feel him there already.'

As I was saying this, I turned the upper part of my body towards her bottom and leaned my cheek against her thigh, while with one hand I took hold of my husband's fully distended prick and popped its glowing head into her open cunt, and with the other grasped his pendant balls and gently churned them with my fingers as, with successive prods, he darted his delightful instrument into her region of bliss.

'Oh, Queenie! how good you are!' she responded. 'How nice to feel your fingers playing about my cunt while you watch your husband's prick filling it with pleasure, Oh, Dick! your prick is like heaven in my cunt. Oh! that was a glorious shove! I feel your wife pinching my clitoris; now her fingers are in my cunt alongside your prick; now, they are in my bottom: fuck – fuck – fuck. And you, my dear lord, are fully repaying her for it; ah – that's right – fuck her well – give her a belly full – drive home your prick – I will press it at the root. Hah! you like that. I will squeeze your cods – you like that too. Now, I will tickle tickle your arse; and that you like best of all! Fuck, my lord; fuck, Queenie; fuck, Dick. And we'll bound and heave – prick and cunt – arse and cods – all together – fuck – fuck – fuck.'

The abundant and rapturous effusion we enjoyed on this occasion so cooled us all down that we agreed to separate until the evening, when with recovered strength and renewed appetite we would again place ourselves in position to listen pleasantly to the continuation of Frances's animating story.

So our two men went off to invigorate themselves by an open plunge in the salt waters of the sea; while we performed our ablutions in the modest retirement of my bathroom.

That evening, after a light supper and a moderate supply of choice stimulants, wearing garments of the lightest description, we gathered round Frances and requested her to continue her narrative. Both she and I were so placed that our cunts and bottoms were well in view, while the men's pricks and appendages were conveniently located for the manipulation of our wanton and inquisitive fingers.

Frances proceeded as follows:

'As soon as Captain Jones had aroused his amorous desires to the highest degree by sucking, smelling and tasting, the great tension in his course but singularly vigorous prick compelled him yield to its demands. So, rising to his full height, he poked its swollen head up to my face, and with a proud look brandished it before my eyes.

'It certainly seemed to promise all that any prick could do, accordingly I offered no impediment when he separated my thighs to the widest extent, and placing the big head at the entrance of my cunt, slowly drove it up the soft and lubricated channel.

'Big as his prick was – and it was among the biggest I have ever seen – my cunt had no difficulty in taking it all in, though it certainly got a good stretching; and as he went on working his tool with increasing rapidity and force, its great size not only caused no inconvenience but made my whole bottom and cunt glow with the most intense satisfaction.

'I had nothing for it but to give myself up to the delight of the moment; so I tightened, as my dear lord had taught me, the pleasure girths inside and each time the captain sent home his prick, I squeezed its head far up in my cunt, and met his onward push with a corresponding heave of my bottom. He quickly discovered that I was enjoying the lively movement of his prick equally with himself and, holding me firmly by the shoulders, he leaned forward, pressing his whole weight on my body, and with a roar of delight poured into my cunt a flood of boiling sperm. I then lay under him, with my eyes closed, while he remained for a few moments with the whole length of his prick soaking in my cunt.

'One of the men, however, attracted by the shout and excited by a view of the captain's ecstasy, now came behind him, and pushing a hand between his legs, felt the lips of my cunt.

'The captain, arousing himself, looked round and seeing who it was said: 'That's right, Darby, hold my balls and tickle her arse while I take another bout, and then you shall have a clear coast all to yourself.'

'I felt the captain's prick swelling in my cunt, and preparing for the second fuck, which you know, Queenie, most women like better than the first, I again compressed its head in the innermost recesses of my cunt, and softly heaved my bottom.

'Meanwhile, the fellow behind, having let down his trousers to give his tool free action, kept one hand between the captain's legs, working his balls and poking my bottom, and passing the other round his hips and catching his prick, made it pass through his fingers as he thrust in and out of my cunt.

' "Go it, captain – fuck her – ram in your prick; how she twists her arse! She is the very devil at a fuck."

' "Man alive, Darby, where are you driving your prick? Do you want to bugger me? Shove it in alongside of mine. Her cunt will hold the two if you can reach it. There I will move higher – now try – push it in underneath mine. Hah! I though so, you've got in – now fuck! – fuck for you life."

'I felt Darby's prick poking in under the captain's; my cunt was awfully stretched, but somehow, inconceivable as it may seem to you, he actually got in the head and shoulders. I verily thought my whole bottom was turned into cunt. The pleasure caused by the friction of the two pricks as they plunged in together was overpowering; I seemed to swim in an ocean of spunk as an unctuous flood streamed forth on every side. Then my sense appeared to fly away from me, and everything became dark.

'When I came to myself, I was lying in one of the berths and the three rascals were tying up their plunder into bundles.

'Then a voice spoke down the hatch, "Make haste, I see lights moving in the harbour, and they seem to be approaching us; let us be off at once or it may be too late."

'The captain gave orders to have everything placed in the boat alongside, and then, turning to me, he pointed to the pistols which he had placed in his belt and said: "Now, miss, you have so far behaved well. I have taken my revenge, I don't want to harm you further, so if you make no stir until the morning you will see no more of us; but if you make any commotion now, we will return at once, scuttle the yacht and slaughter everyone on board – even if we hang for it," he added with a dreadful curse.

'I heard them getting into the boat and quickly pushing off; then I got up, and having carefully dressed myself as usual, took the lamp and went into the fore cabin. I found the steward on the way, tied hand and foot and strongly gagged. I set him free, and together we searched the cabin. In one of the berths we found a young lad, secured in the same manner, and down in the fore hold, lying on the cabin table, poor Roberts, who had been first bound and then thrown violently down; we lifted him up, put him in his berth, and took as much care of him as we could. All the rest of the crew had gone off with the captain.

'I was very thankful to find that beyond plundering all they could lay their hands on, which after all was not very much, they had done the yacht no harm. We therefore decided on doing nothing until daylight; when the steward and I reported the matter to the harbour master's office, and placed the yacht in charge of the authorities.

'I then went to Monsieur Rinaldo, my language master, and when I told him what had taken place, he kindly offered to put me up at his own house until Lord Ferrars returned. I gladly accepted his offer as the best arrangement for the time being, and was forthwith installed as a member of his household. Here, another event, or I should say, series of events took place of a humorous rather than a tragic character, which occasioned my lord much amusement when I related the circumstances to him and which, I trust, will be equally entertaining to our kind friends here.

CHAPTER SIX

The Middy's Tale Continued

Monsieur Rinaldo's family was small, consisting only of one maidservant and his wife, who was some twenty years younger than himself. She spoke my language well, having been born in England, whither her father had gone as agent for an Italian company. This led to my passing much of my time with her, and we soon became very intimate. From the first, she seemed inclined to take me into her confidence, telling me how much older her husband was than herself, and that although a very kind old fellow, he was not able to give her full satisfaction, and hinting that if she could meet a good-looking chap, such as I was, who would be inclined for sport, she might be easily won.

'I knew what she was driving at plainly enough, but thinking I might safely amuse myself with her, I pretended not to understand her. On which, she became still more eager and outspoken, and, one day, when we were sitting together on a lounge, she asked me if I had ever had a sweetheart? I replied that I never had, and indeed did not care to bother myself in that way.

'Then she asked: "Did you ever make free with a girl? Of course, you would not require a sweetheart for that, although a sweetheart would be much nicer."

' "No," I answered, "I don't want to have anything to say to girls at all for I have observed that they are always causing quarrels and leading young fellows into mischief."

' "You are quite right, Frances, as regards common women, and I am very glad to hear you say so, but don't you know what a pleasant thing it is to meet with a nice sensible woman, who could be kind as well as trustworthy. Oh, Frances, you surely know the pleasure such a woman can give to a young man like you?" and she put her hand on my arm.

' "I have never get found such a woman as you describe," I said smiling but drawing away from her a little.

' "Perhaps, you have never looked for one," she answered, moving after me; "tell me, what sort of woman would you like?"

' "Oh, I don't know. I have never thought about it at all."

' "Ah, I think I know; shall I describe her for you?' she said, glancing at me with an arch expression; 'she should be a brunette and moderately stout; she should have a sprightly manner and be sensible in her talk; and above all, she should have a special fancy for yourself; now, is not that the kind of woman that would please you?"

' "Why, I declare, you are describing yourself, Madam Rinaldo, in everything except the last particular."

' "Now, there you are wrong, Frances, for let me tell you, and you know an honest confession is always a good thing, I am very fond of you – perhaps I should say, foolishly fond of you – and I would like above all things to enlighten you as to the pleasure a loving woman can give to a young fellow who has the courage to avail himself of the opportunity." Here, she put her arm around me, and gently drew me towards her, as she whispered: "Now tell me truly, is it a fact that you never touched a woman?"

' "Of course I have touched them when handing them into a boat, or putting my arm round them when dancing.'

' "Ah, you know very well I don't mean that kind of touching, you are only pretending to misunderstand me; or do you want me to speak more plainly?' she asked, as she kept pushing up against me and squeezing my arm with her fingers.

' "No, I assure you, my dear madame," yelding a little to her pressure, for I felt amused at her eagerness, and expected that it might furnish me with something funny to tell my lord on his return, "I do not really understand what you mean, as I have never felt inclined to touch a woman in any other way than as I have said."

' "How charming to meet with such innocence! How happy I shall be if you, like a dear boy, will allow me to teach you what is the truest joy and the greatest happiness of life – " here she took my hand and placed it on her thigh; "don't you know that every woman has a little treasure which she keeps carefully covered up, and the touch of which causes most men great delight; would you not like to feel it for yourself?" and she pressed my hand down between her thighs.

' "I don't much care," I replied, resigning my hand, however, to her wanton guidance. "I really am unacquainted with the pleasure you speak of."

'She seemed almost irritated by my slowness. "What," she asked, with amorous fire blazing in her eyes, "what sort of stuff are you made of? Perhaps you have no article at all! no masculine organs to infuse some heat into your cold blood! Let me try," and she suddenly dived her hand between my thighs.

' "Oh, don't," I responded, firmly closing my legs together, "I cannot let any woman touch me there. I promised my dear mother when leaving home that no woman should make free with me until I came back to her again; and I mean to keep my promise."

'Her face flushed; she had gone too far to recede; and fearing she might be balked at last, she seized my hand and thrust it under her clothes; "Well, at all events, put your hand on my cunt;" she cried in her mad excitement. "You made no promise not to do that! What more can I do except let you see it? Here, Frances, I can refuse you nothing. I know young fellows like to look at a woman's cunt – see, here it is – this is my treasure, hidden from all the world except my husband, and I show it to you; put your hand on it," she said, drawing up her petticoats, and spreading her thighs.

'To humour her and carry on the joke, I placed my face on her very pretty and nicely formed quim. Its lips, which pouted out in ripe luxuriance, were thickly covered on the edges by a skirting of black hair, very crisp and curly. They were not so fair as mine outside, but were of brighter red within, while the clitoris, the fullest I ever saw, projected like the prick of a little boy, and was of a deep ruby tinge. Rubbing my finger down the slit, I said, "And so, this pretty looking mouth is your cunt! And is it through this that you piddle?" I asked, looking very innocent, and touching her clitoris.

' "No, I don't know what that is for, only that I like to have it rubbed; the little hole for piddling is lower down, in the middle of the slit, just here.'

' "How funny! then you must wet your cunt every time you piddle; I like the way a boy is made much better, for he can piss without himself; but I wonder why such a big mouth is necessary for such a small stream to come out of."

' "You little goose, or you little humbug, I am not sure which! Don't you know that the cunt is made for a prick such as you have, or ought to have, if you are a boy at all." I started, fearing she had made some discovery, but it was only a random hit, for she went on: "and perhaps, in your simplicity, you think your prick is only made for piddling too. I wish you would let me put my hand on it, and I would soon teach you the difference."

' "I would gladly let you, my dear Madame Rinaldo, but for my promise, for I would like to please you. Meantime, tell me, as you are so kind, how the prick goes into the cunt, and what sort of feeling you have when it gets in; and if you wish I will go on rubbing this part while you are telling me."

' "Well, Francis, I never met anyone like you before, but I will enlighten you so far as you let me. I suppose you know what it is for your prick to grown large and stiff, and stand up; that is called an erection; and a prick is no good, in a woman's estimation, unless it can stand up, firm and strong. Now if you were fond of me, and your prick in good order, you would take it out for me to see and handle, then you would get over me and I would lean back and let you in between my thighs. Then you would open the lips of my cunt and place the head of your prick at the lower end of the slit and push it up the passage. Then you would work it in and out, which is called fucking, driving it forcibly up, then drawing it slowly out, then driving it up again, while I would hold you in my arms and keep kissing you and saying how much I enjoyed the motion of your prick in my cunt; and heaving up my bottom, I would cry: fuck me, fuck me, my love, oh! what pleasure! oh! what delight! Fuck – fuck – fuck. And you would grunt and cry: Oh! as the pleasure went on increasing; and when at last you felt the hot spunk leaving your cods and darting through your prick, you would give a shout as the great thrill of pleasure agitated your whole body; then plunging your prick as far as possible into my cunt, you would lie panting on my belly.

' "Oh, Francis! you are giving me such pleasure! rub the clitoris harder, now press up your fingers two together, or three if like." Here we were both startled by a shuffling noise outside the door. Madame hastily put herself to rights, muttering between her teeth, what a nuisance when she felt she was just coming. I jumped up, and quickly opening the door saw something like the skirts of the maid, Juanita, disappearing at the end of the passage. I did not tell Madame Rinaldo what I saw, for I thought it better not to arouse her suspicions against her maid, but only said I could see nothing to account for the noise; yet it would be wiser for me to leave her for the present I said, with a significant smile, as I went out and closed the door.

'Curiosity, however, induced me to follow the maid, treading as softly with my slippered feet as I could. She had gone to her own room, hurriedly shut the door and thrown herself on the bed.

'The door was imperfectly fastened and by a gentle push I opened it sufficiently to get a view of Juanita, with her clothes tossed up, her thighs spread open, her head thrown back and her eyes turned up, frigging her cunt with the middle finger of her right hand. In the midst of her muttered exclamations of pleasure, as she endeavoured by energetic friction to satisfy the importunate cravings of her love chink, I fancied I heard the sound of my own name. This of course naturally increased the interest I felt in watching her performance; and besides, she seemed so terribly in earnest, and so carried along by pleasurable emotion, and her cunt looked in such a bursting state of excitement, that I, familiar as I am with the cunt and its longings, could not help admiring her and sympathising with her wanton exercise. So pushing my hand through the opening of my full wide trousers, I placed it on my own chink of delight, and by the friction of my finger speedily allayed for the moment the intense excitement into which I had been thrown by these two exhibitions of wanton female nature.

'That very evening, Juanita made up to me in the most unmistakable manner. She even charged me with deceiving her, and told me, in her own beautiful language, which seems specially adapted for giving utterance to the emotions of love, that I had spoken to her to kindly and looked at her in such a loving way that I had gained her heart and made her expect and long for some more palpable evidence of love.

'I smiled, and offered her a present, she smiled in return, but refused the present and, coming close up to me, said, "That is not the proof of love I wish for. It is you I want," she added, looking down, while a roseate flush suffused her face.

' "My dear Juanita, you have indeed gained my goodwill by your attention, and I enjoy conversing with you in your own language, for you are so kind in correcting me, and take such pains to get me right; but as to love, you know, I am only a boy, and won't be thinking of marriage for many years to come."

' "I don't expect you to marry me, and I don't want you to marry me; I don't think marriage makes people fonder of one another; I know it does oftentimes the reverse. I do want you to love me, and to love me without force or compulsion."

' "My dear Juanita," I said kindly, for I really felt for the poor girl, while I pitied her infatuation, "What proof of love do you want?"

' "What a question to ask me! You tell me, I am pretty, I know I am young. I am healthy. I am a woman, and I tell you I love you and crave your love in return; what can I say more?"

She put her arm round me, and drawing me to her, pressed me to her bosom, and burst out sobbing as she laid her head on my shoulder.

' "Well," thought I to myself, 'this is a pretty fix! what am I to do? what excuse can I make? I must carry on for the present, however, as well as I can, and contrive to get away before she drives me to extremities." So knowing well the soothing effect of such attentions as she was evidently desiring, I first pushed my knee in between her thighs (oh! how readily they opened!) I pressed it up on her seat of love (with what joy she responded by pushing hard against me!) I stooped and raised her petticoats (she made no objection), I ran my hand up between her soft warm thighs, I reached her bush. The lips seemed to open as I pressed my finger in. The chink was very moist and glowing with heat, and the clitoris felt stiff and springy as if endued with life. Wishing to give her all the pleasure I could, I passed my other hand beneath her clothes, and grasped the firm round cheeks of her bottom, while I frigged her cunt as skilfully as I could.

' "Oh, my love! Now you understand me – won't you put it in? where is your prick? let me find it – I will pet it for you and then you can fuck me, if you will."

' "No, dearest Juanita, not just now. I never care for a fuck while hampered with my clothes, wait till I have you naked in bed, then we shall take our fill of love. Meanwhile, let me frig your nice soft juicy cunt; there, do you like that?"

' "Oh, my love! you know how to frig . . . faster – harder – oh! I'm coming – push your finger up. Oh! Oh!!'

She kissed me rapturously, while she hugged me in her arms, then as I gently disengaged myself, I said, "Now, darling, leave me and if I can I will come to you at twelve tonight; but if I do not come at that time, don't expect me, for I might be prevented."

'She left me with reluctance, and I prepared to go out. I had promised to meet on that evening two young men – one whom I will call Henri, a lieutenant in the Italian navy, and the other, Julien, an officer in the marines.

'I made their acquaintance the day after the robbery, when I had to appear in the police court to give my evidence. They were present and took a fancy to me. I passed many evenings in their company, for I thought it a good way of perfecting my education as a boy, though I found, as you may imagine, extreme difficulty in the concealment of my true sex. We generally went to the theatre, or some other place of amusement, after which they usually finished up in the arms of some of their favourite mistresses.

'I was perpetually solicited by those ladies to join in their amusements, but always excused myself on some plea or another.

'On this evening, I had reason to expect that a more determined attempt would be made to overcome my opposition, and compel me to prove my manhood.

'I should mention here that as I often returned late at night, I obtained from Monsieur Rinaldo a latchkey with which to let myself in without disturbing the house.

'I was just sallying forth with this key in my pocket, revolving in my mind various plans of escape from the importunities of my friends, when Madame Rinaldo met me in the passage, and putting her arm round me, without ceremony drew me into her room, and having shut the door, whispered, ' "My dear Francis, don't fasten your door tonight, for I intend making monsieur's evening glass stronger than usual, and I will come to you when all is quiet; you won't turn me out – will you, dear?'

' "Oh! madame, how mad you are! what would you do if Monsieur Rinaldo were to wake up and find you absent from his bed?"

' "Oh! he'll not wake up. I'll take care of that; and if he does, I can easily make an excuse, so don't be afraid. I will come, and be sure that you keep yourself fresh and wholesome for me, and don't stay out too late. Now kiss me, and goodbye for the present," she added, quoting my own expression.

'As I passed out, I thought: How the plot thickens! how strange, to be so beset at once by two most lascivious women, both dying to be fucked! Now, I bet if I were a hot young blade with a glorious prick of my own, instead of being only a poor girl with nothing but an innocent little cunt to boast of, such good fortune would never have happened to me; but somehow, things always go in this world by the rule of contrariness. Then suddenly a light burst upon my mind – why not utilise my two friends! It will extricate me from a great difficulty, be a *bonne-bouche* for them, and given my two randy sweethearts supreme satisfaction. So later when, coming out of the music hall, my two friends seized my arms to carry me with them to meet, as they said, some of the most splendid girls in Genoa, I assured them I would be much better engaged at home.

'Then I described Madame Rinaldo and the maid Juanita, how they were boiling over with lust and wantonness and how I was fairly at a loss to meet their joint demands; "and I must tell you, there is a third girl in the house, whom I love better than either of those, and whom I especially desire to have all to myself this night. But this is my difficulty: madame told me this afternoon that she intends coming to my room tonight and I had already promised the maid, who is, if possible, still more attractive, to go to her about the same time. What would you young fellows think of putting off your other engagement and returning with me. I have as you know the key to the hall door, and we can get in without disturbing anybody. Let one of you take my place in my bed, and receive in my stead the loving Rinaldo, and the other represent me in the arms of the fair waiting maid, while I shall be occupied in another room with the other girl I spoke of; and after you have got as much as you care for – and be assured they will give you enough – I can let you out again, and you may reach home by the small hours." They were both charmed with the novelty of the idea, and gladly agreed to play the parts I had suggested.

So, in due course, we quietly stole into the house. I first let them into a small parlour which I used as a sitting-room. Here we primed ourselves with one extra drink while I gave them more minute instructions, warning them particularly not to speak more than they could possible help, and then only in low whispers, and in everything to imitate me as much as they could.

Then we took of our boots and crept upstairs; on reaching my room, we undressed. Henri ensconced himself in my bed and I, leaving the door on the latch, conducted Julien to the room where the fair Juanita lay awaiting my approach.

I passed in with him up to the bed, and stood there as he got in. I heard her kissing him as she whispered how delighted she was to hold him in her arms at last. Then there was much rustling as they felt and petted one another and she exclaimed, "Oh! what a fine fellow you have got, my Francis! let me kiss him before you fuck me – throw off the clothes, it is so hot, and I will get over you." Then I heard him telling her in a whisper to move her bottom up to his face and let her cunt down on his mouth.

'Then certain sucking sounds informed me, that his prick afforded her a whole mouthful, while his tongue and lips were actively engaged extracting the sweet juices of her cunt.

'In a few moments, she said: "Now dear get over me – I like putting it into my cunt with my own hands – there it is in. Oh! how nice it feels! now fuck." He told her to put her arms round him, and let him know when she felt she was coming.

' "I will dear, oh! how nicely you fuck! how I love to feel your prick in my cunt! let me throw up my legs and cross them over your back. Now your prick gets further in! It fills all my belly! I feel your balls rubbing my bottom! now push – dart in your prick fuck – fuck! there it comes – oh!"

'Now was my time to escape; so I quickly slipped out and returned to my own room. I arrived in the very nick of time. Madame had just passed in, and was getting into the bed where Henri lay in my place, anxiously awaiting her; as she nestled in his arms, she whispered, "What a naughty boy you where this morning, Francis, to give me so much trouble, and force me to expose myself before you; but I know you did it all in sport. And I now find I did you great injustice when I fancied you were deficient. If my old man had as capable a tool as this, I would never think of any other; can you believe it? his prick has not stood for years; and though he loves bawdy talk, and likes fingering and sucking, he only raises desires which he is not able to satisfy. But this fellow is both strong and big. Let me play with him a bit, before you put him in."

' "Well, dear madame, don't frig him at all, for he is on full cock, and almost a touch would fire him off."

' "In that case, you had better mount, and let him fire off in the right direction."

'I heard him getting on her; then, she whispered, 'Oh! what a big head! I am not used to such a great tool! yet it gets in easily enough! Oh! it feels grand! It reaches the small of my back! that's the way now, a good plunge, now another – Oh! Oh!!"

'I heard her teeth grinding and their bellies smacking as she heaved and he drove against her and rammed his prick home. As I listened I grew quite excited myself; my cunt panted; how could I get relief? I abominate self-frigging and only have recourse to it when no other means are available; so I thought, why not try old monsieur himself? – his old tool will at least be better than my own finger and it will be paying off madame in her own coin.

'It did not take me long to make my way to his bed, for I knew the house well. He was fast asleep and breathing heavily. I slipped under the clothes; the bed felt warm and comfortable.

'I am sure, dear Queenie, that though your experience has been very wide, you never had connection with a sleeping man?'

'No, I have never got so far as you describe, though I have often explored the private belongings of a man, when asleep, but somehow he always wakened up as soon as I had got his tool into working order. I am well acquainted, however, with the position you mention and indeed what woman is not; for men are such lazy beings, that whenever they can get what they want without effort on their part, they gladly throw all the work on us poor women, am I not right, old boy?' she asked, putting her hand on her husband's prick, which Frances was softly petting as she told her curious and most exciting tale.

'Quite right, old girl, but judging from appearances, both Ferrars and myself stand in need of some relief at present. The lascivious ideas produced in our minds by the luscious terms and descriptions of sweet

Frances, joined with the exciting effect of your busy fingers, have so stirred up our virile members that they are in full fighting trim, and are prancing like two chargers eager for assault; what say you, Ferrars?'

'I am strongly of your opinion, Dick; and I propose that we maintain the character your good wife has bestowed upon us, of lazy beings, by lying on our backs and allowing our fair friends to appropriate that part of us they most appreciate, and work it to their own satisfaction. In that way, Frances can favour us with an actual representation of what she has described in such glowing terms. And that we may gratify our sense of sight as well as of feeling, I suggest that we denude ourselves of every encumbrance.'

To this we all agreed, and when they stretched their manly limbs in all their naked beauty on the soft carpet at our feet, we readily bent our rounder and more graceful forms over them, and seizing those middle members which women ever prize the most, we placed on the swollen heads the soft pouting mouths which occupy the corresponding region of the female body.

I need scarcely say that it was Lord Ferrars standing prick which I engulfed in my longing gap, and that it was upon my husband's erected tool that Frances poised her amorous bum.

'Now,' cried Dick as soon as he felt the whole of his prick embedded in the hot folds of her thrilling cunt, let us all economise our forces: we will remain perfectly quiescent, and if you fair ladies will move with the utmost deliberation the pleasure of everybody will be prolonged and increased; keep your steeds well in hand, and the final spring will be grander and more effective. I would propose that Frances should now continue her narrative, but it might divert her mind from her present enjoyment; let us rather concentrate all our thoughts on the work we have in hand and draw from it all pleasure it is capable of affording.'

'Right old fellow. Queenie, you may be proud of your husband; he is a thorough-going philosopher, and understands how to attain the *summum bonum*; let us follow his advice, for I am sure we often lessen our enjoyment by giving way to eager impetuosity. But, while I agree with my friend as to the wisdom of deferring the story, I would request you and Frances to carry on between yourselves, as you slowly work up and down, the most lascivious conversation you can devise, as we well know how much the pleasures of fucking are intensified by seasoning the act with the free use of wanton terms and expressions.'

'We will do our best,' I replied. 'Now, Frances, down – press my husband's prick up into the innermost recesses of your belly – ' and down we both flopped, driving the two pricks up until the hairs of pricks and cunt intermingled together. Then Frances responded: 'Up again, dear Queenie, let us see his lordship's noble tool reeking with the rich juices of your cunt!' and immediately the two pricks appeared, shining with moisture after the love-bath in our warm receptacles, and purple tips remaining just inside the clinging lips.

'Now again, down cunts – swallow pricks; now up cunts – disgorge. See the pricks now! how glowing and heated they look! Admire the lips of our cunts how swollen they are! Down again; as our fat round arses rub their hard bollocks; now heave together fuck – fuck – fuck – Oh! smack arses – rub balls – shove in pricks – swallow them, cunts. Now, cunt juices flow – shoot forth spunk – heave – plunge – all together' – and the curtain falls, as the exhausted actors, steeped in spunk, lie rolling on the carpet.

Once again, we agreed that it was expedient to postpone hearing the conclusion of Frances's most interesting account of her amorous adventures until we had rested our organs of delight, and were in a better condition to respond actively to the call to pleasure which her luscious descriptions would be sure to elicit.

So, after a plentiful application of the coldest water we could procure to the realms of love, we sat down to a generous repast of food and mild stimulants.

A little byplay of wanton dalliance and sportive freedoms with naked pricks, cunts and bottoms diversified the scene, and kept the fire bright on the alter of Venus.

Our bodily powers being thus recruited, and our spirits revived, voluptuous desire again resumed its sway; so we placed our naked forms in the most comfortable and convenient attitudes for listening to Frances as she, in highly lubricious language, continued her interesting tale. Playing with loving fingers around my husband's half-erected prick, she commenced.

'In taking up the thread of my narrative, I would remind you how, in the still midnight hour, I was enjoying stolen bliss straddled over monsieur's sleeping form.

'The flood of pleasure was now rising to the overflow, and the throbbing of his prick in my heated cunt warmed me that the throes of emission were commencing; suddenly, to my no small alarm, his steady thick breathing ceased and was succeeded by short gasps and soft mutterings as the sleeper gradually recovered consciousness and realised what was taking place.

' "Oh! wife! how good you are tonight! something like your old self – you bring back the time when you first received me in your fond embrace, and your hungry cunt sucked in my prick with true delight."

'Poor old fellow! I was glad to have been able to afford him a taste of real pleasure once again, for I felt he must have been badly treated; but what was I to do next? I had nothing for it but to throw myself forward on his breast, and stop his mouth with warm kisses as he poured into me the essence of life. The pleasurable sensation passed away and was followed by the usual languor. I remained lying on him without motion, only pressing him gently in my arms in hope that sleep would again assert its power and I might slip away without his perceiving it.

'But every time I moved, he muttered, "Don't get off me yet; it's so new to feel your loving weight!"

'I began to feel rather uncomfortable, fearing that madame might return and find her place occupied by a stranger. I had been there more than an hour, and she might come in at any moment, so I whispered, "I want to get up I will return directly go to sleep."

'As I spoke, I heard madame coming along the passage and enter the room. I had barely time to slip out of the further side of the bed as she came up to that nearest to her.

'For the moment I stood in shelter of the curtains as the foot of the bed, thinking it wiser not to open the door until they had gone to sleep.

'As she was drawing the clothes round her, he said, "You were not long doing that little job, dear; turn to me again – you have been so good to me tonight, that I feel quite happy."

'What makes you feel so happy? Go to sleep, you old fool, you must have been dreaming."

' "Ah!" he said with a sigh, "true, I must have been dreaming when I thought you were good to me; yet, certainly someone mounted across me and gave me such delight as I have not had for many a long day.'

' "What do you mean? I wonder, could that slut have been here! I know she is as randy as a she-cat. I will go at once and try whether she is in her bed."

'She got up, lighted a candle, and made towards the door.

'Now, thought I, the fat will be in the fire, and no mistake.

I therefore followed her, but at a sufficient distance to avoid being seen. Just as she was approaching Juanita's room, which was in the upper storey, someone opened the door and ran up against her. In the concussion, her candlestick fell and the light was extinguished; she had, however, recognised a man's shirt and bare legs; so she took Julian, who had rushed out on hearing her step, for me, and throwing her arms round me, said, "For shame, Francis! what brought you here? did you not get enough for one night with me? I wonder at you."

'Fearing that if he replied his voice might betray him, I sprang forward and violently bumped against her. She tumbled down with a yell, which I did not want, but as no time was to be lost, I put my hand on Julien's mouth and whispered: "Follow me." I led him at once to my room, told him to get into bed with Henri, and cover them both with the clothes until I called them. Then throwing on my dressing gown I lighted my lamp and went out into the passage.

'I met madame returning from the maid's room. On seeing me, she exclaimed: "Oh! Francis! surely this house in haunted! Now, tell me honestly, were you with Juanita tonight?"

' "No, most assuredly, as you yourself very well know."

' "I believe you, Francis, for you certainly had no cause; but my mind is all in a maze; my old man, too, fancies that something in woman's shape got across him, put life into this old tool and gave him pleasure; but I think the old cock must have had a wet dream – or something of that sort," she said with a laugh; "however, let us all get to bed now, and we will talk it all over tomorrow.'

'Going back to my two friends we had a quiet laugh together over the strange events of the night. They were in first-rate humour, as they had enjoyed themselves most thoroughly and thought it the best joke they have ever heard of.

'When all was still, I let them out, and having returned to bed was soon fast asleep.

'Next day, however, my troubles increased. Juanita was most loving, and seemed inclined to hug me every time I was within her reach. "But," she observed, "it is very odd that you seem so big and strong by night, while by day, you look more like a boy than a man."

'I only smiled and said, "Ah Juanita, you must not judge people always by appearance."

' "Oh, indeed, you have taught me that lesson; but when may I expect you again?"

' "As soon as I can manage; I will give you due notice."

' "There is no need of that – come whenever you can – every night if you like. But what was wrong with the mistress last night? She seemed like a hen on a hot griddle, in no way easy with herself. She gave a screech outside my door, just after you left, and when I went out to see what was the matter, I found her sprawling on the floor, where she had been knocked down, she said, by a ghost with a blow of his wing. I looked most innocent, and helped her up; then she asked me, whether I had gone to her room and sat like a vampire bat on her husband's belly and sucked up all the juices of his old cock. I assured her, I had never left my room until that moment. Then she turned her tune, and charged me with receiving you. This, of course, I strongly denied; and I told her that, however much I desired a bachelor, I never aspired to you. 'Quite right!' she said, throwing her arms round me."

' "You are a funny girl, Juanita; when I see your mistress, I will convince her that such a charge against you is a mistake; now kiss me, like a dear, and go for this time, as I am very busy.'

'I tried to keep out of madame's way, but it was no use, for she pounced upon me at the first opportunity.

' "Ah, Signor Gipton, you are very clever! you think to throw dust in all our eyes; but we have ears as well as eyes. You never thought that I was listening at your door last night when you and your friend were making merry at my expense. So it was not yourself that I favoured with my embrace! and you, you naughty boy, preferred the maid to the mistress! How can you be such an arrant deceiver and yet wear so innocent a face! Never mind, I'll pay you off – ah, well – don't make up such a pitiful mouth – I am not so very angry, after all, if you will tell me truly, which was it, your naval friend or the marine officer, who occupied your bed last night, I will not be unmerciful; and if you will let me know when he will be there again, I will overlook your offence of bringing a stranger by night into Monsieur Rinaldo's house."

'Hoh! thought I, is that how the wind blows! How cute she is! and such a wanton jade! but I must answer discreetly, as I cannot tell how much she may have heard.

' "My dear madame, I thank you for your kind forgiveness; it was indeed taking a great liberty to bring a stranger in, and place him in my bed; but as you had already met Lieutenant Henri, and said you liked him greatly and as I knew that from his greater age and experience he would be certain to afford you far more gratification than I could, I devised that plan to give you the more pleasure and enjoyment, and I think I may assure you that he will esteem himself highly favoured by your wish to have him again, and that he will be happy to come at any time you may appoint."

' "Well, Francis, I am trusting you more than I ever trusted anyone – my honour, my life itself is in your hands, if you or your friend deceive me, I am lost; but you could not be so base. Suppose we say then, the night after next; and you, I dare say, will console yourself with Juanita; well I don't mind, if you keep the matter quiet, and take care not to harm her."

' "Thanks again, my dear madame, your are kindness itself. You may be assured that Juanita shall never be injured by me; and as to your honour, it will be precious as my own life."

'She then kissed me and went away.

'I felt considerably relieved by the turn events had taken, for I was thereby freed from madame's importunities, and had her sanction for introducing my friends at night.

'She had apparently recognised only the voice of one, but her permission to bring him in was sufficient for my purpose; and, I argued, if one was good, two would be better.

To make what follows more plain, I should tell you there was a kind of lumber-room near mine where I placed some articles I had brought on shore from the yacht. Among the old furniture laid there, I found a truckle bed, on which I placed a pillow and some rugs for my own use when I needed a separate shake down. And it was here that I used to dress and undress when my room was otherwise engaged.

'My friends, I need not tell you, were delighted when they heard of madam's invite, and thanked me for obtaining for them such an unexpected gratification; and so eager were they, that they asked could they not come that very night? After some pressing, I said they might and that I would try to have matters arranged for their reception.

'I recommended, however, that Julien should occupy my bed, and Henri go to the maid by way of change, to which, they gladly consented.

'So, at the proper time, I brought them to my room as before; Julien took possession of my bed and I led Henri to Juanita, whom I had notified in the course of the evening. Julien had told Henri how he managed on the previous night, so he was prepared as to the line of action he was expected to pursue.

I remained to listen at the bedside, as I had done on the former occasion. I heard plenty of kissing and shuffling about, by which I knew that Juanita's eager fingers were playing round Henri's manly tool while he in like manner was gratifying himself by feeling the soft hairy lips of her lascivious gap.

'After a while, she said, "Stay, I will mount this time – how nice and stiff your prick is! Oh! it goes in – how deliciously it fills my cunt! yes, you may pinch my bottom, and tickle my arsehole. Yes, I will say prick, and piss, and fuck. Do you like this way of fucking? Oh! isn't it nice when I push down and get your whole prick up into my cunt, and my belly presses yours and your balls rub against my bottom. Oh! Oh!!"

'My own cunt now began to water for a fuck, and there was Julian in my bed, with his prick, no doubt, at full stand, waiting for madame's cunt; but she did not know it.

'And here, let me make the confession; I had so planned it that I might have one night's pleasure with my friend Julien, under pretence of being madame herself. So, having undressed in the lumber-room, I came to my own bed, and raising the clothes got in alongside Julien.

'He greeted me with the words – "Dear madame, you are welcome." I groped for his prick, while my cunt thrilled under the touch of his searching fingers. "Isn't he in good order? I have been thinking of nothing else since Francis told me you would favour me tonight. I wonder, though, what he is doing with himself, for it is a marvel to me how he could resign, even to a friend, one so fresh and lovely as yourself!'

' "Oh, never fear, he is amusing himself with someone whom he likes better; he knows how to pick and choose, I can tell you."

' "I have no doubt of that, for the girls are all so devilish fond of him they are ready to open their cunts the moment he approaches; but he treats them all with the greatest disdain. I don't understand him at all – he seems a mere boy, but he is crabbit as old Nick.'

'I could not help laughing at the description of myself, and as he threw his leg over me preparatory to mount, I said – "Don't be in such a hurry; we have plenty of time; let us talk a little longer while your prick is still large and strong. I suppose, with a tool of such dimensions, you are a prime favourite with the girls. Do you fuck a great many?"

' "Yes," he replied, 'I am kept in tolerable practice; I seldom pass the twenty-four hours without fucking someone."

' "Now, tell me," I asked, "do you find much difference in the cunts of the various woman whom you fuck?"

' "Well, not much in the dark, especially if they are young and healthy. Of course, some girls are more randy than others, and then their cunts are hotter and the lips are fuller and stand open, and when you push in your prick they close firmly round it, as if they were sucking it in; and as you drive in your prick, they heave their dear little arses and meet your thrust in the most luxurious manner. They make the best fuck when a man is in full vigour, but if one is at all feeble they are apt to pitch you out of the saddle, and before you can get on again, your strength passes away.

' "Then there are others that lie perfectly quiet and seem to concentrate all their feelings in their cunts and oftentimes more than make up for their inaction by nipping the head of your prick far up in their cunt just at the mouth of the womb. This nipping pleases most men more than heaving or twisting about.

' "Sometimes too we meet with girls that are altogether inanimate. They seem to have no feeling one way or another; you may place them how you will, do with them as you please, and provided that you pay them well, fuck them as you please and in any way or in any place that you like. Some men like this; I don't, I like a soft well-proportioned woman with plenty of feeling. Like you, dear madame; not too big as to size, but having large fleshy thighs, full round bottom and wide smooth belly, with a good bush of silky hair over her cunt, but not too much at the sides. I like to feel the mount prominent, and the lips standing out, so that the whole cunt supplies a good handful the way this does," here, he spread his hand over my cunt, and pressed it all round with his fingers. "I like to feel the furrow between the lips warm and thoroughly moist as yours is," here, his middle finger pressed into the slit, and its tip rubbed my clitoris and the hollow between the nymphae. "And I like to feel the passage inside hot and well wrinkled up, so as to hold my prick in a firm embrace." The finger now penetrated my cunt, and pushed delightfully up the passage; after moving it two or three times up and down, he drew it out and applied it to my bottom-hole.

' "Do you like my touching this little aperture in your bottom?"

' "I do," I replied, "there is great feeling there."

And I put my finger to his own arsehole.

' "Ah!" he said, 'you are wise, you know how to get the most pleasure! Yes the bottom has great feeling. But why not call it arse? It is more exciting, and men when about to fuck love to hear a woman speak of her arse, and talk of prick, and cunt, and bollocks, and fuck, and piss, and all the other words of that kind. Say arse for me, my love."

' "Yes, arse. Do you like me to put my finger in your arse?"

' "I do, now go on, and say the other words."

' "Do you like me to frig your prick and move your bollocks this way?"

' "I do; now tell me how you piss."

' "Yes, well, you know I must first take out the poe; you can piss standing up, but we have to piss sitting down; so I put up my clothes, and if I have drawers on I pull them aside, then I sit down, and spread my thighs so as to open wide the lips of my cunt, and then I hear a swish as the piss rushes out through my cunt and rattles into the pot. If we had light now I would let you see my cunt pissing for I know that men like to watch the amber stream flowing out from between the hairy lips of a woman's quim."

' "Yes, darling, you must piss for me someday when we have light, and then I will kiss your cunt while it is still wet with your piss, for I would like to taste anything that came out of such a sweet little mouth as this cunt of yours. That will be a pleasure on some future day; but now, my love, I can't wait much longer; do you like the feel of my fingers frigging your arse and cunt at the same time? and does petting your arsehole increase the feeling in your cunt?'

' "It does, dear, I have a grand feeling both in arse and cunt now; get over me, poke in your prick and fuck me to your heart's content."

'He moved over me and got in between my wide-spread thighs, and holding his prick to my cunt, pushed with his backside.

'I enjoyed his weight on my body as I felt the big head poking at the entrance of my cunt, then inside, then up, further and further, until the whole length of his grand instrument was lodged in my belly, and the lips of my cunt pressing round its root rubbed against the hairy tuft which grew there.

'Then commenced the old fucking movement – so often told, yet always interesting when our sympathy is called forth – of prodding and heaving; poking and shoving; pressing and squeezing, intermingled with: "Ah's and Oh's; push prick; hold it, cunt; heave bottom; shove arse; fire away, cods; spend; spunk fuck – fuck – fuck."

'Oh! didn't I strain the dear fellow to my breast as the flood of hot spunk poured into my cunt, and his firmly gathered-up stones rubbed luxuriously on the sensitive opening of my bottom.

'Oh, it was a delightful fuck! and brought back to my mind the time when my dear lord first took possession of my cunt and filled it with rapture and delight.

'As Julien lay resting on my breast, with his prick, not much diminished, soaking in my cunt, he said, 'Now love, you asked me if I found much difference in cunts, let me ask you if you find much difference in pricks? and what kind you like best? for I am sure you have had some experience in that line."

' "Oh, I know what a prick ought to be, and can tell when it is able to give the satisfaction I expect. A great deal depends on a man's age; young men naturally have more vigour, larger tools, and being more experienced, if they are temperate in their habits and have not impaired their constitutions by dissipation or disease, are able to give more entire satisfaction.

' "I like a pick then of some experience, of moderate size, and able to stand upright without frigging.

' "I like a man to be cool and deliberate, and not to charge at me as if he were going to stick a spear into a wild beast.

' "I like a man who holds himself in command, and is able to restrain his discharge until the woman has reached the same point as himself and is able to reciprocate his emotion as he darts his spunk into her cunt; in short, a man who consults the woman's pleasure as well as his own. Such you have shown yourself to be.

' "And now you make me recall to mind the reason why empty wine bottles are called marines – because, having done their duty, they are prepared to do it again. So you may recommence. I am ready too."

'He willingly responded, and his second fuck was more than equal to his first; the pleasure was more spun out, all the parts engaged were more fully lubricated and performed their office with more equal force and prolonged enjoyment.

'I was thoroughly satisfied, and soon afterwards wished him good-night, saying that it was necessary to return to my old man lest he should miss me from his side.

'I then dressed and went without noise to Juanita's bedside and gave Henri the signal agreed on; he got up, and we stole quickly away. When they were ready, I let them out as before, and returned to bed. I slept heavily for I was tired and needed rest, but towards morning, I was awakened by someone leaning over me and peering into my fact by the light of the early dawn, while I felt a prying hand searching out the secret of my cunt.

'Then a merry laugh informed me that it was Juanita who had come to my bed and was indulging her wanton curiosity.

' "Well," she exclaimed, "whoever would have thought it! after all your impudence and swagger, Signor Gipton, you are only a girl like myself – and a very audacious one too, to deliver me up to your friends! You must have thought me very easily deceived to bring them to my bed and get me to fancy they were you. I was indeed doubtful of the first, but I soon found out that the one who was with me last night was not the same as the one I had the night before. And didn't I hear your step when you came to call him, and then didn't I watch you letting them both out of the hall door? So I thought I would come here and scold you for trying to deceive me in such a bare-faced manner! though I am not half so angry as I should be, for, I must say, the young fellows behaved well and made themselves very acceptable."

' "Well, Juanita, I meant to give you pleasure. I was not able to gratify you myself, as you perceive, so the next best thing was to get one who could, and who would be trustworthy too, and induce him to represent me; and I am glad to hear you say that my plan was successful. And now, like a dear girl, won't you help me to maintain my secret. Lord Ferrars would be extremely vexed if it came out. He has independent means, and you shall be well rewarded, and meanwhile, you may have as much of the young officer as you please; and you and I will be good friends too." Then putting my hand on her cunt, I continued: "You are very nicely made, dear, and both my friends told me you gave them more pleasure than anyone they have had for a long time."

' "Oh, I don't heed what those young fellows say; they tell that to every girl in succession, and the last is always the best. But how have you satisfied the mistress? I know that she was mad for you. Has she found you out yet?"

' "No, although she came here of her own accord, the night before last, but I had Monsieur Henri waiting for her in my place, and he pleased her well; but she found out who it was, by listening at my door when we thought she had gone to bed. And she is to come her tonight to meet him again by her own appointment; what do you think of that?"

' "It does not in the least surprise me, there never was a woman more insatiable for fucking than she is! Old monsieur is not so bad as she makes him out, but I don't think that any husband, nor a dozen of them, could satisfy her. I know that she gets her draper, her hairdresser and her shoemaker to fuck her at every opportunity, even the poor country boy that brings her flowers and fruit cannot escape. And when all fails, she comes to me to prod her with a dildo, or gamahuche her, which she enjoys most of all, and always repays in kind. I did not fancy it at first, but now I enjoy it as much as she does; and I will do it to you as often as you like.'

'Here she began pushing the clothes aside to get more freely at my cunt but I said, "Thanks, dear Juanita, I am sure it would be very nice, but first tell me more about madame. Did you ever see her fucked by any of those people you refer to?'

' "Yes, I have not only acted as confidante and go-between, but I have at times assisted at the consummation itself. I have more than once held a prick to the mouth of her hungering cunt, and tickled a man's arse and cods until he poured into her a full allowance of foaming spunk.

' "However, I will tell you of her shoemaker first. He is a married man, but she likes him all the better for that, as he has experience and at the same time is able for a right good fuck, being both healthy and strong. The first time he called, madame told me to bring him to her room, as she wanted him to take her measure for a pair of boots. I then retired, but watched them through the door which I had left partially open. She was sitting on the side of her bed, and he went down on his knees before her. She rested her foot on his thigh and pulled up her dress to allow him to measure her more freely. He fumbled a good deal while her praised her neat little foot. Then he pushed his hand up her leg. She drew her dress up somewhat higher as she gave him the necessary directions, all the time working with her toes over his prick which lay along the thigh on which her foot rested. He smiled as his voluptuous feelings became excited, and the prospect of gratifying them opened out.

' "He lifted her leg a little higher and peered up between her thighs: then, as if thoughtlessly, he put his hand on her knee under her dress. She took no notice of it, but went on speaking of some great lady for whom he worked. 'Oh, madame!' he exclaimed, still advancing his fingers, 'she is not half so pretty as you are, nor half so well made! What beautiful legs!' lifting her dress. 'What lovely thighs! Let me open them a little more – what a delicious perfume comes down to intoxicate me.' Here he sniffed up under her dress.

' "Oh, monsieur! What do you mean by lifting my legs? You will make me fall back. I won't let you separate my thighs.'

' "Here he arose, and standing between her legs, proceeded to open his trousers down the front.

' "You must not unbutton yourself – don't attempt to take it out – I won't look at it – I won't let you put it near me – you must not draw me to the edge Oh, my! where are you pushing it?'

' "He held his fine rosy-headed prick in his hand and was directing it between the lips of her cunt now lying open before him. 'Into your swell cunt, madame. Oh, how nicely it goes up!' he said, as he drove it steadily home. 'Don't you like to feel it in there? Isn't that nice?' he asked, as he commenced the regular fucking movement, at first slowly but gradually getting more rapid and vigorous in his thrusts. In short, he gave her such entire satisfaction, that she commended his perform-ance, and promised him a repetition whenever he felt so disposed.

' "With regard to the country lad I spoke of, she adopted a different course. He was a simple country bumpkin, nineteen years of age, with little mind, but well-developed body. He brought a cart of vegetables to the market every Saturday, and then carried a basket of flowers and fruit around the town.

'Madame had cast her eyes on him, and considering that he was well adapted to give her the pleasure she wished for, requested me to take the matter in hand. So the next time he called, I brought him into the parlour, on the table of which I had placed some books of highly lascivious French prints. I told him to wait a few moments while I went to look for the mistress, and pointing to the books, said, 'There are some curious books belonging to the Master; you can amuse yourself looking over the pictures while you are waiting.'

' "I then went out and closed the door, but did not go further than the next room, where I found madame intently peering through a slit in the partition which afforded her a view of the interior of the parlour. She smiled as I whispered, 'I have applied the match, let's see how soon the fire will reach the magazine.' And putting my hand on her cunt. I peered through the lower part of the opening.

' "We had not long to wait; as he turned over the leaves, his face flushed, his hands groped at his trousers, and in a few moments, out sprang a most tremendous prick.

' "Madame gave a start of gratified surprise: 'Oh! what a beauty!'

' "All right,' I added, 'now go and placed yourself on the bed, and I will not be long in fetching him.'

' "Opening the parlour door suddenly, I ran up, and before he could put his prick out of view, I caught it in my hand.

' "What is this for? Ah, I know; come, I will show you how it ought to be employed.' He seemed thunderstruck, and allowed me to lead him out while I still held his prick. I brought him to madame's room, and pointing to her naked bottom as she leaned over the bed, with her head wrapped up in the curtain, said, 'There is what you saw in the picture; come near, and put your hand on it.' He spread his paws over the cheeks of her polished bum. 'And look here,' I said, drawing open the moist lips of her cunt, 'pop in your prick and you will taste such pleasure as perhaps you never felt before.'

' "He grinned; but when I thrust in the head of his prick, he pushed it up with right goodwill. To my surprise, he fell to like an old hand and showed that whatever else he might be ignorant of he knew how to fuck. Nor did he draw rein until he had twice deluged her cunt with his spermy balm."

'Juanita then gave me a delightful gamahuche: after which she went away. And here I must conclude, for that morning I got a letter from my dear lord, informing me that I might expect him in the course of the day, and directing me to lose no time in getting the yacht ready for an early start.

CHAPTER SEVEN

Lord Ferrars' Continuation

Frances's narrative of her strange adventures while sailing under false colours, and the clever way in which she extricated herself from her difficulties, and even turned them to account in promoting her amorous enjoyments, amused us greatly, while her bold expressions and free use of bawdy terms had their usual effect in charging our minds with wanton ideas and causing intense emotion in our generative parts.

Both she and I gazed with delight on the distended state of the two pricks we were fondling with such loving fingers. We admired their size and stiffness, and the saucy manner in which they held erect their uncapped heads; while our cunts, glowing with amorous heat and moist with the dews of love, opened out their ruddy lips in expectation of a coming treat.

I remarked, as I had often done before, the rapid effect produced on the sensitive organs of sexual pleasure by the frequent use of such words as prick, cunt, bollocks, spunk – and even arse and piss; and how thoroughly all their natural coarseness and vulgarity disappear when spoken by a pretty girl and, under the influence of her sweet tones, wanton touches and voluntary self-exposures, what a magic power they possess.

I was not therefore surprised when Frances concluded her narrative somewhat abruptly; for she perceived that we were all too much excited to remain quiet any longer, and she felt that before anything more was said, something must be done, if only for relief.

All this time, Frances was sitting on the soft carpet, while we reclined around her. Dick lay on his back in front, his hand playing with my cunt, while his prick was exulting under the stimulating touches of her cunning fingers; meanwhile, I devoted my attention to his lordship's manly tool, rubbing it to my face and kissing off the pearly drop which appeared from time to time on its rosy summit. Lord Ferrars himself kept both his hands employed touching us all in turn, and, what I deemed a little unnatural, took especial notice of the choice qualities of my husband's fine standing prick. He grasped its firm column in his hand, and slowly pushing down the soft skin made it lift its purple head more proudly than ever.

Frances, putting her finger on it, said, 'My lord, would you not like to see this going into Queenie's cunt? It is such jolly fun to watch husband and wife fucking. They do it in such a businesslike manner. Come, dear Queenie, turn over on your back, spread your thighs and raise then as much as you can, so as to give us a full view of your beautiful bottom and all the luscious chinks there! It is a beauty! Venus Callipyge never made a more magnificent display! and see, my lord, what a cunt! so prominent! so plump, and so ripe and rosy! The view of such an enchanting slit as this, with its deep crimson folds, bathed in moisture and palpitating with desire, makes me regret that I am not indeed a man, able to plunge in my prick and revel in the joy it is longing to feel and impart; but as that cannot be, I must give way to one who can. So, come here, Dick, and after my grand speech, let me arrange you according to my fancy. Now my lord, if you will pop in the prick and tickle her cunt and bottom, I will manipulate his balls and stimulate him behind.'

I permitted her to carry out her lubricious idea, and afforded them every facility for watching our conjugal encounter and seeing and touching all the parts engaged.

They first took a deliberate survey of my cunt within and without; then, while Frances was pouring forth her rhapsody, Lord Ferrars stooped and kissed my cunt, probing both it and my bottom with his penetrating tongue.

My good-natured husband too submitted to be placed in position over his wife, and have his prick rubbed against and then pushed into her cunt.

'Now, Dick,' cried the merry madcap, 'remember you are performing in public, and should be as stately and dignified as a Spanish don; there, that steady plunge was well done; now draw your prick altogether out that it may cool a little after its hot immersion and that I may have the pleasure of introducing it again.' She gave it one admiring glance, and then replaced its soft head in my tingling cunt and told him to push it up.

'Now, out again,' she cried. 'Now in; push,' and she gave him a resounding smack behind; 'push – heave – shove – bang – fuck – fuck,' she urged, giving him a wack on his bottom at every word.

Lord Ferrars laughed as at the same time he delved the fingers of one hand in my cunt and bottom and, slipping the other underneath, lifted me up to meet each thrust of my husband.

The cup of pleasure was now filled to the brim, and I closed my eyes in rapt enjoyment of its rich and abundant overflow.

When Dick withdrew his diminished weapon from its well-soaked sheath, and I raised myself from my recumbent position, I found that Lord Ferrars had precipitated himself into Frances's open arms, and was revelling in the sweets of her oft-used cunt; while she urged him on with delirious cries of, 'Fuck me, my lord, fuck me; fuck me, my lord, fuck – Oh!!'

When we had thus cooled the raging fever of our blood, and were again reclining in various attitudes of repose, I requested his lordship to favour us with an account of all that happened in the interval between his arrival and the sailing of the yacht.

'Ah, my dear Queenie, I perceive you want to hear something more of lecherous madame, and of old monsieur, and their merry maid Juanita; and you shrewdly guess that when I appeared on the scene, my finger, or some other small member was certain to be thrust into the pie so piquantly prepared by my adventurous middy; and you are right, for when Frances, after first releasing my pent-up desires in her loving arms, and still more loving cunt, had acquainted me with all that had occurred in my absence, and described madame's varied charms and accomplishments, I expressed my wish to have a more intimate acquaintance with that peculiarly salacious lady.

'My little darling, without the slightest trace of jealousy, at once undertook to obtain for me the gratification of my desire. She said, that from what she knew of madame's lascivious ideas and habits, she did not expect to meet with the smallest difficulty, nevertheless, she requested me to allow her to secure the assistance of Juanita by taking her into our confidence.

' "All the better," I replied, "for then I can have the maid as well as the mistress; and possibly she may turn out to be the greater treat of the two."

'To facilitate our plans, it was arranged that I should occupy Frances's room and join monsieur's family party during the few days I might have to remain on shore. Frances herself moved into the apartment of Juanita, who in turn was transferred to the lumber-room.

'My design, as you may suppose, was to knock all the fun we could out of madame, and at the same time afford darling Frances and myself all the gratification that could be obtained from her lubricious tastes and fancies.

'As I expected, madame made me the subject of conversation at the next interview she had with Frances. She enquired all about my secret habits; and asked, whether I was fond of women? and whether I went much with girls?

'Frances told her that, so far as she knew, I was uncommonly fond of women; that I have an unusually fine prick; but that I had some queer tastes. This at once excited her curiosity, and she begged Frances to tell her most particularly all my peculiar ways and notions.

' "Well, for one thing, he likes to see a woman's naked bottom turned up before his face, and to fuck her with her head looking out between her thighs, while she cries: fuck my cunt; fuck my arse; oh, my cunt! oh, my arse!'

' "Oh! that's nothing, I would not mind showing him my bottom in any position, and to call it my arse too, and to look up between my legs while he was fucking me would only increase the pleasure."

' "But, further, he likes to fuck a woman just after she has pissed, and he delights to see her piss, and sometimes even to have her piss into his mouth."

' "Well, that is indeed a matter of taste! if a man wishes me to use his mouth instead of a piss-pot, that's his business, not mine. I would not mind that."

' "Oh, but that is not all; he is not quite satisfied unless she lets him piss into her mouth while she holds his prick in her hand and keeps milking it all the time."

' "Ah, that is a queer fancy! I am not sure that I would comply with that, but a woman will certainly do a great deal for a man she likes; what more?"

' "He also takes special delight in having several women at the same time; and loves to have his prick and bollocks handled, and his arsehole tickled by one woman, while he is fucking another; and the more smutty names and bawdy words they use, the better pleased he is. He says his prick always stands stiffer when he hears them talking of pricks and cunt, fucking and pissing, bollocks and spunk."

' "There is nothing unnatural or uncommon in that. Why, his lordship must be a grand fellow for a fuck. I like above all things to meet a man who goes in for fucking with his whole heart, a man who understands and enjoys what I call the necessary preliminaries and indispensable accessories of sexual delight, such as viewing and talking; touching and kissing; smelling and sucking; and pissing, too, which is no doubt most exciting. The man who only thinks of ramming his prick into a woman's cunt and at once discharging his spunk understands nothing of the true science of love, and loses more than nine tenths of its pleasures. Yes, we must make his lordship feel at home while he is with us; and if he does not object to fuck a married woman, and would have any fancy for me, I would be only too happy to afford him every facility – only for appearance sake, you know, I must pretend at first to be very modest and coy. Would he like to fuck me, do you think, Francis?"

' "I am very certain that he would; and as to your being married, I have heard him say that he always enjoyed fucking married women more than others, because the entrance into their cunts of another prick besides that of their own husbands seems to please them especially, and all the more because they are told it is wrong. So I will tell his lordship, if you like, that there is between madame's thighs and hard by her beautiful bottom, a nice cunt ready for his inspection and longing for his prick."

' "No, no; that would never do; but tell him, as if from yourself, that madame's husband, being so much older than herself, cannot, of course, he expected to satisfy a young woman such she is; that she seems a lady of very warm temperament, and that in your opinion his lordship might by a little attention and judicious solicitation bring her to yield to his desires.'

' "Very well. I'll start him on the scent, and as he intends to pay you an early visit today, be prepared for a run to earth; but what about his peculiar fancies? is he to have his way?'

' "Oh, if I grant him the main favour, I may as well try to please him in every other way I can. In fact, I have not the smallest objection to showing him my map of the world with its two hemispheres, curved lines and central regions; and when he has explored to his fullest satisfaction its bosky heights and shaded dells, he may penetrate however and whereever he may chose, and as deeply as he can. Oh, yes, even the thought of his fucking me makes my whole arse and cunt tingle with delight, and as to pissing, I will piss for him, and if he has any special fancy, he may piss himself how and where he pleases. Moreover, if he desires to extend the company, there is Juanita; if you will let her join us, I am sure she won't object, and she will tickle his bottom and talk bawdy for him to his heart's content."

' "Oh, I won't object – I would enjoy seeing his lordship fuck either of you. I have held his prick before now while he was fucking a girl."

' "Ah! you are the right sort of friend for a man to have! Well, bring her to the little closet off my boudoir, and she may come as lightly clad as ever she likes, and you too for that matter; and you can both make your appearance when you think you can join in with most effect. You know best what will please his lordship. So I leave all that to your own discretion. Meanwhile, manage like a good fellow to get his lordship to delay his visit for half an hour, that I may perform my toilette and trim up my cunt fit for so great an English milord."

'When Frances told me all this, I praised her *outré*, but at the same time skilful, arrangement, and said: "Madame is evidently a woman of more sense than I thought; and I feel sure that she is able both to give and receive much more pleasure than the ordinary run of womenkind; however, as the old saying goes, the proof of the pudding is the eating!"

'Frances then went to Juanita, and while she gratified her by according her a survey of her cunt, ending of course with a good suck, she explained to her the situation; it took her fancy amazingly and she declared she must sponge and titivate too.

'They then agreed to go together to the closet mentioned by madame, from which, as it opened into the boudoir by a glass door, they would be able to see and hear all that passed.

'So, while madame was in her dressing-room polishing up her love trap, they entered the closet, Juanita in her shift and Frances in trousers and shirt. Soon afterwards, madame made her appearance in a graceful morning wrapper and fine cambric chemise. She posed on the sofa, so as to show off her voluptuous form to the greatest advantage.

'When I came in, madame received me with much friendly warmth, and made me sit by her on the couch. I will pass over all the preliminary small talk, but presently she asked me if I had seen many pretty women in Genoa?

' "I have seen a few, but none to be compared to the fair specimen before me now," and looking particularly at her neck and shoulders, which were only partially covered with a handkerchief lightly thrown over them, I continued, "and let me say, without meaning to flatter you, my dear madame, that with the exception of the Venue of Canova, I have not seen anywhere a more beautiful throat or more finely proportioned shoulders than these," putting my hand gently on her arm, and moving closely up to her.

' "Ah, my lord, you are crafty; you say you are not flattering, but I know by your eye that you really want to see a little more."

'I accepted the hint, and raising the kerchief, passed my hand down to the rise of her swelling breasts.

' "There now! see, how one favour only emboldens you to look for another; I engage, you are now longing to see what my titties are likes – ah, don't – they are not worth looking at – stop."

' "Not so; they are very beautiful," and I stooped as if to kiss them.

She made a show of keeping me off, as she said, "You English have a funny way of expressing admiration; in love as in war, you are always more ready with deeds than words – ah, don't – don't – now let my bubbies alone; you just remind me of a baby poking about its mouth to find the teat."

' "Just so," I replied taking one of her nipples between my lips, while my stooping posture enabled me to slip my hand under her petticoats and run it up between her legs.

' "Oh! what are you doing down there? Stop – babies don't look for a teat under one's petticoats!"

' "Ah, but I am more intelligent than other babies, for I know there is a teat somewhere here that is best of all – and here it is between two soft lips – oh, it is a delicious little teat!"

' "Oh, my lord! – don't do that – do–n–t – oh – eh," she said, throwing back her head, and letting me open her thighs more widely.

' "What a strange man you are! How you push me back; you must not spread my thighs, I know what you want – you want to be indecent and to see everything I have between my legs; and indeed, there is not much to be seen – ah, don't – you must not raise my dress; how can you expose me that way! oh, I am so ashamed! It is shocking to be opened up to a man's view in such a manner!" and she threw her arms across her face.

' "What are you doing? Oh! how your fingers tickle me! How can you kiss it? Oh, yes, I know that you are only preparing it for something else – there, don't I see you unbuttoning your dress and loosening your braces – don't take it out – why do you wish me to look at it? Yes, it is very nice, and big, and strong; I know it is called a prick, my husband has one too, only not nearly so large and stiff. Does he often put it into me? not very often, he is not able. Yes, I know this is my cunt, and that it is made for a prick, but I cannot let you put your prick into it, you know, that would not be proper. Yes, I am quite aware that fucking is very pleasant, but I musn't let you fuck me, my husband only should do that."

' "Oh! you cannot refuse, now that you have let me see your charming cunt" – and I pushed in between her legs.

' "But you must not see it any more" – and she covered it with both hands, while I tried to thrust in my prick between.

'Her fingers, however, were but a poor protection, for it quickly pushed through them and pressed the clitoris with its head; as soon as she felt it there, she cried, "Well, my lord, there is no resisting you, you are so determined to have your own way, but first, let me see what your champion is like," and raising herself from her recumbent position, and throwing aside even the semblance of modesty, she took my prick in her hands, felt it all over, then moved on to the balls, and finished by touching in the most lascivious manner the aperture behind. As she made this investigation, she said, "Ah, my lord, you have what many a nobleman has not: a right noble tool, backed up with a pair of splendid cods – large and tightly gathered up. But before you bring them into play you would like, I am sure, to get a good view of my bottom – or my arse, if you like that word better, and as I am told it excites some men greatly to see a woman piss, I am quite willing to let you watch my cunt in that interesting act. So, if it would please you to see me piss now, put your hand under the sofa, and you will find a box containing a poe which I sometimes use when taken short. Take it out, and I will piss into it, or anywhere else that you like.'

'I laughed outright while I glanced at the bright eyes which I saw peeping through the glass door of the closet; but thinking it better to go on with the joke I said, "My dear madame, you are right, there is no more beautiful object than the fair, round, plump arse of a handsome young woman like you; and the sight of such a woman in the act of pissing has a most stimulating effect. Moreover, nature has set the pissing hole right in the centre of the cunt, not only to cleanse and moisten it, but also to impart an agreeable parfume; for the smell of fresh piss on a healthy woman's cunt is decidedly pleasant to a man who is going to fuck her; and even its taste as it issues fresh from her cunt is piquant and exciting. So if you are inclined to piss now put your bottom out a little over the edge of the sofa, and I will hold the pot underneath."

'Madame pulled up her shirt behind, and holding back her tights on either side with her hands, thrust forward her arse in all its naked splendour; her cunt, thus drawn widely open, presented its glowing slit in a most lascivious and attractive manner.

' "Now, my lord, are you pleased?' she asked. 'My whole bottom is exposed – hairy lips, rosey cleft and arsehole – nothing is hidden, you see it all. Now, are you ready? Shall I piss?"

' "Yes, I am ready – fire away" – and a watery jet of a clear amber colour darted out of the crimsom chink, and with a hissing, gurgling noise splashed into the pot I held beneath.

'A woman pisses much more rapidly than a man, but before she finished I caused her with my fingers to wet the lips of her cunt and sprinkle its hair with the odorous drops. I then kissed her cunt, and just tasted the dewy froth that hung about the hair. "Is it good, my lord?" she asked, with a laugh; and putting her hand on my prick, said – "It is this fellow's turn to piss now; shall I hold the poe for you? and if you wish to give me a taste, you may sprinkle a little on my lips."

' "Well, my dear madame, as you are so very good, just take its head into your mouth and hold the poe under your chin."

'My intention, of course, was only to try how far she would go: but she made no small bones of the matter, for holding my prick daintily in her hand, she popped its head into her mouth and then worked it with her fingers as if she was milking a cow.

'But finding that nothing was coming, she took it out, saying, "Piss, my lord; why don't you piss?"

' "My dear madame, your abandon is delicious. I came under my good star when I met you. I do not want to piss now, and in fact, you have so well worked up my prick, that something better than piss is much more likely to come. Let me give you all the pleasure I can while I am able. How do you wish to have it?"

' "Place me in any position that you choose but first let me call my maid Juanita. She is very clever, and her blood boils with lust and wantonness."

' "Capital idea; call her by all means."

' "Juanita; Juanita! where are you? Come, and being your friend Monsieur Gipton with you; I am sure, his lordship won't object.' And pointing to me as we entered, she said, 'That young fellow is everlastingly rogering my maid, and I am beginning to think he has got her with child; don't you think her belly is growing big?"

'Here we all joined in a peal of laughter; and Frances, with her trousers well buttoned up, danced round the room, while Juanita ran up to madame, saying: "Dear mistress, how I wish we could get you a big belly! let me prepare you for his lordship's prick; if anyone can do the job for you, he will; but won't you take off this cumbersome dress, it is only in the way, and besides, it hides your beautiful charms – Ah! you have put no corset on, that was wise."

'When she had thus reduced her to her chemise, she drew it down from her shoulders and tucked up the lower part round her waist. Then making her lie back on the pillows she pointed to her breasts, and said, 'Look here, my lord, see these bubbies! aren't they grand? but you have admired them already. I saw you kiss them, and suck them like a baby! Ha, ha; and see here, what a smooth white belly! with this navel, like a pretty dimple in the middle; but look lower down, what a grand tuft of golden brown hair on this rising mound! and see these two thick lips, how they push out as if they wanted something! How fat and unctuous they are! still wet with the piss you rubbed over them to make them smell sweet! Ha, ha; you see, I was watching when you got madame to piss before you and then, with your fingers in the middle of the stream sprinkled all her cunt and bottom! I saw you tasting it too! Ha, ha; you'll taste mine, I engage."

' "That I would, my pretty Juanita; raise your shift, show me your cunt and shoot out your piss, and see if I don't."

' "Oh, well, you can have my cunt whenever you like, and piss too, for that matter; but at present, it is better to confine your attention to madame. She is longing to be fucked – look at the love juice oozing out at the end of her cunt! and, see how her splendid arse is dimpled! and these great white cheeks, how they close in round this dainty little pink arsehole, which seems to invite attention too."

'Madame had been all this time playing with my prick, and gradually drawing me towards her, and she now, with animation, exclaimed, "Now, Juanita, you have prepared me enough; pop this fellow into my cunt, and continue your kind offices by holding the balls and tickling his lordship's bottom, and you, Monsieur Gipton, can act your friendly part behind, and watch us as closely as you like."

'I stooped over her and pressed in between her wide-spread thighs; as I pushed up against her bottom, I placed my hands on her soft voluptuous bubbies. 'I love, you know, to press and mould a woman's breasts when I am fucking her.'

'Then I felt the loving fingers of dear Frances bending my well stiffened prick, and directing the head to the entrance of the hottest cunt I ever penetrated.

'If I had not that very morning poured into the cunt of my sweet

Frances all my super-abundant spunk, I should certainly have discharged at onece, and, even so, it was with difficulty I restrained myself, as I slowly drove up my prick until our hair was blended, and my balls pressed tightly on her arse.

'I remained thus for a moment, enjoying the sensation of feeling my entire prick embedded in a cunt glowing with such an unusual degree of amorous heat. But that did not satisfy her; holding me firmly embraced in her arms, she suddenly jerked up her bottom with such vigour that she must have forced my prick at least another inch into her wanton recess. Then flinging her legs in the air, she pounded on my backside with her heels, and kept heaving up her cunt, as she cried, "Fuck, my lord – fuck, for your life – fuck – drive in your prick batter my arse with your balls," then turning to Juanita, she cried, "Come round here, Juanita, and push your most lascivious bottom up to his lordship's face while I get my head between your thighs and suck your randy cunt; and Monsieur Gipton, I trust your busy hands will improve the shining hour by pressing the honey bag of your friend, and tickling him in the rear.'

'Surrounded as I was by these various appliances of pleasure, my whole body seemed to float in a sea of voluptuous bliss.

'My face was rubbed by the satin cheeks of Juanita's alabaster bottom, dimpling with pleasurable contractions, as madame's penetrating tongue stirred up the nervous organism of her cunt.

'While madam herself, writhing and twisting under me in all the mad delirium of gratified desire, sucked in my prick as into the vortex of a whirlpool.

'All the time, I felt the soft fingers of my middy roving with stimulating touch over each sensitive surface that came within her reach.

'Then the floodgates of pleasures burst open, and madame trembled with eager delight as she felt her heated reservoir brim over with the vivifying stream.

She was indeed voracious in her appetite, for as I lay panting on her bosom, the inner folds of her cunt seemed to be still sucking out with fond compression the last drops that could be extracted from the fountain of love, and, after allowing me a moments to recover breath, she wanted me to start afresh; but the powers of nature would not respond, so I had to retire from that well-contested field, leaving her victorious in the fight, but not quite satisfied with the result.

CHAPTER EIGHT

Old Monsieur's Ingenious Device

'Strange to say, madame's excessive lubricity rather caused me to experience a sense of satiety amounting almost to dislike; so that, instead of seeking, I actually avoided a repetition of such another amorous encounter as I have described.

'Juanita, however, may have had something to say do with; for she certainly was a counter attraction of no mean power.

'Not that she tried, or even wished, to draw me away from her mistress; but she had such a winning and artless manner and manifested a spirit of such thorough self-abnegation that I felt struck with admiration for her, and was singularly drawn to her.

'She accompanied Frances willingly to my room at night, and on several occasions, we had very jolly bouts together.

'After they had entered, I always kept my door locked, but one night just as we were dropping off to sleep after a delightful fuck, in which we had all participated, we heard the handle of the door stirred and then a gentle knock. I made no response, for I guessed who was there, but the wish then arose in my mind to make an effort to compensate poor old monsieur for the neglect and ill-treatment he had experienced at the hands of his wife.

'Frances warmly commended this notion, and we arranged a little plot together for the accomplishment of our design.

'But monsieur was not by any means so simple as we thought; he had not only been carrying on with Jaunita on the sly, but had, by an extraordinary device of his own, discovered the true sex of Frances, with a view to making her subservient to his desires.'

Here, Frances, interrupted, by saying – 'Oh, my lord, don't tell that, for it was a dirty trick.'

'It was indeed, as you say, a dirty trick, but at the same time so ingeniously carried out, that I am sure the account of it will please and gratify our kind friends here.

'But to make the matter more intelligible, I will first relate the commencement of his intrigue with Juanita, as she afterwards described it to Frances.

'The morning after Frances had so kindly consoled monsieur in the absence of his wife, he closely questioned Juanita as to the event of the previous night, and said to her, "I have always admired your candour and truthfulness, Juanita, and I have ever found you kind and obliging – tell me truly, was it you who came to my bed last night and made up so delightfully for madame's desertion and neglect?"

' "No indeed, monsieur, I never left my room, until, as you know, madame herself came to my door."

' "Well then, some good angel must have paid me a visit, for you two were the only woman in the house last night; and certainly a lovely being in female form came and took pity on my loneliness, when madame had gone off gallivanting by herself. You know how she treats me, and I am sure you often pity me; I see it in your eyes even now Juanita." Here the old fellow took her in his arms and began to kiss her.

' "Oh, fie! monsieur! how can you make so free with a servant. There now, you have had enough; let me go; don't keep pushing in your knee between mine! I cannot suffer you to raise my dress – Oh! monsieur. Take your hand away – how you rummage me! Why don't you choose a young lady from one of your classes? She would suit you better than I.'

' "No, sweet Juanita, no one could suit me better than yourself. You are as nicely made here as the finest lady in the land. How uncommonly ripe and plump your cunt is. You must have had some experience in fucking – let me have a peep."

' "Oh, no; not now, at least; mistress might come in, and she would kill me if she caught me with you.'

' "No danger of that; she has gone out shopping, and the hall door is closed. Monsieur Gipton, is out too, so we have the house all to ourselves. Come into my room – sit down here on the couch; you are very pretty, Juanita, and as good as you are pretty; now put your hand inside my trousers and take out my old fellow; he is not so far gone as your mistress makes out there, you have stiffened him up already, dear girl – how nicely you frig! slip your tongue into my mouth while your soft fingers are playing with my prick. Oh! Oh!! now stop – we must not let it come yet; lean back, and let me cock up your bottom with this pillow what a lot of hair you have, Juanita! and the lips of your cunt are grand: so soft! so juicy and so warm! just what a cunt ought to be! may I fuck you!"

' "Oh, yes, fuck away – get all the pleasure you can – your prick is not bad; it is indeed a shame for the mistress to treat you as she does. I am glad my cunt pleases you – yes, I like that – now, fuck me faster – fuck me harder drive up your prick as far you can – fuck – oh! it's coming! there – there. Now are you content? Kiss me."

'You are a darling girl, Juanita, and have given me great satisfaction. Take this little present as an earnest of future favours, and always regard me as a sure and trustworthy friend; and now that I have taken you into my confidence, I want to talk with you about another matter. Tell me truly what you think of young Gipton. He is much with you – do you like him? and has he ever attempted to make free with you?"

' "I do like him, but he has made no advances of that kind to me; what do you think of him yourself."

' "I do like him too, but there is something about him which puzzles me beyond measure. I have a curious feeling whenever I go near him, as if I would like to throw my arms round him and hug him to my breast."

'Juanita laughed until the tears ran down her cheeks.

' "What are you laughing at, dear?"

' "The notion of your hugging in your arms a young man like Monsieur Gipton!"

' "Well, I can't account for it myself; but, I am persuaded there is some mystery connected with him which I will not rest until I find out, and I think from the twinkle in your eye you know more about him than you are willing to confess. However, I shall soon ascertain one point at least – which will help me, I think, towards a satisfactory solution."

'Some days after, monsieur came to her with a broad grin on his face, saying, "The mystery is solved, Juanita, I have discovered his secret. He is a girl – as indeed I have suspected for some time, and you, you rogue, knew it too."

' "You don't say, monsieur! How did you find it out?"

' "Come with me and I will show you."

'He brought her to a room at the rear of the house, which he called his laboratory and in which was a variety of chemical and scientific apparatus. For monsieur was a much esteemed science lecturer. Off this room was a small privy adjoining the one for general house use. They were both what are called earth–closets, and were supplied with fresh earth every day by the gardener; the open space under the seats was roomy and fully lighted by a large aperture behind.

'Monsieur first brought Juanita to the house closet, and having marked with chalk a cross on the underside of the cover, he closed it down; then he took her to his own, and directed her to look through a tube placed slantingly in the seat. To her surprise, she got a clear view of the cross marked on the underside of the cover of the other closet.

'Monsieur smiled, and said, "Now, Juanita, if that were a bottom, don't you think we could easily tell whether it had a prick or a cunt?"

' "I suppose so," she answered.

' "Well, this morning, I watched Monsieur Gipton going to the closet and soon had the satisfaction of seeing a beautiful girl's bottom performing in the usual way; and I saw yours too, my pretty Juanita, and I can tell you, it make my old prick stand again. Come my pet, stoop over and let me fuck you *en levrette*.'

'Then, after pawing over and moulding her posteriors, and nibbling at her cunt, he plunged in his prick; and as he worked it to and fro, loud grunts and snorts proclaimed the intensity of his enjoyment.

When she stood up and had shaken down her dress, as a hen shakes her feathers after passing from under the cock, he kissed her, and said, "Sweet Juanita, you more than make up for madame's coldness and neglect; may I test your kindness a little further – will you help me gain Frances? and then, we shall have fine times, all three together."

'She said her influence was small, but she would willingly do all she could.'

Part of Lord Ferrars' narrative not being quite clear to me, I interrupted him by saying, 'But, my lord, you have not told us by what means monsieur obtained the interesting view of Frances's pretty bottom.'

'True; the fact is, monsieur brought scientific knowledge into operation. He fixed two mirrors, which he was in the habit of using at his lecturers, on the opposite side walls under the seats. There was only the one open space extending under the two closets, and by placing the mirrors at the necessary angles the reflection of whatever was on the seat was thrown up from one to the other; and by using on his side a slanting tube through a perforated cover, the secret was not revealed to any person looking down through the other opening. So, monsieur was able to enjoy at his leisure the interesting, and in some cases, most exciting view of the varied bottoms of the young ladies who attended his classes. And although, in the first instance, he devised this arrangement for the special purpose of unravelling the mystery concerning Frances, yet finding it work so admirably, he maintained it in good order, to his continuing gratification; and while on the subject, I may as well confess that the very last treat I had before leaving Genoa (by which time, monsieur and I had become close friends) was the passing of an hour it that curious place of observation. It was while monsieur was holding one of his largest classes, and as soon as he had placed me in position, he allowed them, as he said, to stand at ease, in other words, to ease themselves if they liked. So, as we anticipated, they at once went off in parties of two or three to the privy. I should mention that I was able to hear as well as see all that passed, for monsieur had arranged an acoustic appliance, by which he could hear even a whisper, while he watched their bottoms at the same time.

'The first thing that struck me was how shameless these girls were to one another; amidst explosive discharges and sundry sounds more loud than musical, they laughed and chatted about their sweethearts and admirers with the utmost unconcern; and secondly, from the violence with which they shot forth their evacuations, I thought how uneasy they must have felt before; and lastly, the extent to which their bottoms and cunts seemed to open surprised me not a little, while the spasmodic action of the latter reminded me of a mouth after a similar discharge.

'Ever since then, when I see young ladies sitting with their hands folded, and looking so demure as if butter would not melt in their mouths, my thoughts revert to the appearance their bottoms would present if we could witness them in the act of complying with the imperative demands of nature.

'But to return to monsieur. The first effect of his discovery was to convince him that Frances must have been the good angel that visited him in the night, and gave him such complete satisfaction. She must be, he thought to himself, the distinguished mistress of Lord Ferrars, and in his absence, she naturally turns to me for relief. Though, how she found out that my wife was not with me in bed, I cannot divine.

'His thoughts, however, were now chiefly concentrated on the possible use he could make of this discovery; for his previous enjoyment of her charms, followed by his stolen view of the whole region of love itself, had fired his imagination and stimulated his desire to the utmost degree.

'So, he only waited for a favourable opportunity to try what effect the announcement would have on Frances herself.

'His success, as I am sure you are all glad to hear, was proportionate to his ingenuity. But as Frances was the party chiefly concerned, it will be more satisfactory, I think, to leave the conclusion of that part of my narrative in her hands.

'We will therefore ask you, my pet, kindly to oblige our friends by relating how the old Gentleman very craftily but most successfully accomplished his design.'

CHAPTER NINE

Frances's Account of Monsieur's Triumph

'Well, good friends, my interlude will not take long to dispose of, for monsieur advanced boldly to the breech (we all laughed at her attempt at a pun but she gravely went on), and by a gallant charge soon made his way into the citadel itself.

'I had remarked for some time that he was growing very kind and indulgent in his mode of imparting instruction, but latterly he had become positively insinuating. And on the very day after Lord Ferrars had spoken to me of his desire to compensate him in some way for the neglect of his wife, he made the first overt attempt.

'When our usual lesson was finished, he told me he was busy preparing a lecture on optics, and then added, "By the way, Francis" – he always called me Francis now – "do you know a very curious application might be made of the law of reflection. Suppose two privies adjoining one another had one open space below sufficiently lighted up . . . " then he showed the action of two mirrors placed underneath, as his lordship has described, and illustrated his meaning by a diagram which he rapidly sketched on paper. Then he asked me: "Do you understand?"

' "Yes," I replied, "I know enough of science to understand that; but you surely will not introduce such an illustration as that into your lecture?"

' "No, but I have carried it out in actual practice. Come, and I will show you how the principle works."

'He brought me to the privies and marked the cover as he had done for Juanita and when he had shown me how plainly the cross could be seen through the tube on his side, he put his arm round me and with a triumphant smile said, "My sweet Frances, I have seen you there more than once, I therefore know your secret now; don't be vexed with me, for I love you with all my heart; and I have reason too, for I am certain you once came in the night and gave me delicious consolation, when madame left her own bed, I suppose, for another. You cannot deny it! Let me, my love," and he tried to kiss me.

' "Oh, no, monsieur, you are under some strange hallucination; it must have been somebody else that you saw."

' "No, my pet, I saw you go in and close the door, and then your lovely bottom was fully exposed to my admiring gaze. And now, sweet Frances, tell me truly, did you not come to my bed that night? Hold up your head and answer me. Oh! what a roseate blush covers your pretty face!"

' "Well, monsieur, we all feel for you; only last night Lord Ferrars spoke so kindly of you; he thinks madame's avowed indifference much to be blamed, and considers you worthy of a better wife."

' "Lord Ferrars is both wise and good; in fact the very beau ideal of a true English nobleman – manly in bearing, off-hand in dealing and gentle and considerate in manner. And as you, dear Frances, resemble him in many ways, be equally good and kind and let me feel once again your charming little nest. I know something already of its wondrous sweets, and I long to know more." He fumbled at the opening of my trousers; and I loosened them for him. "Dear girl, how soft and smooth your thighs are! fit approach to this mossy retreat; and these soft lips, how luscious they feel!" His hand roved over all my cunt and bottom.

' "Oh, monsieur, how your fingers do stir me up! What do you want to do?"

' "To fuck you, Frances," he replied, pressing hard against me, 'to put my prick into your cunt and fuck you. Take it out yourself, my love. Do you remember how you felt for it once before. You thought I was asleep, but I was fully conscious of every thrilling touch. Do it again, my love; put your hand in here, that's a darling! Kiss it for me now – how nice to feel it in your warm mouth. How deliciously your tongue moves round its head! Now take my balls in your hand, press with your fingers. Oh, there! touch me there – push in your finger a little way – how good you are! That is very nice; oh! how you suck! do you wish me to spend in your mouth?"

' "Yes, monsieur," I replied, taking out his prick for a moment, "I want to give you all the pleasure I can; so if you like to fuck me in my mouth, you may. I will suck; you push in and out, and I will play with your balls and bottom at the same time."

'The old fellow patted my head, played with my ears and uttered encouraging terms of endearment, while I compressed my lips round his tool and moved my tongue about its swelling head. I felt it grow stiffer and larger as I went on, while he worked his loins back and forward; what surprised me in one usually so staid and correct was that he poured out, with spasmodic energy, smutty words of the most outrageous character as he became more excited: "Prick; cunt; bottom; pissing; farting; Oh! Frances, darling! How nicely you suck my prick! fuck; bugger; fuck; prick; cunt; arse – oh!!" and a fair allowance of thin watery spunk burst into my mouth and passed down my throat.

' "That was a delicious suck, darling Frances, you have wonderful skill and are as kind as you are skilful. I can do no more now, but tomorrow we must manage somehow to enjoy a good fuck together again."

'I promised to be ready for him, and suggested Lord Ferrars' room as the best and safest place for our rendezvous, saying, "He is very busy about his yacht now, and will probably be out all day. I will let you know, however, when the coast is quite clear."

'My lord was glad when he heard how well I had pleased old monsieur; and said, he would like to remain concealed in his room to watch the fucking scene, and listen to monsieur's smutty conversation.

'So, the next forenoon, he went out with considerable noise and fuss, but returned in a short time, and letting himself quietly in by means of my latchkey, he was able to regain his room without being observed. I shut him into the wardrobe, and then went to call monsieur, as I had promised. He was waiting for me, and gladly followed me to Lord Ferrars' room. As soon as he had carefully bolted the door, he kissed me, and said, "Now, darling, won't you strip – take off every stitch – leave nothing on but your stockings and boots."

'While I complied, he himself threw off everything except his socks and shirt. He then asked me to sit on the carpet and hold open my legs and arms at their widest stretch, like a spread eagle, leaning my head and shoulders on a pillow.

'I of course selected a part of the room opposite the wardrobe.

'He then went down on his hands and knees and crawled towards me; all the while keeping his eyes fastened on my cunt and bottom as he muttered: "What a beautiful cunt. What a lovely arse!" When he came up to me, he put his hands under my bottom and lifted it up to his face; he sucked first my cunt, and then my bottom-hole, thrusting in his tongue as far as he could. Then looking up, he said with a laugh, "How grand it looked poked down through the privy hole and how it did piss such a rush! and such a splutter! and once you gave a delightful fart! How it made my prick jump! I fairly groaned with desire. Could you piss a little now?"

' "I will try if you wish, but don't talk any more of the privies, I am heartily sick of the subject. How shall I do it?"

' "Just over my face. I will place some of these thick towels on the floor and lay my head on them, and you can straddle across me with your bottom over my face; and while you piss, hold my prick in your hand, and you will soon see the effect."

'I got over him as he wished, and took hold of his rather languid affair. I then squeezed out a few drops over his eyes and nose; "That's all I can do now." He put his hands up, pressed down my bottom on his face, and again sucked my cunt.

'His prick stiffened a little while I went on frigging it with my fingers. Then he drew my body down on his, and holding me in his arms rolled over so as to place me underneath and his prick just over my face; I took its head into my mouth, as he still sucked my cunt.

'His prick was now of tolerable size and strength, and seemed sufficiently prepared for its work, but he paused for a moment to ask, "Would his lordship be very mad if he knew that you had been fucked by anyone besides himself?"

' "No," I replied, "Lord Ferrars is not that sort of man, he has too much good sense, and he is most unselfish."

' "Do you mean to tell me that if he knew I have fucked you, his darling mistress, he would not be angry with either of us?"

' "I am quite sure he would not. He feels for you, and would like to have you gratified; and as for me, he knows very well that your fucking me would not make me love him less, nor render my cunt less agreeable to his prick.'

' "He is a wonderful man! I wish there were more like him."

'Then monsieur turned, and making me stretch my legs straight down, he lay over me, heaving his bottom up and down so as to make his prick rub against my cunt.

'Then he drew up my thighs and placing my knees under his arms, he spread open my cunt with his fingers and pushed in his prick, and then with steady but energetic strokes gave me a very enjoyable fuck.

'Monsieur then put on his clothes, and taking me in his arms, kissed me and said he envied Lord Ferrars the treasure he possessed in his sweet mistress.

'When he went out, I refastened the door, and opening the wardrobe found my lord partly undressed, and his prick standing up in grand erection. He thanked me for doing my part to well; and then, lifting me up, he placed me on the bed and himself over me, whereupon his prick soon made its way into my well-moistened cunt, and he finished up with a most satisfactory performance.

'Now, my friends, that is all I have to tell of monsieur's success.'

'Thanks, my pet, you have told it very nicely, and if you now relate how we got monsieur and his wife to banish jealousy and live peaceably together, you will have made a still better finish, and rounded off your story with more artistic effect.'

So, Frances continued.

'You have been wondering, I dare say, how madame acted when she found that Lord Ferrars no longer responded to her amorous advances; she was just furious – it was not safe to go near her. She was highly displeased at me, and she was mad with his lordship; but it was on her poor husband that she poured out the full vials of her indignation, for the had discovered his intrigue with Juanita and suspected him of others.

'I told Lord Ferrars he ought to take her in hand and devise some means both to allay her irritation, and induce her to take a rational view of things.

' "Well, dear Frances," he said, "I am not afraid of any man, living or dead, but an angry jealous woman is the very mischief; however, I really must do something. So, ask her to favour me with an interview by and by."

'I arranged matters as pleasantly as I could, and they had an amicable chat together; but I will merely give the pith of his lordship's wise advice.

' "You know, my dear madame, there must be give and take in these matters. And would it not be a wise thing for you to make a friendly arrangement with monsieur on that principle? Let him have his fling, and take the same course yourself. But let everything be open and above board and then there will be no more of this wretched jealousy and vile recrimination. And in place of continually fighting, you will begin to like and respect one another. I will talk to monsieur too; he knows that he is a little too old for you, and if you accord him full liberty, he will no doubt gladly allow you to have and enjoy as many young men as you can obtain; of course, both of you will observe the greatest prudence and circumspection.'

'He then brought them together, and induced them to consent to his arrangement, and made them promise to act with mutual kindness and forbearance in the future. To clinch the matter, my lord asked leave to call in Juanita, and said, "It only remains now to seal our agreement by an act of open compliance."

' "Dear madame, place your pretty maid yourself in the arms of your husband; and I, before his face, and with his full consent will at the same time make free with the charms of his handsome wife."

'monsieur seemed to relish the proceeding immensely; while madame, looking dubious and making a grimace, pushed Juanita towards her husband, and said, "There, you may both do whatever you like, and finger and fuck to your heart's content – why, I will even help,' and, with a smile, she pulled up Juanita's clothes, and exposed her white thighs and dark bushy cunt to her husband's view.

'Then, turning to Lord Ferrars, she said, "Now my lord, I have done what you recommended; I trust you are pleased with me?"

' "Yes, my dear madame, you have made a fair beginning; if you continue acting in the same, liberal spirit, you will be thankful to me when I am far away."

'He then kissed her, and replaced her on the sofa, leaning back on the pillows. At a nod from him, I lifted her legs up on the couch and drew up her petticoats; she willingly opened her thighs to his lordship's searching fingers, and said in a low voice, "Oh, my lord, why did you not come to me? I have been longing for you so much! You naughty man – I gave you all I could, and then you grew tired of me; just like all your sex. But I must not scold you now that you are good again." Then putting her hand on his trousers, she said, "Let me see it – let me take it in my hand; how proudly it holds up its purple head!"

'I frigged her hot swollen clitoris, while she bestowed all her attention on my lord's superb prick.

'Meanwhile, monsieur had placed Juanita on her back on the floor with her knees raised up and spread open, thus affording him a favourable view of her well-developed cunt, with its thick pouting lips, rosy clitoris and deep crimsom chink.

'Monsieur had let down his trousers and was kneeling by her side admiring and feeling her cunt and bottom, while she played with his prick and balls. His prick, however, presented a marked contrast to that of my lord, for its head drooped, and its body was soft and flabby and quite unable to stand erect.

'Madame observed it, and cried with an air of triumph, "Look here, Juanita, this is the sort of article that would serve your turn! Monsieur's tool is worn and it has no longer any power – it is good for nothing."

' "Not so, madame," replied Juanita, with an angry flush on her face, "with a little coaxing and patience, monsieur's prick can be brought to a very respectable state, quite able to satisfy any reasonable woman – now look at it." By this time, she had her finger in his bottom, and the additional stimulus had produced a very apparent effect. Monsieur's prick had certainly assumed a tolerably respectable appearance both as to size and stiffness.

So madame, in more amiable mood now that her sensitive cunt nerves were being pleasantly titillated, declared, "You deserve your reward, Juanita, for you have shown both skill and perseverance. Shall I go, my lord, and put it in for her myself?"

' "Do, pet, and while you stoop forward to place monsieur's prick in her cunt. I will ram my prick into yours from behind."

'Madame quickly knelt on the floor beside them, and taking hold of her husband's prick popped its head into Juanita's cunt, then laying her cheek on her husband's back, she elevated as much as she could her great voluptuous posteriors to facilitate the entrance of my lord's tool into her longing cunt, as he put himself into position behind her.

'I went to the other side of monsieur, and inserting my hand between him and Juanita, got hold of the root of his prick, allowing it to slip through my fingers as he drove it in and out; my other hand, I passed round his bottom, and seizing his balls, stimulated their action by gently squeezing and stirring them about.

'Juanita meanwhile wriggled her supple body in the throes of venereal pleasure; while monsieur testified to his enjoyment by various snorts and grunts; but my lord, like an accomplished artist, coolly surveyed the scene with complacent satisfaction, as he prodded with scientific thrusts madame's dimpled bottom, making her face and breasts rub back and forward on her husband's loins, while I made an effort to complete the picture, by adding highlights here and there, in the shape of the most bawdy terms and expressions I could imagine or apply.

'Soon all joined in, and amidst a chorus of, "Prick; cunt; bollocks; arse; pissing; sucking; fucking," spunk flowed on every side, and all sank together in one motionless mass of gratified desire.

'So far, my lords's efforts seemed crowned with success, but still one thing remained which he thought necessary to complete the full perfection of his work, and that was to get monsieur and madame once more to join in conjugal embrace, and declare that they had good reason to be satisfied with one another. This was no easy task, for they seemed to avoid each other, and only spoke of one another with aversion and contempt.

'However, Lord Ferrars was not discouraged, and we arranged another little plot together. Our design was to have the young officers invited for a night, and then to manage matters so that madame and her husband should embrace each other in the dark, and both fancy they were enjoying somebody else. But in the meantime, other events occurred which somewhat disarranged out plans.

As our departure was now drawing near, I went to pass a farewell evening with my two friends. We had supper in their rooms, and by reason of drinking each other's health and various friendly toasts, we imbibed rather more than our usual allowance and were inclined to be merry. They again twitted me with never having enjoyed any of their mistresses and Julien, who had latterly grown very affectionate and was constantly throwing his arms round me, drew me towards him as we sat together on a sofa, and pushing his hand suddenly between my legs, said with a laugh and a shout – "Upon my word, he has nothing at all! – no wonder he does not care for the girls!"

'Henri joined in the laugh, saying, "But look, how he blushes – just like a girl! Let me try what you are."

' "No, no; paws off, Pompey – no more meddling with me, I pray; if I had any desire to go with the girls, they would like me, I am sure, as well as any of you."

' "No, they wouldn't, for you have nothing. Let us see what you have – there's a good fellow – come, Francis, don't oppose your old friends in such a trifling matter."

' "It is no trifling matter," I said laughing.

' "But, by Jove, it is." And, emboldened by my laugh, he caught me in his arms, and cried, "Now, Julien, unbutton his trousers, and take out whatever he has to show."

'Before I could stop them, my trousers were forced open, and they discovered, not an insignificant prick as they expected, but a full, ripe, and, as they declared, a most appetising cunt.

' "Well, well," exclaimed Henri, "who would have thought it! what a clever, clever girl you are, Frances, to have humbugged us so long! But somehow, there were always little things about you that made us feel you were no ordinary boy; and we often wondered how it was that we got so fond you! And it proves, what I have often thought that one's sex even when not apparent has a powerful magnetic influence upon others. In any case, however, the discovery tonight is most opportune when we are in such a humour. Why, even the feel of your sweet cunt has fairly maddened us with desire. Look her, see what a state it has brought my fellow to! it feels hard and strong enough to go through a deal board!" and he showed his prick in fine erection.

' "And so is mine," said Julien, drawing out his affair, and thrusting it up before me.

'I could not help putting a hand on each of their pricks, while they both together explored my cunt and its surroundings.

' "Well," I said, "as you have found out my secret, I am quite willing that you should have the full benefit of it, as this is probably the last evening we shall pass together. How would you like to have me – at the same time or one after the other?"

' "Let us have you every way; what do you suggest yourself?"

' "First, I would recommend our taking off our clothes – the night is warm, and dress is only an encumbrance."

'They at once agreed, and after stripping themselves to their shirts they fell to work with me, and soon left me nothing on but my socks.

'After again pawing me all over, they tumbled me on the sofa, and

Julien buried his head between my thighs and sucked my cunt as if he would draw it inside out. Henri presented his fine standing prick to my face. I petted it with my hands and mouth until the fierce titillation of Julien's tongue in my cunt made it impossible to continue quiet any longer. So I said, "This is indeed a fair specimen of the manly organ, Henri. I have tasted it in my mouth, now let me try it in my cunt; sit on this chair, and I will get across you, and you can pop it in underneath; and if Julien will sit in front, I will repay him for his kind attentions to me by stooping forward and taking his prick into my mouth at the same time."

' "Capital idea," they both declared. So in a moment, I was straddling over Henri, my well-rounded buttocks resting on his lap, and his prick deeply buried in my cunt. Julien sat on a chair before us and I leaned towards him, resting my elbows on his knees, while I took hold of his prick and its belongings and crammed the head and shoulders into my mouth.

'As I moved my mouth on it, the motion of my body resembled that of a see-saw: as my head went, down, my bottom went up, while my elbows formed the fulcrum. The combined friction and suction of mouth and cunt, however, soon caused the two pricks to experience the paroxysm of pleasure and just as my cunt was inundated with a hot flood of Henri's sperm, a torrent of spending from Julien's tool poured into my mouth.

'After resting a while, we renewed our sports in another way. Henri lay on the floor on his back; I lay over him with my cunt on his face, and taking his prick in my hand, I enclosed its glowing head between my lips. My bottom was thus conveniently placed for Julien to enter it where he pleased. He wisely selected the natural passage, and plunged his prick into *his* soft and heated folds.

'So I again enjoyed the double sensation of having the prick of one man in my mouth, whilst that of another man was pleasantly titillating my cunt. Henri also had the twofold satisfaction of viewing a cunt just over his face, stretched open by the vigorous strokes of a sturdy prick, while his own prick was fondled and sucked in a woman's mouth, and his bottom-hole honoured with her finger.

'Julien, meanwhile, had the gratification of looking at and feeling the naked bodies before him at the same time that his prick was revelling in a warm and appreciative cunt and his belly rubbing against a pair of smooth and glossy posteriors.

'We soon finished in the usual fashion, and Henri declared it was the most agreeable evening we had ever spent together.

' "True," added Julien, "true, in a double sense; and we must thank sweet Frances for enabling us to spend so pleasantly together; so let us fill our glasses once again: Here's to the dear girl who has so favoured us tonight: a warm farewell, and a speedy and happy reunion to us all."

'A little change, which occurred in our household affairs at this time, also had a bearing on events. Juanita had taken wonderfully to monsieur, whether from his liberality to her, or the attention which he now openly paid her, or from personal liking, I cannot say, but to gratify him in every way seemed now to be the leading object of her life.

'Learning that he had a special fancy for quite young girls, and wishing to please him, she obtained permission to invite a young cousin of hers – aged thirteen, and named Lola – to come and stay with her to learn the duties of housemaid under her direction.

'She was a bright merry little maid, thoroughly unsophisticated in the ways of the world, having always lived in the country. She slept with Juanita, who at once commenced a course of instruction to prepare her for the real design for which she had been invited.

'I will give you only the substance of what passed between them as related to me afterwards by Juanita.

'Before they arose in the morning, Juanita took Lola in her arms, and after a little fondling and petting got full possession of her little fat cunt. Then she questioned her as to her previous knowledge and experience; but Lola knew nothing of the mysteries of love, and was innocent as a babe.

' "And so, Lola, you do not know the special use of this little chink between your legs! Did you never see a bull mount a cow?"

' "Oh, yes, I know he has a long red pizzle, which he darts into her behind; but what has a bull got to say to us?"

' "Just this, that what the bull is to the cow, so is our man, if we have one, to us!"

' "And has a man got a pizzle too?"

' "You little goose, don't you know that a man is made very differently from us. In this very spot he has something like a pizzle, only it does not dart out of his belly the way that of a bull does; and he loves to push it into the slit-like opening we have, for it gives him great pleasure, as it does to us also. How would you like to feel it here? Something nice and soft, pushing in and out, just here?" all this time she had been skilfully frigging her smooth hairless little cunny.

' "I think I would like it, for what you are doing to me feels very nice. Oh! Nita" (as she always called her), "that makes me jump! Your finger is hurting me now, you have pushed it in too far."

' "That is because you are not open enough yet; if you were once fully opened, you would have no more pain, only delightful pleasure; let me try for another moment, and I will make you all right.' She then slipped in two fingers together, and holding the girl tightly in her arms, pushed them suddenly up the as-yet-unbroken passage. She thus burst through the maiden barrier, and cleared the way for monsieur's feeble tool.

'But the pain caused Lola to cry out and with tears exclaim, "Oh! Nita, what a cruel girl you are! you have hurt me terribly, and perhaps done me harm besides."

' "Not in the least; I have done you a real act of kindness, for now you will be able to enjoy the great pleasure of being fucked."

' "Fucked! What do you mean by being fucked?"

' "Having a prick (that's what they call a man's pizzle) put into your slit (which is called a cunt) and worked in and out, the way I move my finger."

' "But there is no man here that would want to put his what-do-you-call-it into my slit and fuck me."

' "Yes there is. Monsieur would like to give you a taste of his prick; and oh! wouldn't you enjoy it! and now, I will let you into a secret, but mind, you must not tell anybody. He sometimes comes to me at night, and then he always puts his prick into my cunt and fucks me, fucks me so nicely; put your hand on it, Lola, and you will know what a full-fledged cunt is like."

' "Oh, my! what a lot of hair you have, Nita! and the lips are so large and thick! and all between is so soft and warm! and so very open too! why two, three, even four fingers go in easily; may I look at it, Nita?"

' "Yes, dear, and kiss it too, if you like."

' "Oh, Nita, what a nice cunt you have! Does monsieur like to kiss it when he comes to fuck you?"

' "Yes, he often kisses and sucks it, and he will like to kiss and suck yours too, and all the more because it has no hair on it."

' "I would not care to have him kiss it now, for it feels wet and sore since you hurt it."

' "Oh, that won't matter; let me see it; yes, a tiny drop of blood is oozing out from the torn membrane. That is the same with everybody at first; you will be all right before evening, and you will feel pain no more."

'That night, when they were going to bed, Juanita began petting the little quim, and asked if the sore feeling had quite gone away. "Oh, yes," Lola replied, I was just trying, and I find that two of my fingers can enter easily and do not hurt me at all."

' "Yes," said Juanita, "it seems in nice order; now just open enough to receive pleasantly a moderately sized prick," and she made her lie back and spread her thighs; then she sucked her clitoris until her tiny chink shed forth its first drops of maiden spend as she wriggled her bottom in all the circlings of uncontrolled enjoyment.

'Just at this moment I arrived and peeping through the open door obtained an interesting view of Lola's shapely form; her limbs were beautifully made and seemed very smooth and fair, while her little slit, after the titillation of Juanita's lascivious tongue, gleamed like a scarlet line from her full white mound down to the furrow between the well-rounded buttocks.

'Juanita had told me in the morning all about Lola, and how monsieur was to have her maidenhead that night, and invited me to be present. She also said that if Lord Ferrars would care to have her afterwards, he might, as monsieur was not capable of more than one discharge at a time.

'My intention, however, was that my lord should have the first of her, if possible. So I took an opportunity when monsieur was sporting with me in the afternoon, to say to him, that it would be a graceful act on his part to offer her to his lordship, and that thus the way would be prepared for himself and he would have more easy work.

'He seemed quite pleased with the suggestion, and promised to take Lord Ferrars with him to Juanita's room, and then present Lola to him as a mark of friendship and regard.

'Lola was expecting me, and looked pleased when I stripped myself as naked as she was. She encircled me in her arms, and praised my breasts and cunt; which latter she was in the act of kissing with her pretty little bottom saucily turned up, as Lord Ferrars and monsieur entered the room. She was startled at first, and ran behind the curtains to hide, but monsieur drew her out, and leading her to Lord Ferrars said: "My lord, here is a fair little maid, and as innocent as she is fair; she knows nothing as yet of the ways of love, but she is willing to be taught; I present her to you as a scholar."

'My lord took her by the hand, and said kindly, "Don't be frightened, my pet, we will not hurt you, nor do anything you don't like. Come, Juanita, show this little maid how to receive a lesson in love, and you, dear Frances, will assist."

'Juanita could not refuse, so she placed her cousin reclining back on the bed, while I lifted her legs; and then my lord got between them, I held the head of his prick to the entrance of her cunt, his lordship pushed and it slipped in. She gave a shout and said, "Oh, it is too big!" He ceased pushing; she drew a long breath, and then said, "Now, my lord, go on – it hurts no longer – yes, I like to be fucked – I like to feel your prick in my cunt." Both Juanita and I urged her to go on talking, and to repeat all the bawdy terms we had taught her.

'Monsieur looked on with interest, and even felt the lips of her cunt as they pressed firmly round my lord's prick while he completed the lesson he had undertaken.

'He had no sooner finished and vacated his post, than monsieur occupied his position and entered the passage so well-moistened and opened by his lordship; but my lord did not remain idle, for he placed Juanita on the bed beside them and fucked her to her entire satisfaction.

'I come now to the final act. The day following the scene I have just described was to be our last in Genoa, so we determined to make an effort that night to bring monsieur and madame to a more cordial understanding.

'But how we carried out our plan, and what measure of success attended out attempt, I must withhold for the present, as I plainly see that you, my friends, are ready to retire but if, when we meet together again, you care to hear more about it, I will be happy to oblige you.

CHAPTER TEN

Jim's Visit

Before Frances had an opportunity of resuming her account of the happy reconciliation between monsieur and madame, our party was agreeably increased by the arrival of our old friend Jim. She was still unmarried, and as full of life and fun as ever.

She seemed greatly struck with the appearance and manner of our jovial middy, who appeared to her to be a very good-looking fellow, of about eighteen years of age, with all the free and easy ways of a thoroughbred sailor, very different from the demure character which she assumed at our first acquaintance.

It at once occurred to me what a capital joke it would be to arrange a love scene between them, in which one at least would be in earnest. So I first praised Frances to Jim and said he was a young fellow any girl might be proud to win and draw to herself by the silken bands of Cupid's chain. I next took an opportunity of privately preparing Frances for the role she was expected to take, that of an ardent and enterprising lover.

Then, in order that they might improve their acquaintance with one another, I sent them to ramble together in the garden by themselves, having first exacted a promise from each to give me afterwards a minute account of everything that passed between them.

This occurred on the evening of the day of her arrival; but another small event happened some hours before which I must not omit to mention.

Jim had come in one of her most excited moods. She told me that the very sight of my husband set her cunt on fire. I promised her a speedy gratification in the shape of a good fucking, either from him or Lord Ferrars, saying that they were both equally ready and equally good. Then I drew up her dress, put my hand on her cunt, tilted her back and, having first surveyed the rosy chink spread open with my fingers, applied my mouth to the feverish orifice, and gave her what she declared was as good as a fuck – a warm and loving suck.

She then returned the compliment, by touching, viewing and sucking my own centre of delight, finishing up by probing with her finger the sensitive interior of my bottom-hole.

Just at this moment, my husband slipped into the room, and seeing how we were engaged, came quickly behind us. As Jim had her head between my thighs, her pretty little bottom was turned up in all its naked beauty. So Dick, without saying a word, placed his hands on its voluptuous orbs, drew them, apart and pushed the head of his prick down the smooth furrow that lay between them, pausing for a moment at the ring shaped aperture of her bottom, as if wanting to enter there; but the start she gave, when she recognised his touch, caused it to pass on until it met the lower end of her slit, all moist with the drops of spend still oozing out of its glowing depths.

There it quickly effected a lodgement, as she turned her head and exclaimed:, 'Oh, Dick! how pleasant it is to feel your prick there again!' then jerking back her bottom, she engulfed it to the root.

I smiled at her eagerness, and said, 'Now, Jim, you will have the fuck I promised you. Now, Dick, put forth all your skill, and ravish her with delight; she has been longing for a taste of your prick; give it to her in all its length and fullness – more slowly, but ram it home hard – make your belly plump against her bottom – there, that was a fine stroke. Are you enjoying it, Jim?'

'Oh, yes, darling Queenie, your husband fucks delightfully; his prick fills my cunt with rapture.' She then moved a little to one side, so as to let him have a view of my cunt, which she held open with her fingers. 'Look here, Dick, admire your wife's beautiful cunt, while you are fucking mine.'

Dick went on prodding away, getting hotter, faster and more

energetic at every shove, while he panted: 'Yes, it is pleasant to watch – Queenie's open cunt – while I drive my prick into yours – now, Jim – now – speak!'

'Oh! – prick – cunt – bollocks – bottom – arse – fuck – fuck!' and Dick throwing himself forward, they both fell prone on my belly. I held them together, while they lay soaking for a few moments in the soft flow from love's fountain of delight.

As soon as Jim recovered herself, she kissed us both, saying, 'Thanks, darling Queenie, and you too, old friend Dick; your prick is strong as ever; and were not Queenie so generous with it to her friends, I would envy her its possession, for there is nothing on earth to be compared to a good fuck.'

I must now tell you what took place between Frances and Jim during their garden ramble in the evening.

Frances was the first that came to me; she told me, with great glee: 'I have succeeded, but Jim, as you call her, is very clever, and acted the part of a modest maiden to perfection. It was only when I praised you and insinuated that you had not been so cold and stiff, that I appeared to make any advance. We were then near one of the summerhouses, so I put my arm round her and drew her inside, and when in shelter there, after a little struggle, I kissed her; as I pressed her to my bosom, our bellies pushed together, and somehow my knee got between hers, and I felt the way was open on a sure and easy conquest. When we sat down I lifted her leg over mine, as, I remarked, we could thus sit more close to one another, and as I stooped my mouth to get more kisses, my hand worked its way up until it reached her mossy nest, amidst many affected starts and exclamations. And, do you know, Queenie, that, girl though I am, I quite enjoyed the feel of its soft unctuous lips, as I pushed my fingers into the humid recess; and I really warmed to my work, while I protested my love and admiration; then slipping down before her, I managed at last to pull up her clothes, draw her to the edge of the seat, and spreading her thighs, to gain full access to her hot and juicy cunt, which I sucked, I think, to her great satisfaction.

'When I stood up, she wanted to investigate my affair, evidently with a view to bringing the matter to its natural conclusion by an agreeable fuck; but I pretended it was then too late, and promised that if she left the door open I would come to her that night when all the house was still.

'She consented and I recommended that we should be careful to make as little noise as possible, and not talk at all. I said this in order that my lord might go to her if he felt disposed and enjoy her in my place.'

Jim came afterwards; she also looked pleased and conscious of success.

She said: 'Your middy is a funny little chap, and has the idea, common to nearly every sailor, that girls are made for their special delectation and diversion, and that they have only to go in and win. However, he was so pressing and persevering that I could not prevent him having his own way and gratifying himself, and me too, by exploring my cunt and its surrounding and then finishing up with a real good suck.

'But when I wanted to return the compliment, and ascertain his qualification as a man, he rather drew back, which surprised me not a little, for as a rule, young fellows are very fond of displaying their manly proportions, and, as you know, Queenie, nothing seems to please them more than for a girl to seek for and handle their precious organs of delight.

'My cunt glowed with excitement but was far from being satisfied, so I would have enjoyed playing with his prick for a while and then feeling it rammed home with energetic thrusts deep into the region of bliss.

'However, he has promised to come to me tonight and then I shall see, or rather, I should say, feel what his person is like in its private development. How I wish, dear Queenie, that you could be present at the same time; it would be to nice to feel your soft fingers titillating my cunt while he was fucking me.

'And I am sure he would enjoy it too, for unless I am much mistaken, you have already proved by your own experience what he is fit for! Is it not so, dear?'

'Well, Jim, to tell you the truth, Francis and I thoroughly understand one another, and as you desire it, I will accompany him; but we must keep very quiet, for your room is next to that of Lord Ferrars, and if he heard any larking, he is so very curious, he would try by all means to find out what was going on and endeavour to make his way in to take part in the sport.'

'Well, a worse thing might happen than that, Queenie! I think it would be great fun if both your husband and Lord Ferrars joined us; and I fancy, you and I would be a match for them all. However, it may be well to keep quiet at least until Francis and I have had our promised fuck, especially as he seems to wish it himself.'

Lord Ferrars readily undertook the part he was expected to perform. The slight deception rendered the affair more interesting and acceptable to him, as it imparted a certain amount of novelty to the enjoyment of a really fine girl. All the evening he maintained a quiet reserve, and resisted all Jim's effort to draw him on to amatory enterprise; but Frances, as a jovial middy, exceeded herself in demonstration as an accepted and expectant lover.

We all retired early, and when Jim had gone to bed and her light was extinguished the Lord Ferrars and I, followed by Frances and my husband, entered room with as little noise as possible. We approached her bed on tiptoe, and Frances whispered, 'I am here, darling Jim, and Queenie is with me, are you ready?'

'I am, dear Frances; and your having Queenie with you makes you doubly welcome; get into bed,' and she held up the clothes.

Lord Ferrars slipped in and took her in his arms, while I drew down the covers, and placing one hand under her bottom and the other on her cunt. He quickly got between her legs, and lifted up her thighs, and I caught hold of his prick and rubbed its head up and down the moist slit of her cunt.

'Now, Queenie,' she said, jerking up her bottom, 'pop it in, dear: oh! how nice it feels! you have a better prick than I expected, Francis! it quite fills my cunt! more slowly, darling, but push it home firmly – that's the way; I love a long steady stroke. Oh, Queenie, I can't help talking when I have a good prick in my cunt. It makes both my bottom and my tongue wag in spite of me; and if Lord Ferrars hears me, and wants to come in, let him do so by all means. I feel as if I could enjoy him all the more after Francis has done all he can.'

'Why, Jim, you are insatiable; I suppose, you would like my husband after his lordship.'

'Aye, that I would, and half a dozen after him. Now Francis, fuck – fuck – fuck.'

Her clitoris felt quite hard and stiff under my fingers, and the lips of her cunt protruded and made a sucking noise each time his lordship drew back his prick.

Lord Ferrars never spoke but fucked steadily on; and now his strokes came fast and furious; she bounded beneath, and spurred him on by every means in her power, ejaculating with increasing fervour and loudness as the crisis approached: prick; cunt; bottom; arse; piss; fuck; fuck; fuck.' She ground her teeth with erotic rage, and Lord Ferrars uttered moans of supreme satisfaction as he sprinkled her womb with the sperm of life.

When he began to stir, she muttered, 'Don't take it out yet, dear Francis, give me the benefit once more; the second fuck is always the most pleasant. Let your prick lie in my cunt; I will pet its root and balls, and I will play with your bottom too and that will soon get you into humour again. How much larger and stronger you seem by night than by day! I did not think much of you last evening, but you are a grand fellow tonight.' And grasping his lordship's hairy bollocks, she began gently squeezing and rubbing his large, firm testicles; and stretching her other hand round the cheeks of his muscular arse, she insinuated her forefinger in his anus, and with great skill and effect played it around the inside of that highly sensitive aperture. These touches acted likes a charm; his lordship's prick swelled in her cunt and resumed all its vigour as he recommenced slowly driving it in and out.

'Don't hurry him, dear Jim,' I cried, 'stay a moment,' and I pulled away her hands and told her to feel out to her right and try what she would find.

'O yes, I declare, another prick, on the stand too! and I know it, Queenie, it is Dick's – I know it by the curve up and the size! Put it to my mouth, Dick, and I will give it a suck while Francis is finishing his second fuck. If we now had Lord Ferrars for you, Queenie, we should be all right! I don't hear him showing any signs of curiosity, however.'

'All in good time,' I responded; 'Put your other hand out towards the left and try what you will find there,' and I pushed up Frances, all naked as she was.

'Why, here is something quite different; but it is only a cunt; that can't belong to Lord Ferrars,' she said with a laugh, in which we all joined.

'Who is it, Queenie? I did not know you had anyone here of the feminine gender beside ourselves.'

'Hold on a moment,' I replied, 'until I get a light, and you shall see for yourself.'

The moment Jim perceived who it was lying over her, she exclaimed, 'Oh, my lord, is it you that have been fucking me all this time? What a shame to drive your noble prick into the cunt of a poor girl under pretence of being somebody else; but anyway, I hope my cunt gave your lordship's prick full satisfaction.'

'Forgive me, darling Jim, for this little bit of sweet deception. I never enjoyed a fuck more: your body is so springy, your belly to smooth, your bottom to big, and your cunt to full of warmth and life that my prick revelled in sweets, and melted in bliss.'

'Well, my lord, I must say, that I have found your prick equally pleasant. But what am I to say to you, Frances, my accepted lover! So you have only a cunt, and not a prick after all! I thought somehow you could not have a right prick when you would not let me put my hand on it. However, as you have a cunt, let us put it to use. With your permission, Queenie, I will ask my old friend Dick to come round and poke it from behind while she leans across Lord Ferrars, who is now going to favour me with another fuck. And if you, dear Queenie, will hold each of the pricks by the root, and push up your bottom in such a way that I can get at your cunt, I will frig your clitoris and enable you to join in the common spend.'

My husband, with his usual good nature, at once complied as I said:

'What a luxurious imagination you have. Jim! You and Frances are well matched.'

Frances only grinned and leaning forward over the bed rested her soft bubbies on Lord Ferrars' loins and gliding one hand between their bellies, placed it on Jim's cunt so as to cause his lordship's prick to slip through her fingers as it passed in and out – a sensation very pleasing to most men. The other, she passed round his thigh and softly moulded his balls from behind.

I on the other side put one knee on the bed and cocked up my bottom in all its luxurious fullness before Jim's admiring gaze; and very quickly I felt her hands playing about my cunt as of yore, plucking the hair, drawing open the lips, pinching the clitoris, frigging between the nymphae and the point of one finger penetrating my arsehole itself.

My own hands roamed everywhere feeling bottoms and bellies, pricks and cunts, giving a sly pinch here, and a knowing touch there, thus helping towards the end we had in view, that each might obtain the highest enjoyment these happy conjunctions could afford.

Suddenly, Frances exclaimed, 'Ah Queenie! your husband has taken his prick out of my cunt and popped it into my belly. All right, Dick, fuck away, fuck my arse, if you like it for a change. And Jim, like a dear girl, push your fingers into my cunt and frig me while Dick is fucking my arse.'

Jim complied and, looking up at Lord Ferrars, said with a smile, 'Do the same, my lord, do the same, fuck my arse' – and she pressed back her thighs so as to present her bottom in the most accessible position. Lord Ferrars did not hesitate, but at once drew out his prick, while I holding open the cheeks of her bottom placed it at the circular entrance, and held it as it gilded smoothly up.

Then arose a universal chorus of lewd suggestions and lascivious request.

'Bang your belly against my bottom,' cried Frances.

'How nice to feel your prick in my arse,' exclaimed Jim; 'shove it in well, my lord, shove it in into my bottom. Do you like fucking in the arse, my lord?'

'Yes, darling, I like fucking your arse. Do you hear my belly smacking against its cheeks?'

'Oh, yes, smack away, it is music to my ears. Oh, Queenie! I feel your fingers everywhere; frig my cunt; fuck my arse; oh! now, Queenie, spend; my cunt flows; my arse is flooded; Oh!!!' and all fell together, and spunk poured in torrents on every side.

After this, both my husband and Lord Ferrars declared that they must take some rest, as the copious and frequent spending in which they had indulged of late was causing them to experience a sensation of languor and physical exhaustion.

So they recommended our calling in external aid if we intended to carry on our amorous amusements, especially as three cunts to two pricks was not a fair proportion.

Women spend in a very different way from men, and never feel the same exhaustion, so we agreed to let them lie down for a time while we catered for ourselves.

Jim told us she had a sweetheart to whom she had already granted her favours, and who, she was certain, would readily respond to our invitation – and could bring a friend too, if we so desired. Moreover, he was eminently trustworthy, and could be relied upon to introduce no one to us who was not as trustworthy as himself.

She offered to give us an account of how she became acquainted with her and learned his good qualities.

So next evening, when Dick and my lord had gone to their club, we three women determined to enjoy ourselves alone; and found that by mutually viewing, and frigging, and sucking each other's cunts we could pass the time very pleasantly together while we listened to Jim's animated narrative.

CHAPTER ELEVEN

Jim's Narrative

'My mother, as you know, suffered in many ways by the death of the late Sir Charles. Her grand hopes were extinguished, his powerful patronage lost, and while a comparative stranger on the island, she was thrown on her own resources.

To the world she maintained the character of a respectable widow lady, who kept lodgings for single men and looked after their interests; to a chosen few she was known as a lady whose favours could be obtained when properly sought, and whose services, even as a procuress, could be secured by an adequate remuneration.

'At the same time she never forgot she had two marriageable daughters, and still hoped by their means to regain her lost position in society; yet, whenever a safe opportunity presented itself, she never hesitated to sacrifice their pretended virtue for a sufficient inducement.

She possessed an intensely amorous disposition herself, which she found great difficulty in containing within due bounds, and took the greatest delight in indoctrinating other women with her own lascivious thoughts and inclinations.

'Mary and I, both by nature and training, acquired similar tastes, but under her management and instruction, we contrived to appear to the general public as very innocent and well-conducted young ladies.

'It is now more than six months since Major Ormund, who holds some civil appointment under the present governor, took lodgings with us. He is a fine-looking man, about fifty years of age, and has a delicate wife who, with two children, resides in England.

'He was not long in discovering mother's weakness, and found that with liberal treatment, she was perfectly willing to take the place of his absent wife, and was able from her vastly greater experience to give him more gratification and more varied pleasure than that washed-out lady ever dreamt of.

'My room was next to hers, and as she never fastened her door, I often gratified my prurient fancy by not only listening to but even witnessing their lascivious exercises.

'My mother has a fine figure and, as you know, Queenie, is remarkably fresh and fair for a woman of her years, while her cunt, in its ripe protuberance, is a sight not often equalled.

'I have always regarded it with the greatest admiration, and especially when I have seen it engaged in the noble act of coition. Nor would she have minded in the least had she known that I was looking on; she kept no secrets from us now, and few things pleased her more than to have 'cunt looked at, petted her and kissed by her own daughters. I have often sucked it until she spent it my mouth, and more than once I have placed a prick in it, and watched and frigged it while she was enjoying a good fuck.

'Once she had disposed of our fictitious maidenheads to any gentleman who paid well for them, she did not care what displays she made of us or herself, or all together, and I remember one occasion when we were all three fucked, one after the other by one of her special friends.

'Major Ormund had us all, and paid for us all, but he began with mother. I think I witnessed their first fuck. The major always took tea with us unless otherwise engaged. One evening I remarked that he and mother were peculiarly affectionate to one another, and I concluded that they had come to an understanding during the day. My notion was confirmed when they were bidding each other good-night.

'He said, with an enquiring accent, "Tonight?" She turned as if to look at the clock on the mantelpiece, and carelessly, as it were, put her finger at half-past eleven. I knew what she meant, and resolved to be an unseen observer of what took place.

'Mother retired about eleven, and after a good wash, and no doubt special titivation, put out her light and got into bed, leaving her door slightly open. Now was my chance. I crept softly into her room and concealed myself behind some heavy curtains that were stretched across the alcove of the window.

'Exactly at half-past eleven, Major Ormund entered the room in his dressing gown and slippers. He closed the door and said, "Where are you, my love?" She replied, "Here, come this way; meanwhile, I will strike a light that we may have the satisfaction of seeing one another." She jumped up, and in her with nightdress, with her hair streaming over her shoulders, lighted six large wax candles, saying as she did so: "You see, I do not fear the light."

'He sat down on the bed and seemed struck with the comfortable appearance of the room, and especially with the large mirror fastened to the wall along one side of the bed.

'When she had finished lighting the candles, she came up to him. He put his arm round her, and placing her on his knee, said: "First, I want a full view of the delicious cunt whose acquaintance I made this morning," and reclining her back on the bed, he spread her thighs and pulled up her nightshift, saying: "No my love, you have indeed no cause to dread the light. What a profusion of beauties are centred here! Such a luxuriant crop of silky hair crowns this swelling mound, while these great protruding lips are comparatively smooth; and such a clitoris, so full, so rosy and so stiff! How it slips about under my fingers! has it much feeling?"

' "Oh, yes, dear Major Ormund, that's very nice, you know how to pet a woman's cunt; and you must let me try my skill on your prick, I want to hold it in my hand," and pushing her hand under his shirt she quickly pulled out a fair-sized tool. It was of the ordinary length but not particularly stiff. She took it skilfully in hand, with the fingers underneath and the thumb uppermost; she frigged it deliberately up and down, drawing the prepuce as much as she could over the glans, then pushing it fully back, until the head stood up firm and erect, while her other hand was equally busy fondling his balls and the sensitive parts beneath.

' "Oh, major, how your fingers stir me up! my cunt is all in a glow, and your prick is in fine order too! would you not like to fuck me?"

' "Yes, darling, but don't call me major, call me, Kit – all my intimate friends call me Kit; and if you will allow me, I will call you Sophy. Well, Sophy, I am quite ready to fuck you, but would not your fanny like to be kissed first?'

' "Yes, Kit, but she has a great longing for your prick while he is in such fine order. Shall I raise me thighs, and then you can take a survey of the contours of my bottom, as well as the secret cavity of my cunt," and mother turned up her great broad rump in all its voluptuous beauty before him.

'He got up and standing back for a moment to get a better view of its grand proportions and exquisite roundness and polish, he plunged his mouth between the hot succulent lips of her cunt, sucking the clitoris and sipping up the soft juice that was even now beginning to exude.

Then she muttered, Now, Kit, put in your prick and fuck me – fuck my cunt, oh! that is nice! Put your hands under my bottom – squeeze the cheeks of my arse – shove your balls against my arse. Do you like this way of fucking?"

' "Yes, darling Sophy, you have a grand cunt for a fuck; your cunt holds my prick as if it had life, and your big fat arse serves as a cushion underneath.'

' "And my cunt has life! it must have life to feel as it does! Oh! that is grand! That's the way, I like to be fucked with a long, firm, steady stroke of the prick! Do you like me to speak while you are fucking me?"

' "I do, darling. I love to hear you talking of prick, and cunt, and bollocks, and arse; go, on, dear."

' "I feel your prick getting harder in my cunt, I feel your bollocks pressing my arse – now, dart in your prick – fill my cunt with spunk – Oh! – Oh!! – fuck – fuck – fuck.'

'He was not equal to a second fuck, which I know mother would have liked, but he asked and received permission to come on succeeding nights at the same hour, and took his departure.

'It was not long after this, that I heard him sounding mother as to her daughters. He seemed at first afraid of exciting her jealousy, but he soon found there was no occasion for dreading that, provided he came across handsomely.

' "Very well, Kit, as you are so liberal, I cannot refuse my consent, if you are able to overcome their maidenly scruples. You see they are quite ignorant of the ways of the world, so you will have to proceed cautiously and prudently, and with every consideration for their innocence and inexperience. I, for my part, will afford you every facility, and render you any help in my power, so far as I can do so without exciting their suspicions; but you had better begin with Mary, for if you win her the younger sister will be more inclined to follow in her track.'

' "All right, Sophy, many thanks for your kind compliance; I will be very careful and prudent. Suppose we begin tomorrow morning; I will ask Mary to take a walk with me, and you can second my request."

'So next morning after breakfast the walk was proposed, and mother said the day was fine, and that it would do Mary good to get a little fresh air, and turning to Mary, she added: Major Ormund, my dear, is a man of the world, he can tell you many things you are no doubt ignorant of, and initiate you into the mysteries of fashionable life and the thoughts and habits of fashionable society in London and Paris.

' "Very well, mother, I am willing to be instructed, and hope Major Ormund will find me an intelligent and docile pupil; but I wish to have Jim with me to share the benefit and prevent scandal.

This was a proposition they neither expected nor desired, but as Mary was determined, there was no help for it; and the major pretended to be cheerful when he included me in his invitation; and he really brightened up when I said I would take a basket with me and gather wild flowers while they were discussing the fashionable world which had no charms for me.

'So we set out; the major put forth all his efforts to be agreeable, and Mary appeared much impressed and gradually permitted him various little freedom. At last we reached a shady grove and he proposed our sitting down to rest. I said, "You look tired, Mary, but I am not. So I will rove about after my favourite flowers, while you rests.

They sat down in a sheltered nook, and I disappeared from view; but I lost no time in making a circuit and creeping softly up behind them under shelter of the thick bushes.

The gallant major had evidently made considerable progress in his suit, for she was sitting close to his side and he had his arm round her waist. At first, I was not near enough to hear what they were saying, so I cautiously approached something nearer. Then I heard her laugh and say, "Yes, I know some girls like to be tickled, it makes them feel funny. Where am I most ticklesome? Well, perhaps on the soles of my feet. Hoh! you can't tickle me through my boots!"

'No, but I am admiring them, or rather the little feet they contain! what prettily shaped little toes! and such well-arched insteps! These can hardly be island-made boots! They are just as well-finished and as good a fit as any Parisian belle could desire, and your fine silk stockings set them off to the best advantage. Let me raise your leg a little – French girls are always pleased when their feet and legs are admired; and the famous actresses, you know, do not hesitate to allow the fair proportions of the whole limb to be seen – and you are just as well made as the best of them.'

' "But you want to see too much – Oh, – your hand tickles me! take it away you are pushing it too far – Oh, – don't, major I cannot let you put it there."

' "Why not there? What harm can my hand do to you?"

' "I don't know, but I ought not to let you – don't."

' "Why? Are you afraid of me?"

' "No, but please take away your hand – Oh! – I cannot bear it."

' "Why? Is it hurting you?"

' "Yes – no – but it makes me feel so queer! Ah! now, you are hurting me! Don't push your finger in – I will not allow that – Oh, stop, it is hurting me – it is hurting me frightfully; and she began to cry, muttering that he was very cruel to cause her so much pain.

'He took away his hand and tried to soothe her. She turned from him, and said with a sob she was sure he had done her some great harm, and pulling her handkerchief out of her pocket she suddenly put it under her petticoats and rubbed between her legs, then looking at it in a sly manner and perceiving that it was marked with blood, she thrust it into her pocket and rose up to return home. He begged for the handkerchief, and after a struggle he obtained possession of it and quietly examined it. Then with difficulty he appeased her, and she at length forgave him and allowed him to kiss her, but would not suffer him to put his hand under her petticoats again as she said she felt too sore.

'When they met me a short distance off, she seemed quite composed and promised to walk with him again the next day on condition of my being with them also.

'Mary and I had a good laugh together that night at the success of our contrivance; before we set out for our walk, we had charged a small sponge with the blood of a freshly killed chicken, and having wrapped it in oiled silk, Mary carefully placed it in her handkerchief. This sponge she adroitely took out and squeezed, and then slipped into the upper part of her stocking, when she appeared to be only rubbing her maiden slit.

'The major may have thought her large, for the finger readily notices difference of size, but when he heard her cry of pain, and above all when he saw the blood-stain on her handkerchief, every doubt was chased from his mind, and he felt satisfied that the sweet defloration of a true virgin was a treat in store for him at the next opportunity.

'Why is it, Queenie, that men almost universally regard the entering a woman's cunt for the first time such a peculiar treat? It seems to me that in the awkwardness and hurry of the first attempt, neither man nor woman obtains half the pleasure that they experience afterwards.'

'Ah, Jim,' I replied, 'these matters are not to be judged by ordinary rules and reasoning; and the sense of pleasure, after all, depends very much on the exercise of imagination or fancy – but go on.'

'The next day being fine, we again set out for a walk. Mary was in good spirits and prepared for any lengths to which the gallant major was disposed to go.

'I have sometimes thought, Queenie, if men could only read our minds, how much less timid they would be! Women, like all female animals, I suppose, require that a certain amount of violence should be used to compel them, as it were, into submission; because, though willing enough in themselves, they like it to seem as if they are forced to comply, and besides they are conscious that if men obtain their favours too easily they will not value them as the ought. However, to proceed.

'I took my basket as before and practised the same manoeuvre. When I got near enough to hear what they were saying, I heard his voice – "Now, darling Mary, you can't refuse me the great pleasure of petting your dear little pussy – open your legs more – what a sweet little nest you have! I trust all the soreness you felt yesterday is gone."

' "Yes dear Kit, but you hurt me very much, and it bled a great deal."

' "I am so sorry, but there is one consolation. I can never hurt you again. Do you know my name for this mossy nest?'

' "No, except that I have heard girls call it their fanny, and you now call it my pussy."

' "But do you now what men call it?"

' "No, I have not the least idea." What a fib, thought I.

' "Shall I tell you?"

' "Yes, dear Kit, I would like to know."

' "Well, they often speak of it as a woman's quim, but the common name which everybody knows is cunt, derived from the Latin *cunnus*. Did you never hear it?'

' "No, I have not been in the way of hearing such words." Oh, Mary! how innocent you are! thought I.

' "Why, most schoolgirls know it well, and I am told they are fond of writing it on their slates, together with the name of another thing that they like still better. Say cunt for me, my love."

' "Cunt, my cunt."

He kissed her.

' "Now, what's the name of this part underneath?"

' "Oh! that's my bottom."

' "Good, but the commoner name is more, exciting – arse. Say arse."

' "Arse, my arse."

' "This cunt is shaped like a mouth, you perceive, with lips and moustache too; you use it indeed, I know, for piddling, commonly called pissing – say that, love."

' "Pissing, my cunt pissing."

' "It has, however, a far nobler use than pissing; piss comes out of it, but there is something intended to go into it, something which is able to fill it with pleasure and delight. Do you know what that something is?"

' "No. I don't know anything that could go into it and give it the pleasure and delight you speak of."

' "Did you never put your finger into it?"

' "Yes, I have sometimes rubbed it with my finger, and then tried to push it up."

' "Did it make you feel nice?"

' "It did."

' "Well, there is something larger and longer than your finger that men have which, when it goes in, makes it feel still nicer, nicer than anything in the world. Do you know what that is?"

' "No, I know of nothing better than my finger." Oh, Mary!

' "Well, let me place your hand here for a moment, and I will enlighten you."

'He had already opened his trousers, I observed, all down the front. So he took her hand, and in spite of her affected opposition pushed it inside and placed it on his prick.

' "Now, does not that feel softer than your finger? take it out, darling, and see what a queer round head it has!"

'He kept her hand on it, while he drew it out. She let her fingers close round it but turned away her face.

' "Look at it, dear Mary, it is my prick, and is just made to go into your cunt and fuck it. Now, say prick, darling."

' "Prick."

' "And what does a prick do to a cunt?"

' "You say, it fucks it."

' "That's a darling; now draw the skin down – this way – see how that makes the head stand up! And look at this ridge round the head, that is what rubs on the inside of the cunt and makes you feel so nice as it goes in and out – this way, like my finger – but don't you think you would like my prick much better?"

' "I cannot tell; your prick is very big; I am afraid it would hurt me too much."

' "No, my darling, it would not hurt you at all, on the contrary it will give you great pleasure, greater than any you ever felt in your life – let me try – there – lie back and open your thighs."

' "Oh, but you must not look, it would be horrible to see me there."

' "How could it be horrible, when it feels to soft and nice!"

' "Oh, it is not meant to be looked at; does not the hair growing about it show that it should be kept covered."

' "Not at all. The hair is only meant to ornament it, and keep it warm and soft. There that's a good girl – open a little more, that's a good girl."

She now lay back quietly and allowed him to pull up her dress as high as he could, and spread her thighs widely apart.

' "Yes, it is a sweet little cunt, fresh and fragrant as an opening rose; and its little clitoris peeps out from between the lips like the tip of your tongue. I am sure, if it could speak, it would say: Put in your prick and fuck me. Shall I try, my sweet Mary? you will like it so much."

' "Oh, it will hurt me, it is to very big, you never could get in."

' "No, it can't hurt you now; your cunt, small as it looks, would easily take in a much larger prick than mine – there – I will rub its head between these moist lips – you are a most loveable girl, Mary – now spread your legs as widely as you can – wait, I will put this bundle of dry grass under your bottom – now – how easily it goes in! Now don't you like the feel of my prick moving in your cunt? Ah! isn't that nice?"

' "Yes, it feels nice. Is this what you call fucking?"

' "It is my love, would you like me to move my prick Faster?"

' "Yes, dear Kit; your prick fucks my cunt very pleasantly. Does it give you pleasure hearing me say these words?"

' "It does, pet – talk to me of your cunt and your arse; and of my prick and bollocks; and spunk; and fucking, and pissing – oh, Mary, its coming – push up your bottom – put your hand on my arse – press my prick in your cunt – oh, there – there."

'She held him convulsively with legs and arms, and her loins and arse worked and twisted during the last quick probes of his prick. Then her muscles relaxed, her eyes closed, and her head lay back in love's sweet swoon.

'You can easily imagine how this fucking scene and these lascivious words affected me. My cunt glowed with intense excitement. I pulled up my petticoats, and stooping forward tried to get a view of it. I would willingly then have shown it to any man, in hopes of being well fucked. Oh, for a prick! I sighed, as I spread the lips apart and looked into the hot recess. My mouth watered to get at it! How I would have enjoyed sucking my own cunt, but I could only frig it with my finger, as I softly whispered to myself, Look at it, Kit, see my cunt, see my arse, put your prick in my cunt – fuck my cunt – fuck it – fuck it – fuck – Oh! at last, and I was relieved.

'After allowing myself a few moments to cool down, I met them looking for me, and we returned home together.

'Next day we walked to the same place, and when I was about to leave them as before, the major put his arm round me, saying, "Stay, little Jim, we don't mind you; do we, Mary?"

' "No, Kit, I don't mind Jim; you may kiss her, or anything else you like. Here, I will hold her, while you kiss her."

' "No, no, Mary," I said. "He may kiss you as much as he likes – you are his pet – but as for me, I prefer being a free nymph of the woods.' And I turned and ran away.

'They both ran after me and, of course, soon caught me, and holding me on either side brought me back to their favourite resting place, and made me sit down with them.

'The major commenced pushing his hand under Mary's petticoats, and winked at me, as he asked, "Do you know what I am doing to Mary, Jim?"

' "No, and I don't want to know," I said blushing, and turned away my face. You see, I can act a little too.'

'You needn't tell us that,' interposed Frances, 'you nearly humbugged me; it may be easy to humbug men, but for one girl to deceive another is something to boast of.'

'Oh, Jim is a regular adept,' I added 'we may all go to school to her.'

'Well, I confess,' she replied. 'I do take delight in a little mild deception. And after all, when we deceive men, it is for their own good. You said that the sensation of pleasure depends very much on the imagination; now, if we can so deceive a man as to make him imagine that he is taking a maidenhead which he regards as a great pleasure, I maintain that by our harmless deception we are rendering him a service. My notion is that women are born deceivers, and their instinct leads them to draw men on by a variety of lures, arts and delusions; and on the other hand, that men from their very nature rather enjoy being humbugged by the women. And in the very instance I am describing, my impression is that the major had an inkling that we were not quite as innocent as we would fain have him believe, but yet for his own enjoyment he rather promoted the delusion; for he touched my chin with his unemployed hand, and said, You may spare your blushes, Jim, they will be more wanted by and by. I am now petting Mary's nice little pussy; and have not you a nice little pussy too – let me try."

' "No, no, major, keep to Mary, one ought to satisfy you."

' "If one is good, two should be better still! Is that not logic, Jim?"

' "And if so, three ought to be better still," I added.

' "Just so, you are right. Three loving girls free from jealousy would be more than paradise. Now, Mary is not jealous, as you see; why not join in our amusement? you will learn many things of which you must now be ignorant, and you will experience greater pleasure than you have ever felt there."

' "Let my hand go!"

' "It will not harm you. Tell her Mary, how nice it feels to have one's pussy petted by a man's hand."

' "It does indeed feel nice, Jim; now that the ice is broken, I love to feel his fingers playing between the lips; and the major has something better than his fingers which can tickle your pussy most delightfully."

'My lascivious nature now became so inflamed that I had to give up all pretence, and allow his hand to make its way up to my burning cunt. Oh! how it glowed as I felt his prying fingers enter the throbbing slit! I involuntarily moved it forward to meet his thrilling touch.

' "That's a darling girl! You have indeed a sweet little pussy. Tell her, Mary, what men usually call it."

' "That's your cunt, Jim, which the major is now frigging with his finger; but he has a better implement, called his prick, which could tickle it with more effect."

' "Take it out, Mary, and show it to her."

' "Mary was now in her element, so she readily unbuttoned his trousers, lifted his shirt, and pulled out his prick, as she said, "There it is, Jim. Now you may study a man's prick for the first time in your life. Look at its fine large purple head! See how this soft skin slips up and down – this is the way to frig a prick. And look at this tuft of hair growing about its root! Oh, it is nice to feel that rubbing against your own hair when the prick is in your cunt fucking you."

' "Stop, major," I cried, as I felt his finger at the entrance of the passage; and fearing he might discover how very open it was, I drew back from him.

' "Is he hurting you?" asked Mary.

' "Indeed he is – he was just pushing his finger in and I could not bear the smart."

' "Well, dear, let him try his prick; that will feel much nicer than his finger, and won't hurt you in the same way; look at this soft shelving head with its rosy top. It will slip in almost without your knowing it, and once it passes the entrance, it will make your cunt thrill with delight. Fuck her, major; lay her back, and I will help to keep her legs open."

' "Do, darling Jim," pleaded the major. "Let me fuck your sweet little cunt. I will be very gentle, and stop pushing the moment you ask me."

Mary had played her part so well, that feeling matters were in a safe train, I allowed them to push me back. She quickly drew up my petticoats, and said, "There, Kit, there – look at that little pussy, how soft and warm it is! Look at these pretty pink lips, all moist and open, waiting for your prick.'

'The major leaned over me, pushed his head between my thighs and gave my cunt a nice warm kiss, saying, "Sweet cunt! Now raise your bottom, that I may push this under it so as to fuck you with more ease."

'Mary, having spread me out to her satisfaction, said, "Now, she is ready; her cunt is beautifully open for you; let me hold your prick.' And taking the major's prick in her hand she rubbed its head up and down the slit of my cunt.

' "How do you like the feel of the major's prick in your cunt?"

' "Oh, it feels very nice rub it – rub it, there Mary."

' "Yes, but we must now get it in, or it will spend its sweet liquor outside – and that would be just a flash in the pan; there now, bear with it for a moment until it gets quite in – "

'Oh, stop, Mary – take it out – I can't bear it; indeed I can't. Oh! you said you would not push if I asked . . . Oh! Oh!! you are making it push harder than ever.'

'I held my hands firmly on the major's loins, and kept him from forcing his prick through the entrance; I felt Mary fumbling about my cunt and at last heard her say: "All right, now it's getting in."

'Then, heaving a sign of relief, I allowed him to push home, and said, 'Oh, major, how you have hurt me! But now that your prick is all inside, I like to feel it, and you may fuck me as hard as you like.'

'Mary, I need scarcely tell you, had the little sponge prepared as before, and while pretending to direct the major's tool, squeezed its contents over his prick and my cunt. And the words "all right" were to be the signal to me that the operation had been successfully performed; so now I felt I could safely give full rein to my libidinous inclinations. I therefore compressed the interior of my cunt, so as to give that pleasant nip to the head of his prick that men love so well. I crossed my legs on his back, pressed up my cunt to meet his strokes, and squeezing him in my arms, kept muttering, "Yes, fuck me – fuck my cunt – I love to feel your prick in my cunt – fuck – fuck – fuck."

'The major's eyes sparkled, his active arse worked energetically up and down making his prick dart in and out of my cunt, and he said, "I am so glad your sweet cunt likes to feel my prick fucking – fucking – fucking," and held me in his arms with a convulsive grasp while his prick flooded my cunt with boiling spunk.

'On drawing out his prick, he noticed the blood marks on it, as well as on my cunt and chemise, and while he wiped both me and himself, he said with a smile, 'What a lot of blood you and Mary seem to have? I have never known girls bleed so freely. I have often fucked girls for what was, I am certain, their first time, without causing them to bleed at all. Indeed, I have wondered why so much is made of it, for all depends on the degree of force used at entrance; when it is very slight the membrane often stretches without rupture, so that the absence of blood is no evidence of the want of true virginity – though its presence must, I suppose, be considered conclusive," he added, bowing to us.

'Mary and I looked quite innocent as we listened to this wise dissertation, then, to divert his thoughts, Mary began to pet his prick, and asked him which he liked best, fucking her sister or herself?

' "What a question to ask, my dear Mary! as if I would make a comparison between two such lovely girls, equally kind, pleasing and susceptible. You are both eminently fitted for the enjoyments of love, each of you a perfect Venus in her way," and he kissed us both and made us sit on either side of him.

'After petting and looking at our cunts separately, he said he would like to see them both together, so he placed us lying side by side with our cunts fully exposed to his view. Then he coaxed us to frig our own cunts while he looked on, hand frigging his prick. Then he lay on his back, and got Mary to suck his prick and pet his balls while she knelt at his side with her naked bottom cocked up in the air; I played with her cunt, and let my own bottom down on his face to enjoy as he liked.

'As soon as Mary felt his seed spouting into her mouth, her cunt began to flow, while the combined effect of his hands, lips and tongue on my bottom and cunt caused my own reservoir to overflow with love's soft juice.

'You may well imagine that after this all reserve was cast aside. The major had the run of the house by night as well as by day. And as he had great experience, and a very kind natural disposition, he gradually acquired extraordinary influence over mother, so that she trusted him with the chief management of our affairs. His arrangement was, that no gentleman should be received by us who was not known to him and did not come to the house as his friend. Thus he maintained the appearance of respectability, and made things smooth and pleasant for us. He settled with each party for the house fees, as they were termed, and they were all handed to mother, while we received our special present afterwards.

In this way, he secured for himself not only the enjoyment of three women, as much as he desired, but what he prized more highly still, the frequent gratification of his lascivious taste in seeing and hearing all that passed between us and the different parties whom he introduced; for, with mother's consent, he contrived that each of our rooms should be commanded by peepholes or spying places, to which he had free access.

'We are well satisfied with his management, for he saves us much risk and trouble, and always selects, when possible, men that are comparatively young, have gentlemanly manners and are possessed of independent means.

'Personally he dispenses his favours equally amongst us three and he is very careful never to neglect mother; yet I think I am his favourite, for he seem to take me more into his confidence, and consult me about all his own special enjoyments.

'If you wish, I will endeavour to describe some of the scenes in which I was either a witness or partaker.'

We said we would be delighted to hear all about them, and begged her to give us the details as minutely as possible. And in order to stimulate her more, Frances turned up her cunt and bottom more fully before her, and I manipulated with more energy her own pretty little love chink, while she kept her hand on mine, giving my clitoris a pinch every now and then by way of emphasis, as she continued.

The first friend whom the major introduced was an officer, named Captain Stuart, a very nice young fellow, exceedingly wealthy, and heir to a Scotch title. He was passionately fond of women, and seemed to make the pursuit of them the great object of his life.

'The major brought him home with him one evening after a mess dinner, and they had supper by themselves in his room.

'To make what follows intelligible, I must tell you that there is a small room adjoining that occupied by the major, which Mary and I use for a dressing-room; it contains a bath and other toilet requisites, and we often sit there to read and work. Between these rooms is a large aperture in the wall, which has been formed into a double press, opening with doors into each room, and having a common back composed of boards. The major has removed the lower shelves so that when the doors are open any person in one room can see and hear all that passes in the other; and this arrangement has often been found very convenient on both sides.

'On this occasion, he notified Mary and me of the coming of Captain Stuart, and told us to listen particularly to their words and suggestions that we might shape our conduct accordingly.

'After supper, the major entertained his friend with a portfolio of very lascivious French prints. And you may be sure, we were at our post of observation, listening to every word and watching every movement.

'The captain was delighted with the pictures, he praised their beauty, and said there was nothing in the word he so much admired as a naked woman, especially when her cunt and bottom were fully exposed to view; and that next to the reality, the well-drawn and highly finished pictures had the most effect.

' "How they do make a fellow's prick stand! My blood seems to boil already! I would give a good sum tonight for the view and the use of a hot randy cunt. Could you put me in the way of such a thing, Kit? Just look at this chap of mine; you have seen it before, but I doubt if you ever saw it in so distended a state," and he drew out a strong muscular prick with a great swollen red head.

'This was just what the major desired, both on our account and his own, for while he thoroughly enjoyed a woman's cunt, he had a particular fancy for seeing and handling a fine prick.

'So putting one hand round his friend's manly tool, he pushed the other in underneath and pulled out his hairy bollocks as he said, "Well, Alick, if you are prepared to pay handsomely, I may be able to gratify you to the fullest extent of your desires. My landlady has two remarkably fine daughters. They are young and handsome, beautifully made, and they possess, what you so much admire, splendid cunts and arses, which they have no objection to displaying before such friends as can appreciate their beauty and value their worth. In short, they are just the kind of girls you seek, for they love fucking, and think that a fine prick like this of yours, Alick, is the most interesting object in the universe." And looking admiringly on his friend's prick, he tenderly frigged it up and down.

'All right, old fellow,' he replied, apparently much pleased with the major's attentions, 'get me your cheque book, and I will put my name to a sum that will satisfy your beauties. To whom should it be payable?" he asked as he commenced writing.

' "To the widow herself – Mrs Sophia Bond," the major answered.

Captain Stuart filled in the cheque and handing it to his friend, said, "Will that suffice?"

' "Yes, it is most handsome, and will ensure you the fullest gratification; and I think I may offer you also the additional pleasure of making your own selection. The room adjoining this is used by the young ladies as a dressing-room: they always come to it before going to bed, and when they are in the humour, they play like two wantons together, and indulge in every kind of amorous sport with one another. I know this, for I have made an opening in the back of that press through which I can watch at my ease all their erotic games.

' "I sometimes lend them pictures and books like these, which they are fond of looking at, and invariably try to copy. I left a famous book on their table this evening, together with a dildo, which I have been promising them for some time. And as this is about their usual time for undressing, I would not be surprised if they were there now; so if you will sit on this stool and apply your eye to my spying place, and tell me in a low voice all that they are doing and which of them you prefer, I will keep this chap of yours in working order, and we shall both share the fun.

'The captain placed himself in the required position, with his legs apart and his prick projecting, and looked through the opening into our room, while his friend Kit sat before him and manipulated his fine standing tool, which was on a level with his face.

'After waiting a moment, he asked, "Well, Alick, are the girls there? Can you see them? And what are they doing?"

' "Yes they are both there, and have just commenced to take off their things. What a lucky dog you are, Kit, to have such a scene presented to you every night. There are few things so interesting as watching a woman undressing – she has so many funny little ways, and seems to slip in and out of her clothes so easily. It must be warm in there, however, for these two appear disposed to denude themselves altogether; and I hope they will.

' "The one with dark hair has now thrown off everything except her shift. She has got hold of your book, and has sat down just opposite, with her shift tucked up and her legs wide apart. You are right, Kit, she has a splendid cunt with magnificent lips, ripe and plump, and her clitoris like a bit of bright coral gleams in the centre. She is holding the book in her right hand while the left is occupied with her cunt, the middle finger working in the slit. Oh! how she frigs! She must be first-rate at fucking. The one with fair hair has come up behind her and is leaning on her shoulder as she looks down on the book. She too has pulled up her chemise, and her hand is busy with her cunt.

' "They are indeed a fine pair of girls, and I will be well content with either of them – but stop, they are talking about the pictures, let us listen."

'We of course heard all this, and now that the cheque business was satisfactorily arranged, we were quite ready both to please them and gratify ourselves by doing all in our power to stimulate and satisfy their prurient curiosity.

'The picture on which Mary seemed so intent at this moment, while her ears were drinking in every word spoken in the major's room, contained a group of three pairs of partially naked men and women, all eagerly engaged in the pleasing sport of exciting each other's lascivious feelings to the highest pitch of amorous enjoyment. Looking down at this picture, I said, "What a grand exhibition of pricks, cunts and bottoms you have there, Mary; that man sitting on she chair, with the girl straddling across his lap and holding his prick as the stoops forward to watch it passing up into her cunt, while he has his hand over her shoulder petting her bubbies, and at the same time sips sweet kisses from the girl at the right – he looks particularly happy! Don't you think so, Mary?'

' "Yes, he seems to be enjoying himself, but my attention was rather directed to the girl he is kissing; look at the lascivious spread of her thighs, as she stands over the man on the stool; observe the wanton bend of her body as she presses her bosom against his face to enable him to suck the nipple of her breast, as he holds his standing prick to the mouth of her cunt, which looks ready to absorb it in the heated folds within. She has thus a threefold enjoyment: she is pleasantly kissed by a man who is at the same time fucking another girl, while she has her nipple sucked and her cunt penetrated by the man below her. You know, Jim, I have a special fancy for being enjoyed by different men at the same time; and you have felt that pleasure too.'

' "Yes Mary, I thoroughly agree with you that our pleasurable sensations are both increased and multiplied by having different men engaged with us at the same time; and I was just thinking that perhaps we might have that very enjoyment tonight: for who can tell but that the handsome young officer whom the major brought home with him might take a fancy to pass the night here. And if we had him and dear old Kit together, what fun we should all have! Did you you think, Mary, in the passing glimpse we had of him, that he looked like one who could give a woman satisfaction?'

' "Aye, he looked like it at all events; and I fancied that he eyed me as if he desired some further acquaintance. So let us wait here a little longer, and if the major does bring him in, certainly they will find us in rare dishabille.'

' "I do hope they will come in, for I feel awfully randy tonight. Lean back, Mary, spread your thighs, and I will give your pussy a suck just to keep her in good humour."

'Mary willingly complied, and I knelt on the floor between her wide-spread legs, taking care to turn my own naked bottom towards the aperture through which, I was certain, Captain Stuart was intently watching us. As I sucked Mary's cunt, I made as much noise with my lips and tongue as I could, and cocked up and twisted my arse in as wanton and lascivious a fashion as I could devise, my ears being strained all the while to ascertain the effect on him.

'I was not disappointed, I first heard him draw a long breath, then give a short gasp as he muttered, 'Oh, don't, Kit, don't press my prick any more or I shall fire off. The fair-haired girl is sucking her sister's cunt, with her own voluptuous arse turned up in all its naked beauty, and she wriggles it in such a way as to show every inviting cranny it contains. I can stand it no longer. They are wishing to have us. Let us go in; and mind, Kit, we must have them conjointly, and one after the other."

' "All right, old fellow; I was inclined to make you discharge, and take it in my mouth as I did once before, but that would lessen your power afterwards, so let us strip and go into them in our shirts. They will perhaps pretend to be much alarmed, but after all we have heard, we can have no doubt as to their being immensely delighted."

'While they were getting ready, I whispered, "Mary, let us give them a surprise! It won't do to let them have such an easy conquest as they expect. Let us put out the lights, and at least they will have to hunt for us in the dark; and if we apparently do all we can to escape from them, they will enjoy us all the more when they succeed in catching us."

' "Capital idea – let us do so – out with the lights, and let us strip to the buff; they will find it harder to hold us, and we can play them all manner of pranks in the dark – now be still."

'So when the door was opened, our room was found to be in total darkness, and seemed quite deserted.

' "Hallo!" exclaimed Captain Stuart, as soon as he got inside, "the nest is warm, but the birds are flown."

' "I am not sure of that," said the major; 'they love sport, and that merry little imp with the fair hair is the very devil for fun. She is never happy unless she is up to some lark or another. Feel about man, let us see who will catch a bird first."

'They at once began to grope round the room. I was standing behind the door when a pair of arms enclosed me. Putting up my hand I felt the hair on his chin, and recognising the major, I whispered: 'Stay with the little imp, Kit, let your friend catch Mary, for she is wishing for him."

' "Good, my little duck," he replied, giving me a kiss as he pushed his knee between my legs; then placing one hand on my bottom, he directed the other to my cunt, and said aloud, "Well, Alick, how are you getting on? Have you captured a bed-fellow yet?"

' "Not yet; I just touched something warm but it eluded my grasp and slipped to one side. Now I feel a soft hand at my prick! Hah! I have somebody now, with a great round arse and big hairy cunt!"

' "Hold her fast, Alick, or she may slip from you again. You have got the dark-haired houri, with the splendid cunt that will draw in your prick like a sucking calf. As for you, Jim, you rogue, this hunt in the dark is all your devising, I am sure; well, make amends by now giving us all the light you can!"

' "Very well, Kit, but won't you spare our blushes by suffering us first to cover our nakedness."

' "Don't think of such a thing; we are as naked as yourselves. Light every candle you have, that you may see how gloriously our pricks stand, longing for your cunts, and that we may view and explore every delicious cranny of your bodies."

'With Kit's help, I then lighted half a dozen candles. Meanwhile, Mary had thrown herself on her face on the couch, and Alick was busy pushing open her legs and examining all the secrets that lay snugly hidden between them.

'The major went to her and, turning her round, said, "Sit up, Mary; look at my friend Alick's grand tool! I have been petting it myself all the evening to keep it in good order for your cunt" – and taking Mary's hand he placed it on Alick's standing prick.

' "Put your hand on it too, Jim; Alick, like myself, delights to have two loving girls play with his prick at the same time."

'Alick smiled as Mary and I together petted his prick and balls. She leaned her breast against him, while I rubbed my cunt on his knee, and to complete his satisfaction, passed my hand round his loins and titillated his bottom from behind. Mary then, wishing to include Kit, placed her other hand on his prick, and drawing it up, playfully rubbed the noses of the pricks together.

'This seemed to excite them more than anything, and Alick exclaimed, "Mary my love, are you ready for a fuck? My prick is bursting with eagerness. I must lodge him somewhere or he will discharge outside. Where shall I put him?"

' "Into my cunt, Alick, at least at first, and afterwards, anywhere else you please."

' "Very well, lie back, turn up your bottom, and I will slip my prick into your cunt; and if Jim will place herself by your side so that I can kiss her cunt, and if you take Kit's prick into your mouth, we shall all share the fun together."

'In a moment I was lying on my back beside Mary, with my bottom close to her face. My hands soon found their way to her cunt, where Alick's prick was beginning to lunge in and out as, leaning towards me, he drew open the lips of my cunt, and with ravenous eagerness sucked my clitoris and thrust in his tongue.

'Meantime, Mary's hands were occupied with Kit's balls and bottom, while he pushed back and forward the head of his rampant engine of love in her widely distended mouth. She was thus gratified in her favourite fancy for being enjoyed by different men at the same time, and she did seem to relish it exceedingly, for she twisted her arse is unison with the prods of Alick's vigorous tool, and she rolled her tongue with wanton savour round the neck of Kit's prick.

'The major then turning to me said, "Now Jim, all we want is a finishing touch from you; give tongue for us all – use every stimulating word you can remember or imagine."

' "Prick – Mary!" I responded. "Cunt – Alick! Bollocks – Kit! Suck his prick, Mary; squeeze his balls; put your fingers in his arse. Suck my cunt, Alick: push your tongue into it; tickle my arse with your finger. Fuck her, Alick – fuck her cunt – fuck her arse – bugger her arse!" Just then, Mary gave a bound, and Alick's prick was thrown out; I held it in my hand, however, and as her bottom-hole was so near, and so invitingly open, I popped the prick into her arse. She gave a muttered; Oh! as she felt the well moistened prick glide up into her vitals, and I cried: "She has it in her bottom! Fuck her arse, Alick, fuck her arse."

'This last was indeed the finishing touch and brought on a simultaneous burst of sperm from prick, bollocks and cunt.

'After this night, Captain Stuart was a frequent visitor at our house; and as he was liberal with his money, and kind and pleasant in his manner, we did everything in our power to please and gratify him.

He soon found that mother was equal or even superior to her daughters in ability to satisfy his lustful desires. Owing to the great care she had taken to preserve her personal charms, she rather excelled us in smoothness of skin and in plumpness of form. And though her cunt is capacious enough to take in any prick – no matter how large – her power of internal compression is so great that she can adapt it to the smallest size. Moreover, her vast experience, and peculiar skill in manipulating the male organ, enable her both to impart and sustain the highest amount of sensual gratification.

'She also, as you well know, Queenie, takes delight in planning and arranging wanton exhibitions of herself and others, and luxuriates not only in lubricious postures and attitudes, but at the same time the most lascivious terms and expressions roll off her tongue with unctuous relish.

'Alick's youth and confiding dispositions commended him to her goodwill, and she spared no pains to make herself and her daughters agreeable to his taste. He especially delighted in having us all three together, and then strip to the buff was always the order of the day. Mother would take his prick in hand, spreading her light touches over all the most sensitive parts of his prick, balls and bottom, while she had her own bottom so elevated that he could see in a conveniently placed mirror a reflection of the whole of her voluptuous arse and cunt. Meanwhile we displayed before him our various charms in the most exciting manner we could devise.

'I would call his attention to the several beauties of our cunts and bottoms; or Mary would describe a fucking scene in the most lascivious terms.

'Then, mother would cry: "Now, he is just ready to sport – which of you girls will take it in your mouth?"

'Mary who loves to suck a prick at once came forward, and stooping down, received the swollen head between her lips, while mother placed me straddling over his face, and told me to hold open the side of my cunt as I slowly let myself down until my cunt rested on his mouth. She then went behind Mary and told her to lift her bottom as much as possible in order that she might get at her cunt to suck and frig it with her tongue.

'I wriggled my arse on his face, as I felt his tongue winding round my clitoris and penetrating the hot inner folds; and just as my own dissolving flow commenced, I leaned forward and got my hand on the root of his prick in time to feel the convulsive spasm as he poured his rick sperm down Mary's throat.

'Alick took special delight in watching us suck mother's cunt. He said the view of one woman sucking another woman's cunt always strongly excited his lustful desires, but when it was a daughter sucking the cunt of her own mother, the lubricious effect was increased to a tenfold degree.

'So to please him, mother would pull up her clothes, throw herself on the bed and spreading her large fleshy thighs, call Mary to kneel on the floor, suck her cunt and at the same time present her bottom to Alick. He would then kneel behind her and ask me to hold his prick and balls while he fucked Mary and leaned over her shoulder to watch the sucking operation. Then to gratify him still further I would ask, "Are you looking at my mother's cunt, Alick? Move your head a little to one side, Mary, that Captain Stuart may see it better. Look at those fat lips, how they press out on each side of the rosy chink! See how they separate just in the middle of the great hairy tuft that covers the mount. What a fine thick clitoris she has! It sticks out of her cunt like a boy's cock! See how red the nymphae are! They once pressed round father's prick. Do you remember, mother, the time before I was born when father injected me into your cunt? or, at least, set to work to get me into being?"

' "No, dear, that is, I am not sure of the exact time. Your father fucked me almost every night, and always gave me great satisfaction: so that I could not fix on any one occasion. Some woman can tell, so they say, the precise moment in which they conceive. When the woman and the man get the feel together and she it conscious at the time of a kind of nervous tremor in the interior of her cunt, that, I have heard, is a sure indication that conception has taken place; but I cannot say that from any own experience."

' "Well, anyway, I am sure that both you and father must have had great pleasure when you were getting me. Had he a fine big prick like this of Alick's?"

' "Your father's prick was fair enough when he was in health, but it shrivelled up to nothing before he died. But let us talk of something else. I hope Mary is able to nip your prick in her cunt, Alick? I have endeavoured to teach her that trick which so much increases the man's pleasure. It can only be done by a woman of warm temperament who really loves fucking."

' "Like me," interposed Mary, raising her head for the instant.

'Mother only smiled, and continued, "Yes, you may laugh, but I tell you that failure in that respect is one chief reason why men grow tired of their wives, and naturally turn to those who are both able and willing to give them full satisfaction."

' "Very true, Mrs Bond, and if ever I have a wife I hope she may be like Mary, for she thoroughly understands that trick, and nips my prick most delightfully – there, I feel it now. And darling Jim is pressing my bollocks most lasciviously, and now she is tickling my arsehole with her finger – Oh! how voluptuous!"

' "Go it then," cried mother who had delayed the crisis purposely by her apparently ill-timed observations; "go it; I am ready too. Jim frig your own cunt, and let us all spend together."

'I at once obeyed, and turning my bottom towards the mirror placed alongside, into which Alick was now intently looking, I frigged away crying, "Suck dear old mother's quim, Mary; poke Mary's randy cunt, Alick; and now, prick, bollocks, cunt, fuck, fuck away and spend together."

'Now, Queenie, and sweetheart Frances, what say you to having my two friends, Alick and Kit? Shall I send them an invite?'

'By all means,' we replied, 'and you may tempt them too in any way you think fit: but don't let them imagine that we are only waiting like ripe cherries to drop into their mouths, or more correctly speaking, to let them like ripe cherries drop into ours.'

'You may trust me for that,' was her answer.

CHAPTER TWELVE

Jim's Two Friends

Jim accordingly wrote a letter which after much consideration and various emendations was sent by a special messenger to her friend the major.

In this letter, she told him that she was staying with Dr Harpur whom he already knew, and that Lord Ferrars, whose yacht was lying in the harbour, was his guest. The yacht, she added, was in good trim and ready for a cruise, but his lordship was so taken with his friend's wife that he could not tear himself away.

She mentioned also that Lord Ferrars was accompanied by a handsome young fellow named Gipton, to whom he seemed much attached, and whom he always called 'his middy'; but that there was some mystery about him she was very desirous to have unravelled. For this Gipton had made great love to her at first, but as soon as she let him know that she was inclined to yield to his solicitation, he drew back and never availed himself of the opportunities she put in his way, which passed her comprehension. And, what was still more extraordinary, this young fellow has taken up with Dr Harpur, and they went on for all the world just like two lovers. Moreover, Lord Ferrars seems to encourage them by every means in his power.

'Altogether,' she wrote, 'the position of affairs here, though very enjoyable, is decidedly queer, and in my opinion just what would afford you a splendid field for the study of human nature from the amorous point of view; and also afford you a grand opportunity for stirring up lewd thoughts and practising wanton exercises, things which you so thoroughly understand and appreciate. So come over and spy out the land. I am confident that you will be warmly welcomed as a very acceptable addition to our social party; for, when I happened to mention your name yesterday, Mrs Harpur said she had seen you more than once, and judging from your fine physique, the kind expression of your face, and the loving light in your eyes she would much like to number you among her more intimate friends. So lose no time in coming over, and bring Alick with you; ask for me, and I will introduce you both in due form. What I would suggest, is that you and Alick drive here tomorrow about twelve o'clock. The Gentlemen of our party are going in the morning to search out some wild goats, which they have heard are to be found in the neighbouring heights. The middy will be otherwise engaged. And so, Queenie and I shall be alone nearly all the day. We can therefore managed to meet you in the avenue, and then conduct you to the more sheltered part of the grounds, etc. Ever your fond and faithful "little imp", Jim.'

The major showed this epistle to his friend Alick. He was delighted with the prospect thus held out to them and they decided to accept the invitation and start early on the following morning.

At the time appointed, Jim's two friends presented themselves at the entrance gate. We met them in the avenue in our garden costume as if going for a walk; and when Jim had gone through the usual form of introduction, we offered to return with them; but they would not hear of our going back to the house of their account, and asked leave to accompany us in our walk. We consented and led them to the pleasure grounds.

Alick and I took the lead, while Jim and the major fell behind: but as we were passing near a convenient summerhouse, they suddenly disappeared, leaving us to pursue our walk by ourselves.

I must pass over the ordinary small talk we indulged in at first, during which we discussed many of the island celebrities – Alick's eyes sparkling whenever I laughed at the free remarks he made respecting some of them – until I come to that more interesting part where we felt emboldened to make a decided advance to a little personal familiarity.

We had reached a garden seat in a sheltered spot and sat down to rest, wondering what had become of the major and Jim.

Alick said, with an expressive smile, 'They are old friends, you know, and are, no doubt, enjoying themselves in some comfortable nook.' I smiled in return, and complaining of the heat of the day, I tried to take off the silk shawl I had over my shoulders, but had difficulty in unloosening it at the front where it was fastened by my brooch.

Alick gallantly undertook to do it for me, and when fumbling about my throat, he cleverly managed both to press my breasts and playfully chuck me under the chin. I laughed at his awkwardness, but he only leaned more against me until his moustache brushed my cheek. I still laughed while his face flushed and, with panting effort he exclaimed, 'Dear Mrs Harpur, you are one of the most fascinating women I ever met and you are as kind as you are fascinating; the mere touch you with my hands has agitated my whole body of and putting his arm round my waist he pressed me to him.

'Oh! Captain Stuart! you are forgetting that I am a married woman.'

'No, my darling, but I was thinking what delight your husband must have every night when he holds you in his arms' – and he tried to kiss me.

'Oh, stop – I must run away from you, Captain Stuart; you are too demonstrative!' and struggling to free myself from his embrace, I accidentally placed my hand full on his swollen tool. I felt it bound under my touch, and as I could not affect ignorance of what it was, I withdrew my hand and exclaimed: 'Oh!'

He pressed me all the harder, and cried in the most eager and passionate tones, 'My darling, do place that dear hand there again; your delicious touch makes all the nerves in my body vibrate with pleasurable excitement,' and taking my hand, he forcibly replaced it on his prick.

'Why, Captain Stuart, what a funny man you are! What on earth good can my hand do you there?'

'Oh, don't you know? Darling, press it, rub it – stay, let me put your hand inside' – and hurriedly opening his trousers, he pushed in my hand.

'Fie! Captain Stuart, you are audacious! You mustn't hold my hand on it. You mustn't – but what a fine fellow you have!'

'Yes, let me show him to you – there – that's what you may call a prick!' And he looked quite proud of it as it pushed up its great rosy top through the midst of my encircling fingers.

'Frig it, Queenie, frig it; I always take special delight in the favours of a married woman, for she understands and values a fine prick, and knows how to get it into working order,' and opening his trousers more, he continued, 'Put your other hand on my balls, they are worth feeling too.'

I did so, moving one hand slowly up and down the smooth shaft of his throbbing tool, and gently working and pressing his large firm stones with the other.

'Do you like it, Queenie?' he asked, as he saw me looking down with admiring glances. 'Tell me its name, dear.'

'Prick.'

'Now, tell me what you think of my prick.'

'It is a very fair specimen, Alick; just the sort of prick a woman likes to see and pet,' kissing it as I spoke.

'And, Queenie, what have you here yourself?' he asked, as he stooped and ran his hand up between my thighs.

'My cunt, Alick; a soft brown-haired cunt.'

'What would your cunt like my prick to do for it?'

'To go into it, Alick, and fuck it.'

'Would it be safe to fuck you here?'

'No; but there is a place not far off where we shall be quite safe and find every accommodation.'

I brought him to a small building at one corner of the garden which Dick had constructed for a smoking lounge and other luxurious purposes. It consisted of two rooms opening into one another by a concealed door; and in the door was a secret spying hole which could be used from either side, and which we often found very convenient.

In the interior room, I felt sure that, according to previous arrangement, Jim and the major were now comfortably settled, waiting to witness the performance we were going to enact, and very likely to express their sympathy by indulging in similar pastimes themselves. Meanwhile overhead in a snug little hiding place next the roof, reached from the outside, I thought it not improbable that Frances lay ensconced, in expectation of enjoying the view of both parties underneath.

As soon as Captain Stuart and I had ascended the steps and entered this retreat, he exclaimed: 'What a jolly place! so smugly furnished too! I am so much obliged to you. Queenie, for bringing me her. Come, and sit down with me on this comfortable couch.'

'I will, but you must promise to be good and not to shock my modesty too much.'

'Very well, I will be as good as is in my nature, but let this sweet mouth answer for itself' – and taking me in his arms he placed me recumbent on the couch and deliberately pulled up my clothes.

Then, separating my thighs, he kneeled on the floor and began to kiss and suck my cunt; then growing more excited as he went on, he proceeded to kiss and suck my bottom-hole.

Every woman knows what a grand stimulant this is to her erotic feelings. So I writhed my bottom about, and spread my thighs to their widest stretch to give him freer access. At last, I could restrain myself no longer, and I cried, 'Come, Alick, you have sucked my arse long enough; the hot spend is welling in my cunt; get up, ram your prick into it and fuck me, fuck me with all the force you have.'

Alick at once obeyed, and taking off his trousers altogether, he placed the head of his prick at the mouth of my highly excited cunt and with one thrust drove it up to the hilt.

All the sensation of my body seemed now concentrated in my cunt. The introduction of a new prick of such fine prorportions imparted a feeling of novelty, and the vigour and rapidity of Alick's movements caused my nerves to vibrate with emotions of unusual pleasure, while he asked at every fresh prod, 'Do you like it, Queenie? Is your cunt enjoying my prick? Does this style of fucking please you?'

'Yes, dear Alick, your way of fucking is delightful, and your prick fills my cunt to its utmost satisfaction. Do you like to hear a woman talk lewdly when you are fucking her?'

'Oh, the lewder the better. I like to hear a woman talk lewdly at any time; but when my prick is rummaging her cunt, then it makes one almost wild with pleasure to hear her indulge freely in the most lascivious terms and expressions. So be as lewd as ever you can – now, heave your arse.' I did so, and in plunged his prick; as his balls flopped against my bottom, he cried, 'Oh!! that's grand! How greedily your cunt sucks in my prick! How it clasps my prick in its hot folds! Go on, Queenie – you know how to enjoy a fuck. There – you have it. Oh!'

He sank over me with his head on my shoulder and his prick buried in my cunt. After a moment, he raised his face and said, 'What would your husband say if he saw us now?'

'He would say: fuck away, Captain Stuart; fuck her as hard as you can, and I will hold your prick and handle your balls to urge you on; and you would soon feel his fingers round the root of your prick and touching you up behind the balls to start you afresh.'

Just the very thing I was then desiring most, for like every woman who possesses any experience in these matters, I enjoy the second fuck more that the first. I am therefore always glad when my man allows his prick to remain soaking in my cunt. And as soon as I think he has had sufficient rest, I endeavour, by the warm pressure of my cunt, lascivious heaves of my bottom, wanton touches of my fingers and, above all, by bawdy words, to resuscitate his powers and incite him to renewed enjoyment.

In this instance my efforts were speedily crowned with success; for I felt his prick stiffening in my warm sheath, as he replied, 'Why, your worthy husband resembles the major in that. He loves to handle a prick, especially when fucking. I sometimes think he has more than a woman's passion for a prick; he seems so thoroughly to enjoy holding it in his hand, frigging it and, when he get greatly excited, even kissing and sucking it; and once he made me spend in his mouth, while he pressed my balls and squeezed the cheeks of my bottom just as a woman would; but oh! – the talking about it, added to your wanton play, has given me full vigour again – there he is, able for his work – now, Queenie, talk as bawdy as you please!'

'Heave your arse against me,' I said, holding him tightly in my arms, as I kissed out the words; 'Arse; prick; cunt; bollocks; arse; arse; arse.'

Then I felt a second deluge of spunk flooding my cunt and bubbling out at the sides as we sank almost lifeless in each other's arms.

We soon recovered, however, and Alick lay back on the couch to rest. I was wiping and fondling his somewhat exhausted tool when I heard a slight tapping at the door, and Jim's voice saying: 'Let me in, dear Queenie.'

I opened the door, and she entered smiling as usual. Her eyes twinkled in answer to our enquiring looks as we asked what she had done with the major.

'What have I done with the major! Just what you have been doing with one another, unless I am much mistaken. As soon as the major and I gained the shelter of your summerhouse, he induced me to kneel on the seat and present my nether beauties for his investigation, and indeed his investigation was a little rough; for he pinched and slapped my poor bottom until it smarted again; then he kissed it to make it well and rubbed his grisly beard up and down the tender furrow until my cunt became inflamed and I felt as randy as a she-cat. Then he whipped out his tool to give me ease, and after first poking my cunt, he finished up in my bottom-hole.

'That's what I have done with him, in one sense, and in another, I am not done with him! I can tell you that he has gone to exercise his ingenuity by undertaking a course of philosophical, of rather I should say physiological, enquiry. Is not that grandly put? but it is a fact. He had just satisfied his vile propensity with me and we had scarcely put ourselves to rights, when who should appear but Mr Gipton, looking as smart and impudent as ever. We had been speaking of him before, and the major, having plied me with a variety of questions respecting his manners, habits, and antecedents, and said, "From all you have told me, I perceive he is no ordinary character – in fact, he must be either a girl-boy or a boy-girl, if you understand the difference. And more, he must be decidedly clever to have bamboozled your sharp wits. But rest assured, I will find out before long whether Gipton is a Mr or a Miss."

'Just then Gipton appeared and I said, "Well, here's your opportunity, I will introduce him to you, and then leave you to work out the problem together."

'They soon became great friends, and began to converse about the yacht and Lord Ferrars; so I set out to look for you.'

Jim turned to investigate the state of Alick's tool, and said, 'Ah, Queenie, just as I expected, you have squeezed every atom of starch out of this poor prick. It can only be compared to a sock taken out of the wash-tub. Reach your hand and let us try together to re-infuse some life into it.'

Meantime, I must report progress as to our other friends. But as both Frances and the major favoured us with full details of all that took place between them, it will be more satisfactory to combine their account into one united narrative, and let it constitute a chapter by itself.

CHAPTER THIRTEEN

The Major and Frances

The major was exceedingly anxious to unravel the mystery connected with our young friend. He accordingly put forth all the skill derived from his varied knowledge and long experience to gain his confidence, with a view, in the first instance of obtaining access to his private belongings, no matter to which sex they appertained, and secondly, of discovering his secret, whatever it might be.

So he opened the campaign by commending the personal appearance of Francis, and offered to bring him to the regimental mess; he promised also to take him to all the best places of amusement, and introduce him to some of the most fashionable ladies, who would grant him every favour without expense or trouble on his part.

Frances, who only maintained her disguise for the sake of increasing the fun and enjoyment of the final denouement, received his overtures very gracefully, and consented to place herself in his hands and follow all his directions.

She told him that she always considered the enjoyment of women the greatest pleasure of life, and that she also found that enjoyment much increased by men being more free and unreserved among themselves.

The major said he was charmed to hear such sentiments uttered by his young friend; that it was precisely his own opinion on the subject; that he never could understand the prudery of some men; that women, as a rule, had more sense in these matters than men, for they were rather partial to looking at, fondling, kissing and even sucking each other's private parts. 'And that reminds me,' he added, 'I happen to have in my pocket a few remarkably fine prints, which a friend lent me just as we were starting, and I had no time to put them away. Let us look them over together; they will serve to illustrate the subject we are talking off.

So saying, he took out the packet and placed it in the hand of Frances who was sitting by his side.

Now the major, who was very sly, had planned all this beforehand, intending to watch very closely what kind of picture would prove to be most interesting to his young companion. For he said to himself: If he be indeed a man those in which the female charms are best displayed will excite him most; but if he be only a girl in disguise, those in which the manly organ is fully exhibited will be the most attractive. And in either case, they will prepare the way for my seeing and handling those parts which are the special objects of my desire.

So he first directed the attention of his young friend to some female figures, in which the feminine charms of voluptuous bubbies, invitingly open cunts and exuberant bottoms were most suggestively displayed, saying, 'What an exciting exhibition of randy cunts we have here, Gipton! Enough to make a man's prick burst his breeches! Don't you find it so?'

'Yes,' he said, without showing much emotion, 'but on one accustomed to the real thing, pictures have but small effect.'

'Very true,' the major replied, 'but they serve to refresh the memory and excite a pleasant anticipation of joys to come. But see, here you have the male organ in grand development. Does this stir you at all?'

'Yes; it may seem strange to you, but the sight of a fine standing prick has an equal, or even greater, effect on my imagination than that of a randy cunt. I can quite enter into the feeling of that girl who holds the man's prick so lovingly in her hand and frigs it up and down while she gazes on its glowing head, which she loves to see standing up proudly in all its bare and naked beauty.'

'And what do you think of this, Gipton?' pointing to a picture in which one man was fondling the prick and balls of another.

'I think that more exciting still. The artist has well depicted the expression of pleasure in that young fellow's face as he alternately caps and uncovers the rosy head of his friend's prick. But this one here, the last of the series, is perhaps the most exciting of all. He has now taken his friend's prick into his mouth, and while he churns his balls and tickles the sensitive parts behind, sucks out the rich creamy juice which his friend is spurting into his mouth – yes, major – why not? – take out your prick and show it to me. I will frig it for you, and play with it as long as you like.'

'Well, Gipton, here he is – I am quite willing to show you mine and you may do with it whatever you please, but I expect you will favour me in like manner afterwards.'

Frances took the major's prick in hand and began to frig it, as she said, 'You shall see mine afterwards. I love to have it looked at and petted by a man. Meanwhile, go on viewing the pictures, and leave your affair to my management; I know how to excite a prick and get it into first-rate working trim; but I would enjoy hearing you describe the prints at the same time, and as we are both thoroughly excited now, the more wanton and lascivious the terms you use the better.'

'You are a grand fellow, Gipton; no woman could work up my prick better than you! but don't be too energetic, unless you want me to spend in your mouth.'

'Oh! you may spend as soon as you like, and I don't at all object to your spending in my mouth if you wish,' and she commenced sucking the major's prick.

'Well, the picture before me is the same we were looking at last. I will call the two figures Jack and Tom; Jack is sucking Tom's prick, just as you are sucking mine. If affords him a good mouthful, and he seems he enjoy it, for while he sucks he frigs softly with one hand, and touches up his friend behind the balls with the other. And you are doing the same. Oh, Gipton! Oh! how I enjoy the feel of your fingers playing about me there; but to return to the picture. Tom's eyes are fixed on the naked arse of a girl who leans back on a chair before him, holding open her thighs with her hands, so that he may see the whole of her cunt and little round bottom-hole, as well as a good portion of the fat cheeks of her arse. She seems to be asking him, "What are you looking at Tom?"

' "Your arse, Sally; push your cunt up higher, spread the lips wider. I like to see she rosy folds inside – frig your clitoris and put your finger in your arsehole. Now Jack – suck hard," squeeze my prick, press my balls. Oh! there! suck! it spouts, oh!'

'Did you swallow it, Gipton?'

'Of course I did,' replied Frances, wiping her mouth, 'and good lot you gave me; it shot down my throat whether I liked it or not.'

'Well, take a pull at this flask; I'll do the same; and after a few moments' rest, we will proceed with the second act of our play; for I must have a frig and a suck too.'

They rested together for a short space, during which the major made several attempts to get his hand inside Frances's trousers, but she always begged for a little longer delay. At last, the major, sitting up, said, 'Come, Gipton, time flies, let your trousers down and plant your naked bum here on my lap' – and with a determined effort he unbuttoned her trousers and thrust his hand in between her thighs.

Frances laughed, as he exclaimed. 'By Jove! – just what I expected – What a charming girl you are! I suppose I must call you, Frances, now. How admirably you acted the part of a sailor lad! You would deceive any man unless he saw or touched your cunt. And how well you have disguised your bubbies too.'

Here, he took her in his arms. Frances made no objection; on the contrary, she now afforded him every facility to feel and examine her as much as he desired. As his hands were roving over each voluptuous prominence and entering every inviting crevice, he suddenly looked up and said, 'But what about Lord Ferrars? I don't wish to come to loggerheads with him.'

'Oh,' replied Frances, 'you may make your mind easy on that score. You will meet neither loggerheads nor maidenheads here just now, they took their departure long ago. I don't mind telling you that I have accompanied Lord Ferrars as his mistress; that I am very fond of him, and that he is very good to me. He gives me everything I wish for, and, best of all, the most perfect liberty. He does not care how often I am fucked by others, provided I am always ready for him. Indeed he tells me that he enjoys my cunt more just after I have come from the embraces of another man. Not only that, but he likes to see me fucked, especially if he can hold the prick which is fucking me. I think he shares your taste in liking to see and handle a good prick, and watch it doing its work. I have, in fact, a suspicion that he is more pleased when his own prick is frigged by a man than by a woman. And, now that you know so much, I may as well tell you in addition that one reason why he and the doctor are such great friends is that they go shares in every woman they enjoy and are fond of petting each other's prick.'

'Why, Frances, it seems to me that I have fallen into clover. And does he share his friend's wife too?'

'Aye, that he does, and the doctor takes the greatest delight in watching his performance and urging him on by every means in his power.'

'Well, I guess we shall yet have some fun together; but we must not part, until I have had some play with this little fanny of yours; how shall I get to her?'

'Shall I place myself like the girl in the picture?'

'Yes; I am just longing for a view of your lovely arse.'

'Well, major, I will, for I feel randy to the last degree, and ready for anything; but it would not be safe to strip here. Come along with me, I will show you a snug retreat where we shall be safe from intrusion and able to enjoy ourselves as we like.'

Frances led him to the inner room of the smoking pavilion, and having secured the door, she pulled of her trousers, and sitting down on the couch opposite to him, threw up her legs and held open her thighs with her hands on each side.

Then, smiling up at him through her wide-spread limbs, she cried, 'There, major! behold my arse, cunt, and everything; what do you think of them?'

'I think your charming arse beats the picture hollow. It is lovely! Do you often show it that way to Lord Ferrars?'

'Yes, when I wish to excite him very much I show him my arse and say: come! out with your prick and fuck me! but kiss and suck it first, and we shall both enjoy it more.'

'What does he do then?'

'If he is dressed, he lets down his trousers, and shows me his prick, and presents it for a kiss and a little suck; then going on his knees, he pushes his hands under the cheeks of my bottom to raise it higher; then he applies his mouth to my cunt, and after nibbling the clitoris and rolling his tongue about inside the lips, he passes on to my bottom-hole, sucks it and thrusts in his tongue as far as he can.'

'Do you like having your bottom-hole sucked?'

'Yes, greatly, I like it more than anything.'

'Well, I will suck you bottom-hole for you, but, like Lord Ferrars, I will begin with your cunt' – and kneeling down, he applied his mouth to the rosy slit, moist with love's dew and redolent with that hot cunt-perfume which Frances, when excited, possessed in a marked degree. Then moving lower down and drawing open the fat cheeks of her bottom, he sucked the pursed up edges of her little brown orifice, and then worked his tongue a short distance up the passage itself.

This was just what Frances was longing for – it was her passion, and she groaned with inexpressible delight: 'Oh! how sweetly you suck my bottom! push in your dear tongue.'

After sucking for a few moments, while she wriggled her bottom and did all in her power to open her arsehole to facilitate the entrance of his tongue, he asked, 'Do you like that, Frances?'

'Yes, it is most delicious! I love to feel your tongue just inside there, and your breath blowing in the hair of my cunt,' and she hoisted her arse in the most lascivious manner, rubbing her cunt across his nose and jerking her arse against his chin. 'Oh! its coming, major! suck my cunt – put our finger in my arse – pinch the cheeks – pinch hard – oh!'

The major quickly transferred his mouth to her cunt, and licked up the drops of spend that oozed out of her fragrant slit.

Frances then closed her eyes and lay back to rest, while he sat on the ground still playing with her cunt, drawing open the fat, hair-skirted lips that he might see their glowing inside and sniff up the rich salty odour that exhaled from their inner folds.

It was at this moment that we entered the outside room, and Alick's exclamation at once aroused the interest of his friend.

'Hallo! I hear Alick's voice in the other room! Who is that his is talking to?'

'That is Mrs Harpur, our friend Queenie, you know. They have made up matters, I perceive, and are coming there, no doubt, for a quick fuck. We shall have great fun watching them and listening to their bawdy talk. See, place yourself here, look through this little opening and tell me all that you observe, and I will play with this poor tired fellow until I have him in good humour again.'

She then knelt before him, and holding his prick in her left hand, she rubbed its soft head about her nose and mouth, and passing her right hand round his hip, pushed it under his bottom until she reached the bag holding his large firm stones.

Meantime the major continued in a low but distinct whisper.

'What a splendid arse your friend Queenie has! Alick has spread it wide open before him. How he kisses and rubs his face over its glossy surface; now he has drawn open the lips of her cunt and is admiring its rosy chink! Now he sucks it! Don't you hear him! Now he has moved lower down and is sucking her bottom. Alick, my boy you know what voluptuous pleasure is! You are wise – you stop at nothing which promotes it. But listen to Queenie! How delicious to hear her talking of her arse, and telling him to ram his prick into her cunt. Now he is in her; how pleased she looks! How smoothly his prick rushes up between the soft hairy lips of her cunt! How eagerly he plunges against her arse! How promptly she heaves it up! Oh, it is a grand sight! Alick has a splendid tool and uses it with skill and effect. Now, Frances, it is your turn to look, and let me have your bottom to play with.'

'Well, there it is, major,' she replied, pulling up her dress behind as high as he could and stooping forward, 'bottom, cunt, and everything, for you to view and kiss and suck as much as you like; and I will describe, as well as I can, all that is going on in the room outside.'

The major paid due homage to the beauties of her turned up bottom as she continued, 'They are now commencing their second fuck, which Queenie always enjoys the most. She is still on her back with her thighs lifted up and wide apart. Alick is fucking with science and deliberation. He draws the whole of his prick out before every renewed plunge, while Queenie is panting below him, twisting her arse and talking with extreme lewdness to spur him on – "prick and piss; fuck and arse; spunk and bollocks", are the words which sound in his ears at every plunge of his prick into her heated and closely grasping cunt. Oh! major! how nice it is to feel your tongue moving about just inside my arsehole! How is your prick? Is he stiffening up again? Let me put my hand on him. I am longing for another fuck. Stay, I will suck him for a moment – that will put him into good humour. But, hark! Jim has come in, and they are talking about you. Let us listen.'

'Oh, the little imp! with what gusto, she tells how I fucked her arse! Why, she herself cocked up her bottom and asked me to bugger her. There is nothing she enjoys so much as to have Alick fucking, or still better sucking, her cunt while I bugger her arse.'

The major then asked, might he go into them?

'Oh, yes, whenever you please; but won't you fuck me first? My cunt it in a terrible state – oh, it is so hot! Feel it – look at it – kiss it – suck it – fuck it' – and Frances, leaning back and spreading her thighs, jerked up her cunt before his face.

The major said he never saw a cunt look so hot as hers did then: the very lips were swelling out with voluptuous desire, and a hot steam, charged with the spiciest cunt flavour, issued from the heated charm.

How differently constituted women are from men! The previous fucking, which Frances so thoroughly enjoyed, in place of satisfying her had only whetted her appetite for more; while the major began to show signs of exhaustion. However, he could not refuse to attempt a compliance with her request. So leaning over her, he placed the head of his languid prick between the lips of her excited orifice. As soon as she felt it there, she gave on upward plunge which buried it in her cunt to the very balls. Then seizing him in her arms and crossing her legs on his back, she made her belly smack against his at every thrust, and catching his shoulder between her teeth, she nipped him sharply in the agony of her delight.

When she felt major's crisis approaching, she threw back her head, and cried aloud, 'Pour it in, major! Saturate my cunt with spunk – rub your balls against my arse – press hard upon my cunt – oh, fuck!'

Meanwhile, the practised ears of Jim recognised the voice of Frances in the inside room and learning from her ecstatic words that the denouement had taken place, she said to me, 'Don't you think, Queenie, it would be well to go and look for the major and Mr Gipton?' And with a knowing wink and nod towards the inside room, she added, 'You know we have still to introduce the latter to Captain Stuart, who is expecting, I am sure, to find in our young friend not only an agreeable acquaintance but an interesting study. I dare say we shall find them near the place where I left conversing together.'

CHAPTER FOURTEEN

Frances and Captain Stuart

I readily understood that Jim wished Alick to have the gratification of finding out Frances for himself. So agreeing with her proposal, I said, speaking loudly that our friends inside might hear, 'Come Captain Stuart, you are quite rested now; let us go and look for the major; we have allowed him a long time to make acquaintance with that young scapegrace, Gipton; and we wish you to know him too.' I added, as I got up and led the way down the steps.

Jim and I walked on either side of him as we passed along under the trees; taking advantage of the opportunity he put his arms round our waists; then, gently lowering his hands, he ran them up between our thighs from behind, and began to play with our cunts as we moved slowly on.

'Why, Alick,' I exclaimed, 'I thought you must have had enough cunt for one day. After such a performance as yours, most men would have felt disinclined for any further appearance in the lists of Cupid. But, judging from the energetic action of your active fingers in our cunts, there must be some life still in your manly tool. Unbutton him, Jim, and let us see what effect our charms have produced.'

Jim quickly opened his trousers down the front, and drawing out his prick declared, 'He is not at all too bad as to either size or stiffness. With a little more fondling he will be well able for another fuck; especially if we can get him a fresh cunt.'

'Well,' I replied, 'who can tell, but that a fresh cunt may turn up for him before dinner.'

'Why, Queenie,' he asked, 'what do you mean? Do you expect any more girls?'

'Perhaps,' I answered, 'but that will depend of your own smartness; you will have to find her for yourself – and those who would find must seek.'

'Ha! Queenie, I am beginning to smell a rat,' he said, with a knowing look; 'one thing I find: the longer I live, the more I discover the depth and roguishness of your sex. Women are a rich mine, but the quality of the ore is not always revealed by the surface – you must work hard and dig deep to obtain it; is that not the truth?'

'I perceive you are a bit of a philosopher, Alick; let us see how your philosophy will help you in the case in hand. But here comes our young friend – Mr Gipton allow me to introduce you to Captain Stuart. And where have you left the major?'

'He has gone in the other direction, looking for you.'

'Well, we must not leave him to wander alone; come Jim, we will go and find him; and you, Frances, can show the fruit garden to Captain Stuart; I think the melons and mangosteens are ripe.' And Jim and I turned away and left them together.

Frances told me afterwards, that she could hardly help blushing when she observed how intently Captain Stuart regarded her.

He seemed already to have penetrated her secret when he said, 'What a lucky fellow you are, Gipton, to have free intercourse with two such fine women as Mrs Harpur and Miss Bond; and so ready to bestow their favours too. But I suppose you know that better than I do. Eh, Gipton!' and he gave Frances a sly poke in the ribs. 'Come now, meet me halfway – I want your confidence, and I am ready to give you mine. Our friend Queenie has a splendid cunt, and she knows how to make it give a warm reception. I spent twice in it today. When did you fuck her last?'

'Oh, she and I get on well together. I know the excellent qualities of her cunt; it is an old acquaintance of mine.'

'She has a wonderful talent too for manipulating a prick,' Alick added, 'she and Jim had just succeeded in putting renewed life into mine as you came up, and I feel it stiffening now at the thought. Show me what sort of fellow you have, Gipton, and you may investigate mine as much as you please.'

'Very well, captain, where is your prick?' said Frances, putting her hand towards the fork of his trousers.

'In there – unbutton – take him out.'

Frances was not long in bringing to light a large fresh-coloured though rather soft-looking prick, which she took fondly in one hand while she felt for his balls with the other.

'That's a good fellow,' said Captain Stuart, and stooping forward, he ran his hand between her thighs before she had any idea of what he was going to do. 'Hallo, Gipton! what have you done with your middle thumb? You are as soft and smooth here as a pincushion! Open your legs,' and he commenced unbuttoning the trousers.

'Ah! Alick, what a sharp man you are! I am a girl; and you were very quick in finding it out. You may feel my cunt if you like – there, I will show it to you, and you may fuck it too, if you are so disposed.'

'By George, Miss Gipton, you are a clever piece. What a magnificent bush you have over this rosy cleft! How red it looks and how hot it feels! And it is reeking with spunk! Tell me the truth, like a darling girl, has not Kit – the major, I mean – been fucking you?'

'Yes, Alick, he discovered my secret by some lascivious prints which he brought with him. I don't much care to look at pictures of cunts, but I love to see that of a fine standing prick; and especially when it is being frigged by a man. He soon found this out, and drawing forth his prick, got me to frig it for him, and suck it too. Then he tried to get at mine, saying that he greatly enjoyed fondling a friend's prick, and forcing in his hand he met with a cunt instead of a prick. He was so pleased with his success that he wanted to fuck me then and there: but I brought him to the inner room of the smoking pavilion, for the sake of more security and greater comfort.

'He then examined me all over, and kissed and sucked everything I have. After which he fucked me twice in grand style.

'While thus engaged, we had the additional gratification of hearing you and Queenie carrying on in the room outside, and I can tell you we heard no end of kissing, sucking, fucking and bawdy talk.

'Had I not been so well satisfied myself with the major's perform-ance. I would have envied Queenie the great pleasure she expressed on the entrance of your prick into her cunt, and the groans of rapture she uttered at your final discharge. As it was, however, they served to fire my imagination and intensify my joy. But, Alick, you have examined me enough now. Oh! how your moustache tickles me! I declare, you will suck out every drop of spend left in my cunt. Whatever should we do if anyone saw us now?'

'Well, let us go farther in among the trees. The notion of fucking a boy-girl out here in the open has stirred me up with fresh desire. Though my prick is not so large and strong as he usually for, as you know, he has done a fair allowance of work already today, nevertheless you have given him new life. See how he pants! Will you care for him, do you think?'

'Yes, he is by no means to be despised, indeed on the contrary; he seems in admirable order. I like his nice fresh colour and elastic spring. When I press him down, how nimbly he jerks up again! And see how this little slit-like mouth opens when I squeeze the head. There, a tiny drop of spend, like a white pearl, glistens on the top! Now, I will lie back, raise my thighs and turn up my bottom to let you get more easily at my cunt, and enable you to drive your prick farther in when you are fucking me.'

'That's a darling; you are now most conveniently placed, and your cunt looks charming. So your trousers open up behind as well as in front. What a capital plan!'

'Yes, I have to get them made in that manner to accommodate me on my own occasions when I want to piss, you know.'

This little word, 'piss' fired Alick as she designed. With one hand he held open the soft hairy lips, while with the other, he directed the head of his prick to the sensitive entrance at the lower part of her moist slit. Then giving one heave of his muscular backside, he thrust in his prick, and watched it as it slowly disappeared amidst the rosy folds.

Frances gave that peculiar expansive movement of her thighs, joined with a slight upward heave of her bottom which is so strongly indicative of extreme enjoyment, while the most lascivious fire gleamed in her eyes, as she asked him, 'Can you see it, Alick? Can you see your prick fucking my cunt?'

'Yes, I am watching how the fat hairy lips of your cunt suck it in and how red and moist it looks when I draw it out, while the lips seem too follow as if loth to part with it – there, do you like that?' he asked, as he pushed softly up the whole length of his new well-stiffened prick.

'It is delicious, I like your slow quiet style of fucking. It gives one time to relish the prick. How sweetly the head opens up the inner folds of my cunt! Oh! that is so nice! I feel it ever so far up, while the lips of my cunt are stretched round its root and your large hairy balls rub my bottom. Press against me – hold the cheeks of my arse – you may squeeze them as hard as you like, yes, I will say all the bawdy words I can think of for you. Queenie has a lovely arse, and the most lubricious way of showing her arse and cunt together.

'Yes, I have often seen her fucked, and watched her pissing too. That is great fun, you know, to watch the yellow piss shooting out from the hairy lips of a big randy cunt. Yes, I will piss for you some other time; and will hold your prick while you piss for me. And I will suck your prick just after pissing. You want to bugger me, do you? Very well, you may; I'll hold open the cheeks of my arse – can you see the little round hole? Oh! I feel your prick there – its going in – don't push in too far – the most feeling is just inside the opening – yes, that's the way. Do I find your prick too large? No, it feels so well moistened after my cunt! Now, watch – see how I rub the clitoris – this way; then down the slit so. Oh! the feel is coming! Oh! are you ready? Shoot your spunk into my arse, while I frig my cunt – fuck – fuck. Oh! Alick – hold me; arse, cunt and prick are all on the flow together. Oh!! Oh!!!'

Alick said afterwards, that he enjoyed this spend more than any he had that day; that Frances not only gripped him with peculiar tightness in her bottom, but presented her cunt in such a wanton and lubricious manner, that his amorous feeling was worked up to the highest degree.

He also told us that he suspected her true sex from the first moment that he saw her. For in spite of her affected boldness of manner, he perceived that there lay underneath a conscious timidity that did not quite accord with her assumed character.

Besides he detected traces of that habit of keeping her legs together, which is so characteristic of most women, and therefore felt encouraged to proceed the more boldly in his pleasurable enterprise.

CHAPTER FIFTEEN

A Sacrifice to Venus Followed by Lord Ferrars' Narrative of his Boyish Amours

When Jim and I returned after finding the major, Frances ran forward to meet us. Her clustering curls of golden hair were tossed and disordered, but her eyes were bright and her voice cheery as she exclaimed, 'Queenie, I have been vanquished. Both the major and Captain Stuart have proved too strong for my weak defence. My armour has been penetrated, and every vulnerable crevice discovered and laid bare. Let me go in and throw aside my harness as useless and unavailing.'

We only laughed, as the major replied, 'No, my sweet Frances, your disguise is admirable and tends more than anything to enhance your surpassing charms. Is not that your opinion, too?' he said, turning to Alick, who had just come up.

'Most assuredly,' replied Alick, 'Frances would be lovely and lovable in any dress, and better in none at all, for to her the poet's words might be justly applied:

She is, when unadorn'd, adorn'd the most.

Yet I fully agree with you that her boyish costume renders her charms still more piquant and irresistible.'

We then went into the house to prepare for dinner and get ready to welcome Lord Ferrars and Dick on their return from the hunting expedition.

Our new friends were received there with great cordiality, and we were soon as familiar together as if we had been friends all our lives. When the servants were got rid of after dinner, we retreated into my snug little boudoir, and then, as usual, undress became the order of the day.

The gentlemen did not object to our making free with their engines of delight, and we placed no difficulties in the way of their full and free investigation of our secret charms.

We handled and frigged their pricks one after the other, and they fingered and viewed our cunts and bottoms in every variety of attitude and position. My husband and Lord Ferrars, being tolerably fresh, had their pricks in fair fucking order, while those of the others were rather languid after their late services with us; so it was decided that Lord Ferrars was to sacrifice to Venus, and that Jim's cunt was to be the altar on which the libation should be poured forth, while the major was to act what was to him a very pleasing duty – the part of presiding priest, that is he was to hold the sacrificial knife and see that the victim was duly penetrated and the sacrifice in all respects complete.

Jim was accordingly stripped to her stockings and boots, which by universal consent is judged the suitable amount of dress for these occasions, and laid on her back on a broad couch in the centre of the room. We gathered round her, and the major commenced his duties by lifting her legs, pushing a pillow under her bottom and spreading her thighs to their widest extent.

This posture, of course, opened out the charm of love, and presented it in the most favourable aspect for examination and for viewing the entrance of the sacrificial knife.

Then the major, taking a position a little to one side, proceeded to direct our attention to its varied beauties and capabilities. Passing one hand under her bottom, he placed the other on her rising mound as he said, 'Observe this voluptuous hillock, called the mount of Venus, how luxuriously it is crowned with this thicket of silky hair! And here, in the thickest part, see the commencement of the furrow of love, bounded on either side by large well-rounded lips! How they project in ripe luxuriance! How soft and unctuous they feel, while their interior lining is mantled with all the blushing hues of morn. See how this rose-bud clitoris uprears its saucy head!' Then, drawing open the nymphae, he continued: 'But look in here. This sweet clink, adorned with coral sides, redolent with most stimulating perfume, and wet with ambrosial dew, is the very seat and home of love. And observe how instinct with life it is! It actually pants with desire as I titillate its sensitive nerves! See how the soft cheeks below sympathise with amorous emotion! How they compress themselves as, with wanton heaves, the open cunt invites the hot and moist encounter!' Then passing his hand over her smooth belly, he pronounced: 'This altar is now prepared, and this luscious cunt is only waiting to receive its libation and then lie soaking in the flooded streams of love. Come forward, my lord, and do your part.

'But let me first inspect the weapon. My duty is to see that it is fully qualified for it work, and then that the work itself is duly performed and satisfactorily completed. Mrs Harpur, let me ask you, as priestess on this auspicious occasion, to place the weapon in my hand.'

I at once complied by pulling his lordship's shirt over his head, and placing one hand under his balls, I grasped the prick with the other and drew him forward to the major's side.

The major's eyes glistened with pleasure as he took in hand the firm standing prick, and having gently drawn down the soft movable skin, regarded with admiration its glowing head.

Meantime, Jim had passed her hand from behind between the major's thighs, and catching his bollocks, had drawn him nearer to herself, so that while she still lay back with her cunt fully opened to our view, she was able with her other and to clasp his prick and frig it up and down.

The major smiled as he gave one glance at his own affair, so pleasantly captured, and then turned all his attention to the more vigorous prick he was manipulating himself. He was now quite in his element, for he loved above all things to hold in his hands the tool of another man, and he watched it admiringly while his fingers played round its firm shaft and gently moved the loose skin up and down, covering and uncovering the large rosy head and making it elevate its crest in proud defiance.

Lord Ferrars, having somewhat similar tastes, did not object to the major's familiarities. Nay, he evidently enjoyed his skilful manipula-tion, for he pushed forward his prick, and looked down upon it with satisfaction as with successive jerks of his bottom he made it pass backwards and forwards through the major's circling fingers. The latter then pronounced the sacrificial weapon fit for its work and said: 'Now, Ferrars, let me place in at the exact spot where it can most easily penetrate the victim and pass through the opposing folds until it reaches those hidden recesses where the libation must be made which completes the sacrifice of Venus.'

Lord Ferrars, yielding himself to his directions, passed between the wide-spread thighs of Jim and bent down over her recumbent form.

Then the major, having rubbed the swollen head of his lordship's prick two or three times up and down the juicy chink of her cunt, placing its point at the critical spot, and, transferring his hand to his lordship's manly stones, cried: 'Strike home, my lord.' And suiting the action to the word, he gave him a resounding smack on the backside.

The whole length of his lordship's prick rushed up the moist and heated cavity, his hips pressed hard between her open thighs and his balls rubbed the sensitive edges of her arsehole.

'Now it is for the victim to cry aloud and utter her dying song as she feels the weapon of Venus reaching her very heart and yields herself to the maddening ecstasies of love.'

'Oh, yes, sir priest, I perspire and spend. I am penetrated to the heart. I feel the glowing weapon in the very centre of delight. O divine prick! O happy cunt! O sweet fuck! Ram your prick home in my cunt, Lord Ferrars. Batter my arse with your cods – Oh, my arse! – Oh, my quim! major, put your prick in my mouth. Alick and Dick, let me hold your pricks in my hands and rub them to my titties.'

She clutched Alick's prick in her left hand and my husband's in her right, and drawing them towards her rubbed them against her swelling bubbies. She thus attained the highest degree of voluptuous enjoyment. Her cunt was gloriously filled by Lord Ferrars' noble prick; Frances pinched her bottom and tickled her arsehole with her finger. Her mouth was crammed with the major's tool, now stiffened up again, while his hairy appendages rubbed her face. Alick worked away at her left side, as she kept his prick pressed against her breast, while my husband was equally active on her right, making the nose of his prick – now in first-rate order – plunge against Alick's at every push.

Outside of all, I passed around, frigging bollocks and pricks, arses and cunts in succession, stimulating each by the most wanton expressions and lascivious touches I could devise.

Then the floodgates of pleasure opened, and Jim literally swam in a sea of delight as streams of spunk poured on every side, saturating her cunt, belly and breasts and accompanied by excited cries and sonorous groans.

Then the major declared that the sacrifice was a complete success, and that the all potent goddess was delighted with the devotion of her ardent and persistent votaries.

We accordingly arranged ourselves in various attitudes of repose, taking care that each prick should be conveniently placed for the gratifying touches of a female hand, and each cunt open to the inspection and feel of the masculine members of our social party.

Lord Ferrars reclined between my legs, his cheek resting on my thighs, his fingers toying with the curling hairs of my cunt, opening and shutting its pouting lips and pressing the clitoris that lay between.

It occurred to me that some lascivious story or lustful narrative was just what we needed to rekindle our smouldering fires and cause them to burst out afresh into amorous flame; and that Lord Ferrars, for his experience and well-known ability, was the very man to help us in that way.

So, rubbing his prick softly between my feet, I said, 'My lord, you once told me of some of your boyish loves, which interested me greatly. I am sure that if you would kindly favour our present company with a similar sample of your early reminiscences, they would be highly gratified, and we should all feel so much obliged.'

'I have nothing of any special interest to relate, my darling Queenie,' replied his lordship, 'but if it would gratify you and our friends, while we are resting together, I will be happy to do the best I can. In the early days of my boyhood, much of my holiday time was passed with my aunt, Lady Flora, who was a young widow with independent means; but though of a very ardent temperament, she had determined not to encumber herself, as she said, a second time with a husband. She preferred, in fact, being her own mistress, able to carry out her own programme of enjoyment without restriction or restraint. She strictly observed all the social proprieties of life, so far as outward observation extended, but with great prudence and skill she secretly indulged her wanton propensities with the utmost freedom, not only with men of her own rank, but with her grooms and gardeners, and indeed with anyone disposed to enjoy her favours with discretion and ready to submit to her wanton caprices.

'She had a special fancy for boys just budding into manhood and delighted in playing with their partially developed pricks, taking great interest in observing the first signs of sexual pleasure, especially when aroused by acquaintance for the first time with the appearance and uses of the female parts.

'When I first went on a visit to her, I was nearly twelve years old. I had learnt from the more knowing of my schoolfellows that my little cock was called prick and that the little slit which girls have between their legs was called cunt, and that putting the prick into the cunt was a very pleasant operation, but as yet I had not had experience of the matter.

'My aunt commenced by pretending that she was very particular that I should have a good bath every morning and said she must come to my room and see that her wishes were fully carried out. So next morning, before I was up, she came into my room, and having arranged the water in my bath, told me to get up, take off my shirt and step into it.

'I hesitated, for I then felt somewhat bashful about displaying my nakedness before a lady, even though she was my aunt. Observing my hesitation, she quickly pulled down the bedclothes, and said, "You need not mind me, Fred. I am your mother's sister, and often nursed you as a child. There is no reason for being ashamed in front of me, so pull off your shirt and jump into the bath."

'I did as she asked me, for I was really fond of her, and besides felt amused at her fancy. I sat down in the bath and sponged my back and shoulders, with my face turned away from her. She watched me for a few moments, and then offered to help me herself. She uncovered her right arm, and taking the sponge poured the water over my neck and shoulders. In doing so, a large portion of her snow white breasts became exposed to view, which excited my liveliest emotion and made me willing to comply with any further demand, however wild or extravagant.

'She quickly perceived her advantage, and told me to stand up. I did so, this time facing her, with my little prick much larger than usual in full erection before her. She looked at it with admiration, put her hand on it, and said, "What a funny little thing! What do you do with it?"

' "Ah, don't you know! I do my pee with it," I said blushing.

' "But it was meant for something far nicer than doing pee," she replied with a smile, frigging me as she spoke.

' "What's that? Oh, auntie, do tell me. I will be so fond of you, and do everything you wish."

' "Well, we will see; but first I must give you a good drying."

'She rubbed all the upper part of my body with a towel as I stood before her; then slipping of her seat went on her knees to get more easily at my lower limbs. When she had carefully dried all between my legs, she took my little prick tenderly in her hands, and drawing the skin back as far as it could go the kissed the head and then took it into her warm mouth.

'Then placing her hands behind me, she caught the cheeks of my bottom and moved me back and forward, so as to make my prick pass in and out through her tightly pressed lips.

'I actually shivered with delight, and placing my hands on her head, said, "Oh, auntie, how good you are! Oh!! That is so nice! Don't stop, I do not know what is going to happen, but I never felt anything so nice in my life."

'Then a warm glow passed through my whole frame followed by a delicious languor, so that I should have fallen if she had not caught me in her arms and held me up.

'I do verily believe, that, young as I was, I enjoyed then my first spend, or, at all events, felt for the first time the pleasurable emotion caused by the spasmodic action of the organs of ejaculation; and the feeling was so overpowering that for a few moments I lost all consciousness.

'When I came to myself, I was lying on a sofa. My aunt was still bending over me, fondling my prick and playing with the little balls which had lately come down. She looked up and said.:

' "Well, Freddy, my pet, how did you like that? Is not that better than piddling?"

' "Oh! it is delicious – nothing can exceed it."

' "Yes, there is something better still. But I think I have taught you enough for one lesson. Perhaps tomorrow, I will teach you more. Meanwhile be a good boy; ride your pony; take plenty of outdoor exercise, and eat plenty of beefsteak. I want you to grow up strong and healthy, and then you will be a favourite with all the ladies.'

' "I shall be quite satisfied if I am a favourite with you, dear auntie,' I replied, with all the gallantry I could muster.

'During the day following, my thoughts often recurred to the pleasant sensations which my aunt's touches had shown me were so richly stored up in a part of my body I had hitherto been led to despise on account of the obligation to keep it covered up and concealed. But now the attentions and admiration of my aunt had enlightened me as to its value and importance; and I longed for the further instruction she had promised me.

'Besides, the glimpse she had given me of the soft beauties of her bosom, and the rich valley that lay between those swelling orbs, had made me eager to explore farther down.

'I had seen the pouting slits of little girls, and fancy painted for me a similar slit – of course – larger and deeper – that must lie at the bottom of her belly and extend in between her thighs, and I wondered, would she let me feel it with my finger?

'That night when she kissed me as I was going to bed, she said: "As you have been such a good boy all the day, Freddy, you may come into my room in the morning, if you like."

' "Thanks, dear aunt, what time shall I come?"

' "About seven o'clock – after you have had your bath; when you are warm and dry, wrap something about you, and come just as you are."

'My first thought in the morning when I woke was the lesson my aunt had promised to give me; and putting my hand to my prick, I was surprised to find how much larger it seemed to have grown in a single night. My aunt's touches on the previous day and above all the suction of her lips had caused it to develop its power with unusual rapidity. It now felt uncomfortably stiff, and I longed for my aunt's help to relieve its tension as before. I accordingly lost no time in taking my bath, and though it was half an hour before the time mentioned by my aunt, I stole softly to the door of her room. It was closed but not fastened and opened without noise when I applied a gentle push.

'Inside, the air felt warm, and pervaded with a perfume highly suggestive of voluptuous enjoyment. In the subdued light which entered through the richly curtained windows. I perceived my aunt's bed, under a canopy of gauze. I heard a gentle breathing as I approached. She was fast asleep, lying on her back, and to my great delight partially uncovered. One beautiful knee, white as alabaster, and part of the adjoining thigh were exposed to view. I stood at the bedside for a moment in mute admiration. Her arm lay across her face, and her bosom heaved at regular intervals as of one in deep sleep. The outlines of her beautiful limbs were clearly indicated under the light covering that spread over them. I could not resist the desire to see more, so I gently raised the sheet. As she did not stir, I felt emboldened to make further attempts to gratify my prurient curiosity. I gradually uncovered the whole thigh until my wondering eyes caught sight of a thick bush of light curly hair that seemed to cover the bottom of her belly and fill all the angle between her thighs. I felt irresistibly impelled to put my hand on it, at first very lightly and then more boldly, as she did not move.

'Looking at it with scrutinising eagerness, I perceived through the hair two swelling lips, and I pushed the tip of my finger between them. The furrow felt warm and moist, and seemed to open of its own accord. I bent over its and drawing the hairs aside peered into its pink recess. A peculiarly subtle odour exhaled from it, which I sniffed up with delight, for it caused my prick to tingle with lascivious desire. I stooped and kissed the pouting lips. My aunt heaved slightly against me. I started with alarm: and though she was going to waken up; but it was only an involuntary stirring. Of her limbs, for she quickly relapsed into heavy sleep as before. On recovering my self possession, I perceived to my great delight that her thighs were now much more widely spread than at first. And as I bent over her again, I could see that the pink furrow extended down between the cheeks of her lovely bottom. I spread it open with my fingers, and found that the upper part was filled with a fleshy lump, which has a soft outer skin, but felt inside to be a gristly substance, that had considerable elastic firmness when I pressed it.

'I felt intoxicated by the sweet smell it had: I applied my lips to it and rubbed it with my tongue, and finally took it into my mouth and sucked it. My aunt then gave a sudden start, put her hand on my head, and pushed up her cunt, as she said: "Freddy, you naughty boy, you have anticipated me in discovering all my secrets! What are you kissing me down there for?' at the same time placing her hand on my prick and pushing the skin back from its tingling head.

' "Forgive me, dear auntie, for being so bold; when I came in, I found you asleep and partly uncovered, and I could not help feasting my eyes on the beautiful little nest you have at the bottom of your white belly."

' "Well, Freddy, I forgive you. I meant to let you see it – you may kiss it as mush as you like. Get over me, rest your belly on my bubbies, and put your little prick to my mouth – my upper mouth, you know. How do you like my lower one?"

' "It is lovely, aunt; it has such thick fat lips, and such a delicious smell! May I draw it more open?"

' "Oh, you may do anything you like with it – kiss it, and suck it, and push your tongue into it. Do you know its name, dear?'

' "Yes, auntie, our schoolboys say it is called cunt – is that what you call it?"

' "Yes, that is my cunt, and below it is my bottom. Can you see that too?'

' "Aye, that I can, and admire it as well. Your cunt runs down to it. Your cunt and bottom, auntie, seem to be all one.'

' "No, no, they are very different; my cunt opens to the front, don't you see? and my bottom opens behind, and they are separated by a ridge. I am sure my cunt is much nicer than my bottom, and has a nicer smell besides."

' "Not at all, dear auntie, I love your cunt, but I admire your bottom too. Like your cunt it has a savoury smell, and sweet. Would you like me to put my finger in as you do to mine?"'

' "Yes, Fred, if you wish. You are a dear boy, and do that very nicely. I like to feel you kiss and push your tongue into it. Do you know any other name for it besides bottom?'

' "Yes, auntie, I have heard it called arse."

' "Well, we will call it arse too, for the fun of the thing. Do you like me to tickle your arse while I suck your prick?"

' "Oh, yes, auntie, it is delicious! but it is making that feel come again – take out my prick, or I shall piddle in your mouth."

' "That's not piddling, Fred, it its called spending; and though spending in the mouth may be very nice, yet spending in the cunt is better – that's called fucking, you know. Would you like to fuck me,

Fred? – to put you prick into my cunt and fuck me."

' "Yes, dear aunt, if you let me and show me how to do it."

' "Well, get over me and lie on my belly, and I will put your prick into my cunt myself and teach you how to fuck."

'I got over her, with my breast resting on her soft bubbies, my belly lying along the smooth expanse of her belly, and my prick buried amidst the thick hairy bush at the bottom of it.

'She pressed me in between her wide-spread thighs and threw her arms round me as she said, "What a nice soft little arse you have, Freddy!" And heaving herself up and grinding her cunt against my prick, she went on, "And so you are going to fuck your aunt, Freddy, and you want her to show you how to do it? Well, she will teach you!" and pushing her hand in between us, she took hold of my prick and rubbed its head up and down the slit of her cunt. It felt deliciously warm and soft as my prick slipped along its unctuous sides. Then holding its point lower down, she said, "Now, Freddy, push – push in your prick," at the same time shoving up her cunt; "fuck me now," she cried, as my prick plunged into her hot recess.

'Who can describe the rapturous joy I then for the first time realised! My whole prick seemed clasped in living folds which surrounded it and embraced it on every side. My aunt, however, desired more vigorous action; seizing the cheeks of my bottom, she made me work up and down with a motion corresponding to the rapid heaves of her own body, while she said, "Now, work your arse, Freddy, drive in your prick and fuck me like a man – that's the way – fuck – fuck;' and she rolled from side to side and pressed me into her as a discharge like liquid fire seemed to pass from my backbone through my prick into her cunt, and I sank powerless in her arms.

'I soon recovered, and asked permission to continue playing with her cunt: but she stopped me, and said, "You are a wonderful boy, Fred, but I must not suffer you to do anything more now, lest you should injure your health. Go and bathe this good little fellow in cold water and return to bed for an hour or two; and I promise, you shall have other opportunities of fucking me yourself or seeing me fucked by another."

' "Dear aunt, that would be delightful. I would so like to see a fine big prick working in and out of your cunt: and perhaps you will let me touch it at the same time."

' "Well, hurry off now, and I may let you someday soon."

'As I went towards the door, the thought occurred to me: she is on for sport, and if I could only stay and hide, I might see some fun. So instead of going out I only made a slight noise with the handle and slipped behind some clothes that hung near.

'The event proved I was right. After allowing sufficient time for me to regain my room, she called in a low voice: "Tomkins, are you there?" "Yes, my lady," replied the footman, a tall young fellow, as he stepped out of the wardrobe, "I have been watching the young masters' first performance, and I am in a condition to give your ladyship a real treat."

'He then walked up to the bedside, and with the boldness of long familiarity pushed up his prick for her approval and caress. She took it in her hand, and drawing down the skin, looked at it with an approving glance. It was indeed a noble specimen, fully nine inches long, and thick in proportion, and its large glossy head was of a deep ruby tint. I had never seen anything like it before, and it filled me with great admiration.

'She kissed it and said: "Yes, he'll do. Now, Tomkins, feel my cunt. It has been irritated rather than satisfied by Master Freddy – though indeed he did wonderfully well for a boy, and if he grows to be a man he will have a fine tool."

'Meantime, Tomkins had drawn her across the bed, and going on his knees had laid her up-lifted legs on his shoulders; then pushing his hands under her, he began to kiss and suck her cunt.

' "Dear mistress," he muttered, "your sweet cunt is indeed in a most excited state. I never knew it to feel so hot or smell so savoury! Shall I put in my prick?"

' "Wait a moment, Tomkins, go on sucking, while I call Susan. Nothing pleases me more than to have a woman spend in my mouth when my cunt is so excited as it is now."

'She pulled a bell-rope near at hand, and immediately a young woman, whom she retained as her special attendant, entered the room through a door concealed in the panels.

' "Take off everything, Susan, and jump up on the bed."

'She loosened a string or two and her clothes fell on the floor.

'As she got on the bed, my aunt smiled at her and said,

' "Stand over me, Susan, with your legs wide apart. Good, your cunt looks red and inflamed; when was it fucked last?"

' "This morning, my lady. James was just beginning to give it the second poke when your ladyship called me."

' "So much the better. I hope you did not wipe it on the way?"

' "No, my lady, it is still dripping with his spunk."

' "Very good, that's the way I like to have it. Now let down your arse, place your cunt on my mouth and talk to Tomkins."

'She squatted down and settled her cunt on my aunt's mouth; then twisting her bottom about, she said: "Tomkins, her ladyship is sucking my cunt. She is pushing her tongue where James had is prick ten minutes ago. She wants me to spend in her mouth, while you are sucking her cunt; so tickle my arse with your finger – now, my lady – there – its coming – Oh! – Oh!!" '

CHAPTER SIXTEEN

Lord Ferrar's Narrative Continued: Lady Flora and her Confidential Domestics

'Susan remained with her cunt pressed on the mouth of my aunt, who seemed to sup up with peculiar zest the unctuous drops which exuded from that lustful gap. When her ladyship had finished licking round the sides, and had probed the hot juicy passage with the full length of her penetrating tongue, she told Susan to lie on her back with her legs drawn up and her bottom turned towards Tomkins.

'Then, addressing her footman – who might be more correctly termed her cuntman, she said, "Now Tomkins, my man, give me a good bellyful of prick while you feast your eyes on Susan's randy slit."

'Tomkins made no delay, but getting up at once rammed his prick into his mistress's cunt, and began fucking her with such tremendous energy that I felt the room shake with the concussion of his strokes – more than that, I could hear the sucking sound made by the lips of her cunt each time he drew out his prick, and then the loud smack of his loins against the fat cheeks of her arse every time he drove it back again.

'She showed equal vigour in plunging up to meet the prods of his prick, while she gripped him tightly with one arm and to excite him more placed her other hand on Susan's cunt and, spreading open the lips, cried: "Look at Susan's cunt, Tomkins, open for a prick and begging for a fuck. What a pity it is that my page James is not here to finish his poke and fuck her before us!"

' "I am here, my lady; knowing your ladyship's good-nature, I made bold to fellow Susan. Shall I get on the bed and fuck her now in your presence?"

' "Do James, you are just in time, and be quick about it, for Tomkins is coming to the short strokes,' and turning to the latter, "Hold back a minute, Tomkins, until James gets into Susan. I will put his prick into her cunt myself, and we will both watch them while they fuck."

'James darted between Susan's wide-spread legs, and with my aunt's help soon buried his prick in her cunt.

' "Now fuck away, both of you," cried Lady Flora, "and let everyone repeat after me aloud: Heave cunts – press pricks – shove bottoms – get ready bollocks – fire away pricks – swallow cunts – prick – cunt – arse – fucking – pissing – farting – prick – bollocks – cunt – fuck – fuck – fuck."

'Then gripping one another with a convulsive grasp, the lustful discharge flowed from each simultaneously, and with a universal groan of gratified desire, they rolled upon the bed.

'As you will readily understand, this scene had a powerful effect on me. The view of two randy women fucked at the same time, the writhing of their naked bodies, the working of their fat bottoms and the evident satisfaction with which their cunts received the thrusts of two such fine pricks as these young men possessed, all combined to produce in me an impatient longing for fresh enjoyment of my aunt's favours, while the familiar footing on which she placed her servants removed all my apprehension of giving her offence.

'Her free use too of such bawdy language, though it surprised not a little, stirred up my strongest sensations of voluptuous desire. The word pissing especially arrested my attention. I had never seen a girl piss, but as I watched my aunt's fine large randy, looking quim, I thought what a beautiful sight it must be to see her piss streaming out from between those soft hairy lips – thus indicating, as it were, the cunt to be the very fount of love itself. So I determined, at the next opportunity, to ask her to let me see how she pissed.

'But I was to be gratified sooner than I expected. My prick had stiffened up wonderfully during the exciting scene I had just witnessed. I grasped it with one hand while I pressed the heated balls with the other. I was on the point of leaving my hiding place and stealing up to them, with a view of joining in, when further activity arrested my intention and inclined me to wait until I had witnessed more of their lascivious proceedings.

'My aunt having absorbed all the spunk which Tomkins was able to inject at one time, raised herself up and made the two men sit on either side of her while Susan knelt on the floor and with a wet sponge cleansed her reeking cunt. But during this cooling operation she kept her hands on the two pricks, and commenced softly frigging them, as the said: "Now we shall see which of you will come to life first."

' "Well, my lady." replied Tomkins, "although the touch of your ladyship's delicate fingers about one's prick is most exciting, yet allow me to suggest that if you will permit us to sit on two chairs in front of you, while you lean back and turn up so that we may have a full view of your ladyship's splendid arse, with its little round aperture and the luscious slit of your cunt over it, while we frig ourselves with our own hands, I think that your ladyship's wishes will be more speedily accomplished."

' "Very well, Tomkins, get the chairs;" said my aunt, throwing herself back while Susan propped up her head with a pillow. Then lifting her thighs she held them open with her hands, and looking through them, she laughed and said, "Is that the sort of view you want? See, you have all the secrets of my bottom before you – cunt, arsehole and everything."

' "Thanks, my lady, such a sight ought to raise the dead. You ladyship's arse gleams like the full moon, your little round arsehole, fringed with hair, looks waiting for a prick; and your fat pouting cunt, so red, so moist, and so open, would draw a monarch from his throne."

' "Bravo, Tomkins. What do you say, James?"

' "I have only to add, my lady, that if Susan would place her naked bum alongside that of your ladyship, we shall have the double excitement of seeing two bottoms instead of one."

' "Quite right, James. Come, Susan, lean forward at my side, with your nether beauties uncovered; rest one leg on the floor, and extend the other along the edge of the bed. Now, boys, I'll act showman for Susan's fat bottom," and she turned herself half round, thus presenting us with a most lubricious side-view of her own cunt and bottom, as she continued, "Now then, churn your cods and rub up your pricks, while I describe Susan's arse. Observe first, how these plump cheeks tremble with lascivious motion as I stir them about. Then view this luxurious furrow lying snugly between them, and in the centre of it this little round, pink, pursed-up opening. Wouldn't you like to stretch these wrinkles with your prick, and feel the purse string holding it tightly as you rammed it in and out? or perhaps you would find this rosy slit, which nature has prepared expressly for the use of the prick, both sweeter and more satisfying? See how these thick lips project! and observe what an inviting look pervades the whole cunt, as if it is expecting to be sucked or fucked, according as your fancy might incline. Now Susan, sit up; it is your turn to act showman. Tell them what you see here," and the turned her bottom towards Susan, still holding her thighs at their widest stretch. Susan, who had been frigging her own cunt with the middle finger of her left hand, now placed the four fingers of her right in the slit of her mistress's cunt and rubbed them up and down the open chink.

' "Oh, Susan, that's grand! I'm going to spend."

' "Will your ladyship get over me and spend in my mouth, while I frig my own cunt and tickle your ladyship's arse."

'My aunt then got over Susan with a knee on eeither side and her cunt pressed down on her face. I could hear the sucking of Susan's lips in my aunt's cunt while she frigged away at her own and thrust the forefinger of her other hand into the hole of my aunt's arse. Then my aunt's whole body seemed to writhe in voluptuous contortions as she poured into Susan's mouth the rich liquor of her cunt.

'Then they lay side by side to rest, with all the interesting parts of their palpitating forms still uncovered and in full view of the two men and myself.

'But Lady Flora, whose appetite for prick seemed unappeasable, did not continue long in this inactive state. She soon sat up again, and looking inquisitively at the men's prick, said, "They seem in tolerable condition; if you would now frig each other, it would give them the finishing touch and gratify me. I love to see one man frigging another man's pricks. Somehow, it is more lust-provoking than when women do it for them." They at once crossed their arms, and taking hold of each other's prick frigged it as only a man can do.

'Tomkins prick immediately stood up in all its glory, fully distended, and with it great purple head swollen and pointing upward to the skies.

'That of James did not look so vigorous. So he said, wishing for a little longer delay, "There is one thing more, my lady, which if your ladyship would oblige us by doing, it would put our pricks at once into first-rate working order. I have often heard your ladyship pissing, and wished so much to witness the sweet performance. If your ladyship could piss now, and let us see your ladyship's cunt in the act of shooting it out, it would be a very great treat to Tomkins and myself."

' "Well, James, I will do it if I can." And pushing herself forward, so that her bottom projected over the edge of the bed, she told Susan to hold the pot below her arse.

' "Now, boys, I am going to piss – watch – make ready – present – fire!" And a clear amber stream spouted out from between the plump lips of her cunt and rattled into the vessel which Susan held carefully underneath.

'I could stand this no longer; the sight of my aunt's cunt pissing in full view of the two men, who watched it with lust-inflamed eyes while each frigged the other's prick, drew me irresistibly towards them.

'I darted in between, and pressing up to my aunt's bottom, cried:

"Forgive me, dear aunt, for coming back. I heard you pissing, and I could not avoid peeping in. And then your cunt looked so beautiful with the yellow piss streaming out between its lips that I ran up to ask you to let me fuck it while it is still wet with the hot piss."

' "Well, Freddy, I can't refuse you; you may fuck me now if you like. But let me show you a new way, which will give you fresh pleasure. Sit here on the bed – now lean back, and I will get over you, as if I were the man."

'My aunt then threw herself upon me, almost smothering me with her bubbies, while Susan guided my prick into her wanton gap. Her cunt felt indeed as if soaked in hot piss as my prick glided up into its heated recesses, and the moist clinging folds inside held it with a tenacious grasp.

'Then addressing James, she said, "You might push in alongside Master Fred, James; it will not be the fist time that I have had two pricks in my cunt at once."

Immediately, I felt the soft head of James's prick pushing in over mine and rubbing deliciously against it as he worked it in and out, while the grinding together of our cods every time he drove his prick home was a new and most agreeable sensation.

'In my ecstasy, I cried, "Oh, auntie! what a cunt you have! to hold two pricks at the same time! How nice it feels! May I pinch your bottom?"

'My aunt wriggled about over me, as she answered, "Yes, Freddy, pinch away. It is grand – and you, James, fuck – fuck me – yes, you may fuck my arse if you like; and Susan will hold open the cheeks."

'Then James drew out, leaving my prick almost lost in the wide cunt, but very soon I felt the pressure of his tool from the adjoining channel and its rubbing motion nearly the same as before, showing how thin the partition between the two passages must be.

'My aunt then cried out, "Tomkins, what are you waiting for? See, Susan's bottom is ready for you. You may fuck or bugger her just as you please. Which would you like best, Susan, to have his prick in your cunt or your arse?"

' "Oh, my lady, it is all one to me. Let him poke my cunt first and then finish up in my arse if he chooses."

'Susan's arse was well cocked up, and Tomkins very quickly commenced agitating behind her, whether in her bottom or her cunt, I could not decide. All the while, however, I felt her fingers busily playing round the root of my prick, stirring my balls and poking my bottom. The movement of her finger about in my bottom just inside the entrance of my arsehole gave a new sensation of peculiar delight;

and I understood then, what I afterwards more fully realised, the great augmentation of amorous excitement which is caused when the arsehole is entered by a finger, or still better by a prick, while one's own prick is titillated by and or embedded in cunt.

'From this time forward, my aunt threw off all reserve and freely admitted me to all her secret orgies. These pleasant gatherings generally occurred either early in the morning or late at night. During the day, everything was conducted with the strictest propriety and decorum.

My aunt treated her servants so kindly and judiciously that they found it in their own interest to make themselves as agreeable and useful as they could; and although, in private, she permitted and encouraged the most unbounded freedom and familiarity, yet on every other occasion, she expected to be treated with the greatest deference and respect. And they were quite prepared to go along with, for they were well assured that, if at any time they showed the slightest disposition to presume or deem their services indispensable, they would be at once dismissed without compunction or delay.

CHAPTER SEVENTEEN

Lord Ferrars' Narrative Continued: His Last Term at School

'My affections were strongly drawn towards my aunt. I admired her cleverness and tact, and I was delighted with the new sphere she opened out for the gratification of my amorous propensities. At the same time, she proved her regard for my welfare by impressing on me the importance of never overtaxing the powers of nature; and she assured me that if I wished to preserve my physical oganism in full working order I must practise much self-restraint and allow those parts that occasional rest which nature requires and prudence enjoins.

'She also warned me against too great indulgence in self-frigging; and she told me that many boys and young men destroyed themselves in that way. That the obtaining of pleasure in connection with another was natural, but that solitary gratification unless used in great moderation was not only very injurious to health but unfitted one for the true enjoyment of love.

'However, when I was returning to school for the last term, she said that as I should now be some time away from her, a discreet indulgence now and then might be a relief, and besides would tend to keep alive my affection for her and my desire for renewed enjoyment of her favours.

'To assist me in this matter, she cut a nice little lock of hair from her cunt, and having steeped it for several hours between the odoriferous lips of her moist slit, she gave it to me to sniff and rub about my nose whenever I handled my prick and thought of her cunt and the various delights I had enjoyed with her when petting and feeling, kissing and sucking, frigging and fucking together. And she made me promise to write to her regularly and give her a minute account of all my lustful feelings, acts and observings; and in every letter to say something of pricks, cunts and fucking.

'She told me also to endeavour to establish a familiarity with one or more of my companions, and keep her duly informed of the result.

'I promised faithfully to carry out her wishes, and left her with many assurances of affectionate regard.

'I can only give you in a general way the substance of the numerous letters I wrote to my aunt, but as they were written with great care and consideration, I have a perfect recollection of their contents.

'I related to her how I used to frig myself after school hours, lying in the grass. How I would unbutton my trousers, take out my prick and watch it stiffening up as I frigged it up and down. How I used to hold to my nose the lock of hair which she gave me, and which had still a strong flavour of the sweet perfume of her cunt; and that as I frigged, I always repeated all the words she had taught me – prick – cunt – arse – spunk – pissing – farting – fucking – and tried to recall the look of her cunt, as it used to gleam upon me when she spread her thighs and twisted her bottom from side to side.

'I told her that on one of these occasions, one of the elder boys – Charley Cox, who was always very friendly towards me – stole upon me unawares, and before I discovered his approach, witnessed the nature of my amusements.

' "Excuse me, dear Fred," he said, observing my startled and half-angry look, "I wanted to see and talk with you on the very subject on which you have been now engaged. The other day, when we were the changing-room together, turning round suddenly, I saw your prick and was much struck with is remarkable size, and wondered was it through any effort of your own that it had grown so large. But I think you have let me into the secret today; and as I only want a lesson, pray forgive my interruption. So take out your prick again; and see, here is mine, though not half so well developed as yours, but if you can teach me how to make him grow as big I shall be truly thankful."

' "Well, Charley, sit down here; I shall be glad of your company, and will do what I can to gratify and oblige you," And reopening my trousers, I again pulled out my prick, and as Charley placed himself beside me, put my hand on his soft and pendant tool He at the same time took hold of mine and commenced frigging it slowly up and down, as he said, "I always thought you a good fellow, Fred, but now I find you a real brick. I like the feel of your prick in my hand, and mine is already developing under the magic of your touch."

' "Yes, this double frigging is pleasant enough, but I think we should on the whole enjoy the thing more thoroughly by doing it to each other turn about; what do you say?"

' "I don't doubt but you are right, Fred, and as I feel inclined to spend, if you go on with me, I will polish you off afterwards."

' "All right, old fellow, then lie on your back spread your legs, and I will take a stretch between them." I then laid myself between his legs, and resting on my elbows held his balls with one hand and his prick with the other. "Now, Charley, tell me exactly how you feel and when you are going to spend."

' "Well, Freddy, your watching my prick and holding it so close to your face while you are frigging it, greatly increase the feeling of pleasure. Now it is all in aglow and I feel the spunk bubbling in my cods."

'I at once took the swollen head between my lips, and quite relished its sweet taste, as I sucked with all my force while I still frigged its shaft with my hand.

' "Oh, Freddy, old fellow, have you put it in your mouth – Oh! There – I can hold it no longer – oh!! – oh!!! Did you swallow it, Fred?"

' "Yes, why not? – indeed, I could scarcely avoid doing so, for you shot it out with such force that it made its own way down my throat."

' "I don't wonder at that, for I never enjoyed a spend so much in my life. I had my first fuck the other evening but the pleasure I had then was not to be compared with what you made me feel now."

' "Had you a fuck the other evening, Charley? Tell me all about it and I will frig you as often as you please."

' "Well, lean back and spread your legs, so that I may take possession of your prick while I recount the ins and out of my little adventure. You know Dolly, Farmer Jones's girl, who often comes to sell buns and sweetstuffs to our fellows. They are always chaffing her as to which of them she will choose for a sweetheart. She has an answer for everyone, while her eye twinkles and her pouting red lips seem always soliciting a kiss. I happened to be the only one in the schoolroom when she came last. So after a little joking, I placed a half-crown in her hand saying: 'Now Dolly give me a nice soft luscious kiss.'

' "She put her money in her fob, and allowed me to take her in my arms. I pressed my lips to hers, which she held up for me and readily opened to admit the point of my tongue. While kissing her, I passed my hand down her back and squeeze her fat buttocks. She responded by a gentle pinch of my prick with the fingers of the hand which hung down between us.

' "All right; thought I, so I said, 'Dolly, I would like a little further play with you, but have not time just now, but if you will come to the little grove behind the hangar this evening at eight o'clock, I will meet you there and give you half a sovereign.' She smiled and gave me a nod, and turned away, as some other fellows were coming in.

' "At the time appointed, I asked leave to go out, and found Dolly waiting for me among the trees. It was nearly dark, so I again took her in my arms, this time, however, thrusting my knee it between hers, and as I pushed it up against her cunt, she opened out a little to give me more room.

' " 'You are a good sensible girl, Dolly, and very pretty; are you as nice down here as your charming face above?' I asked, as I rubbed my hand over her cunt outside her dress, and then lowering it to the bottom of her short frock, said: 'May I try?'

' " 'What an impudent boy you are, Master Charley! What do you want to do with your hand under my petticoats?'

' " 'To feel your cunt, Dolly.'

' " 'Don't – you mustn't do that.'

' " 'Ah let me – there's a good girl – open your legs – Oh! what a fine big cunt you have, Dolly! Such a lot of hair! and such big fat lips!'

' "I now felt her hand playing about my trousers.

' " 'Good girl, take it out.'

' " 'What shall I take out? Master Charley.'

' " 'My prick, Dolly. Ah, you know well where to find it. Your cunt is made for it; shall I put it in?'

' " 'I didn't say you mightn't Master Charley.'

' " 'Well, lie down here on the grass – now spread your legs.'

' "She stretched her legs open, and I got between them and pushed my prick between the moist lips of her cunt. Somehow I could not find the entrance – it was my first attempt, you know.

' "At last she put down her hand and said, 'Stay I will direct it. You are pushing too high up – there – that's the spot – now push – Hah, it's getting in.'

' " 'Oh! Dolly! that's nice; but don't heave or you'll knock me out.' Then a gush of spend and it was all over.

' " 'Oh, Master Charley, you were too fast; but don't take it out – lie on me little longer. Did you never fuck a girl before?'

' " 'No, Dolly. I once felt my sister's cunt, but she would not let me fuck her. Were you often fucked, Dolly?'

' " 'Scores of times. Master Charley!'

' " 'Who fucked you last, Dolly?'

' " 'Old Doctor Scratchem, the headmaster. This afternoon, as I was going away, he called me into his study and said: "I feel awfully randy today, Dolly, and I want you to give me relief, so take my old fellow out and pet him a bit."

' " 'I did so, while he fingered away at my cunt and bottom.

' " ' "Here's a book of bawdy prints' " he said, "lay it open on the sofa, and you can look it over while you lean over the arm and cock up your naked bum; I want a good view of your fine arse."

' " 'He then took his old prick in hand and looked at my bottom, first from the right side and then from the left. At last, going down on his knees, he looked up from underneath, while I occupied myself looking over the pictures.

' " ' "Wriggle you arse, Dolly, and open your cunt as much as you can, and tell me what pictures you are looking at, while I work up my prick for a fuck."

' " ' "I see lots of men and women fucking. Here is a girl lying on her back with her bare arse turned up before a naked man with a fine big red-headed prick who is just going to stick it into her cunt. Here is another girl straddling over a man whose prick is deep into her while another fellow is driving his prick into her bottom"

' " ' "Can't you say: Buggering her arse."

' " ' "Well, buggering her arse – but I don't want you to bugger mine. Its a good honest fuck that I like. Stick in your prick and fuck me. There – that's the right place – now, doctor, fuck, oh! are you done so soon?"

' " 'He pulled out his prick after spending a drop or two, and left my cunt only half satisfied; so I want you, Master Charley, to finish what he left half done. And I think that my story has put you in the way of doing it, for I feel your prick is as large and strong as ever.' Then she gave a sudden heave up, almost pitching me off as she cried, 'Now fuck, and don't be in a hurry – take your time and fuck me with long steady strokes – that's right, now your are making me like it – put your hands under my bottom, and I will cross my legs over your back and keep you in the right position.

' "Her cunt seemed to grow larger every moment, and sucked in my prick like a calf's mouth. I felt her hands too, trying, as I fancied, to shove in my balls along with my prick. I never thought that a girl's cunt could be so large – and Dolly is so short; but her cunt seems to begin at her navel and extend to her bottom. Somehow I got too much of it, and I did not feel half the pleasure you have given me. Do you like the way I am frigging you? Are you near spending?"

' "Yes Charley – it is just coming."

' "Then I will take it in my mouth as you did for me."

'After this, we often had Dolly together; we used to fuck her one after the other, turn about, and sometimes both at the same time, in every variety of attitude we could imagine. Our favourite way, however, was for one of us to lie on his back with Dolly kneeling over him sucking his prick, while the other fucked her from behind just above his friend's face.

'Charley and I, being older boys, were allowed the privilege of sometimes walking by ourselves, and one afternoon, availing ourselves of this liberty, we met Dolly in a wood at a little distance from the house, and thinking ourselves secure from observation, freely indulged in our favourite sport. But we were unfortunate, for the doctor's wife, taking her afternoon walk, came suddenly upon us, and before we were aware of her presence, witnessed all our proceedings. She said nothing, but after taking a good look, passed on. Terror filled our hearts, for we felt certain that condign punishment would quickly descend on Dolly and ourselves.

'I was not surprised therefore where I got a message that evening from Mrs Scratchem that she wished to speak with me for a few moments before going to bed.

'Now, I must tell you that the doctor's wife, who was comparatively young and rather good-looking, managed all the internal business of the house. She had a small room upstairs where she kept her laundry lists and accounts and in which she used to see us when she wanted to make enquiries about our clothes and washing.

'I went to her as I had often done before, but this time I found her seated on a sofa and not at her desk as usual. When I entered, she told me to close the door; having done so, I went and stood before her, looking considerably foolish and embarrassed. At the same time, I scanned her face and observed that although she looked agitated, she did not appear so angry as I expected, while there was a gleam in her eye which I could not then account for.

'She began by saying, "I feel constrained to speak to you of what I unavoidably witnessed this afternoon. Thinking the matter over, I consider it prudent not to tell the doctor. He might deem it necessary too inflict some public punishment, which perhaps would only make things worse, to I have decided on speaking to you myself. But it is not my intention to scold you. You and Charley are the oldest lads in the school, and cannot be treated like the younger boys. And besides, for young fellows of your age there may be some excuse. I believe that young men growing into manhood have certain necessities which require to be gratified in some way – I mean by intercourse with the other sex. You see, I am speaking very plainly as a woman of the world and as one who takes a rational view of such things; and therefore your going occasionally with a girl, safely and prudently, I don't altogether condemn. But going with Dolly I consider neither safe nor prudent. I therefore feel bound to give you warning, not merely as being responsible for your health and general well-being, but from the great regard I feel for your excellent aunt, Lady Flora, whom I am proud to be allowed to reckon one of my best friends, and also, I may add, from a personal liking for yourself." Here, she blushed and looked down. "But," she resumed, looking up, her face very red and her eyes very bright, 'you will be tired of standing, Freddy; come and sit down here beside me."

I gladly complied, and as I sat down, she put her hand on my knee as she continued, "The ground of my warning is that I have reason to know that Dolly is almost common to the neighbourhood, and I believe that girls under those circumstances are apt to acquire a very painful and disagreeable disease, which they are sure to communicate to the men who have connection with them; this is what I am dreading for you."

'She paused; so I replied, "My dear Mrs Scratchem, I thank you for your kind warning; but as regards Dolly, I think you are mistaken. She may go with a few – but she is very select and very particular about her own person; and I have no reason to fear that I have suffered in the past."

' "Well, that is just the point I am a little uneasy about. The symptoms do not always appear at once. You perceive, I am speaking almost professionally; before my marriage I acted as lady nurse in one of the London hospitals and several cases of this kind were brought under my notice. Now, as you know the motherly feeling I have towards you, perhaps you would allow me to examine you myself, and then my mind would be easy on the subject," and she moved her hand towards the fork of my trousers.

' "My dear Mrs Scratchem, I have not the least objection. You have already shown me so much kindness that I am ready to please you in this, or indeed, in any way in my power," at the same time unbuttoning my trousers down the front and pulling out my prick.

She took it in her hand and stooping towards me examined it closely, pushing back the prepuce and turning up the glans, while she pushed her other hand underneath and felt my balls.

' "Your parts are very nicely made and well developed, Freddy, and seem in a perfectly healthy condition. Was the whole of this inside Dolly today?"

' "Yes, the whole of it was in her – "

' "Go on – you may speak to me freely. What does she call it?"

' "Cunt."

' "And what does she call this?"

' "Prick,"

' "And when you put your prick into her cunt, what does she call that?"

' "Fucking."

' "Yes, those are the common names. They are not used in polite Society, you know, but when people are talking confidentially as we are now, they are more convenient and direct. Now tell me, for I want to know everything, when you had this in Dolly's cunt, fucking her, did she seem to like it very much?"

' "Oh! that she did; she held me tightly in her arms and heaved up her bottom every time she felt my prick driving up her cunt."

' "Well, I don't wonder to her liking it, and I suppose you liked it too."

' "You may be sure of that, Mrs Scratchem, there is nothing in the world I like so much as fucking a nice cunt.

' "Yes, I believe you; but would you not like it better to fuck a lady than a common girl, such as Dolly!"

' "Perhaps I should if I could find a lady equally kind and agreeable as Dolly."

' "What would you say if, out of regard for your aunt, and to save you from harm, I should be kind and agreeable too?"

' "I would say that you were the dearest, sweetest lady in the universe."

'She stopped my mouth with a kiss, and taking my hand placed it on her thigh and whispered, "You may."

'I lost no time, you may be sure, in passing my hand under her petticoats and running it up between her warm thighs. How easily I spread them open. How readily she leaned back and allowed me to draw up her clothes! The viewing and handling of my prick had thoroughly aroused her wanton desires, and when she felt my fingers playing about the sensitive lips of her cunt, she muttered, "Oh, Freddy, you won't tell anyone, that's a good boy – do you want to see it? There, what do you think?"

' "That you have a lovely cunt, Mrs Scratchem. It is so soft and warm, and smells so nice! I love to open its lips and see the inside."

' "Would you like to kiss it? To kiss my cunt and then to put your prick into it and fuck me?"

' "Yes, dear Mrs Scratchem, I will kiss your cunt first and then fuck it."

'I pushed my mouth well in between the full unctuous lips of her cunt, while I clutched firmly the smooth elastic cheeks of her fat bottom.

' "Oh! how you suck my clitoris! You make it throb with pleasure, and your tongue winds deliciously round my cunt. You may squeeze my bottom as hard as you like. Oh! you are pushing your finger in! Yes, I like that. Does Dolly like to have her bottom tickled?"

' "She does, but she calls it her arse."

' "Well, we will call it arse too. Dolly has an impudent arse, for I noticed she did not seem at all ashamed when she held it up naked before you this afternoon. But what was she doing to Charley?"

' "She was sucking his prick while I fucked her cunt over his face, and he held my prick and watched it passing in and out."

' "And when Charley fucks her, what part do you take?"

' "Sometimes, I lie underneath and she sucks my prick and I hold Charley's and watch him fucking. At other times, she straddles over him with her bottom turned up, and then I fuck her bottom while he fucks her cunt."

' "Does she like that style of fucking?"

' "Yes, she says, it doubles the pleasure to have one prick in her cunt and another in her bottom at the same time."

' "What a strange idea! We might try it someday," she muttered, as if speaking to herself. 'But now, Fred, I think we are both ready for our fuck. Now listen to me and try to follow my instructions. Introduce your prick quickly and with deliberation into my cunt; and when you have pushed in as far as you can, press firmly against my loins and bottom, then draw out slowly until only the tip of your prick remains between the lips of my cunt; then drive it steadily back, gradually increasing the strength and rapidity of your strokes. Meantime, if we are able to keep on talking and use plenty of bawdy words, the pleasure will be both increased and intensified. Now put in."

'She lay back with her thighs at their widest stretch and, holding her cunt open with her fingers, awaited my approach. I placed the head of my prick between the lips and slowly pushed it up. Her cunt felt very hot, and though abundantly large, had such elastic power of compression, that I felt it squeezing my prick all round like the fingers of a closed hand.

' "Are you enjoying it, Freddy?"

' "Oh, yes, it is grand. Do I fuck you right, Mrs Scratchem?"

' "Yes Freddy, you fuck wonderfully for so young a man."

'I was now coming to the short strokes and beginning to breathe hard. "Don't be so noisy." She whispered, "or we shall be heard; however, don't stop – shove away – smack against my bottom as I heave my cunt – if you must make a noise, do – just fuck – ram in your prick. Ho! Hah! that's delicious!"

'Then, as we rested, she said, "I don't blame you and Charley for going with Dolly; there is no pleasure like that of a really good fuck, and she has taught you well. The next time Dolly comes, tell her I would like to see her by myself, and I expect we shall be good friends – but remember I rely on the secrecy and discretion of you both. Now, good-night.'

CHAPTER EIGHTEEN

Lord Ferrars' Narrative Continued: Dolly and Mrs Scratchem

'It so happened that Dolly called next morning, being anxious to ascertain what evil consequences had followed the discovery of the day before. I was just able to say to her: "The mistress wants to see you. Dolly – but don't fear, she means well; and my advice is, give her your full confidence; and if you can, let me know the result, by and by."

'When I saw her again, she told me all that had taken place in her interview with Mrs Scratchem and I carefully wrote it for my aunt.

'Dolly was directed to the same room where I had seen Mrs Scratchem and found her sitting on the same sofa. She looked kindly at her and said – ' "Why, Dolly, how you manage to steal the hearts of all the men! My old man raves about you. I have been wishing for some time to have an opportunity of telling you that you need not fear my being jealous – in fact, I gave him free rein to go with you as often as he likes. He loves a little variety and so do I. We therefore mutually agreed to leave each other quite free, and so we get on in first-rate style. But as regards our young men, that is a different matter, Dolly. You know we are responsible for their morals and good conduct, and we must maintain the respectability of the house. At the same time, I am quite aware that young fellows in the hot flush of youth require some outlet for their superfluous energy, and if they can't obtain it in one way they will be sure to seek it in other and perhaps more injurious ways. So I consider it the wiser plan to allow a certain amount of liberty, yet under some control and prudent direction. Now I have heard that you Dolly are very particular as to whom you admit to your embraces, and I am sure that if anything was wrong with you you would not suffer our young men to incur any risk of infection. Is not that your own feeling, Dolly?"

' "It is indeed, dear Mrs Scratchem; and as you have spoken with so much kindness and consideration, I am ready to trust you in all these matters. I do try to be very select, and I seldom have a connection without a thorough ablution as soon as possible afterwards. But of you have any with to examine me yourself, I have not the slightest objection."

'Mrs Scratchem replied, "I am glad to find that I have not been disappointed in you, Dolly. You seem to be a good sensible girl, and as I wish to have your full confidence, I accept your offer. I confess, too, that it will gratify me to see and inspect the little cunt which my husband tells me give him more satisfaction than any he ever fucked. So lean back and open your legs."

'Dolly obeyed, and Mrs Scratchem proceeded to raise her clothes and expose all her belly and thighs.

' "What a quantity of hair, you have. Dolly! It covers all the lower part of your belly! Your whole cunt, too, is large and well developed, and the lips are unusually plump and full, while the inside lining is exceedingly hot and moist. You must be a very lascivious girl, Dolly; and I am certain you are very fond of being fucked! Are you not?"

' "Yes, I am fond of fucking,' replied Dolly, laughing; 'I know of nothing that can be compared with having one's cunt crammed with a good sturdy prick. When I meet with a really well-made man, I often feel rather more disposed to pay him for fucking me than to look for anything at his hands."

' "Dolly, you are right," responded Mrs Scratchem "The mercenary spirit of some women is detestable. Now I understand why the men are all so fond of you. And I am sure your cunt gets a good share of admiration too. Do you enjoy having it petted and played with?"

' "Yes, I love to feel a man's fingers fiddling about my cunt. It always causes me a pleasant thrill and makes me wish for a fuck. But somehow your frigging, Mrs Scratchem, has a stranger effect. I suppose that is because you know that exact spot – which men seldom do. Oh! that is so nice!!"

' "Do you like having your cunt sucked, Dolly? A tongue frig is generally very agreeable."

' "Oh, yes. I think a tongue – frig delicious! I always try to get every man to suck my cunt before he fucks me; and sometimes the sucking is the best part of it."

' "Was your cunt ever sucked by a woman?"

' "No, Mrs Scratchem, I did not think that one woman would care to suck another woman's cunt."

' "Quite the contrary, most woman like it very much – especially when the cunt has plenty of feeling like yours, Dolly, and above all, when it is kept nice and sweet. Would you like me to suck yours?"

' "I would, Mrs Scratchem, if you don't dislike it yourself."

'Mrs Scratchem spread Dolly's cunt open with her fingers, pushed in her mouth and ravenously sucked her clitoris with her lips and tongue, while Dolly twisted about her bottom and muttered, "O – oh la! Mrs Scratchem! How nice! Oh, dear. How you suck! Oh, Mrs Scratchem, your tongue is setting me wild! And now I feel your finger up my bottom!! This is beyond a fuck! Oh, my cunt! Oh, my bottom! Oh, my arse! I'm spending! Oh, I'm spending," and Dolly with a mighty groan lay back, while Mrs Scratchem, grasping the quivering cheeks of her bottom, licked up the sweet juices that poured from Dolly's fountain of delight.

'After a while, Dolly came to herself and said, "Dear Mrs Scratchem, I never enjoyed anything like that. I had no idea that it could be so nice to have one's cunt sucked by a woman. And now you must favour me with a full view of your own cunt and bottom, and I will suck everything you have."

'Mrs Scratchem lay back in her turn and spread her thighs wide open while Dolly pushed a pillow under her, and said, "Why, Mrs Scratchem, you have a beautiful cunt of your own, with red-brown hair, the colour of gold, and such a luscious chink, as hot as an oven and steeped in voluptuous dew! What can the old doctor mean by turning from such a cunt and looking at a poor affair like mine."

' "Oh, he is tired of it, Dolly; he has frigged it and fucked it so often that he needs something new to stimulate his old cock. And as he does not mind my getting a stray fuck when I can, he is welcome to you or anybody else. I saw you between Charley Cox and Fred yesterday afternoon, one of their pricks in your mouth and the other in your cunt; which of them has the largest prick, and which fucks the best?"

' "Charley's prick is not bad, but Fred gives the best fuck, for he seems to have had more experience and goes about his work in a more artistic manner."

' "O Dolly, you are sucking my cunt and tickling my bottom very skilfully and pleasantly, but I don't want to spend just yet; let us have a little more talk first. Tell me now, of all the men that fuck you, which of them has the finest prick?"

' "Farmer Jones has the largest and strongest, and if powerful action and a tremendous discharge constitute a good prick, I must place him in the foremost rank. And here, I should tell you, he is not my father – at least, so far as I know. I am a foundling. He took me out of the workhouse, and as he had no child, he adopted me as a daughter. I was scarcely fourteen when he first made free with me. Shall I tell you how?"

' "Do Dolly, it is the very thing I would especially like to hear."

' "Well, then, I was passing through the yard in the dusk of the evening, near where he was standing in the shadow of a wall with his face turned in. I did not notice him until he suddenly wheeled about, and putting his arm around me said, 'Dolly, put your hand here – I have something to show you.'

' "His dress was all open in front and his great tool was sticking out. He put my hand on it while he still held me with his arm around my waist. I had never either seen or felt that part of a man before, and it excited both my wonder and curiosity. However, I pretended modesty and trying to draw away my hand, said, 'Oh, Mr Jones! how can you? – let my hand go.'

' " 'Now, Dolly, you are no longer a child; come in here,' still holding me, and drawing me towards the stable. 'I want to teach you what every girl ought to know.'

' " 'No, Mr Jones, I mustn't – you would harm me.'

' " 'Afraid of me? Don't you know me better than that, Dolly.'

' " 'Well, tell me what you want to do?'

' " 'Come here and I will tell you.' He pulled me inside the door, and having carefully closed and fastened it, he said, 'Come sit down with me on this nice clean straw.'

' " 'Now, Mr Jones! Where are you pushing your hand? oh! don't – ah – how you tickle me! You mustn't pull up my clothes – what a disgrace!'

' " 'There – let me look – take away your hand – what a nice fat cunt you have, Dolly! But it is very tight!'

' " 'Oh, Mr Jones! Oh! Your finger is hurting me – don't push it in so far. You'll force me to call out.'

' " 'Well, let me kiss it to make it well' – and putting his hands under my bottom he lifted me up and then buried his face between my thighs and gave my cunt its first experience of a man's kiss. He not only kissed, he sucked and licked my cunt all round. I began to find the situation decidedly pleasant, and made no objection when, raising himself up, he pushed his prick against my cunt and said: 'Now Dolly hold my prick in your hand and rub it between these soft lips – that won't harm you.'

' " 'I rubbed its great head over my clitoris and said: 'Yes, but you must not try to put in, Mr Jones. It is too big – it would kill me.'

' " 'No, my love, it will go in as nicely as possible, and once inside, it will give you more pleasure than ever you felt in your life. There, rub it up and down the whole way' – and forcing it down to the lower end of the chink, where he well knew the entrance was, he gave a vigorous thrust, and to my surprise the enormous head popped in, and with a shout of triumph he drove it up. I fairly screeched with the sudden pain but in a moment it passed away, and I felt my cunt agreeably gorged with the huge morsel. Mr Jones then hugged me tightly in this arms, and working his loins with tremendous vigour drove his prick back and forward until every nerve of my body tingled with amorous emotion. Then he pressed home and in a moment I felt his fiery discharge flooding all my cunt, bursting over the sides and trickling down my bottom.

' "After the first exchange, not a word was spoken by either of us during that first fuck. But when after lying in me for a few moments, he commenced the second, he said, 'Dolly, you are a splendid girl; you seemed to enjoy that silent fuck most thoroughly. Now, like a darling, let me hear you say how you like the feel of my prick going in and out of your cunt – this way. Just tell me exactly what you feel, and it will make you enjoy it all the more. Isn't that nice?'

' " 'Oh, yes, it is very nice. I like to feel your –'

' " 'What?'

' " 'Your prick.'

' " 'Where?'

' " 'In my cunt.'

' " 'Doing what?'

' " 'Fucking me. And I like to feel your hands –'

' " 'Where?'

' " 'Squeezing my bottom.'

' " 'That's right. Now heave your bottom up – so – and your arse.'

' " 'Yes, I like what you are doing to me. I will heave my arse and say prick, cunt, arse, fuck – fuck – fuck . . . Oh! Now! give me all you can – arse – arse – arse.'

' " 'Darling, you are a first-rate fuck. Now that I know how good you are, you shall be mistress here, and I will fuck you day and night.'

' " 'But won't that get me in the family way, and how shall we manage then?'

' " 'True, Dolly, it would be well to avoid that danger, and I well know one way of doing so, but I am unwilling to recommend it, unless you are disposed for it yourself.'

' " 'What way is that, Mr Jones?'

' " 'To get yourself fucked as soon and as often as you can by other men. The mixing of the seed of different men in the same cunt has been found to prevent conception in the womb.'

' " 'But who is there here to fuck me besides yourself?'

' " 'Well, there is Sandy, the herdsman. He is a mere country yokel, but he is the best hand I have. And, as it happens, he is now near at hand, in the cowshed preparing for the night. So go in and speak kindly to him, getting as close up to him as you can, and I wager a crown piece you will feel his prick in your cunt before ten minutes.'

' " 'Well, Mr Jones, as I would do anything to avoid getting in the family way, I will do just as you tell me. But won't he know that I have been fucked quite recently?'

' " 'No matter, he will like your cunt all the better. However, I will give it a good wipe and a parting kiss.' He carefully wiped my cunt, and having given it a good sucking kiss, sent me in quest of Sandy.

' " 'Sandy, is that you? Are you preparing beds for the cows? I hope you make them warm and comfortable' – and I walked close up to him.

' " 'Yes, Miss Dolly. You are a good girl to be so thoughtful for the poor dumb beasts! Wouldn't you like to have someone to make you warm and comfortable?' he said, putting his hand on my shoulder.

' " 'Yes, Sandy, if I could find someone that could do it.'

' " 'Then you haven't far to look, Miss Dolly, for I'm the boy to make you warm and comfortable,' he said, putting both arms round me and pressing me against his belly so that I could feel his prick bounding between us.

' " 'Stop, Sandy, don't squeeze me so hard.'

' " 'Darling Miss Dolly, how can I help it when you are so nice and good!?' His hands were now on my bottom and I felt his fingers pushing in between my thighs from behind. 'Let me just touch you for a moment – that's a love – let go my hand, I won't hurt you;' and he began to raise my clothes and tried to push his hand up under my petticoats.

' " 'Sandy for shame, that is not the way to make me warm or comfortable.'

' " 'Yes it is, dear Miss Dolly, oh! what a darling little cunt! How soft and moist it is! I know it is longing for a fuck, and that will make you warm and comfortable. Lie back here.'

' " 'Oh, no, Sandy, you must not lay me down – I can't let you between my legs – Oh, don't uncover me – you mustn't get over me. Oh! What are you pushing against me?'

' " 'My prick, Dolly, my prick – there – let it in – it will make you feel grand – open your thighs. Hah, it is in! – now, do you know what it is?'

' " 'I do, Sandy, you are doing to me what you make the bull do to the cow.'

' " 'Just so, the bull fucks the cow and I fuck you. Don't you like it, Dolly? The cow shoves up her rump to get all she can of the bull's pizzle, and won't you do as much for my prick?'

' " 'I will, Sandy, push in the whole length of your prick – Oh, yes – that's very nice – fuck me hard – fuck me fast – now! let me have all you can give,' and Sandy roared as he shot a torrent of boiling spunk into my well-satisfied receiver. I got up and shook myself, while Sandy kissed me and made me promise to give him another treat soon. Then slipping quietly out, I sped away towards the house.

' "Mr Jones met me on the way, took me in arms and said, 'Bravo, Dolly, you have made a good beginning, you have taken a fair dose of spunk from two different men within the hour. But now, to make matters still safer, I wish you could get another from a third – it would make assurance trebly sure. Let me see, I will write a line to neighbour Harris, and invite him to pass the evening with me as I am quite alone, and send you with the note, and ask him to take care of you on the way back. I know that he admires you, for it was only last week that he remarked to me what a fine girl you had grown! and he is one of the hottest fellows after women I ever met. You have only to let him have his way, or at least not hinder him too much, and you are safe to be well fucked before you get home. So put on your traps while I write the note.'

' "In due time, I delivered the note to Mr Harris. He was very kind and brought me into a snug little parlour where he was taking his evening glass of punch. He prevailed on me to sip a little out of his tumbler. It was very strong and made my heart beat and my eyes swim.

' " 'Oh! how strong it is! it will choke me.'

' " 'Not at all, take a little more. It will make you feel jolly and prevent the night air giving you cold.'

' "To encourage me, he put his arm round me and pressed my bottom with his hand. It is amusing how almost universally men begin

with the bottom before they attempt the cunt. It is like stealing a march
behind. So now when Mr Harris found that I did not object very much
to having my bottom squeezed, he thought he might safely take
another step, and drawing me to him, he said, 'Come, Dolly, you and I
are old friends. Come sit on my knee while you sip a little more
punch' – pulling me down and at the same time slyly lifting my dress. I
pretended not to notice him until I felt his hand on my bare thigh, and
there could be no mistake as to his design.

' " 'Oh, Mr Harris! do you want to ruin a poor unprotected girl?'

' " 'No, my pet, I'll not ruin you, but I mean to be fond of you and
take the best care of you – there – open your legs more – what a
luscious cunt you have, Dolly! and plenty of it too! These are grand
lips! Lean back a little more.'

' " 'There – you have felt it long enough – now, let me go – you
mustn't see it – oh my! I feel so ashamed to have you looking into it that
way. Don't bring the lamp any nearer.' He had drawn the lamp to the
edge of the table, and with the light full on my exposed cunt, was
kneeling between my thighs and holding my cunt open with his fingers.

' " 'Your cunt is something to look at, Dolly, I only wish I had more
light to see is better. It has the deepest, reddest slit I ever saw! And
these great fat lips swell out on either side in the most lascivious
fashion. If you don't love fucking all I can say is your cunt belies you;
now tell me the truth, you do don't you?'

' " 'What a question to ask me! How can I tell?'

' " 'Well, see here, Dolly, this will open understanding.' And rising
up, he placed his prick in my hand.

' " 'No, Mr Harris, put it away; I must not look at it, nor touch it, nor
let it near me.'

' " 'Why? it won't bite. Feel how soft it is! And what an innocent
head it shows when you draw down the skin this way' – making my
hand move down to the root and causing its red head to stand up stiff
and inviting.

' " 'Now, let it in,' and going down on his knees he pushed it up
against my cunt.

' " 'I was making a show of covering my cunt with my hand, but he
shoved it aside, saying: 'I like your hand there very well, but keep it out
of the way while I am getting in.' Then, directing the head of his prick
to the entrance, he drove it quickly in and it filled up all the cavity
inside. My cunt throbbed, my thighs opened to their widest extent and,
in spite of me, my loins worked up, responsive to his thrusts.

' " 'Ah! Dolly, I am right, you do know what fucking is, and you love
it well. Don't you, Dolly? Isn't that good?'

' " 'Yes – Oh! – yes.'

' " 'Tell me if my prick pleases you?'

' " 'It does – Oh, it does – let me hold it in my hand while you are fucking me. Now fuck – push again – Hah! I'm coming – Oh!

' " 'Are you done?' I asked, as after a big thrust, he stopped shoving and drew out his prick.

' " 'For this time, my pet, but I expect we shall have another fuck before the night is past.'

' "Then, opening a desk, he took out a note and, handing it to me, said, 'This is only a fiver, darling – as a little remembrance, you know; and I am still in your debt, for you have given me one of the finest fucks I ever had in my life. Now let us start.'

' "All the way back he continued fingering my cunt and bottom, and keeping up the most bawdy conversation. He said he delighted in hearing me speak of pricks, cunts and arses. Of course, when I felt the five-pound note in my pocket, I did and said everything I could to please him. When we came to the last stile, he asked me to lean forward on the top of it and poke out my bottom. 'I want to enter you from behind – it is my favourite mode of fucking. Your arse feels like a cushion when I plump against it as I drive home my prick.'

' "While fucking me, he kept poking his wet finger into my bottom, until he had my arse as randy as my cunt.

' " 'Tell me, Dolly, were you ever fucked in your arse?'

' " 'No, Mr Harris, surely no one would do such a thing as that.'

' " 'Yes, they would, Dolly, it is a delightful way of fucking. Just let me get in and you will soon agree with me; put your hands back, like a darling girl, and hold open the cheeks.'

' "How could I refuse. I poked my bottom out, and drawing the cheeks apart tried to make the narrow way as open as I could. He presented his prick and began to push; its well-moistened head slipped in and quickly passed through the surrounding wrinkles; it smarted for a moment as it was passing in, but when once it was inside, working up amongst my entrails, the most extraordinary sensation of pleasure pervaded my whole belly. Bottom, loins and cunt. I groaned with ecstasy and writhed my body in the most wanton and lascivious contortions, while he held me round the hips, worked his fingers in my cunt and banged his belly against my bottom as he drove his prick in and out of my arsehole."

' "Now, dear Mrs Scratchem, I have given you an account of my first experience in the fucking line, and your cunt is on the flow for the third time; let me sup the juice which is oozing out."

' "Very well, dear Dolly, but let us lie on the carpet. You can get over me and put your warm cunt on my mouth, and we can indulge in a nice suck together."

'After this mutual relief had cooled down their amorous heat and allowed their blood to revert to its normal flow, they returned to the sofa and sat down side by side. When they had sufficiently recovered breath, Mrs Scratchem said, "And, Dolly, did you find Mr Jones's, plan effectual in preventing your being afflicted with a big belly?"

' "Well, something has prevented it, for, though I have had no end of men's seed poured into and over my cunt, I have hitherto escaped that evil; and I have heard from others that it has had the same effect in their case."

' "It may be as you say, Dolly, and certainly if one strays at all from the straight road, a few steps more or less won't make much difference. Anyway, it was a knowing dodge of Mr Jones, for it freed himself from the sole responsibility."

CHAPTER NINETEEN

Lord Ferrar's Narrative Concluded: Mrs Scratchem on the Spree

'Mrs Scratchem who in love matters was a thorough-going socialist, put her arm round Dolly's neck, kissed her and said, "You are not at all the kind of girl I thought you were, Dolly. I admire you warm disposition, and I love you for your candour and the confidence you have reposed in me. I greatly envy the free life you lead, and if I could only see my way, I would gladly participate in some of your wanton enterprises. Are there any of your lovers to whom you would consider it safe to entrust our secret.

' "My dear Mrs Scratchem, I shall be only too happy to prepare the way for your free enjoyment of your natural gifts; and I think I know a mode of doing it without reposing too great confidence in the fidelity of anyone; for my rule is never to put more confidence than is absolutely necessary in any but a tried friend. However, my plan is simply this; come out with me occasionally in the evenings, and I will present you to some of my most select acquaintances as a visitor from the neighbouring town. If you alter your hair, darken your eyebrows, put on one of my dresses and come along with me, I will defy anyone to recognise in my friend the fashionable Mrs Scratchem; and from what you tell me of Doctor Scratchem and your agreement with him, I don't suppose he will place any obstacle in the way of your following your own inclinations."

'Mrs Scratchem listened thoughtfully, and then replied: 'Dolly, your plan seems feasible, and it would certainly be very agreeable. When would you propose to carry it out?"

' "Well, let me see. I must first prepare Mr Jones, but as he is rather a blabber-mouth, we must not let him know too much. I will only tell him you are a friend who wishes to visit me occasionally for a spree, and that you might not object to a little sport with himself, on condition of his asking no questions and being content to shut his eyes and accept what his good destiny has sent him. I could have everything settled and ready by tomorrow evening, and after dusk meet you in the grove with a bundle of the things we need and you could make the changes there and then come home with me."

'Mrs Scratchem met Dolly at the time and place appointed, and very soon under her skilful management was transformed into a fair specimen of a country belle of the artisan class. A pair of flashy earrings and a gaudy brooch, with a few touches of rouge on her cheeks, completed the disguise.

'It was dark when they reached the house. Mr Jones met them at the entrance and received Dolly's friend – Miss Lydia Fox – with a warm welcome. Dolly had already told him of her coming to pass the evening and described her as: "A young artless girl, inexperienced in the ways of the world, but of an amiable disposition; and what will please you more to hear, she is very amorously inclined – in fact, whenever we get together, and can conveniently manage it, we soon have a finger in each other's quim and indulge in a little bawdy chat together; so you won't find it very hard to gain her consent, but you must set to work with courage and determination. "

' "Very well, Dolly,' he replied, 'where I succeeded with you, I expect I shall not fail with her."

'So Mr Jones, thus prepared, and assuming his best manners, gallantly conducted. Miss Fox into his sitting-room and complimented her on the bright tinge of her cheeks after her walk.

'Meantime Dolly got ready cakes and coffee, which she made more exhilarating by the addition of something strong, and all three became very merry together.

'In the midst of their fun Mr Harris dropped in – unexpectedly, of course – and was hailed as a welcome addition. He quickly exploited the familiar footing on which he felt himself to be by taking Dolly on his knee and pinching her soft bottom.

'She laughed, but Miss Fox blushed and cried: "Oh! Dolly, oh!"

' "Dolly is a sensible girl, Miss Fox," said Mr Jones. "She never objects to a bit of fun, and so we are all very fond of her. Besides I am sure she finds her seat very agreeable. I wish I could induce you to follow her example," and he threw his arm round her.

' "Oh, Mr Jones! you are forgetting yourself," she exclaimed, trying to look grave but with a wicked twinkle in her eye. "I am not in the habit of allowing gentlemen to make free with me in that manner."

' "Don't be foolish, Lydia. Mr Jones won't harm you." And she pretended to give him a sly wink to go on. Mr Jones, thus encouraged, not only kept his arm round Lydia but put his other hand under her bottom to lift her up.

' "Oh! Mr Jones, you stop at nothing. I suppose, you will be wanting to kiss me next."

' "Aye, that I will and I'll do it too" – and he boldly seized her in his arms. She squealed out and tried to push him away.

' "What fun to see Lydia kissed! Let us go and hold her, Mr Harris," cried Dolly.

'Miss Fox did not seem very much put out by this general onslaught. She laughed, but yet appeared to resist as strongly as she could. However, by their joint efforts they soon had her lying on her back. As she kicked her legs about, her clothes were thrown up above her knees; still she did not mind but kivked away harder than ever. Dolly held her arms but her legs seemed the most interesting point of attack for the men; as she fought a thrilling glimpse was afforded them of a red gaping cunt propped up by a pair of gleaming white globes. And while they tried to grasp her fleshy thighs their hands slipped along their smooth surface until they reached her fat projecting posteriors.

'Still the struggle went on, and amid shrieks of fun and laughter, her clothes were tossed higher and higher until at last the great bush of golden hair that covered her mount was brought clearly into view, together with the pouting lips below.

'Then, Dolly, with exultant laugh, cried, "Now's your chance, Mr Jones, take a kiss from that sweet mouth which Lydia takes such pains to hide."

' "No, he mustn't," cried Lydia, working her legs in such a way as made her cunt open out and display in the most wanton manner the pink lining of that glowing slit.

'Mr Jones said nothing, but at once pressed his head between her struggling thighs and soon had his mouth in close contact with her hairy chink.

' "Now keep quiet, Lydia, and let him kiss your cunt. You always say you are delighted when I kiss and suck it, and Mr Jones will do that much more agreeably than I can.

'Miss Fox made no reply, but as if acknowledging herself vanquished, ceased struggling and, spreading her thighs widely open, pressed up her cunt to meet Mr Jones's warm caress.

'Mr Harris, observing the turn that matters had taken, drew back from Lydia and commenced pulling up Dolly's skirts. Dolly smiled lasciviously and said to him, "You naughty man – you are copying Mr Jones; you want to have my cunt exposed as well as Lydia's! Well, I won't prevent you, but let me place myself in a more convenient position." And throwing herself down beside Lydia, she pulled up her petticoats, and spreading her thighs, invited Mr Harris to possess himself of her secret treasure in any way he liked.

'He was not slow in accepting her invitation, and applying his moist lips to her lecherous gap, he rolled the soft clitoris about with his pliant tongue.

'Now sounds of delicious suction were heard, and both women twisted and writhed as they pressed up their throbbing cunts against the men's mouths, while the latter embraced their soft bottoms with encircling arms.

'After enjoying this pleasing suction for a few moments, Dolly raised herself and said, "Now, Mr Harris, you have cleared the ground, let me see what you are going to plough it with!"

'Mr Harris already had his prick out, so standing up between Dolly's thighs, he projected it towards her face. She took it in both hands, and drawing it to her mouth, first kissed and then sucked its glowing head.

'Mr Jones taking his cue from his friend pushed up his prick towards Lydia's face to induce her to take it in her hands and apply it to her lips. But she kept on jokingly thrusting it aside and saying, "Oh, fie, Mr Jones! How could you expect me to do such a thing – to kiss its impudent head! Oh, fie, and who can tell where it has been, or what it was doing last" – all the time, however, rubbing it with the back of her hand and, unintentionally as it was, giving it the most wanton and exciting touches.

' "I can tell you. The last place it was in was Dolly's cunt; and Dolly's cunt sucked it clean and nice. There's no cunt like hers!"

'Dolly laughed: "Well, you men are often the greatest fools. Don't you know that the cunts of women who have been often fucked are more or less alike." '

Lord Ferrars' luscious story, told with such consummate grace and skill, produced the full effect: every cunt was now gaping with desire and every prick swelling with eagerness and power. A general mélée followed and each, adopting their own fancy or whim, obtained the desired gratification.

Before we separated, I got Lord Ferrars to promise to give us a further account of his aunt, Lady Flora, and especially a description of his own *amour* under her auspices with a certain young lady named Clara Alcock.

And as the major and Alick had consented to come to us again next week, we hoped for an early opportunity of hearing the continuation of Lord Ferrars' pleasing narrative.

Wordsworth Classic Erotica

◆◆§❧◆